Orissers

by

L. H. Myers

First published December 1922 by G. P. Putnam's Sons.

This edition published by Bookship, 2024.

ISBN 978-1-915388-08-7

Cover design © 2024 Murray Ewing. Illustration by Randolph Caldecott.

The
Orissers

BOOKSHIP

Contents

Part One 9

Chapter 1 11

Chapter 2 18

Chapter 3 25

Chapter 4 32

Chapter 5 38

Chapter 6 47

Chapter 7 54

Chapter 8 63

Part Two 71

Chapter 1 73

Chapter 2 79

Chapter 3 86

Chapter 4 90

Chapter 5 97

Chapter 6 102

Chapter 7 108

Chapter 8 118

Chapter 9 127

Chapter 10 132

Chapter 11 136

Chapter 12 143

Chapter 13 147

Chapter 14 151

Chapter 15 154

Chapter 16 163

Chapter 17 169

Chapter 18 177

Chapter 19 182

Chapter 20 187

Chapter 21 196

Chapter 22 201

Part Three 209
Chapter 1 211
Chapter 2 215
Chapter 3 218
Chapter 4 223
Chapter 5 226
Chapter 6 233
Chapter 7 240
Chapter 8 246
Chapter 9 251
Chapter 10 258
Chapter 11 263
Chapter 12 270
Chapter 13 278
Chapter 14 284
Chapter 15 290
Chapter 16 298
Chapter 17 303
Chapter 18 307
Chapter 19 314
Chapter 20 320
Chapter 21 326
Chapter 22 330
Chapter 23 338
Chapter 24 344
Chapter 25 350
Chapter 26 355
Chapter 27 360
Chapter 28 363
Chapter 29 370
Chapter 30 378
Chapter 31 384
Chapter 32 388
Chapter 33 395
Chapter 34 400
About L. H. Myers 405

Four species of Illusions beset the human mind, to which (for distinction's sake) we have assigned names: calling the first, Illusions of the Tribe; the second, Illusions of the Den; the third, Illusions of the Market; the fourth, Illusions of the Schools.

The Illusions of the Tribe are inherent in human nature, and the very tribe or race of man....

The Illusions of the Den are those of each individual. For everybody (in addition to the errors common to the race of man) has his own individual den or cavern, which intercepts and corrupts the light of nature....

There are also Illusions formed by the reciprocal intercourse and society of man with man, which we call Illusions of the Market, from the commerce and association of men with each other....

Lastly, there are Illusions which have crept into men's minds from the various dogmas of peculiar systems of philosophy....

— Bacon's "Novum Organum," Book I, ¶¶ 39-44.

Part One

Chapter 1

Allen was standing in the passage outside a closed door. The night was dark, sultry, and still. The window behind him was open, but no air entered, nor any sound of traffic. Two or three minutes had elapsed since he had bidden Cosmo Orisser good night; but he could neither bring himself to go away, nor find the resolution to go back into the room.

For the time being he was completely tired out. The alternatives which Cosmo had just presented, overwhelmed him with dismay. His mind had a tendency to circle higher and higher above the points at issue, until the past, the present, and the future, all seemed equally remote, and he was reduced to smiling helplessly at his vision of himself, standing there on the sixth floor of that dirty tenement-house, at one o'clock in the night,—the very embodiment of indecision and discomfort.

One instant he was in the clouds, and the next he dropped heavily down into actuality. He became aware of the whistling of the gas-jet at the head of the stone staircase, of a step sounding upon the asphalt below, and of his own heart-beats telling off the seconds as they slipped by. Then he lost sense of everything but his position of agonized arrest; and his mind would gather itself, like a cramped muscle, into a knot of anguish.

During the last few days he had been clinging obstinately to the belief that he might yet detach himself from Cosmo and stand aloof from the uncertain consequences of that unrepentant prodigal's return. But now he knew better. He saw that he was caught—or very nearly caught. The breath of adventure had been wafted to him in the hot, dusty town of Tornel, and his spirit had leapt to the call of excitement and romance. Already he was surveying the last eight years of his life with the eyes of one who has sailed forth from a smooth, shady river into the tossing sea.

An hour ago his companion had brought matters to a head by making a definite proposal and demanding an immediate answer. But he had temporized. And now he was beginning to feel that he ought to have been ready to obey the impulse of the moment. In life there were such occasions. His refusal to answer had been a sign of weakness and insincerity.

Yet how could you be sincere with a man whose standard of sincerity was so extravagant? Besides, it was not in human nature to be more sincere with others than you were with yourself. And that was what Cosmo really demanded. He had the exorbitance—as well as the insight—of a madman. But his insight was apt to be falsifying. By interpreting you to yourself in terms of his own abnormal mentality he frequently did you an injustice. That was one of the things that made commerce with him so exasperating. He gave you distorted reflections of yourself. You found your self at last enclosed with him in a psychological "Chamber of Mystery," where it amused him to make himself and you the objects of unpleasant experiment.

The fact was that during the last few days Allen had had a good deal to put up with. And now, as he wavered outside Cosmo's room, it suddenly struck him as possible that the other had guessed that he was still there. Was it not indeed conceivable that Cosmo was actually standing on the other side of the door? And waiting—waiting, with a satirical grin upon his face, for just the right moment to throw the door open in order to catch his victim at the acme of discomfort?

The conjecture was intolerable. And for that reason all the more likely to be correct. Indeed, with Allen's rising exasperation, it expanded into something approaching a conviction. Positively, he could feel waves of intelligence passing between himself and that other presence, close but unseen. An odious exchange of intuitions, a ridiculous tussle of wills, was taking place. . . . By heaven! he would not stand it! And stepping forward, he flung open the door.

Cosmo was there, sure enough! Yes! there the man stood—squarely facing him, and with eyes levelled straight at his own.

Allen burst out into a furious laugh. "The devil take you!" said he. Not a word did the other reply.

Then he saw that Cosmo, too, was angry. The candle on the table beside him lit up a countenance pale, frenzied, despairing.

For a moment the two men regarded one another in silence; then a new sentiment, akin to compassion, stirred in Allen's heart. The grimness of Cosmo's physical and spiritual presence overpowered him. He received the impression that he was looking through the man's fleshly covering at the skull and skeleton underneath. Something ineffably pathetic disengaged itself from that tall, minatory figure, relieved against the dimness of the small, poverty-stricken room.

Of a sudden his mind was made up. He would give his assent to Cosmo's proposal—no happy assent, alas!—but a dreary, desperate assent.

A few minutes later he was walking homeward through the empty streets. His spirits, for whatever reason, had gone down into the depths. Of a truth, there had been nothing encouraging in the brief passage which had just taken place. Awkwardly, even sheepishly, he had said his say. And Cosmo, after frowning upon him for some moments more, had nodded, stepped forward, and closed the door in his face.

Allen walked slowly, with bowed head. His echoing footfalls vexed him. The air was hot and stagnant. The grey, blind frontages of the houses expressed misery.

On reaching his rooms, he paced to and fro across the floor. Solitude and leisure for reflection were what he craved. But he soon found that his thoughts could not move freely within the confinement of four walls; and presently the idea came into his mind that it would be pleasant to ascend to the roof of the building which, he recollected, was flat, and accessible through a trap-door. Acting forthwith upon this impulse, he mounted to the attic landing, and by means of a ladder at the end of it made his way up into the outer air.

On the edge of the leads he stood and looked down; the street lamps were shining in ordered rows; he looked up; not a star was visible, not one.

Behind him was a corner-tower of masonry, which lifted itself still higher into the night. He noticed an iron ladder affixed to it, and conjectured that this ladder must give access to another and loftier expanse of roof. At its upper end, however, unless the darkness deceived him, a projecting cornice caused it to bend outward and overhang. After a moment of hesitation he started climbing. It pleased him to put his nerve and agility to the test. In a minute he had reached the protuberant stonework; in another minute he had writhed himself around it; and there, finding the level space that he had looked for, sprang erect to send his gaze out over the wider prospect.

The building upon which he stood was lofty and situated upon a rise of ground. By day he would have had a broad view of the surrounding plain. Now all he could see was the street lights and coloured railway lights scattered spaciously into the darkness. For some while he gazed out northwards, where, three miles or so over the sand-dunes, stretched, invisible, the long line of the sea.

The thought of the sea made the atmosphere seem less oppressive; and by a like movement of fancy his elevation over the mass of sleeping humanity raised him above the pressure of common human cares. Yet, presently, when he turned to stare into the east, his brow clouded again and he breathed a long, slow sigh. Far away, across that slumbering countryside, lay Eamor, the place haunted by his banished memories and regrets—Eamor, the homestead of the Orissers, which he had put out of his mind to no purpose, since Cosmo's return had brought all these memories back to him.

After another and a yet deeper sigh, he settled himself with his back against a chimney-stack, and there fell into profound meditation.

Allen Allen (for his parents had given him a Christian name identical with his surname) was the son of an army officer, who had died in middle age, leaving a widow with three young boys on her hands. His mother, however, was fortunate in possessing a small income of her own, which enabled her to send her sons to a public school and to the University. The least satisfactory of the three was the youngest, Allen. He had ability, but was indolent. It proved impossible to assign him in advance to any profession; and, after a year at the University, he betook himself, without notice, abroad. His mother ordered his return; he refused, upon which she wrote to say that for as long as he chose to remain away he must earn his own living.

Allen was then nineteen. So far from having acted on impulse, he had laid by with great regularity during the last three years a good portion of his quarterly allowances; and, before taking flight, he had used considerable ingenuity in borrowing all the money he could from his two brothers. He was consequently in a position to break himself in gently to the hardships which he was wise enough to expect, whilst keeping in reserve a small sum as a security in case of illness. Such was his scheme; and, characteristically, having laid down the framework, he left Fate to fill in the details. Living the life of a vagabond, and never drawing seriously upon his resources excepting when confronted with a passage of unusual discomfort, he drifted southwards through France, Switzerland, and Austria—southwards, because he loved the sun, and then, because he hated seafaring, towards the east. With his mother he exchanged letters occasionally. She was not by temperament sympathetically inclined towards him, and she disapproved his ways; but she was wise enough to bear him no lasting grudge for following them. A year after his departure she died, and Allen learnt that he could look forward to obtaining on his twenty-first birthday the control of funds amply sufficient for his modest needs.

It so befell, moreover, that at this same date he made the discovery of an interest which was to give him a fixed and enduring purpose in life. He had recently become acquainted with a small band of archaeologists, who were starting on a journey into Asia Minor. One of their party fell sick; and Allen, having succeeded on very slender grounds in convincing himself and his new friends that he would make an efficient substitute, was offered and accepted the vacant place. His self-confidence proved well justified, and it received a signal reward. He discovered the key to his happiness. The coming years of his life lay sunny and golden before him in their opportunities for studying antiquity, for discovering all that could be discovered of ancient man.

After parting with his friends, Allen went to Egypt and there in library and museum devoted himself to a disciplined course of study. It was in Cairo, about three years later, that he fell in with Sir Charles Orisser. The name of this distinguished savant was familiar to him; and he had formed a definite conception of the man's character through his writings. He enjoyed Sir Charles's acerbity, he chuckled over his humour, he delighted in the irritation which that pen aroused among the more pedantically-minded of his *confreres*. There was no taint of logrolling or jealousy discernible in anything Sir Charles wrote; and Allen, who had tasted by this time the peculiar flavour of professionalism, felt sure he would like Sir Charles just as much as the large majority of workers in the same field disliked him.

When at last he succeeded in obtaining an introduction, he found himself in the presence of a tall, thin man between forty and fifty years of age, whose colourless manners and stereotyped gentlemanliness of aspect were at first a disappointment to him. It was not long, however, before he made the discovery that this exterior was expressive of little more than an inborn desire to attract the minimum of notice. At the end of one hour's conversation he liked the man as much as he had thought he would, but he had no notion whether the other liked him. As a matter of fact his new acquaintance did like him, but, not being accustomed to liking people, he was more than usually careful to conceal what he felt. Sir Charles had an aversion to the popular man; Allen seemed to belong to that class; and Sir Charles had to make certain that he was not of the type which predominates within it. It was only after he had assured himself that Allen's countenance was not noticeably frank, nor his manners conspicuously cheerful and unaffected, nor his conversation remarkable for its ease and humour, that he felt safe. If Allen was rather obviously likeable, the reasons were unobjectionable. It was not easy to define them, but no doubt a good deal could be put down to the complete absence in him of that spirit, which, disguised and subtle in operation, so largely insulates man from man,—the spirit of competition. As a specialist, he was inoffensive because untainted by professionalism, and in other respects his society was agreeable, primarily, because he suffused an air of physical and mental well-being.

Sir Charles had planned to resume, with the beginning of the cooler season, his excavations in the Nubian Desert. A few days before starting, he made up his mind to ask Allen to accompany him; and that was the beginning of an alliance that was to end only at his death, some five years later.

It was a strange life the two men lived together during the greater part of those years. Few and short were the periods when they were not at work. For at least six months out of every twelve they lived in tents pitched on the hot sand, and the rest of the year they would spend in the study of their finds. Allen had met an enthusiasm that outstripped his own. When he looked at his friend gazing in deep abstraction at some small, unearthed fragment, and bethought him that twenty years of hard, solitary application lay behind the worker, who asked for nothing better than another twenty years of similar toil, questions, which his own case had never suggested to him, rose, unwanted, to his mind. What force was it that spurred them both on? What was the secret of their peculiar enchantment? Why should their voices sink and their hands tremble, as they sifted out of that limitless aridity some relic only remarkable because the hands that fashioned it had become dust so many centuries ago? He could find no answer; he could only invoke the mystery, the fascination, of Time. That desert soil, upon which they both crawled—it spoke to them of Time. And they worked it with the blind pertinacity of insects who have a big task appointed for their little day. At night the stars—they, too, spoke of Time; beneath their light the generations of Earth seemed as transient as the glitter upon heaving water, civilisations rising and subsiding on a quiet ocean swell.

The present, and all the affairs of the present, were here subdued into insignificance. So completely, indeed, did the world of actually existing men and women fade away from his ken that sometimes, by a healthy

16

turn of thought, Allen summoned to mind all that he was choosing to ignore; and then, suddenly curious to know more about his fellow-worker, he would regret that their intimacy, greatly as it had developed, shed so little light upon Sir Charles's attachments to contemporary life.

All that he knew as yet was that his friend came of a good old family with an estate in the Midlands. The Orissers had been wealthy in their day, and Sir Charles, the only surviving representative of the main branch, was reputedly well off. Later, however, Allen learnt that the estate had deteriorated, and that its master was spending far more than he could afford. For his neglect of his duties as a landlord many blamed him, and were only partially reconciled to his way of life, when the country, waking up to the fact that he had acquired an international reputation, conferred on him the honour of a knighthood.

Allen knew, too, that Sir Charles was married. It was in their second winter together that his wife died. To attend the funeral the two friends made a hurried journey home and returned to their work at the earliest possible moment afterwards, leaving the widower's small son, Nicholas, then seven years of age, in the charge of his mother's relatives. In this domestic interruption of their affairs Allen came, too, rather surprisingly, by the further knowledge that she who had just died was a second wife, and Nicholas a second son. Sir Charles, it appeared, had contracted an earlier alliance in his youth—a most unfortunate alliance, the woman proving "absolutely impossible"; and the issue of that marriage, Cosmo, was, he said, absolutely impossible too. The subject was evidently a painful one, and although Allen's curiosity was now fully aroused, his information remained for a long time confined to the facts that Cosmo was alive, and that his father paid him a regular allowance on the condition that he should live abroad and go by another name than that of Orisser.

Chapter 2

As time passed, it was borne in upon Allen with ever greater incisiveness that the community of feeling between his companion and the contemporary world was singularly slight. At first he thought that Sir Charles must suffer from this isolation of spirit, but later he perceived that his friend was troubled by no desire for a closer connexion with humanity. It was not that Sir Charles had become embittered, but that, apparently, he had been born with few natural leanings towards his kind. This mental disposition Allen viewed at first with perfect complaisance. *He* knew what things they were for which that lonely spirit reserved its ardour. He had witnessed Sir Charles at work. And on no other brow had he seen, or did he expect ever to see, the tokens of such penetrating speculation; in no other eyes the glow of such sustained and patient inquisition. The light of all his days was concentrated by that man upon the vestiges of the past, and at night, as he sat musing outside his tent, you saw him seeking a further inspiration from the ancient light of stars. Well might he have said:—

> Ganz vergessener Völker Müdigkeiten
> Kann Ich nicht abthun von meinen Lidern,
> Noch weghalten von der erschrockenen Seele
> Stummes Niederfallen ferner Sterne.*

Whatever was censurable in this attitude, Allen, whose enthusiasm followed a similar bent, was predisposed, as we have already said, to condone. Yet, as time went by, his sentiment underwent some alteration. There would arise moments when it became tinged with impatience and even, finally, with disapproval. Sir Charles displayed negligences and indifferences so sweeping as to shock him; and the worst of them, to his thinking, was the father's treatment of his son, Cosmo. Allen's interest

---

* "Interdependence" by Hugo von Hofmannsthal, translation: "From the weariness of forgotten peoples / Vainly would I liberate mine eyelids / Or would keep my startled soul at distance / From the silent fall of far-off planets." (Translation Charles Wharton Stork, *The Lyrical Poems of Hugo von Hofmannsthal* (1918, New Haven).)

had early fastened upon Cosmo. He spared himself no pains in enticing Sir Charles to talk about him. It was not easy to get the subject accepted, but by dint of perseverance he extracted the whole story at last.

All communication between Cosmo's parents had already ceased before the child's birth. His mother, then living in France, undertook entire charge of him from the first; and, when she died, Cosmo, then ten years old, was transferred to the care of her French relatives. Sir Charles paid for his son's maintenance, but never gave evidence of any wish to see him. Once or twice, however, when complaints touching the boy's disposition became urgent, he had been constrained to go and investigate them. On these occasions he received, on his own statement, the impression that Cosmo was no whit better than he was represented. No, even at that tender age the boy was already "a terror." "He came into the world raging," said a witness of his childish career, "and he has not ceased to rage ever since."

Cosmo was certainly intractable both as an infant and as a small boy; on reaching adolescence he took to running away; and as he grew older, his disappearances became more and more prolonged. At length the exercise of authority was abandoned; the youth was left to follow, unmolested, his own incomprehensible way of life.

Such were the bare facts, which the father, when he was so minded, was able to illustrate here and there with a touch that added to their singularity. But in general he would not be communicative about Cosmo, and invariably closed his recitals with the comment that his son, although no fool, was hopeless.

Allen, however, continued to think a good deal about this young man, who was of his own age, and the only person in the world possessed of the power to penetrate Sir Charles's indifference. He liked to talk about him for this reason; he liked to see the flush of a human emotion gradually rise to his companion's cheeks. He constituted himself Cosmo's champion. "When you come to think of it," he would say, "the discouraging thing about children—and about adults, too, for that matter—is the passive, unimaginative way in which they accommodate themselves to life as they find it. Men commonly accept the conditions in which they are born and bred, as inevitable and unchangeable; and end by yielding them a superstitious respect." And then, continuing rather maliciously to sound an echo of observations that were often on Sir Charles's own lips, he would observe that to this characteristic was certainly due the sluggishness of humanity's development from its dawn to the present era—that great era which had witnessed the birth of the self-conscious, the critical, and consequently the Satanic spirit—the very spirit in which Cosmo so notably abounded. It amused him to start from these grounds in his championship of Cosmo, whom in the end he would paradoxically uphold as the embodiment of that noble dissatisfaction with accepted systems of living and thinking, which, more finely than personal ambition, leads to mankind's advancement.

Sir Charles's reply would be simply that Cosmo had never in his life advanced himself or anybody else. The fellow was a wastrel.

But to this Allen found a good deal to retort. He had been shown some of Cosmo's letters (for greatly to his father's annoyance, Cosmo could not be dissuaded from writing), and it was easy for him to point out that a passage such as the following was not one that an ordinary wastrel would indite:—

> "Why are you angry with me for being what I am? Is my life happiness? And could I not, at a price, make myself more happy? Ah, you know that to bend my desires to happiness would be for me an infamy! Greater than my determination, my spirit would not obey! For my brain is lit by its own burning, and my limbs move to the impulse which is a fountain within me. I see men only as shadows on my way; they flit like shadows, unless I arrest them to give them some portion of my reality. I must go forward always in pursuit of Vision; which alone is reality. This world is a caricature, a changeling, substituted by some ugly trick. We are not in the Real World; but apparently I am alone in perceiving it.
>
> "Do you tell me that this is the Real World? A thousand times no! I cannot be deceived; for I behold the other! I assuredly remember what existed, the wonderful, the Lovely—before that accursed trick was played. I go for ever stalking the old reality, as by flashes it reincarnates itself.
>
> "Over the brow of a hill I see it redly transfiguring the plain. I surprise it on the sea rising from its bed, and tossing and towering in excitement. I discover it everywhere. I even detect it peering out at me from behind the faded curtains of this dark gin shop."

Did Sir Charles claim that this was the language or the spirit of an ordinary wastrel? Well, no; the father was prepared to admit that Cosmo's worthlessness was of a different stamp. Allen was indeed at liberty to consider him a mystic in the savage state, a visionary, a prophet, anything that he pleased! But what then? What was there to do about Cosmo? What the devil did Cosmo want? He was already receiving money—more, indeed, than could be afforded.

These questions would have been difficult to answer had not Cosmo at about this time himself provided a reply. He begged his father to see him. He had conceived, it seemed, the notion of some sort of reconciliation. Previous attempts had no doubt been failures; but he wanted one more chance.

This appeal came at a not inauspicious moment, for Sir Charles had been a little shaken by Allen's zeal on his son's behalf. He listened quietly when Allen pointed out that Cosmo unquestionably nourished a strange, fanciful kind of affection for him; and in the end he deferred to Cosmo's reiterated entreaties. He consented to a meeting.

This was in the fourth year of his companionship with Allen. It was summer and the two friends were in England. The meeting was to take place in Spain, through which they arranged to travel on their way to Egypt. Cosmo would join them in Madrid.

Allen was much excited. How would it go off—this trial for which he had so urgently pleaded? On arriving at their hotel, they found not Cosmo, who should have been there to greet them, but, as chance would have it, a young cousin of Sir Charles's, a penniless orphan, Lilian Orisser, who was travelling in the company of a rich lady by whom she had been adopted. The presence of these two upon the scene had not entered into Sir Charles's calculations; but intercourse with them was not easily to be avoided; so he accepted the situation with simplicity, making no mystery of the expected advent of his ill-famed and half-mythical son.

No word had been received from Cosmo, when, two days later, the combined party went off on an early ride over the arid uplands that surround the city. Sir Charles had designed to visit some flint pits, in which, it was reported, prehistoric implements had recently been discovered. The expedition did not prove very exhilarating, and, as the little cavalcade was trotting back to town, dusty and hot, the sun being now high overhead, one and all they fell silent. It came to them, therefore, in their separate reveries, all the more as a surprise, when, on a desolate stretch of the way, a man stepped out from under a clump of gnarled cork-trees and, with uplifted hand, strode towards them over the white sand. Startled, they drew rein. The stranger, tall, gaunt, and with a hard smile about his lips, approached and saluted. It was Cosmo.

On recognising his son, Sir Charles dismounted and, after making him known to the others, fell back. For a brief space the commonplaces natural to the occasion were exchanged. Cosmo informed them that he had just arrived in Madrid, had learnt at the hotel in what direction they were to be found, and had ridden out to meet them.

After he had thus declared himself, silence again fell, and with it a certain constraint. Abruptly Sir Charles remounted. Indicating a miserable bodega half hidden by the trees, Cosmo let it be known that he had a horse there tethered, and said he would accompany them back. Before long the whole party were clattering once more over the scorching cobbles to their hotel.

When, in after days, Allen looked back over the passage of the next three weeks he always found himself baffled in his attempts to extract an interpretation of the untoward event with which the period closed. Nothing, in the interval between Cosmo's first apparition and the incidents of the climax, stood out with any particular significance. Perhaps his mind, set on the wrong tack, missed all the clues; but the clues, he thought, if any there were, must have been faint.

The birth of an understanding between father and son was what he stood principally on the look-out for; but his admiration for the latter also fired him with a desire for a friendship between Cosmo and himself. Cosmo was a magnificent creature. His great physical vitality was matched by the fire of his spirit. One felt that his body with all its energies was subjugated to his imperious mind. What, then, was the reason of his failure in life? Why did that spirit, brought into touch with the world through such a noble vehicle, find no satisfying channel for its activity? Why had it so little power of accommodation? Why such a constant rejection of reality? And in favour of what?

In both his desires Allen suffered almost immediate disappointment. Not only did Cosmo ignore him, but he gave no appearance of considering his father either. He had arrived in Madrid in the company of a young French nobleman, sleek, silent, and self-possessed; and he seemed to prefer the society of this youth to that of any other member of the party, not even excepting Lilian Orisser. Yet this girl, barely eighteen, was so pretty, so attractive in her youthful freshness and elegance, that it did occur to Allen at the time that Cosmo's indifference to her might have some tinge of affectation. For his own part, he was faintly intimidated by her charms. She pleased him so much to look upon that he asked for nothing further. Besides, his whole mind was occupied by the mysterious and exasperating figure of Cosmo. Nothing was happening

22

in accordance with his pre-vision. The period of Cosmo's probation had turned into a social holiday, through which they were drifting without discernible purpose.

Two weeks later they reached the southern coast, and Sir Charles suggested that they should cross over to Morocco to spend a few days at a villa some five miles from Tangiers, which had been placed at his disposal by a friend. The idea pleased everyone, so the whole company crossed the Straits, with the exception of Allen, who was temporarily incapacitated by a knee cap bruised in riding.

What subsequently happened—what led up to the occurrences of the second night, and indeed what those occurrences actually were— Allen was not to learn till many years after; and a relation of them takes its proper place at a later point in this chronicle. The reader must be content for the present with the scant knowledge which came to Allen by report. The villa was in charge of two native servants; the party installed themselves, it seemed, comfortably enough. The change from hotel life to these rougher, freer conditions was a source of amusement to them.

On the third day after their departure, however, to Allen's utter astonishment, Sir Charles, accompanied by Lilian and her protectress, made a sudden reappearance in the hall of the hotel. In answer to his inquiries, Allen was informed curtly that the Count had been stabbed by Cosmo, and was lying at the villa in danger of his life. "And where is Cosmo?" he asked. Sir Charles waved his hand and smiled wryly. "In the villa, over there, nursing the Count!" Allen could only stare.

The return party were evidently weary and disinclined to offer further explanations. Nor was more light to be obtained later. Sir Charles himself seemed to lack the key to the mystery. He could only say that he thought the Count would probably die and that Cosmo would attempt to make off in some coastal vessel before information was lodged with the police. For his part he went on bitterly, he washed his hands of Cosmo, and the Count's death would not cause him any great sorrow. But it was desirable that they should not remain in ignorance of the way affairs were moving, and therefore he begged that Allen would go over to the villa the next day and see.

Allen went. The journey was tedious, and his curiosity intense. When at last he descried the white walls of the house shimmering within its grove of tamarisk and other shrubs, his heart leapt with excitement. He was ushered into a room where he found Cosmo sitting by the Count's bedside, a cigarette between his lips and an open book in his hand. The injured man's face was flushed, and he breathed with difficulty. He greeted his visitor however with a smile that was not only composed, but much more disdainful than any he had yet permitted himself. (He and Allen had disliked each other from the first.) He asserted that he was already on the road to recovery; there was no necessity to call in a doctor; everything needful had been procured, and—with a gesture towards Cosmo—he had an excellent nurse.

On the subject of the night's affray neither of them offered one word of comment. While the Count was mockingly polite, Cosmo was taciturn. In a short time Allen saw nothing for it but to take his leave.

Sir Charles and his party remained in the south of Spain for another fortnight. Once during this period Cosmo, without giving notice, crossed over to them. On that day by great good fortune Sir Charles and Lilian Orisser had gone off on an excursion; so that if, as Allen suspected, Cosmo's desire was to provoke some scene, he was baulked of his object. He saw no one but Allen, to whom he gave further assurance that the Count's injury was after all trifling, and that he would soon be on his feet again. For the rest, he revealed himself in a black and forbidding aspect. Not that he was unfriendly; on the contrary, to Allen's surprise, he treated him rather as an intimate. Before you, he seemed to say, it is unnecessary to wear a mask. What he disclosed, however, was more his sullen, despairing temper than the actual substance of his thoughts. With downcast eyes he stood and brooded.

As was natural, Allen had formed the suspicion that what lay at the bottom of the drama was jealousy; but it was particularly difficult to fit this explanation to the observed behaviour of the persons concerned.

With the candour of youth Lilian Orisser had done little to conceal the fact that she positively disliked the Count, and at no time had the Count appeared to pay any attention to her. Moreover, between her and Cosmo Allen had not noticed anything pass.

After a prolonged silence, during which Cosmo never once raised his head, Allen, impelled by irresistible curiosity, made some remark into which, pointedly enough, the young girl's name was introduced.

Cosmo's head came up; he fixed on Allen eyes of a quite unearthly glitter, and turning on his heel, stalked silently away. He had not gone far, however, before he halted, looked back, waved a hand, and shouted an amicable farewell. That was the last Allen saw of him until after Sir Charles's death.

Chapter 3

A few weeks later Sir Charles and Allen were back in Egypt, where the latter found plenty of time to ruminate on the whole episode. He could hold to no one mind about it, however; but regarded it according to his mood with varying degrees of amusement, vexation and disappointment. Unquestionably he now understood much better what Sir Charles meant when he called his son hopeless. Yet, largely as a result of his last talk with Cosmo, he preserved for him a feeling akin to friendship.

During the weeks that followed Sir Charles and he abstained by tacit consent from discussing what had occurred; and Allen imagined that his companion's silence signified that he had put out of mind once and for ever their journey to Spain and everything connected with it. Not until they had been in the desert for about two months, was he undeceived. One evening, as they were sitting outside their tent, Sir Charles informed him that he intended to marry Lilian Orisser in the spring. The news fell upon Allen like a thunder bolt. He was speechless; and although the other affected to smile at this astonishment, it was plain that he had not found the announcement easy to make, and was a good deal embarrassed by the manner in which it was received.

What made Sir Charles's news not merely amazing, but positively dreadful, was the knowledge Allen had recently acquired regarding his friend's financial position. When last in England Sir Charles had spent much of his time in the City, and had finally confessed to Allen that during the last three years he had been resorting to desperate expedients to scrape up the funds needful for his work. His business associates, he further intimated, were rascals, and their activities no benefit to mankind. Allen's moral sense was not offended by these admissions; if ever the old adage "all is fair within the law" was applicable, it surely became so when the good cause of Egyptology was in question. But had Sir Charles kept within the law? It presently appeared not. It looked in fact as if the law, like an old friend too sorely tried, might of a sudden turn into an enemy. The situation was black. And while it was likely that Sir Charles's negligence and passivity would, in the event of a public inquiry into the affairs of his associates, deflect from him the major weight of blame; it would none the less be patent to all the world that he had sold his good name to dishonest men, and not troubled himself about the use they made of it. Not only was ruin probable, but some measure of disgrace.

And now—this projected marriage! What, in heaven's name, was one to make of it? After the first shock of surprise, Allen brushed aside all its other circumstances of unexpectedness, to stare aghast at the economic spectre by which it was overshadowed. His friend, who admitted that the girl's guardian would never become reconciled to it, suddenly appeared before him in a guise that would have seemed villainous, had it not been so tragic. Tragic it undoubtedly was. The understanding of that gradually soaked into him—without the use of many words on Sir Charles's part. The latter had nothing to say in attenuation of his intent except that Lilian Orisser realised to the full what she was doing. He simply revealed himself as yielding to an overmastering desire to make the girl his wife; and she, moved, one had to suppose, by an answering passion, had likewise surrendered to her fate. There was something awful in Sir Charles' clear sighted appreciation of the conditions, in his composure, and in his acceptance of whatever the future had in store.

In the spring the two friends went to England, and a few weeks later the marriage duly took place. It caused, as had been anticipated, a breach between Lilian and her protectress, who had to suffer the additional vexation of seeing her charge reject the hand of a man of immense wealth. This man, John Mayne, although he did not have any advantage over Charles Orisser in point of youth, was at the opposite pole as regards money. An international financier, his name was synonymous with riches. No wonder, then, that the poor lady's chagrin was great. So great, indeed, was it, that when, a few weeks after the marriage, she died, common report insisted that disappointment had hastened her end.

Sir Charles and his bride accordingly started married life under very poor auspices and without the approval of a single friend on either side. After the wedding Allen went down to Sir Charles's country seat, Eamor, to prepare it for the later arrival of the newly wedded pair. He had been to Eamor once or twice before, but on hurried visits only, when Sir Charles's single-minded aim had been to appease agents and bailiffs with the utmost dispatch. Since the death of young Nicholas's mother the beautiful old house had lain empty. It was now Allen's task to superintend the opening up of the establishment—just as though a new departure in life were really being made. But all this preparation for the future he felt to be a mockery; and, as he talked with the people about the place, their cheerful anticipations made him look into himself with an ironic sadness.

No doubt it was in great measure due to this sense of his, that all was going for nothing, that he became affected so unhappily by the external beauty of the scene. In his heart the dusty magic of Egypt gave way to another. He beheld, as for the first time, and as though they were emerging from an early morning mist, the green and dewy undulations of that English land scape. This was what had been forfeited;—this was what had been offered in sacrifice to the beast-headed gods of old Nile!

The morning came, when, standing upon the front steps of the house, he descried in the distance of the shaded avenue the old-fashioned victoria in which Sir Charles and his wife were rolling leisurely up to their abode. Already, as it seemed, they had sunk deep under the peaceful influence of the place. Arriving, they slipped into the placid sequence of the days without a stir. Young Nicholas, then ten years old, came with them.

Although Allen had thought a great deal about Lilian Orisser, since his return to England he had seen scarcely anything of her. He now had ample opportunities for studying her closely. First of all, he observed that the light and animation in her eyes, which had attracted his notice in Spain, if softened, were still there. But about the colour of the eyes he had been mistaken; they were not blue, as he had imagined, but grey. The half-smile habitual to her lips was still there too, and was still, as it seemed to him, tell-tale of a contained exuberance, of a readiness to confront life with audacity—with more audacity perhaps than she cared wholly to reveal. She took joy in life without a doubt, but a joy, he must hope, that was filtered through a delicate sensibility—else how should she be a companion for her husband?

Not long after her arrival she and Allen went for a country drive together. The occasion stood out in his memory for ever after, because the barrier of faint mistrust, which up to then had stood between them, was at length removed. The air was full of the sweetness of bean-fields still in blossom. She had pinned a dog rose into the soft grey of her dress. She looked so flowerlike that in his thought, dreamy from the cadence of their slow advance, she became wholly identified with the perfume, the freshness, and the grace, of the young summer's day. As they jogged on in silence, he wished that they need never speak, and that the drive might continue without end. Her face he could not see;

but her gloved hands, lying in her lap, seemed to express her to him wholly. Was she happy? He could not disbelieve it. She seemed the very mirror of serenity.

In a little while, the silence having been broken, she began talking to him very quietly about Sir Charles. By her manner she made the long stillness in which they had both been steeped, seem a passage into comparative intimacy. Without emotion of any kind she told him that she was not allowing herself to fall dupe to all the lovely, reassuring appearances at Eamor; she was not forgetting anything, nor hoping vainly. But she thought her husband was as happy as might be—and, for her part, she was too.

He felt that there was little for him to reply. In his answer, when it came, he made no attempt to draw the future out of the gloom which shrouded it.

For a few minutes no more was said, then, with a smile she asked whether he had not made up his mind to quit the sinking ship. After all he had his own career to think of.

He gave a little laugh. "As soon as I discover that I'm in the way, I'll go. But, until then . . ."

They looked at one another, and again she smiled. It was surprisingly unnecessary to say more. She did point out, however, that, in the event of a scandal Allen would find his association with Sir Charles tell heavily against him.

"Oh, as to my career——!" he rejoined with a shrug; and at that they left it.

The days went by in immense tranquillity. The summer expanded and deepened over the countryside, driving the cattle under the shelter of the trees and veiling the horizon with a drowsy haze of heat. On the fringe of the wood, where it ran up to within a short distance of the house, Nicholas and his stepmother, now great friends, would sit together upon the grass and read aloud or play chess, a game of which the boy was already very fond. And during the long twilight of the evenings husband and wife might be seen pacing by the hour with linked arms along that same border of the wood. From the terrace Allen could see them, and this spectacle, more than any other, had the power to pierce his enforced tranquillity with a pang of invincible anguish. He could no longer hide from himself how miserably he was suffering from a hidden sickness of the mind. Each day he apprehended better how passionate was the attachment which bound those two to one another; and he wondered each day with a greater bitterness at the passivity with which

Sir Charles awaited the end. The serenity of these days was their most poignant quality. In the beginning he had been able to forget for hours together that the peace and quiet of them was not real; but later the spectre was always by his side; and, finally, life as a whole lost its freshness; he saw it as dependent, everywhere and always, upon the practice of ignoring, and ignoring, and again ignoring.

During this period he, like the other two, turned instinctively to Nicholas. Here was someone who had the right to call himself happy. And young Nicholas certainly was happy, albeit with a gravity beyond his years. At first he had been inclined to resent Lilian's amused teasing of him; but so soon as he had perceived that his deeper sensibilities had nothing to fear from her mockery, his attachment to her had become complete.

Had there been anything to attempt or to contrive, Allen no doubt would have been less susceptible both to the unholy sweetness of these days and their invisible cruelty. Once or twice, when a feeling of desperation came over him, he marched determinedly into the library and insisted on being made privy to his friend's calculations and expedients. But in the end he had always to give up. A brief survey of the field was sufficient to reveal its uncompromising barrenness. By themselves, he saw, they could do nothing. Help from outside, and on a large scale, was needed. Was there no one to whom an appeal could be addressed?—Alas, there was not.—No one at all? Was not John Mayne among Sir Charles' acquaintances? And might not——?

But no! At Allen's hesitating mention of that name, the other frowned impatiently and shook his head. In his view, as Allen understood easily enough, John Mayne's previous relation with Lilian was an obstacle rather than a bridge to any such approach. Besides, as a further impediment against invoking the outside help of an expert, there stood the very questionable nature of the financial operations that would have to be revealed.

So one came back to it that there was nothing whatever to do— except to wait for a miracle. And one day Allen leapt to the fancy that such a miracle was in effect shaping itself. This, one afternoon, was suggested to him by the unexpected sight of Lilian and John Mayne, sitting together under the trees; but it turned out, merely, that John Mayne, who had taken a house in the neighbourhood for the summer months, had motored over to pay his respects. The visit was void of special significance; and Allen slipped back into despair.

John Mayne, who called again once or twice, was about their only visitor. The district was lonely, and Sir Charles had long ago lost touch with the few neighbours that he possessed. Under these conditions, and while a summer of unusual brilliance and intensity brooded over the countryside, inevitably and imperceptibly there fell upon the inmates of Eamor the sense of something preternatural in their moral and material isolation,—a sense to which they submitted in a kind of languid enchantment, becoming passive spectators of themselves, as they moved through the routine of existence in surroundings too beautiful, too unchanging, too still. A tendency to dreaminess in Lilian, a moodiness and increasing retirement into his library on the part of Sir Charles, were the visible signs of this creeping listlessness. When they paced to and fro over the lawns in the evening, they would be silent; and at any time during the day, in the midst of their usual occupations, one or the other might be detected standing in a condition of pensive arrest, to awaken presently with a start or a sigh, and enliven, maybe, the next few minutes with a little burst of factitious animation. Sometimes, waking in the night, Allen felt he must flee the place. Nay, it came over him that they must all flee! Husband and wife loved each other; and assuredly this awful resignation into which they had fallen was an outrage upon themselves and upon their love. Why not gather together what money could be found and fly the country? He propounded his scheme to Sir Charles with a desperate urgency, and, to his joy, the latter had little or nothing to say against it. In fact he seemed to acquiesce.

"You must act at once!" insisted Allen.

"Yes, yes," assented the other vaguely, "at once!"

But the summer slowly burnt itself out. Autumn came upon them. And still Allen waited; and waited in vain.

One evening at sundown he was standing in the embrasure of the hall window, looking westward over a lawn that went shelving down to a low bank of trees, whose rounded masses stood out in dark definition against the ruddy sky. His thoughts were wandering, or rather his brain seemed empty of thought. The coloured light made a glow about him on the dark panelling; the house behind was, as usual, very still.

Then from upstairs there came a short, sharp sound, so much muffled that it might have been no more than the snapping of a piece of wood. But it might also have been a pistol-shot; and his mind fastened with awful certitude upon that—and no other—conclusion.

For perhaps thirty seconds he stood where he was, then turned, and, as he mounted the stairs, found that his knees were trembling. On reaching the long corridor, half-way down which was Sir Charles's room, he saw, at the other end of it, Lilian. She was coming towards him, pale, and with a look in her eyes that must have matched his own. With a helpless gesture he tried to stay her advance. She came on, however, and, reaching the door at the same moment as he, entered the room with him.

Chapter 4

The next morning, when Allen awoke, he noticed first of all that it was another sunny day. Then he lay still for a while, collecting his thoughts, and in the meantime heard about the house the usual morning stir.

Although the bullet that ended Sir Charles's life was equally fatal to the whole baseless structure of existence at Eamor, everything was going on as before; the rooms were being dusted, the horses exercised, the silver was being laid out;—all would continue, for a period, unchanged, just as the sap continues to rise in the trunk of the uprooted tree.

The next day an inquest was held; and he stated that in Egypt in the spring of the year Sir Charles had suffered a violent sunstroke and had lain at death's door. His friend, he averred, had not been the same man since. This facilitated the usual verdict, and perhaps stilled certain forebodings on the part of Sir Charles's creditors.

The funeral over, Lilian and he began to examine the dead man's papers. For three days they worked hard, each taking a different part of the task; and at the end of that time he was able to pronounce a rough and ready conclusion. Affairs, he said, were just as bad as they had reason to fear; but it might be possible to defer the hour of reckoning for a short time,—say, for three months.

Here he paused. They were sitting, as he ever afterwards remembered, in the library with a great array of papers between them; and he had paused because he so hated—and by the look on her face he could see that she too hated—what was to come.

Well! they could put off the day of reckoning for a little, but it was no use doing so unless—unless they saw a chance of rescue—unless someone could be found to come forward . . .

At this point Lilian frowned and looked away. As they both knew, there *was* a chance of rescue. And perhaps she, on her side, knew that it was more than a mere chance. She had had letters from John Mayne. One of those letters was at this moment clutched in her hand; Allen had not read it, but she had told him whom it was from.

Here, then, lay the opportunity, the choice, which, even from the first night after her husband's death, Allen had forecasted with something resembling hope, mingled with something akin to despair. He had not met John Mayne many times, but he did not like him; and he could not conceive Lilian's liking him. Yet, if that letter contained an offer of assistance, it was not in his conscience to urge her to hold back—even though her acceptance were to carry with it the implicit promise to marry John Mayne. The extent to which the idea of this marriage outraged his feelings was a clear—though premature and unacceptable—revelation to him of the actuality of his own desire to marry her. The situation was abominable, and he hated it. His friend had been dead scarce more than a week; yet here were John Mayne and he confronting each other, as it were, in rivalry over the widow. But John Mayne had an excuse for his position. He was coming forward with the offer to save Charles Orisser's reputation and to re-establish the fortune of the Orissers upon a sound basis. What had his rival to show? Nothing. Allen was not quixotic; he had, indeed, a prejudice against fine feeling; but the situation was so pointed, the contrasts were so marked, that he really did not find it in him to utter a word. Besides, he had no reason to suppose that Lilian's thoughts had already detached themselves from her husband sufficiently to regard him, Allen, as even a prospective suitor. John Mayne's great pull lay in his ability to come forward with a business proposition, whilst leaving sentiment discreetly in the background. But of course Lilian would have to marry him in the end; it would be an unspoken bargain.

So Allen, his brief report ended, sat sullen and mute, while she, crumpling the letter nervously in her hand, appeared to find speech equally difficult. Pale in her black dress, she looked the very picture of distressful irresolution. Presently she rose to walk undecidedly about the room. When at last she broke silence, it was only to touch the fringes of the subject. But Allen soon saw, as the broken sentences came out, that what had to be had to be; and he applied himself with a will to concealing the bitterness in his heart. Before she left him, it was understood that John Mayne should be "consulted," should be permitted "to give advice"—that John Mayne, in a word, should be allowed to play the part he had it in mind to play.

From this time on everything developed in the manner Allen expected. Half-truths and half-measures proved impossible. Before long the big man had assimilated the whole of Charles Orisser's financial history; a few days more and he "had the situation well in hand." He had in truth taken absolute possession of it, just as he had taken possession of

Sir Charles's desk, over which his broad shoulders studiously hung. Henceforward poor Allen was no more than John Mayne's clerk. The close intimacy of his painstaking, but hopeless, labours with Lilian was a thing of the past. Every day his instinctive antipathy for John Mayne increased, and he made no doubt that it was reciprocated, although it was no part of the newcomer's design to betray any such feeling. On the contrary, one was made acutely conscious that John Mayne felt the position to afford him a signal opportunity to display all his tact, and, especially where the lady was concerned, all his delicacy of sentiment. So much so that Allen, bitterly sensible of the rising barrier between himself and Lilian, could not refrain from seeking her eyes, when on certain occasions her benefactor's manners were more than usually suggestive of the movement of a well-trained elephant treading among glass bottles. To do her justice, however, her recognition of such glances was of the fleetest. After all, John Mayne *was* doing her a service. His task was turning out to be a heavier one than any of them had imagined; and he was applying himself to it without flinching.

Allen sank into an ever deeper dejection of spirits. It was months since he had given thought to his archaeological work; and he had no heart to resume it, although by now John Mayne was quite able to dispense with his assistance. He was accordingly well pleased when a task, involving a change of scene, presented itself before him. He undertook, on Lilian's behalf, a mission to Cosmo.

Very soon after the catastrophe at Tangiers Cosmo had betaken himself to Mexico. Letters arrived which showed that he saw, or affected to see, nothing in that incident to warrant a stiffening of his father's feelings against him. It was noteworthy, however, that his letters were now addressed more frequently to Allen than to Sir Charles. Evidently he understood that in Allen he had a friend.

The news of his father's marriage to Lilian Orisser had taken singular effect upon him. He had written to Sir Charles to say that, had he guessed what was on foot, he would have hastened to England to shoot the woman dead. In the same letter, too, he brought abominable charges against the young bride; exactly what they were Allen was not told; but Sir Charles's anger against his son was raised to white heat.

This letter and others of similar import came into Lilian's hands soon after her husband's death; and when Allen made the suggestion that he should go to Mexico to inform Cosmo of the event, and to come to terms with him as regards his future allowance, the alacrity with which she seized upon the proposal revealed how deeply apprehensive she was of mischief from that quarter. In his talks with her at this time Allen obtained, in truth, some surprising glimpses into her mind. She, who had shown such strength of nerve in the great tragedy of her life, lost all her coolness before the prospect of conflict with Cosmo. The ridiculous, the meaningless, hatred which the latter evinced for her, she actually appeared to return—and with an admixture of dread. In excuse of her feelings she told Allen that Cosmo in his letters to his father had denounced her as his slanderer and supplanter and had sworn he would be revenged. The absurdity of the charge and the emptiness of the threat were no reassurance to her; Allen found himself combating an irrational fear against which argument was useless.

Armed with a certified copy of the will by which Sir Charles had left everything to his wife, and authorised to promise Cosmo that his present allowance would be continued, Allen accordingly set off. Where the money was to come from he did not ask. That was, alas, only too plain! And yet, in all this affair, John Mayne was not consulted. It was doubtful whether he had ever heard of Cosmo; and even if he had, it was most unlikely that in the present juncture he had found time to give a thought to that far-off, negligible creature. So, as Lilian seemed particularly anxious that they should keep the matter to themselves, Allen took his departure without informing John Mayne where he was going, or what his business was.

On the journey the young man's spirits revived. He found it a relief not to have Lilian constantly before his eyes. Her grief had pained him; but her rapid, bitter mastery of her grief pained him still more. In the short lapse of six weeks she had turned into a different person. "She is preparing," he said to himself, "to become John Mayne's wife. She is forcing herself to forget everything she has cared for—and she is succeeding!"

The contrast between Eamor and the central Mexican plateau, on which he eventually tracked his quarry down, was strong enough to satisfy even the most immoderate desire for change. The actual scene of the meeting was a strip of desert, a bleached expanse, blinding under the raw, white light. Behind it quivered an iridescent and chimerical mountain-range. In the foreground the shadows of a dozen earthen huts made blots of darkness upon the wide-flung tawny brilliancy. These, with a few red and yellow blankets stretched as awnings, were the only objects to arrest the eye. The air and the light sent a shock of joy through the blood; one's nerves, taut and tingling, received from the space and the stillness a noble challenge to alert and turbulent life.

As for Cosmo, Allen's first impression was that he had changed but little. He looked perhaps more gaunt and dry, and his movements were more febrile than in Spain; but his general air was the same. The healthy, primitive existence lived by his companions—an existence varied by occasional bouts of debauchery—was congenial to him. Theirs was essentially a masculine society, and Cosmo's genius was male. If civilisation had rejected him, it was in great part, as Allen now told himself, because the feminine spirit governed it. In any distinctively manly community Cosmo was sure to be popular—at least until his arrogance excited a reaction against him. As a stranger he would generally find a welcome, but he might not remain welcome for very long. The sociality for which his temperament rendered him specially unfitted was that of the modern state,—a sociality grounded upon a tacit acceptance of materialistic ends. His contempt for received opinion was so openly displayed that those who most depended on received opinion for protection, comfort, or self-respect, lost no time in combining together against him.

Because of his virility he was not the kind of man that women would ignore. And, to judge from his own tales of his past life, their feeling towards him generally took the shape of vengeful hostility. Possibly some intuition came to them that Cosmo's amatory propensities were as unconventional as the rest of his character. His attitude towards the other sex was, moreover, by no means gallant. To provoke feminine antagonism was one of his foibles.

Allen spent two months with him, sharing his life; and at the end of that time he felt disillusioned. The man's mind now appeared to him to be as hard, arid, and empty, as the desert upon which he chose to live. The visions that floated over it were mirages; and Cosmo himself had well-nigh lost the will to pursue them. His long, sullen reveries, his hours of dreamy apathy, gave token of a gathering sense of frustration and defeat.

He received the news of his father's death with indifference. His inquiries into the situation at home were superficial; he accepted the terms offered him with a shrug. Europe and all that it stood for appeared to be fading out of his ken. Allen parted from him without regret, and was firmly persuaded that they would never meet again.

On his arrival in England he betook himself to Eamor to make his report. He found Lilian more distant, more estranged, than ever. The rigid conventionality of her manner was an offence to him; and he was about to cut their colloquy short, when an astonishing thing happened.

In an instant he lost control of himself; pacing the room vehemently before her, he poured forth in a torrent of words all the anger, disappointment, and bitterness, in his heart.

The woman listened without speech or movement; then burst into tears and left the room. For his part, after wandering about the grounds for half an hour in an indescribable state of contrition and anguish, he drove to the station and returned to Tornel.

A few days later he received a summons from one, Walter Standish, who had charge of John Mayne's home office, and was the latter's confidential secretary and right-hand man. He went and was offered a well-paid post at the Tornel Museum of Antiquities, a foundation which owed much to Sir Charles. After a moment's reflection he accepted the position, and was about to take his leave, when Walter detained him. During Allen's absence several questions, he said, had arisen in connexion with Sir Charles's estate—questions upon which Allen could probably throw some light. In the course of the long, business conference that followed, particulars of Lilian's arrangements with John Mayne became known to Allen. He learnt that John Mayne had discharged all Sir Charles's debts, liquidated certain of his financial undertakings, and was putting the others upon a sound basis. Furthermore, the mortgages on the Eamor estate had been paid off; but a new mortgage was being prepared in favour of John Mayne—this new mortgage being accepted by the latter as a sort of return for his vastly more important expenditures. The new mortgage, however, was a heavy one; and Allen at once made the observation that the estate could hardly be expected to produce the sum required yearly as interest, and that without taking the cost of living at Eamor into account. Moreover, neither Lilian nor Nicholas had any private means.

Walter smiled. "To you," he said, "I need make no secret of the fact that Lady Orisser will before very long become Mrs. Mayne. In these circumstances the whole question of the mortgage and of the interest on it becomes insignificant. My impression is that Mr. Mayne is taking the mortgage more as a concession to Lady Orisser's feelings than for any other reason." And in carefully chosen terms he went on to intimate that his chief, imbued with a deep sense of chivalry, had no other desire than to preserve Eamor for the family whose ancient homestead it was, and already looked upon young Nicholas as a son.

Chapter 5

Allen came away from this interview with feelings of mistrust and dissatisfaction that he could not wholly account for. Walter's personality was unsympathetic to him. "A prig!" he said to himself, as he strode impatiently down the street. "One who takes care only to see the righteousness that lies on the road to worldly success. Standish and John Mayne are certainly well coupled."

In his pocket he had a memorandum that Walter had insisted on his taking away with him. It set forth in what fashion John Mayne—acting in the name of Lilian Orisser, the titular executrix—had proceeded in the heavy work of winding up Sir Charles' estate. This paper, Allen divined, had been pressed upon him with a double purpose; there was the intention, first, of exhibiting how much it was costing to save the name of Orisser from dishonour; and, secondly, the idea of safeguarding the generous intervener against any complaints, objections, or claims, which Sir Charles's presumably unscrupulous associate might attempt to raise against him in the future. "I am being paid off and dismissed," thought Allen. "They have one and all finished with me. My connection with the Orissers ceases. The post at the Museum is a parting gift—but a gift, by the way, that can be withdrawn at will, for Walter is on the committee, and can turn me off, if and when he pleases."

In a flash of anger he considered taking back his acceptance. Then he thought better of it. He was Sir Charles's literary executor, and the post at the Museum would give him just the leisure and freedom that were needed for the important work involved.

On getting back to his rooms he found a letter from Lilian. He opened it flinchingly. It contained no allusion to their last meeting, however, nor showed what impression his outburst had made upon her, unless some inferences were to be drawn from the very gentleness of its tone. She begged him to accept the post at the Museum, if only in justice to her husband's memory; she spoke of an early marriage between herself and John Mayne as of an event long since decreed; she reminded Allen that she owed John Mayne her deepest gratitude, and begged him not to think that her sense of this obligation diminished her gratitude to *him*. No; she valued his friendship as much as ever; and in proof of this would ask him yet another favour. In all the business that John Mayne was now transacting for her she found herself quite out of her depth. Would Allen give those affairs the intelligent examination that she was unequal to giving them? so that when the day came upon which she would be required to sign the documents pertaining to her executorship, she might do so with the sense that they had satisfied him. Furthermore, would he—conformably to a suggestion of John Mayne's—come down to Eamor on that day, and be a witness of the final proceedings?

This letter did much to assuage Allen's wounded sensibilities. He was very ready to execute the first part of Lilian's request; but he would gladly have excused himself from attendance at Eamor. As that ceremony, however, was to constitute the closing incident in the arduous task of setting right what Charles Orisser had left so ruinously wrong, he did not see how he could refuse. Accordingly, on the appointed day he found himself standing once more before the fireplace in the library, waiting, constrained and despondent, for the others to enter. In a few minutes they all came in, Lilian, John Mayne, Walter Standish, even young Nicholas. It was plain that John Mayne intended the occasion to make up in formality for what it lacked in pleasantness. From Allen's point of view it was not improved by the fact that a week ago he had had another and a still less agreeable interview with Walter. On Lilian's behalf he had quite definitely objected to the plan of a new mortgage on the Eamor Estate. Why, he asked with bluntness, why did John Mayne take the lustre off his magnanimity by keeping alive the memory of a debt that could never be repaid? The mortgage, doubtless, signified little to *him*, but it was bound to occupy quite an important place in the mind of his wife.

To put this before John Mayne's representative had been an ungrateful task; and Walter had done nothing to make it easier. He had looked blank, then raised his eyebrows, finally smiled a little and courteously professed his inability to view the matter from Allen's standpoint. He had adopted, in short, just the attitude which the situation conveniently offered him. But an inward rage fortified Allen's determination to say his say. Not delicacy, nor tact, nor good taste, should debar him from looking into the future and formulating those unpleasant—but conceivable—eventualities which John Mayne's proved generosity enjoined that he should ignore. It was too much, indeed, to hope that he could alter what had been arranged, but he reckoned that he could take out some kind of insurance against future troubles by enforcing a very clear prevision of what those troubles might be. He could expect that Walter would report this interview to his chief, and that the memory of it would arise to put John Mayne upon his mettle and prick up his sense of honour, should a quarrel with his wife ever tempt him to use his mortgage as a weapon against her.

The procedure in the library was ceremonious. One by one the documents were put before him, and he was called upon to declare that each was in order before it was tendered to Lilian for her signature. Several times he caught John Mayne's eyes resting upon him with a shrewd dislike. Before the production of the mortgage, the old man squared his shoulders and prepare to make a speech. It was far from his desire, said he, to take any material compensation from his future wife for the assistance he had been privileged to render her. In the document that she now proposed to execute he saw nothing but a token of her generous wish to make every return to him that in her power lay. That she made this offering and that he accepted it, was to be regarded simply as a sign that their two minds were as one. Eamor, he declared, and his fist struck the table, Eamor had belonged to the Orissers for some five hundred years! Well, it was his intention and desire that it should continue to be the homestead of the Orissers for another five hundred years and more!

As a semi-public pronouncement this was eminently satisfactory. Allen secretly flattered himself that his downrightness with Walter had not been entirely without effect. He had not expected anything so explicit, and shrewdly suspected that the speaker had been a little carried away by a complacent consciousness of mastery. This was an hour of triumph for John Mayne. He had paid the price, got what he coveted, and earned gratitude and admiration as well. Poor John Mayne! it was unfortunate that his self-satisfaction should make such an unattractive creature of him!

Alas, too, for Lilian! Throughout the proceedings Allen had instinctively avoided looking in her direction; and, when the speech was finished, it was not on her but on Walter that he fixed his ironical regard. The latter frowned and turned his head away.

A few minutes later he had appended his signature as witness to the deed, and shortly afterwards was driving back to the station.

The days, the months, the years, that followed were uneventful ones for Allen, although full of study and thought. His duties at the Museum being, as he had foreseen, light, he was able to devote his main energies to the ordonnance and critical examination of the great mass of material that Sir Charles and he had collected. And this work conducted him into regions over which his mind had hitherto done little more than skim—like a bird flying in the dusk over an unknown land. His studies in Egyptian mythology gradually led him to the exploration of the whole dark body of primitive lore. He was carried some little distance into the provinces of anthropology and psychology. He had to adventure at times into the territories of biology and even of metaphysics. Indeed, he would probably have smothered himself at last under a blanket of erudition, had not his temperament been of the selective, rather than of the collective, order. Discovery, not learning, was his aim. He believed that his subject-matter might be made to reveal the subconscious intuitions and desires of all mankind. He kept the sense of following an invisible thread. When the thrill of an intimate personal interest in his subject left him, he took it for a sign that he was off the track.

For a long time his romantic attachment to Lilian Orisser (who had soon become Lilian Mayne) caused him pretty constant heartache. And it remained capable of kindling into heat whenever circumstances led to an exchange of letters or some chance turned his mind in her direction, Its decline would have been more rapid had not a stimulus been applied to his imagination by a very early breach of her relations with her husband,—a breach, which resulted in her sudden return from the continent to Eamor, there to follow an unattached and lonely way of life. While John Mayne continued to spend the greater part of his time abroad, Lilian remained in seclusion. And the picture Allen created for himself of her solitary existence in that spot acted as a perpetual irritant to his tenacious romanticism.

Once or twice in the course of her first years of retirement, questions relating to Sir Charles's literary remains gave him an excuse for paying her a half-day's visit. In those meetings there was no ostensible renewal of intimacy, but he always came away with an increased insight into her position. She did not confess, but neither did she conceal, that she regarded her husband with nothing short of loathing; and Allen's intuition told him that it was unnecessary to look for a specific cause for this aversion. She had not married John Mayne from natural inclination, and sheer incompatibility of temperament was answerable for the rest. That she had not, however, yielded to her antipathy without a bitter struggle was evident from the several attempts at reconciliation to which she lent herself during the three years following the original separation. Indeed, it was certain that she was miserably oppressed by a sense of failure, and had not settled down to live alone at Eamor until she perceived that the case was desperate. How desperate it was Allen realized when he ventured to ask her about her financial arrangements with her husband, and discovered that she had accepted a position of virtual imprisonment. For the allowance she received was given her upon the condition that she should never leave the place. When Allen cried out against this stipulation, she explained ruefully that her own unwisdom had been largely responsible for it. She had cherished the past too openly. She had permitted her passion for everything that spoke to her of Charles Orisser to kindle a fire of jealousy and rancour in his successor. The old man had evidently said within himself that if she cared only for Eamor and Nicholas, Eamor and Nicholas were all that she should have. Let her live there, with the boy at her side, in her own fashion! Whilst she lived there he would allow her just what was sufficient for the boy's education and the upkeep of the place. But should she leave Eamor without his consent, the whole allowance would be stopped.

Later, on rare occasions, Allen came across Nicholas in Tornel, and at every meeting did his best to reestablish the amicable relation of old times. But he found the youth more difficult to approach than the child had been, and in the end he desisted. As the years passed, everything tended to make him feel that his connexion with the family of Orisser had melted away. Sometimes he asked himself with a shrug why it was that he regretted it.

Yes, that had been his position, that his attitude of mind, until the other day, when, of a sudden, Cosmo—Cosmo, from whom he had received no word since their leave-taking in Mexico—Cosmo, the world abhorring and by the world abhorred—Cosmo, who, if not dead, was as good as dead—had appeared before him in the flesh. It spoke much for the vitality of his ancient memories that, when his eyes fell upon Cosmo, his heart dropped a beat. It was the flying open of the swing-door to a dismal public-house in one of Tornel's most dismal streets that put the apparition before his eyes. Cosmo had stepped forth blinking, like a vulture, and, like a vulture, lean and bald and grim. It was impossible not to recognise him; yet so changed was he that recognition seemed an insult. True, his still erect carriage of himself and the savagery of his rheumy eyes made a denial of decrepitude; but the violence of that denial was mocked by its futility. What in heaven's name was the man still alive for? And what could be the reason for his return?

For a while the two men stared at one another; and to Allen's mute interrogations Cosmo's answering scowl replied that this encounter, at any rate, had not formed any part of his programme. Soon recovering himself, however, Allen stepped forward with cordiality. Indeed, his perception that the meeting was undesired caused his greeting to be a good deal warmer than it might otherwise have been. This manner, too, had the advantage of enabling him to ply Cosmo with questions. When had he arrived? Where was he lodging? Why had he not written? And how long was he intending to stay?

To all this the other, looking down through eyes contemptuously narrowed, answered either curtly or not at all. His bearing clinched Allen's conviction that his designs, whatever they might be, were assuredly not amiable. And again, for that very reason, his friendliness remained proof against all snubs. He accompanied Cosmo back to his dreary quarters and spent a long evening with him.

This was the beginning of a complete and painful change in Allen's way of life. Not daring to leave the other to his own devices—for what was to prevent him from taking the next train to Eamor?—he fell into the position of Cosmo's attendant, entertainer, and nurse, in conformity with the man's physical and mental requirements at every moment in the twenty-four hours. Of course, it was a ridiculous situation. He himself ruefully recognised it. What made him persevere from day to day was his persuasion that he was rapidly gaining influence over Cosmo. He assured himself that he would very soon succeed in inducing his troublesome companion to go back whence he came; and that then he, on his side, would have the satisfaction of going back to his routine with the sense that he had done Lilian a very useful service.

In the meantime, however, Cosmo's designs remained more or less shrouded in mystery. At the end of five days Allen's understanding amounted to this: he apprehended that Cosmo had put in his appearance at Tornel chiefly because he was at the end of his tether. He could bear with himself no longer, and needed some novel diversion. Lonely, reckless, suffocating under the weight of an immense ennui, and confident that his cud was not far off, in what direction would his thoughts naturally turn? They would turn to the satisfaction of a last curiosity, to the stimulus of a last excitement; they would turn towards "home";—home, for a last fling of revenge, and for death with a whoop of derision at the world which had rejected him, and more particularly at her whom he chose to objectify as his especial enemy.

His days in Tornel, before he fell in with Allen, had been spent, it appeared, in solitary brooding. For most of the time he had been, by his own confession, under the influence of the drugs to which he had recourse when neuritic pains, caused by the virus of a terrible disease, prostrated him. In this condition, and amid the depressive surroundings of a squalid, busy, indifferent town, moments had undoubtedly come when he lost heart for the game. With increasing incisiveness the question must have cut into his mind: what grip could he take upon the hard surface of this life, where part fitted into part with the exactitude of squared masonry? In a word, how should he open his attack? Eamor and Tornel were bits of the same mechanism; and what use was it to fling oneself into the wheels of a machine powerful enough to tear one into fragments and continue running with undiminished smoothness?

Such, Allen conjectured, were the misdoubts that were inclining Cosmo to hearken to the suggestion that he should give up and go back. But he was soon to learn that he had only guessed a part of what was passing in the man's mind. The final revelation, and the climax, came upon that sultry night in which we discovered him standing in a trance of irresolution outside Cosmo's door. The latter, in the course of an interminable monologue, had declared—with dreadful emphasis—that he would never leave the country unless Allen were to accompany him. His words had filled his auditor with dismay. What! thought Allen. Was he to abandon his work? Exile himself? Lead a life of vagabondage? And all for what? For what? Or rather, for *whom?* The idea of such a sacrifice staggered him. But still more did it stagger him to find that he was almost prepared to make that sacrifice.

Various and complex were the impulses, intricate and even contradictory the considerations, that had finally clenched his mind. Many of them he hardly understood. But he was willing to confess to himself that if he preserved a strange kind of affection for Cosmo, he was none the less counting heavily upon the man's early death. But further back in his mind there lay of course quite another set of motives; and these he was less willing to examine. He did not like to concede to his sentiment for Lilian an important part in his decision.

And still less was he prepared to recognise certain cravings of his own nature which an unadventurous life at Tornel had been systematically starving. When he asked himself whether he was taking the plunge for Cosmo's sake, or for Lilian's, or simply for the sake of a change, he did not know what to reply. He was certainly not doing it out of devotion to Cosmo alone. And this aggravated his uneasy sense that the basis of his connexion with the latter was not perfectly sound. He was aware of harbouring equivocations, reservations, ambiguities, particularly impermissible in relation with such a man as Cosmo. Cosmo might be cunning and secretive; and Cosmo would lie, when he chose; but he knew how to be sincere with himself better than any other man alive. His scrupulousness in this respect was of a higher order than was generally attempted or even conceived. The article called truth, and commonly exchanged as such in the commerce of life—the article that most persons consider good enough to offer to themselves and to others—that article, compared with the stuff that Cosmo dealt in, was shoddy. Nor did the reflection entirely satisfy Allen that his motives in this case were probably well gauged. He was either a true friend of Cosmo's, or he was not. Alas, alas! it was not going to be an easy relationship!

Such were the strands that went to make up the loosely-woven tissue of his reflections, as he sat, wakeful and perplexed, upon the roof. When the early dawn came to suffuse the overhanging fog, he was still resting in the same place. But, by then, he had sunk into that dreamy condition, when the mind, no longer controlled, plays idly with every small impression it receives. The emergence of the city out of the greyness was proceeding before him like the slow development of a photographic plate. And in his mood of detachment he wondered why he lacked the power to watch his life—yes, and all other lives—with even such a quiet, unimpassioned interest as pervaded him now. For he seemed to float above life—to be raised above the small coercions of life. And yet—and yet something was present even at this hour to vex the peace of his spirit. What was it? It was a little noise—a small persistent noise, which, as he at last realized, must have accompanied all his thoughts. It was the small, vicious hiss of a steam-jet, ejaculating at regular intervals from the rear wall of a contiguous factory. That busy, unremitting sound was beginning to oppress him. It even infected him with apprehension. That was the voice of matter,—a reminder of the wear and tear of quotidian things, and of the abject condition of earthliness. That was what went on and on—and beat you in the end!

Alas, poor Cosmo! A vision of the man arose before his eyes—of the old Cosmo, as he had appeared upon the hot plain of the Castille. Stalking along, magnificent of gait, the black splash of his shadow behind him, Cosmo had rightly presented himself as the very genius of that brilliant, arid fervency. And now, how fallen was that son of the morning! How tattered the banners of ecstasy that once he flew!

Chapter 6

His decision once taken, Allen was in a fever to be off. Life in Tornel, with Cosmo as a companion, was becoming more unbearable every day. Fortunately, berths were available on a ship sailing for South America at the end of the week; and, as Cosmo did not care one jot whither he went, Allen lost no time in booking a passage.

The next thing was to come to some arrangement with the Museum authorities. It would be best, he thought, to call on Walter Standish, to whom he would declare that a breakdown of his health made a holiday necessary. Walter might not believe him, but that could not be helped. And Walter would not wish to raise objections.

About the date of his return he must necessarily be vague. His private hopes, in so far as he made bold to formulate any, were that Cosmo would soon either die or grow weary of his society. But the future was too obscure to peer into. He looked no further than to the hour when Cosmo and he, safe on ship-board, would watch the land fading out of view.

To this hour he looked forward with impatience. Then, and not till then, would he allow himself to compose a letter to Lilian telling her what he had done. The thought of that letter was his present consolation and reward. That it should be so was absurd;—but so it was.

Of recent years he and Walter had met only at the Museum and only for the discussion of matters relating thereto. It was accordingly with a small touch of curiosity that he now prepared to seek the man out in his own distinctive surroundings. Walter, he knew, had recently moved into a modern block of office buildings, erected by John Mayne, where he had reserved for himself, his secretary, and his stenographer, a little suite on the topmost floor. At once upon stepping into the edifice Allen received a visual impression of intense cold and cleanliness; but the cold, he inly commented, was only an appearance; for the building, in all its parts, was mysteriously and suffocatingly warm. As for the cleanliness—well! the air, at any rate, was not clean; the frosted windows being closed to everything but a white, polar light, which penetrated everywhere. Entering a steel cage, he was shot upwards to a great height and turned out upon a marble corridor that extended pale, inhospitable vistas for equal distances to the right and to the left. His resonant footsteps took him past innumerable glass-panelled doors, inscribed with the names of companies over which John Mayne had the control. The silence of the place was metallically pitted by a clatter of frenzied typing machines.

"Strange," said Allen to himself, "that civilisation should have evolved a race of men of whom this is the natural habitat,—men, who are most at their ease in surroundings of smooth marble and polished mahogany,—men whose lungs inhale the atmosphere of steam-heated apartments with more satisfaction than the hill top breeze!" Yet Walter, he went on to reflect, could not be said to be a specimen of the regular business type. His aspect, to begin with, was by no means urban. His large frame was well covered, and seemed to call for tweeds rather than broadcloth. If a sedentary life had imparted a certain looseness and oiliness to the texture of his flesh, his carriage of himself was still erect and free. His complexion, too, was fair and ruddy, and his blunt, benign, mobile features informed the world that he was a man of liberal culture and varied interests.

Walter's entry into the sphere of business had been, as he himself often said, rather of the nature of a happy accident. The only son of a highly successful portrait painter, he had been trained for the bar. After a short period of unsuccessful practice he had been taken into John Mayne's office. How he had risen to his present position was something of an enigma. Had John Mayne, with his famous insight into character, early discovered in him those mysterious qualities that constitute financial genius? Was he joking when he said: "That young fellow, Standish—well, you know, he has the flair!" People wondered, following Walter with their eyes, speculatively. His career certainly seemed to justify his chief's encomiums. In a short time he had built up a large fortune; and when, later, he ceased to make any visible effort to grow rich, money continued to pour in upon him. Poverty appeared to dread his look of reproachful censure; and well she might! for, not content with his own immunity, Walter pursued her relentlessly into the slums. In company with John Mayne, he recognised that the modern industrial world presents a fine field for philanthropic effort; and, accordingly, his principal energies had been concentrated for many years on the administration of charity. This was his speciality. The amount of money that passed through his hand for the construction of schools, libraries, churches, and polytechnics was, as he himself said, simply amazing. It was amazing, too, how much the poor could absorb without ceasing to be poor. However, he never lost heart.

Ushered into a comfortable ante-chamber, Allen prepared to wait, for he had been given to understand that, not having an appointment, he could hardly expect to see the man of affairs immediately. The room was empty, but scarcely had he settled himself with a newspaper, when another visitor arrived, and was escorted obliquely across the apartment to another door which gave access to Walter's sanctum. This young man, who on his brief passage across the room had evidently not noticed him, was recognised by Allen as Nicholas Orisser. Nicholas, apparently, did have an appointment with Walter, or, if not, possessed superior claims to admittance. Allen overheard the two men greet each other with pronounced cordiality—a cordiality which seemed to denote that the occasion was a particular one. And, indeed, during the next minute, while the door still stood ajar, a key to the situation was provided. Walter was being congratulated on his engagement to be married; and the pronouncement of the name of Madeline was sufficient to indicate that his fiancee was John Mayne's favourite niece. Furthermore, there was question of John Mayne's near arrival at Tornel, and——But that was all the listener was destined to hear; the door closed, and he was left to go back to his newspaper.

These items of news, however, had a disturbing effect upon him. In the present unsettled state of his mind he was liable, without doubt, to attach undue importance to every occurrence that could be related, however remotely, to the affairs in which he was interesting himself. He knew that it was an unusual thing for John Mayne to come to Tornel, and, although Madeline's engagement might well be held to account for the approaching visit, he was fancifully inclined to look for some other, more important, reason. For one thing, Madeline had been living at Eamor for the last three or four years, and he had often wondered on what terms she stood with Lilian. So now he fell to speculating whether John Mayne would go down to Eamor to see his niece there,—and how the marriage would affect Lilian,—and even whether it might have any reactions upon her general situation.

These imaginings so wrought upon him that all at once he rose and went quietly down into the street. It was his intention to waylay Nicholas, and snatch a few minutes' conversation with him. He would return to Walter afterwards. What exactly he would say to the young man was a question he had not determined with any precision. The truth of the matter was that he hungered for news of Lilian, and had made up his mind to extract all he could from her step-son—even at the cost of appearing somewhat intrusive.

He was destined, however, to meet with disappointment. After he had hung about the street for twenty minutes, the vexatious suspicion came to him that there might be another exit from the building, and that Nicholas might have made his way out into another street. He inquired and found that this had in fact occurred. So greatly was he put out that the idea of interviewing Walter became unbearable. After a moment's reflection he turned his face homewards. He did not like to leave Cosmo alone for any length of time. Besides, he had nothing to say to Walter, after all, that could not be expressed just as well in writing.

During the next two days he found little time to think about Nicholas or Walter or indeed about anyone but Cosmo. The latter was now inclined to regret the abandonment of his first purpose. He could not resign himself to giving up his campaign against Lilian in particular and civilisation in general without feelings of humiliation and self-disgust. The depth and genuineness of his sentiment affected Allen at times with an answering sense of guilt. There were moments when he actually saw himself as the serpent in the stark and flinty Eden of Cosmo's mind; and, knowing that he would never succeed in changing Cosmo's ideas, he could not help wondering whether the man's rancour might not one day boil over and put a violent end to their precarious alliance.

Every hour spent in Cosmo's company added to his wonder at the strange combination of wisdom and folly, insight and blindness, that his companion presented. Unreasonable as Cosmo was, there was yet much to admire in his extreme sensitiveness to all that was unlovely and mean in the spiritual as well as in the material life of a town such as Tornel. He discerned with an extraordinary keenness and hated with an extraordinary hate. Between his emotional reaction and that of other men there was all the difference that lies between the palate of a child and that of a seasoned toper. And it was Cosmo's peculiarity, too, that the abstract verities of which he did stand possessed lost nothing of their fiery compulsiveness with time and familiarity. They had come to him, not through that gradual process by which the essential is ordinarily distilled from out the inchoate mass of presented experience, and the Ideal mistily and tardily disengaged,—as a goal, indeed,—but as a goal so remote, so dim, that the world in the meantime must needs be accepted with all available complacency;—no, they had come to him rather by direct intuition; and the Ideal was present before his eyes, so sharply visualised, and so tantalizing in its splendour, that his spirit was stung into a perpetual rebellion against actuality—hideous actuality, to which humanity was, on the whole, brutishly resigned.

The compromises that mankind made without being aware of it, were those that drove him to the worst desperation; for in this compounding on what is he saw a propensity to deny or ignore what could be imagined. No matter if that vision was unrealizable; it was a vision to preserve. And it was not being preserved. Another and a poorer ideal was being put in its place. The temper which prompted Society to glorify itself was a material temper. For a society which glorifies itself can see no excellence excepting in service to itself, and gradually, but infallibly, loses sight of all but material services. It consequently exacts terrible renunciations from its members,—the deadliest and easiest being the suppression of the sense of renunciation.

In the wilds life with such a man might be tolerable, but in civilisation it was misery. When you entered into Cosmo's sphere you stepped into a spiritual world of different values or dimensions from those of other men; the forms and movements of other minds became indistinct and incoherent; a metaphysical barrier stretched between yourself and them. The everyday world was all around you, but you were not in it; you were alone with Cosmo.

Very rarely did the man give evidence of interest in practical affairs, even in the direction of his own personal concerns. The curiosity that he evinced regarding Lilian and Nicholas—for there were times when he plied Allen with questions—was singularly detached and analytical. And if he looked for points that might furnish a handle for his malevolence, that malevolence was, so to speak, abstract in character.

On the table in Allen's room there stood a snap-shot taken eight years ago at Eamor. It showed Sir Charles with Lilian and Nicholas upon the lawn. Allen would have put it away, only Cosmo's first visit to his rooms had taken him by surprise, and afterwards it was too late. Thereafter, too, whenever Cosmo visited him, the man's eyes would sooner or later travel round to that picture. And the day came at last when he picked it up and took it to the window for scrutiny. A deep flush overspread Allen's features, as, covertly, he watched. After a minute Cosmo put the picture down; his face was cold, hard, smiling. Without a word he resumed his pacing up and down the room.

What were the thoughts that stirred within that brain, while his steps took him to and fro, to and fro, between window and door? If that pictured scene had the power to inspire Allen with a sense of exile, what sentiment did it arouse in Cosmo? Once, in his boyhood, Allen remembered hearing, he had visited Eamor. Did he have no repinings? Or did the light that slanted upon that peaceful group gleam in his eyes, too, as the low gilded sunshine of regret? There was no telling. His face showed nothing—nothing, except an occasional glimmer of amusement, at the passage of some unconjecturable thought.

On the eve of their departure they set out from Allen's rooms to dine more sumptuously than usual at a restaurant. There was a tacit understanding between them that, if his fancy so inclined, Cosmo should make a night of it.

Dusk was falling; it had been a day without brilliance, and the evening was without freshness. In the street, as was his custom, Cosmo strode along a couple of paces ahead. For the last hour or so he had been indulging a savage kind of jocularity,—whether in anticipation of their approaching deliverance, or at the near prospect of raw spirits in satisfying quantities, Allen could not say.

The streets were thronged. Sombre-clad, white-faced workers were hurrying home under the spluttering arc lights. Taller than they, Cosmo stalked along, his gaze going straight out before him with lofty, unseeing disdain. He had the air of one who is steadfastly keeping some distant goal in sight; his limbs seemed to move under the spell of an inspired purpose.

At last, before a large square in the commercial quarter, he halted and contemplated darkly—as if the finger of God were pointing at it— an eating-house of exceptionally jaded aspect, which thrust a blunt wedge of plate-glass between two noisy streets. The establishment apparently struck his fancy; for, presently, he crossed the street and went in. Seating himself at a marble-topped table near the entrance, he ordered meat and drink, then waited; following with bright-eyed impatience the bringing and uncorking of a bottle.

The prospect of an inexpressably dreary evening unfolded itself before Allen, but his mood was one of resignation. Having steered his craft to this point without disaster, he could allow himself some measure of relief from anxiety, some measure even of self congratulation.

"Here's damnation to Tornel!" exclaimed Cosmo, raising his glass, and the look he sent round now showed plainly enough what impulse had moved him to celebrate his farewell to the town in this particular establishment. With its imitation marble pillars, its dirty gilding, and fly-blown mirrors, the big hall achieved second-rateness to perfection. Here they were in the very temple of pretentious squalor; this, if not the pinnacle, was at any rate the emblem, of civilisation.

Ah! could he but have seized an armful of those miserable pillars and buried himself in the rattling rubbish of their collapse. As it was, he fell wolfishly upon the greasy food set before him and drank from a thumb-marked tumbler as from the skull of an enemy.

Chapter 7

Meanwhile the place was rapidly filling. Persons vaguely congruous to the establishment hovered round, looking for seats; and Cosmo, whose table would accommodate more than two, was soon the centre of a little company. He was paying very freely for drink, and those creatures of cheap elegance and facetiousness made a fine show of conviviality around him, while among themselves they were full of rapid asides.

As time wore on and the atmosphere grew thick and heavy with smells of food, liquor, and tobacco, some drifted away, but others remained. Loungers, too, came up, leaning against the pillars to listen; for, as the spirits worked within him, Cosmo got into his stride; and none better than he could hold an audience when he was in the vein.

Allen moved out of earshot. That life of crude exploit and rank adventure which it now pleased Cosmo to flaunt—how little it was truly significant of the dreams that urged him along! And the man himself knew this well enough. In his present recitals he was instinctively suppressing what was fine; or rather, he dissolved his pearls in the acid of a brutal cynicism before casting them before his audience.

Allen had turned away to stare through the great pane behind him into the grey aridity of the lighted street. There figures drifted by like clouds across the face of the moon. Many looked as indefinite, as purposeless, as wan; and those who showed gaiety and animation, seemed possessed of a life that was merely factitious. Their expressions were grimaces, their gesticulations puppet-movements, their laughter was soundless, through the thick plate-glass. Watching them, Allen fell into a stupor, which endured until something in the outline of one of the passers-by snatched at his attention, causing him to lean forward with a start. He followed that figure with his eyes for as long as he could, then involuntarily rose to his feet. A glance at Cosmo showed that the latter would not be stirring for a long while yet; and his own departure, he fancied, would scarcely be noticed. Picking up his hat, he left the hall, and, once outside, had little difficulty in refinding the object of his interest, who had passed on no more than a hundred yards down the street. It was Nicholas without a doubt.

To his former desire to speak to Nicholas there was added a new curiosity. Why was the young man promenading this quarter at this hour? It was not the hour for business, nor the quarter for pleasure.

Whilst hesitating whether to accost him or not, he kept Nicholas in view. The latter was trending towards a region of shuttered stores and warehouses—a gloomy region intersected by long, ill-lighted streets, which at this hour were almost empty of traffic. He was walking in a hurried, unobservant manner, yet stopped now and again to look around him. The line he was following would, Allen knew, take him before long right out of the town. He would reach a place where buildings abruptly ceased, and a broad, rough road went down between fields of refuse to the waste track that lay between the town and the sea.

To Allen's increasing wonderment Nicholas tramped steadily on. Not until he had come to the edge of the town did he falter and finally draw up. A dreary expanse, dotted with smoking brick-kilns and rough wooden shanties, lay before him, dimly revealed in his immediate vicinity by the street-lamp under which he stood. A long straight avenue of similar lights marked the further course of the road. A smell of roasting clay hung in the air; the oppressive silence of the place was broken only by the occasional rumbling of a dray among the warehouses behind.

Nicholas was plainly unaware that he was being followed, and Allen, now fully determined upon entering into conversation with him, was wondering how he should set about it, when a number of black-shawled figures—factory girls, to judge by their appearance—came trudging in twos and threes out of a side alley, and, after passing down the road for a short distance, disappeared across a field to the left.

Nicholas watched them for some moments without moving, then suddenly struck out after the last group. Allen followed in turn, to come presently upon the shine of lighted windows, which he perceived to be those of a wooden conventicle, set down like a box in the middle of a rough piece of ground.

He had by now convinced himself that the young man's actions were governed simply by caprice;—a conclusion that was supported by the restlessness which the hot, stagnant air of that night had engendered in his own veins. A succession of windless days had enveloped the town under a blanket of vapours that bred a fever in the blood and sent one blindly out in search of some avenue of escape. It was too much, however, to suppose that the curiosity which had brought Nicholas to the doors of this prayer-house, would carry him so far as to attend the meeting within. Great was Allen's astonishment, therefore, when the youth actually entered; and the next minute he, on his side, was pushing his way into the building, to take up his stand only a few feet behind him among the crowd of men at the entrance. The rest of the interior, up to a platform at the farther end, was packed with women on benches. An uneasy silence reigned, every-one staring fixedly at the preacher, a thick-set, heavy-jowled man, who sat with his face tilted heavenward and eyes closed in an attitude intended to be suggestive of prayer.

The meeting had begun; the constraint momentarily augmented; but not until it had reached breaking point did the man on the platform rise and give voice. His utterance came as a deep-toned, muffled vibration, the source of which would have been doubtful, had his lips not been seen to be moving. This sound increased in volume and in articulation; his eyes at the same time gradually opened; the message of salvation unfolded itself.

The building was unendurably hot; its very walls seemed to sweat, their yellow varnish glistening in the light of many furious gas-jets. Faces shone with perspiration; a haze collected overhead.

But the hardest thing of all to bear was, unquestionably, the surge and swell of that indefatigable voice. Here and there beneath their shawls emaciated shoulders shuddered, and anaemic faces became strained in a smile of half-voluptuous anguish.

Allen was watching Nicholas. But at last, under the weight of his own discomfort, his vigilance failed; and when, after some minutes, he looked again, it was to see by the young man's livid face that he was on the point of fainting. Vigorously elbowing aside the stupefied figures that stood between, he succeeded in reaching him before he fell, and managed without too much difficulty in drawing him forth into the comparative freshness of the outside air.

At first, moved by an instinctive desire to get away, the two stumbled forward for some yards in the direction whence they had come; then, perceiving that the other was hardly equal to keeping on his legs, Allen propped him up against a shanty which stood on their path. Leaning against the wall, one arm across his face, the young man kept silence; and Allen was not quite sure whether he had been recognised. Nicholas's first words, however, removed this doubt.

"How did you come to be there?" he gasped. "As for me, I had no conception what it would be like!"

So saying, he laid a hand on Allen's shoulder, and again started to move across the field to the road. There they took rest once more, Nicholas seating himself upon a broken piece of fence.

"You did not know what it would be like?" repeated Allen in reflective tones. "Well! is that why you went?"

Nicholas laughed uncertainly. "It was like turning up a stone with one's foot, and finding underneath a congregation of horrible insects."

The other looked at him with curiosity. "Anyhow, it was an experience!" said he.

"I don't want experiences."

"Ah! Why not?"

"They are not in my line," the young man muttered.

"What do you mean, 'not in your line'?"

Nicholas made no reply, and Allen repeated his question. He intended to make his companion talk. In the matter of place and circumstance, fortune had oddly favoured him.

"Well!" replied Nicholas after a pause, "haven't you noticed that when anyone makes a fool of himself, he takes refuge in the thought that he has gained experience? Intelligent people are those who manage with the least experience—at least so it seems to me.

"I see." Then after a moment: "Are you an intelligent person?" Allen laughingly inquired.

The young man looked up with gravity, as if giving the question serious consideration.

"Intelligent? Yes!" he returned. "But nothing else!" At the same time he detached himself rather shakily from the fence as a sign that he was ready to go on.

Allen made no corresponding movement. "You had better wait a little longer," said he. "Besides, there are several things I want to ask you about. Yes," he went on with an emphasis which was called forth by the look of surprise that came into the other's face, "it is a long time since I had news of your step mother—or of you. I knew you as a boy;—have you forgotten that?"

"No. I have not forgotten."

"But you are astonished that my interest in you—and in your family—should continue?"

Nicholas was slightly taken aback. "I am always astonished when anybody takes an interest in anybody," was his reply, given after a moment's silence.

"Are you interested, then, in nobody but your self?"

"To lose interest in oneself is a symptom of middle-age," returned

Nicholas with some sharpness. "Besides, I am interested in ideas rather than in people."

Allen glanced in the direction of the conventicle and smiled.

"Those ideas?"

"No. Those are not ideas, but emotions. And very crude ones at that!" He paused, put his hand up to his head, and added whimsically: "The devil! I've lost my hat in there!" Then, catching Allen's eye, joined him in a laugh.

"However, but for you I should have fared much worse!"

Allen smiled. "I saw you in John Mayne's office the other day," said he with abruptness.

The other looked surprised.

"Yes. And I overheard you talking to Walter Standish. So he is going to marry Madeline Mayne, is he?"

Nicholas nodded.

"And John Mayne is expected here shortly?"

"Yes."

"When exactly?"

"I don't know. In four or five days."

"Is it this marriage that brings him to Tornel?"

Nicholas hesitated. "Partly, I suppose. But also—he is ill."

"Ill!" Allen gave full expression to his interest. "Do you know *how* ill?"

The other shook his head.

"You see," Allen said, with a troubled look, "I am going away." He paused. "I don't like to hear that John Mayne is ill!"

Nicholas regarded him with gentle amusement. He clearly meant it to be seen that he had fallen in with his catechizer's humour and was ready to indulge it.

"Why not?" he questioned in turn.

"I should have liked to be on hand when he died."

"Ah!" The young man turned this over for a while. "You mean . . .?" he began doubtfully.

"Yes," said Allen, although he was not certain how the other meant to finish his sentence. "I might be of use."

On this there was a pause. The lamp under which they were standing afforded Allen some opportunity of studying his companion's aspect. The greenish light from above gleamed upon the young man's smooth, fair hair, to which it imparted a metallic lustre, and upon a square forehead, which it made inordinately pale. His eyes, one of which Allen knew to have a cast, were now in shadow. The nose, the mouth, the chin, so finely modelled as to be slightly effeminate, completed a physiognomy which, to Allen's sense, was not altogether agreeable. The face was expressive of a melancholy that would easily turn to scorn.

From the meeting-house behind them there broke forth long, dreary wailings. Nicholas lifted his eyes with a look of disgusted interrogation.

"Some of those people are being moved to confess their sins," explained Allen with a smile. "They are receiving grace."

"Sins! Grace!" And the young man first frowned, then uttered a short laugh. "How beautifully simple!" The next moment, however, he sighed. "Well! shall we move on?"

In silence they started up the road towards the town. But after they had gone a little way Nicholas suddenly stopped short.

"When you said, just now, that you might be of use to us—what exactly did you mean?"

His features were all but indistinguishable on the spot where he now stood, and his voice was devoid of expression. Allen gazed meditatively down the street.

"There was nothing definite in my mind. . . . But I cannot forget that I was present when John Mayne promised that Eamor should eventually be yours—yours, free and unencumbered." He paused. "You were there, too; do you recall the scene?"

"No."

"Not at all?"

"Well—perhaps dimly."

"How do you and John Mayne get on together?"

Nicholas laughed. "I don't think I have seen him more than three times during the last three years. And he only comes down to Eamor for the day. I don't like him."

"Does he like you?"

The young man laughed again. "It would surprise me very much to hear that he does."

"And his relations with your step-mother,—they have not improved?"

"No."

They had moved on and were once again within the precincts of the town. The tall fronts of the houses gave an echo to their footfalls. Allen was seized with a lassitude and depression which he felt the other to share.

"Tell me," said he, "are you not sometimes bored at Eamor?"

"No," returned Nicholas with vehemence. "I ask for nothing better than to spend the rest of my days there."

Allen was silent, and presently to his surprise Nicholas took up the thread of speech. "What has been spoiling Eamor during these last few years is Madeline Mayne's presence in the house."

"Your step-mother doesn't like her?" Allen asked quickly.

"No, she does not."

There was a pause.

"It pleases John Mayne to keep her there," continued Nicholas in a voice of extreme bitterness. "And it is not difficult to guess the reasons why."

"What are they, then?"

Nicholas evaded the question. "I don't say it is pleasant for her to live with us; she stays because she cannot help herself. John Mayne has virtually adopted her. She is not going to risk a quarrel with him. Besides, her skin is thick. She knows how we feel about her. But what does she care?"

A sudden desire to communicate had evidently seized hold of him, for the next moment he went on:—

"To-morrow evening Walter is taking me to some idiotic function at which he is to make a speech. Afterwards I am to drive him down to Eamor—in our new car. He will stay with us a couple of days—until John Mayne arrives in Tornel."

"And will John Mayne go down to Eamor later?"

"I don't know," returned the young man gloomily.

For a while Allen brooded. He was oppressed by the feeling that he was hurrying off into exile at a time when affairs might well be quickening out of the stagnation of years into a swift, eventful flow. But presently, brushing these preoccupations aside, he said:

"Do you say you have bought another car?"

"Yes?"

"Forgive me! But can you afford it? As you probably know," he continued, taking pleasure in a certain grimness, "I had a good deal to do with your family affairs at one time. That's my excuse for asking."

Nicholas hung fire, then: "Of course, *we* can't afford it!" he returned in a hard voice. "But John Mayne can!"

By a common instinct they both slackened their pace. Under the street lamp their glances sought one another.

"I admit," Allen conceded, "that the matter is not, fundamentally, a money matter, and yet ..."

"What?"

"You cannot afford to be provocative!"

Nicholas threw back his head with a short laugh.

"Provocative? Really, I don't think we are! But, to tell you the truth, I know nothing, or next to nothing, about our affairs. If you are interested in them, why don't you question Walter Standish?"

"Why don't *you?*"

"Because the whole position sickens me. Besides, have you ever known Walter tell anyone anything worth knowing? Of course not. However," he went on with growing excitement, "don't think I am annoyed by your questions! I am not. And please don't carry away the idea that I despise money. I am not such a fool as that. I know that money is the most important thing in the world."

Allen smiled.

"No, no," cried Nicholas, "I mean it. And you, would you deny it?"

The other hesitated.

"Surely," pursued Nicholas with measured emphasis, "surely it is perfectly obvious that to a really civilised human being, brought up in luxury, money is the indispensable means to everything that makes life worth living? Such a man's faculties, aptitudes and tastes are adapted for exercise within the sphere created by money—and in that sphere alone. Cast him out of it, and he will deteriorate—or even perish—miserably! One need be no cynic to recognise that! The spirit, like the body, can only thrive in the environment proper to it; and it is sheer cant to say that a man's spiritual environment is independent of his material environment. Self-culture—and I am not using the word in a snobbish or pedantic sense—is what the civilised man lives for;—and culture is impossible to the man who has to struggle for his daily bread."

Allen looked at him. "I see, at any rate, that you have given this matter some thought," said he with quietude.

Nicholas laughed harshly. "Do you suppose——" he began, and then broke off with a shrug.

They were approaching a point where it seemed natural that their ways should diverge; and Allen, although his mind was full, could find nothing more to say. Indeed, the disproportion between what there was to say, and the opportunity for saying it, was paralysing. In perfect silence he walked on to the cross-roads and there stopped.

"Good-bye!" said he, holding out his hand. "And let me assure you from my own experience that poverty need not be so dreadful as you imagine." He paused. "I sail to-morrow afternoon for South America.

You can tell your step-mother that I shall write to her from on board ship. Good-bye!"

The young man gripped the hand that was extended to him with more warmth than Allen had expected. For a moment they stood looking at one another, each possessed by a certain shyness. Then, with a parting gesture, each went his way.

For his part, Allen said to himself, he had certainly gathered plenty of food for meditation. And what occupied him most of all was the spiritual equivalences or analogies that he discovered in the characters of the two brothers. It would have interested him to make them known to one another. . . .

When he reached Cosmo's restaurant he stood at the window for some minutes, gazing at the scene within. There was Cosmo just as he had left him! Yes, there he was, thrown back in his chair, his chin lifted and his eyes slanting downwards with the same cold brightness upon his audience! A wisp of smoke was going up from his cigarette; the crude light of an incandescent gas-jet fell upon his fair, close-cropped, shapely head; and hanging above it from a tawdry bracket was a festoon of glued string, black with dying flies.

Chapter 8

On his way to Cosmo's lodgings at noon the next day, Allen kept reminding himself with mingled anxiety and relief that in less than five hours he and his companion would be safe on board. He had given careful thought to every detail of the departure. So careful had he been, indeed, that he might almost have detected traces of misdoubt or superstition in that very meticulousness. For thus do men cannily insure themselves against the sting of self-reproach in an enterprise of which they half expect the failure.

As he drew near to his destination, his nervousness increased. Instinctively he braced himself against the vexations and surprises which commerce with Cosmo so generally involved. And it was well that he did so. The living-room, when he entered it, was empty; and, passing through into the bedroom, his first glance showed him that Cosmo was seriously ill.

Yes, Cosmo was ill! Too ill, probably, to set out upon a journey! Standing in silence at the bedside, Allen looked down upon the man's haggard visage and cursed the Fates in his heart. Not many hours ago he might perhaps have welcomed an upsetting of his plans; for the news concerning John Mayne's health had added to his disrelish of departure. But, like many other persons, he was apt to cherish his decisions as much for the pains undergone in giving them birth as for their intrinsic attractiveness; and the confounding, at the eleventh hour, of a decision so deeply considered and so painfully reached, awoke in him a spirit of rebellion which stifled all other feelings. As he stood there, the idea of taking the man away rooted itself in his heart with a fanatical attachment. He vowed that if it were humanly possible to get Cosmo on board ship by five o'clock that day, he would do so. And if Cosmo were to die on the voyage out, well! that could not be helped!

The fact was that the bygone week had strained Allen's patience to the uttermost. He was tired out. It was intolerable to see oneself mocked for all one's pains! He swore that to bring to the vulgar business of practical affairs delicacies of calculation, scruple, taste, and feeling, was never anything but folly! In life's welter of hazard and accident the best things went for nothing.

As he looked down upon Cosmo and made his inquiries, there was as much rage as pity in his heart. The solicitous tone of his own voice sickened him. When he urged Cosmo to let him send for a doctor, he knew that he was counting secretly on a refusal; and when the refusal came, he accepted it without difficulty. He accepted, too, Cosmo's statement that he knew well enough how to treat these attacks. Without remonstrance he assisted him to administer to himself another injection of morphia. After that, all he could do was to sit down and wait.

In silence they both waited. He knew that if Cosmo could find the strength to rise, he would. He had seen in Cosmo's eyes a look of horror and panic, and he could read its meaning. He knew that the man's spirit was dashing itself against the walls of this odious little room like a wild bird that finds itself caged. The wanderer from the Mexican plateau saw himself dying here—here, in this compost of abjection and dirt;—here, with the smells of cooking and washing in his nostrils, and in his ears the bustle and clatter of a humanity that he loathed. Each ingredient in the squalor of his surroundings magnified itself, as Allen could guess, to mock his present helplessness. Oh, yes if Cosmo could summon the strength for it, he would rise and flee!

And so an hour passed by. After having given his companion a cup of tea, Allen withdrew into the next room, seated himself at a table which had been laid out for a light meal, and automatically went through the movements of eating. His face was now a perfectly expressionless mask, and his consciousness seemed to have become a mask too. It hid from him what was going on below. When again he looked at his watch it was two o'clock. His fingers drummed upon the table; his eyes stared out of the window.

At length a stir in the next room shook him out of his stupor. Without moving his head, he turned his eyes towards the open door.

Cosmo's figure, incredibly tall and emaciated, appeared in the doorway.

"In a few minutes," and the man's voice was both husky and harsh, "in a few minutes I shall be ready."

Allen drew a deep breath and nodded.

It was in good time after all that the two travellers started forth. Cosmo, to all appearances, had made a miraculous return to something like his normal health; and with an insane obstinacy, to which Allen dared risk only a feeble opposition, he insisted on setting out on foot. A woman, an inmate of the building, who happened to be watching her child at play under the archway leading from the court into the street, was a witness of their departure. She described afterwards how she had seen the tall man, who was looking much as usual, emerge from the stairway and stalk across the court, the other, who carried a bag, following a few paces behind.

When the tall man came to the arch, her little girl was sprawling in the middle of the way. He stooped, picked her up, and swung her high aloft. The child smiled and crowed, for playful treatment of this kind was not unfamiliar to her; but quite suddenly the sound died from her lips and the expression of her face changed to the extreme of terror. The next instant the man behind bounded forward, and with outstretched hand clutched the tall man, who with a snarl set down—indeed, one might almost say, threw down—the poor babe.

The occurrence was startling and inexplicable. As the mother rushed to her infant, which was still convulsed, the two men passed on through the gloomy archway and disappeared. She, herself, was seized with a fit of trembling, which, however, a moment later she overcame, and, moved by an overpowering curiosity, ran out to look down the street.

The long thoroughfare was nearly empty, and she at once descried the two figures she was looking for about three hundred yards away. The tall man was now again some few paces ahead; he moved in big, swinging strides down the centre of the street. She remained staring after them until they were lost in the grey dust-haze.

The port of Tornel was about three miles north of the town, from which it was separated by a waste expanse traversed by a network of tramlines, railway lines, and canals. It had never entered Allen's head that his companion would attempt the whole journey on foot, but when the latter continued deaf to every suggestion that they should engage a vehicle or take a tram, he began to suspect with consternation that such, in very truth, might be Cosmo's senseless intent. A demonic kind of energy seemed to be animating him. He moved forward with a violence and stiffness of gait that suggested the operation of his body machinery by a spiritual agent other than the ordinary. There was a glitter, too, in his eyes and a fixity impressed upon his features, which, when Allen pushed abreast, warned him against attempting intercourse, and sent him, with a pang of dread, back to his customary position in the rear.

The way that Cosmo was choosing brought the two men to the outskirts of Tornel not far from the scene of Allen's conversation with Nicholas. As they descended the slope out of the town, the port-works were to be seen, low, black, and bristling, across the intervening flats. But instead of continuing along the main road Cosmo presently struck off along a path which, although direct enough, was certainly not the route Allen had it in mind they should take. It ran by the side of an old, unused canal; it was deserted; there was little likelihood of finding any kind of assistance—still less a vehicle—upon the way, in the event of Cosmo's collapse.

The latter, however, was betraying as yet no signs of weakness. On the contrary, it was Allen, burdened as he was with a bag which contained a residue of Cosmo's belongings, who was hard put to it to keep up the pace. During the whole of the forenoon the air had been growing steadily more sultry and oppressive. By all evidences the electric storm that had been hanging over Tornel for the last week was about to break. The steadfast gloom of the morning sky had sensibly deepened since they set out; and when, on reaching the open, Allen scanned the horizon southward behind the town, he had a moment of veritable consternation at sight of the wicked blackness now spreading rapidly overhead. However, the gods could not stop their going now! So with set jaw, and without even troubling to wipe away the perspiration that kept trickling down his forehead, he plodded doggedly on. He could note for his satisfaction that they were half-way already, and the pale, glassy surface of the canal alongside had not yet been indented by a single rain drop, nor was thunder yet to be heard even from afar.

Deep—and to his nervously strained imagination, singularly ominous—was, nevertheless, this hush, this process of silent preparation for the oncoming storm. The portent gained in intensity from the desolation of the surroundings, and these seemed the more desolate for being so little removed from the throng and bustle of the city's life. Here, but a few yards outside the torrent of humanity, no human shape was in sight; smoke, rising in a straight column from a railway engine stationary in the distance, was the only thing in all the landscape that moved. And the only sound that came to his ears was the remote screeching of tram wheels somewhere in the suburbs behind. Almost could he imagine that the townspeople, amongst whom he had been jostling not more than a few minutes ago, had all been stricken down in one general visitation of death.

And in such wilful phantasies did his mind take refuge, hiding itself from the hauntings of a more indefinite, and yet more intimate, dread. With every step that he took, he hated more this sluggish canal with its fringe of coarse grasses and weeds; the sweet, vile smells of the refuse dumped on every side; and, above all, the brutal solitariness of the region, itself by humanity so brutalized.

His single solace in this condition of nightmare lay in the reflection that the present chapter of his trials was drawing swiftly to a close. What manner of catastrophe would it be that could now interpose itself between him and his goal? There lay the port and the ship before him! Another half-hour and he would be aboard. What mattered it, then, when, looking back over his shoulder at Tornel, he saw that dusky monstrosity itself looking pallid against the blackness behind? What matter? The gods in their wrath might be pursuing, but already the fugitives had made good their escape!

Yet—what was that? The inscrutable figure in front was separated from him by a smaller interval than before. Had his own pace without intention quickened? No; the cause lay on Cosmo's side. Until this instant the man's stride had not shortened, nor his eyes wandered from the straight line before him; but now he was intently scanning the prospect on either hand, and, as he did so, his forward march abated.

Allen stared aghast. And when, a moment later, Cosmo stopped short, so did he.

Cosmo faced about. For a minute he looked Allen straight in the eyes.

"I have done with you!" said he.

He took a step nearer. "I have done with you. Do you hear?"

Still there was no reply.

Then Cosmo took another step forward, and swiftly raising his hand, struck Allen with his open palm as hard as he could across the cheek.

This movement once accomplished, he fell back; and the two stood facing each other exactly as before.

The unexpectedness, no less than the impact of the blow, paralysed Allen. For several seconds after all was over, the sound of the percussion was still, to his sense, ringing out over the flats. Then suddenly he became aware of a great stillness; and simultaneously he was filled with an unimaginable shame. Something monstrous had taken place. That sound; and then this stillness!

He saw Cosmo standing there and looking at him. Cosmo was smiling, as it might have been in contemplation of a lay figure. He was smiling as an artist might, who had just put to his canvas a successful, finishing touch. The man's relish of his handiwork was terrible; it raised the black and freezing passion of his face to an intensity that was positively inhuman. For the first few moments it welded all Allen's other emotions into a sentiment of wonder, almost of awe. He returned Cosmo's look with the unselfconscious steadiness of a child surprised.

Only gradually did anger unfurl itself. But at length its hot pungent fumes began to curl upwards into his brain. A cauldron had been uncovered, and was now belching forth passion, black and rusty red. At the same time, however, underneath this seethe and surge his thinking mind leapt secretly into activity. While a fiery flush was spreading over his face, his brain held him there, alert, steady, biding his time and building up his purpose.

Cosmo was still smiling. "That means," said he, "that our little farce is ended."

"Farce?"

"Yes—farce!"

Allen regarded him, as it seemed, thoughtfully.

"Look here, my friend!" said Cosmo. "You go your way, and I go mine! Do you understand?"

The colour was already ebbing from Allen's face. His mouth had hardened. For a minute there was no sound but that of his heavy breathing.

"Cosmo!" said he at last, "I hold you to your agreement. Come!"

At this Cosmo's expression became really extra ordinary. "Hell!" he cried with unexampled violence. "Can you not understand, you dog, that I refuse?"

"It will be better," replied Allen in a low, dull voice, "much better for us both, if you will come."

"And better no doubt for Lilian!" mocked his adversary.

Allen took in a slow, deep breath. The pronouncement of that name seemed to revive the sting of the blow. His eyes were still fastened upon Cosmo's face with a singular intentness, and it may well have been something the latter now discovered in that gaze, which caused him suddenly to step backwards, at the same time drawing a revolver.

Keeping close watch upon Allen, he cocked it; his fingers handled the white steel lovingly.

"You can go now," he jeered with full-flavoured insolence, "to the devil!"

"What if I chose to stay by you?"

Cosmo smiled and snapped the breach of his weapon.

"My present intention," said he, "is to go for a little stroll among the sandhills. Don't let me find you here on my return."

Flinging behind him a grin of minatory triumph, he sauntered off obliquely in the direction of some dunes, which, at a small distance, rose in sandy hummocks out of the flat. With Cosmo's bag lying at his feet, Allen stood looking after him. But at last, when some two hundred yards lay between them, he bestirred himself. Slowly he struck out in Cosmo's track.

Part Two

Chapter 1

For the last half-hour, ever since the early breaking of the summer dawn, the car had been rushing along sandy roads bordered by forest trees. Nicholas at the wheel and Walter huddling at his side had the grey looks of those who have come round to the small hours in wakefulness. Their departure from Tornel had been delayed until after midnight by the violent recrudescence of a storm which had broken over the town in the afternoon. But the greater part of their journey now lay behind them; Eamor was not many miles away.

A wonderful, yellow light was streaming through purple bars of cloud that lay across the east. The trees by the wayside dripped heavily; the road glistened; the air was still and marvellously sweet.

Although he had not been away for more than a few days, it seemed to Nicholas that long years had passed since he had left home. The cross-glades that flashed out, rain-drenched and sparkling, as the car sped by, were now familiar; and their beauty so wrought upon him that the tears started to his eyes. His nerves, he realized, were stretched to an exaggerated sensibility by fatigue. He hoped that Walter was not looking at him; and began forthwith to increase his speed in order that he should no longer be able to gaze upon the landscape.

Some twenty minutes later the open lodge-gates came into view. With a practised movement the young man swung the car round into a long avenue of beeches, the lower branches of which shone luminously green. Higher up the foliage had already been tinted by the sun, and already a few leaves lay curled and crisp upon the road,—leaves that the car rustled aside with the wind of its speed.

At the end of the avenue they came out upon a lawn, and presently halted before the sunny porch of the house. Rising stiffly from his seat, Walter yawned and stretched himself. It had been a pleasant journey, he said, though a trifle long. How good the sun was after the chill of dawn, eh?

The house stood upon a rise, clear of trees, open to all the light and warmth of the sky. A grey, weathered structure, it sprang out of the turf, which in places rolled up to its very walls, as simply as a rock from an Alpine meadow. On every side, excepting the north, the slopes went down to a woodland fringe, like a beach going down to the sea; and far around were tracts of forest, which, seen from the upper windows in a tempest, moved with the undulations of driven water.

Light airs, still damp with night, blew in through doors and windows, filling the house with freshness. In the hall, where the two men threw off their coats, a big, gentle draught was moving. The deep quiet that reigned was still the quiet of night-time. Presently a servant came and escorted Walter to his room; but for a while Nicholas loitered below, and, as he looked about him, sighed with something more than content. This hall, where young flowering plants nodded against a background of old oak, was endued with a twofold charm. Here a gracious antiquity was brightened by all that is pleasantest in youth. There was something mellow, and springlike too, in the atmosphere of the place,—a quality which he likened to the mingled fragrance of fresh rose leaves and the rose leaves of pot-pourri.

In the dining-room he found some fruit, which he ate with avidity, and took a deep draught of water. And again, upstairs, as he bathed, the delightfulness of pure water appealed to his senses with an exquisite intensity, joining with the limpid quality of the silence that was exhaled from the countryside,—a green and peaceful silence that poured in through the casement with the sunlight and the scent of verdure.

Two hours later he knocked at his step-mother's door and, receiving no answer, went in and passed through her bedroom to a little chamber beyond. Lilian Mayne, who was reclining on a sofa with a breakfast tray beside her, looked up as he came in and gave him a long, slow smile.

"Well, Nick dear, I heard you had arrived. It was a great way to drive through the dark. Aren't you very tired?"

While she was speaking he let himself fall into a chair, and they regarded each other with a visible content. She had just finished her meal and was smoking a cigarette. He accepted the cup of tea she offered him, watching her with keen pleasure as she poured it out. The tray, bright with silver, her hand deftly moving, her forearm from which the loose sleeve of her wrapper had slipped back, the even pallor of her face beneath dark coils of hair;—it was all of it delightful!

"How glad I am to be back!" he exclaimed.

Her eyes lifted upon him with gentle malice. "Why are you always running off to Tornel then?"

"Always? Once every three months, I should say."

Lying back in his chair, he let his gaze wander vaguely about the small, lofty room. Its dove-grey walls and the general absence of ornament were particularly refreshing after the gilded mouldings of his hostelry at Tornel. In the subdued light that filtered through a white blind drawn down against the sun, everything was shadowless and colourless—colourless but for the china-blue of his companion's dress, the vivid gleams of silver on the tray, and the blue, transparent tuft of flame under the tea-kettle.

"Nick, I am sure you must feel bored here—sometimes!"

His gaze came back to her quickly. "Why do you always say that? You know I'm not bored."

Her lips and eyebrows moved in mild contestation, but she made no reply. He frowned a little.

"Why should I be bored?" he continued. "Haven't I got—everything?"

It was to be seen that this was a familiar point of dispute; but that did not prevent the young man, on this occasion, from plunging with even more vehemence than usual into his old arguments. Eamor offered all that was to be desired—at any rate by a person of discernment. Were his studies in question? Well, books, papers, periodicals, reviews—all were to be had at Eamor. "All the thought of the world," he protested passionately, "can be drawn to this house. And yet——"

"Walter thinks you ought to go to the University," she interrupted briefly.

"Are you going to quote Walter to me? I have been to a public school, and that has done me quite harm enough."

She looked away; and in a minute he went on: "Walter is a fool. I know myself better than Walter knows me."

"And the world?" she mocked at him gently. "You know that, too, better than Walter?"

"Walter doesn't know the world! How can he? He is *of* it. But from Eamor one can observe and understand. As for Walter's life, it is utterly futile. It would drive me to desperation in one day."

Out of her dim smile there shone a kind of pity, She gave a small head-shake.

All at once he rose and took a turn down the room. "I, for my part, might well ask you if *you* were bored," he observed with an abrupt change of voice.

"Oh, my dear," she returned quickly, "I've got beyond that!"

He sighed. "I know all about boredom. There are two kinds, intellec-

tual and emotional. The first fastens on you, when your mind has nothing to feed on, or when it has food thrust upon it that it doesn't want—
at school, for instance. But in the library here I'm my own master. . . .
Oh, I find plenty to think about, I assure you!" And he laughed. "Why! I
sometimes lie awake at night from excitement, asking myself what I
shall fall upon and devour the next day!"

He had halted before her; but the next minute went over to the
window, and, pushing aside the blind, leant forth over the sill. The light
outside was dazzling; the flower-beds were quivering and vibrating
under the sun; surges of scented warmth rose from the ground and
reverberated against the walls of the house. Across the lawn his eye
caught the gleam of a white dress. It was Madeline, and Walter was with
her. The two were sauntering along under the shade of the trees. In a
minute they passed out of sight. Far away he heard the whirr of a
mowing-machine; now and then a bird chirped plaintively in the caves;
in all the air there was the hot murmur of summer, full of somnolence,
full of ecstasy in mere living. And these sounds rose into the spacious
silence of the country-side, making it rich and deep. It seemed to him as
if silence were being distilled by the woods and the warm turf; as if in
waves it enwrapped and overflowed the house. And he felt the house to
be standing there in beauty and in peace to receive the warmth and the
silence, and to luxuriate in them.

When he drew back the room was dusky to his eyes. "Walter is out
there with Madeline," he said.

Lilian made no reply.

"Thank heaven!" he continued, "we shall soon see the last of her!"

"You have heard that John Mayne is ill?" said she after a moment's
pause.

"Yes."

"Can you make out how ill?"

"No." He hesitated. "But somehow I fancy it is serious."

She looked at him for a moment with wide, meditative eyes, then let
her lids fall and sank back on the couch. Seating himself, he closed his
eyes in like fashion; and there followed an interval of musing.

Between the woman and the boy there was a family resemblance.
She was of slightly larger build and not so fair, but in the poise and
shape of the head and in the proportion of the limbs it was discernible
that they came of the same stock. That this affinity, moreover, was
temperamental as well as physical received illustration at this moment
from the similarity of their postures. The immobility and relaxation of

the body might be divined, in each case, to be the mask of a mental activity.

On this occasion, however, the young man's mind was quick to lose its energy. He was in that condition of weariness when the brain is disposed to hearken only to the sensual world's appeal. As, presently, he studied his companion through half-raised lids, to him it seemed that a sweet, enervating indolence was breathed out of her. How fine were the lines of her figure in that straight-flowing, silken robe,—the throat firm, the shoulders broad, the limbs with their supple attachments long and strong. She had one hand behind her backward-tilted head, and her gaze—for she too had now opened her eyes—went up dreamily to the ceiling.

All at once she broke the silence. "Nick, what are you thinking about?"

"I don't know," he replied slowly.

"Have you seen Isabel yet?"

"No."

"Then go and find her! I must dress. It is time I went down to give Walter his welcome."

He rose unwillingly. "Must I go?" Then with a yawn: "Madeline won't be sorry to leave us, will she?"

"I suppose not."

He looked as if this did not satisfy him. "She hates being here, I imagine."

"Not exactly."

"I find that very difficult to understand," he threw out with a certain petulance.

She smiled indulgently. "Of course you do."

"Are women's lives so empty," he retaliated, "that any emotional excitement, however unpleasant, is welcome?"

"You can put it that way if you like."

"I see." And he became pensive. "Well, poor Walter! it is a bad look-out for him—unless he really counts for more than we think he does."

"Oh, he'll count for more with *her*—in the long run."

"I wonder if he will ever find her out!"

"From his point of view there is really nothing particular to find out."

He seemed struck by this. "Perhaps not!" he mused. Then, after a pause: "It's curious to think that they will come to know each other very well in their fashion, and quite probably continue to consider each other delightful persons, and grow deeply attached. The domestic life of a pair of professional poisoners, or rattle-snakes, may of course be idyllic. And this wonder I feel about Walter and Madeline, they feel—or might equally well feel—about you and me. But if anyone ever told me that Walter knew Madeline, or would ever know her, better than I do, I should laugh." He fixed his listener with a look of humorous inquiry. "You wouldn't maintain such a thing, would you?"

"No."

He considered. "But you would maintain that *you* know *me* better than Madeline knows me?"

"Yes!" she smiled.

His manner became judicial. "Well!" he returned, "that looks as if we were not being scientifically impartial. Indeed, when I come to think of it, *I* am by no means sure that Madeline, who hates and despises me, doesn't know me better than you."

"Oh, Nick, what wonderful detachment!"

He laughed.

"Shall I describe my character, or yours, as Madeline sees it?"

"No. For pity's sake! But ring the bell—and go!" She was sitting up now, her hand wandering vaguely about her hair.

"You look a little tired," he said suddenly. "Are you well?"

"You know, I'm always well."

She rose and, putting her arm around his shoulders, drew him with her into the next room. A light kiss fell upon his forehead before he left.

Chapter 2

For a while he wandered about, looking for Isabel. The house, with its awnings and blinds let down against the heat, was ghostly dim and still. Flickering lights and empty resonances met him wherever he went. In the corridors there was a rustle of cool airs passing. The blinds over the open windows stirred gently. Fierce patches of sunlight darted like birds across backgrounds of obscurity; a glimpse of his own form, shadowed forth upon the liquid depth of a mirror, held him wrapped for quite a time in half-metaphysical wondering.

He was tired and Isabel was nowhere to be found. In the end he decided to go out under the trees, and lie down, and go to sleep. It came across him that Isabel might be hiding herself purposely; they had been falling out quite often of late. But of course that did not matter; Isabel was not like Madeline. Isabel and he understood each other well enough!—too well, perhaps, for he knew that Lilian, who had taken the child under her protection some five years ago, did not consider her a good match for him. Isabel had no money; her parents were persons upon whom the world was inclined to look askance; besides, there was Orisser blood in her veins; and Lilian was quite sure that the family needed new blood.

Stepping out of doors, he paused under the shock of the heat and light. The whole surface of the earth quivered with the exuberance of a life intoxicated by the sun. On the strips of lawn that intersected the flower-beds heaps of freshly-mown grass were smouldering like incense; sprays of heliotrope and mignonette, torn off by the passing knives, lay tossed upon the green mounds, withering. In the hottest regions of the garden enormous poppies, erect under the blaze, dropped at moments their heavy crimson petals; and, quivering with almost human trepidations, above each heart, so bared, the pollen-weighted stamens hung. As he passed by, an old thought came to Nicholas,—the thought that these mute beings were pointing a way of beautiful, and perhaps not impracticable, simplicity. They yielded themselves to the whole heat of life, and then died—how easily! Why must his own little spirit be so trivially restless and intricate?

On the borders of the wood where the lawn-grass merged into wild grass he lay down and awaited sleep; but his drowsiness sank him no further than into reverie—into that condition when memory reconstructs the past to make it live again with the intensity, and under the strange illumination, of dream-life. So the house and the garden of Eamor dropped away from him; and he was again at Tornel. While a physical lethargy held him powerless, he was forced again over the old scenes step by step. And his brows, above closed lids, were frowning.

In point of time he was passing once more through the hours of the morning that had followed his meeting with Allen. The heavy urban sky was hanging over his head; the sense of threat, without which he never entered beneath the city's pall, pressed more massively than usual upon his spirit. He was restless, apprehensive, and full of self-reproach. Why, the evening before, had he responded with so little grace to the friendliness which he discerned in Allen? Why, when affairs of the past came into question, had he displayed an unconcern, which, if not insincere, was at any rate superficial? Was he really content with scarce more knowledge to-day about his father's suicide than he had half-instinctively gathered as a child of ten? To the bare facts, which were all that he possessed, Allen, he reflected, could have given colour and meaning. Allen, he believed, would have been willing to enrich his mind with an understanding of the past;—and was the past nothing to him? The conception dawned that the past, which a callow superciliousness had hitherto led him to disdain, was of all fore-ordaining powers the greatest and most relentless. The ocean upon which his present being tossed was moved to the winds and currents of the bygone years—years that had the mastery of his fate. Yes; and as regards man's captaincy of his soul, was that, he wondered, ever much more than an ornamental command?

Under the stress of these reflections he had entertained for a while the notion of seeking out Allen at the Museum, which was the only address of his that he knew. The resolution failed him, however; so in the afternoon he tried to distract himself by taking out and testing his new car. Very soon he found himself driving it towards the Docks, but stopped to realise how absurd his half-unconscious project of a resumed conversation with Allen really was. Consequently, in a gust of impatience, he turned off from the main road, and amused himself by picking his way along rough tracks over the marshland in the direction of the sea. It was his fancy to get down to the very shore. At last, after abandoning the car, he proceeded on foot to the crest of the low line of dunes from which he could look out over the shallow, muddy water.

With sluggish weariness the long, low heave of the sea travelled shorewards to topple in a lethargic wave upon the sand; and at long, slow intervals the noise of each wave shook the apathetic air. Without sun the heat was intense; it sapped all energies, and pressed down gigantically upon the plain. Cattle, scattered in the distance, stood inert, with head outstretched; and above, no twittering of birds, no flutter of a passing wing.

Then, whilst he was looking out over the steely sea, suddenly from behind a bank of western cloud the sun darted a swift ray. The light struck a point far out upon the watery horizon, and the rest of the world fell into greater gloom by contrast. Presently, however, a coppery glow advanced over the swell; a moment later he noticed his shadow shape itself upon the sand; the reeds in the marsh behind shone out ruddily like swords.

Drawing a long breath, he rose and trudged along the shore until he came to the estuary of a small river, left half empty by the ebb of the tide. Its sluggish surface was flecked with refuse which caught the yellow scum. A little farther he reached a place where the channel narrowed and deepened between rising banks, and here he noticed that the water which came down was turgid and thickened, as if with freshly stirred mud. For some reason this circumstance arrested his attention, and for a moment he debated whether he should go on. At last a moody obstinacy forced him to proceed. With rising aversion he picked his steps along a strip of evil smelling mud which skirted the base of the hither bank. The river, flowing smoothly beside him, made no sound; and, as he went, the periodic rumour of the sea died away. He began to walk faster, urged by the sense of trouble that was oppressing him; he was now filled with a strong desire to escape from the damp and gloom of the river banks that rose above his head. Hurrying and stumbling, he increased his pace, until, turning a sharp corner, he came out on a wide, open space bathed in a rich glow from the sun.

Dazzled, he came to a halt, and stood gazing before him. A group of men were moving slowly over the gleaming sand; their silhouettes were cut out in sharp definition against it; their long shadows lay purple behind them.

The vehement light that swept across the place caught up his consciousness and bore it irresistibly along. He stood in an isolated present, possessed by an unreasoning wonder at what he saw—the copper-coloured sky above, the fiery earth beneath, the silently advancing men.

As they drew nearer to him, however, curiosity over came his dazedness. The men were toiling under some heavy burden; and his whole mind became engrossed by the desire to learn what it was. Approaching, he questioned in low rapid tones: What had they there? A dead man? A suicide?

But they turned away from him with a frowning taciturnity that was hardly without contempt. Their mumbled answers baffled him, and he was becoming prey to a kind of desperation, when, to his utter amazement, in one of the men who was following in the rear he recognised none other than Allen.

Allen was looking strange, and his manner was strange too. His clothes were drenched and mud-stained; he moved like a man in a dream. In answer to Nicholas's repeated questions, he avowed that it was he who had pulled the body out of the water.

"The body? Then he is dead?"

"Yes. Dead."

"How do you know he is dead? And who he is?"

Allen made no reply. Nicholas, however, persisted in his interrogations; and at last one of the men trudging alongside intervened. He explained that Allen was suffering from shock; no good questioning him. As for the fellow they were carrying, no one knew who he was; they fancied he was dead; but they were taking him to a little hut near by, there to try the usual methods of resuscitation. In reply to his questioner's suggestion he admitted with indifference that a doctor might be of some use.

On hearing this the youth set off at the top of his speed back to his car. He vowed to himself that in less than thirty minutes he would have a doctor on the spot. Of a sudden his energies had awoken; he was now all action; indeed, he hardly knew himself in the violence of his resolution to play a vigorous part in the little drama upon which he had so curiously stumbled. Having raced back to Tornel, he soon found a doctor and presently was racing out again. After that, a dreary period of waiting ensued. One among the little huddle of loiterers gathered outside the cabin where the doctor was at work, he wearied himself with impatience and anxiety. He was strangely excited, strangely desirous that the man should live. Providence had thrown the would-be suicide into his hands. He, Nicholas Orisser, would be the man's destiny.

Long after the rattle of thunder and the fall of heavy rain-drops had caused his companions to disperse, he remained crouching under the dripping eaves. His imagination was busy with phantasies about the person of the unknown. Passing over Allen's share in the business, he determined that the unknown was *his* man. The unknown had rejected life. Well! he, Nicholas, would give him a new life. And in return the unknown should initiate him into the secrets of humanity. There should be an end of his own terrible sense of isolation, of his feeling that he stood outside humanity. He had a claim on this man; they should understand one another as no two human beings had ever understood each other before. Had he not always felt that men shared some secret in which he might not participate? Well, now he would learn that secret. He would tell the unknown everything; and the unknown should tell him everything. He saw himself and the unknown sitting together deep into the night, talking, explaining, until the inner-most mysteries of the human spirit lay stark and bare before them.

At this point the day-dreamer under the green boughs at Eamor stirred and shook off his dream. To his opening eyes the spreading beech overhead appeared as an old and kindly friend. He welcomed it. He needed reassurance and comfort. All that had passed at Tornel partook of the character of nightmare. Already he repented him bitterly of what he had done. He had actually arranged that the would-be suicide, who, though resuscitated, was suffering severely from the shock of his experience, should be brought for his recovery to a cottage on the outskirts of Eamor village,—a pretty little place, embowered in the trees, which Lilian kept open for the use of convalescents. On putting forward this proposition, he had been strongly opposed by Allen; but the doctor, on the other hand, had thought well of the scheme. Between them, they had made short work of Allen's objections, which appeared both un-reasoned and harsh. If Nicholas desired to perform this act of charity, what possible grounds could the other have for gainsaying him? At the time, Nicholas remembered, Allen's antagonism had surprised and angered him; he now, however, regretted the obstinacy with which he had overborne it. Of his own will he had established a link between Tornel and Eamor. He had created a bridge between those two spheres that he had every wish to keep apart. He flinched before the thought that at this very moment the poor half-drowned wretch must be upon his way. He was travelling down in company with Allen, using the old car, which had been available for this purpose. Some comfort was to be taken from the offer which Allen had ultimately made to instal the newcomer in the cottage and look after him—at any rate for a day or two. This mitigated Nicholas's sense of responsibility. It did not, however, alter the species of shame he took upon himself for having acted throughout in a manner which would appear little consonant with his established character. It was not like him to interfere in other people's affairs. And this doubtless was the reason why, as yet, he had lacked the courage to tell Lilian what he had done. She would be surprised, and he embarrassed.

His former phantasies of a deep intercommunication between himself and the unsuccessful self-murderer had vanished into nothingness. He saw them now as puerile, hysterical, and altogether outside the order of reality. The white, drawn face, the staring eyes, the muteness and rigidity of the being seen dimly and but for a few instants in the twilight of the cabin, inspired him, reminiscently, with a feeling something akin to terror, and gave body to his presentiment that, in bringing the creature to Eamor, he was introducing a tainting and corrupting part of that other world into this.

Somewhat similarly, too, he sustained the illusion that he had lost something of himself at Tornel—that a portion of his own spirit had been left behind to wander over those dreary flats, to hover over those serrated perspectives of mean roofs, to listen endlessly to the rattle of trains, the roar of furnaces, the hum of dusty thousands labouring in irremediable squalor.

And then he thought of John Mayne, the man who held the balance of their fate. In one scale were those tenements, those factories and their stunted denizens; in the other was Eamor. Tornel was the pit into which Lilian, and Isabel, and he, might all be cast, if John Mayne so willed it. And John Mayne was but the temporary embodiment of something far stronger and more ruthless than himself, of something that watched and approved when it saw, spawning over the whole earth, this poor human kind, ignorant of the past, more than half insensible to the present, reckless of the future,—a brutish thing, a pitiable thing. But these men and women, they were his like, you would say? No, he denied it! He would concede, if you would, that they had made him; he and his were their product, evolved through many generations—their inferior, if you pleased,—their parasite! But their like; no, only cant would maintain it!

And so the better part of the day passed by. He had a book in which, however, he read but little. In sleep and in somnolence he sped the hours upon their way, and with each hour the spirit of Eamor gradually reasserted itself, sinking him deeper and deeper into the stream of its established life. Here was his home! this was his life! the rest—thank heaven!—was all alien. More vividly than ever before he resuscitated old sensations that were the ghosts of memories—delicate traceries of feeling comparable to the pale skeleton of a leaf from which the grosser substance has rotted away. He felt himself rocked in a cradle of associations that stretched back into infancy. He watched the light fall upon the walls of the house as it had always fallen, and the shadows fall as they had always fallen; and now and again a leaf from the great beeches detached itself and fell, and finally the twilight fell, just as he remembered it, summer after summer, always to have fallen.

Chapter 3

Dusk had gathered over the woods. The huge heavens, empty of light, were like the hollow of a silver cup. Underneath, the trees stood motionless, covering the earth with mystery. From time to time a bird with slowly flapping wings rose up from amongst them, hovered awhile against lonely spaces of sky, and sank down again.

The garden, with its sun-baked lawns open to the twilight, was pale. Moths trooped out of the shrubberies, fluttering ineffectually; some went to the evening flowers, some strove towards the warm, yellow lights that shone from the windows of the house.

It was from one of these windows, high up under the eaves, that Nicholas was leaning, watching the soft flight of the bats beneath him, and the faint stars above, and the closing of the dusk.

And then, from the terrace beneath, there mounted up a thin jet of melody, puerile, expressionless, but sad. Sad! For it seemed that the sky and the earth and all hearts had lost their passion—that the world's energies lay buried for ever under sheer indifference.

"Isabel!" he called, but not loudly, and she did not hear.

She was there below, leaning over the balustrade. Presently she ceased; and all was still again.

He went down to her.

"We shall be alone to-night," she said, as he approached, "we three! Madeline has a headache, and Walter has decided to go back to Tornel to-night instead of to-morrow."

"Don't tell me they've quarrelled!"

She laughed. "No. They have not quarrelled." And turning away, she fell to crooning the same little song.

"I heard you singing that from above."

"Was I singing?"

"Yes."

"I was not thinking about it."

He was now leaning over the balustrade beside her, and, as she breathed out the notes, he inwardly repeated the words: "Dis qu'as tu fait, toi, que voilà, de ta jeunesse?"*

He turned to her with a smile. "Well! what have you done with your youth, Isabel?"

"I have it still."

"And I?"

"You have it still."

"And what—what do you think we shall do with it?"

She made no answer. She had risen on tip-toe and was stretching for one of the tobacco flowers in the bed beneath the terrace.

"Can you reach that for me, Nick, I want it."

He was still looking at her. She drew herself up, a shade of rose upon her cheeks.

"I want it for my dress. Pick it for me, Nick."

She had on a frock that in his eyes wonderfully became her. Indeed, she hardly looked even her sixteen years. She was delicious. Nature in fashioning her had wrought the transient beauty of immaturity to an unusual finish.

He picked the flower she wanted, and they moved to the dinner-table which had been set in an angle of the wall, where the big blossoms of a trellised magnolia hung pale against dark foliage. So quiet was the air that the candles under their colourless shades burned without a flicker. White and silver the table stood, the centre of a little halo of light.

"I was in the village this afternoon and I heard that the cottage was to be occupied by two men from Tornel. Who are they, Nick?"

"Have you told Lilian about them?"

"No. Haven't you?"

"Not yet."

She laughed.

"How funny you are!"

"I am," returned Nicholas gloomily.

Lilian now appeared, and they seated themselves one on each side of her.

At first the conversation flowed rapidly, Madeline's absence giving them all a pleasant sense of freedom. But, as time went on, silence gained upon them and, when the moon rose, they fell into a deep hush.

In stillness they watched that sea-green radiance spreading from the east—a clarity that welled up from behind the dark barrier of the trees until at last the full and tawny disk appeared, pouring its light over the

* "Tell me, what did you do with your youth?"

rugged surface of the wood. Across the lawn the trees stood forth mountainous and dark; the terrace gleamed with a cold, false distinctness of outline; inky shadows formed themselves about the angles of the house; patches of blackness slanted out over the whitened turf; in all the landscape nothing moved save one tenuous spiral of cigarette smoke tremulously mounting.

"The dew is falling," said Lilian at last, and she got up.

Strolling to the edge of the terrace, they hung over the pale, upturned faces of the tobacco flowers, whose sweet scent mingled with the smell of the freshly-watered earth.

Nicholas sighed. "'The present,'" he quoted, "'the present, like a note of music, is nothing but as it appertains to what is past and what is to come.' That is what Landor says. And I think I agree with him."

"No! No!" protested Isabel with fervour. "It is not true!"

Nicholas made no reply. He was surrendering himself to the silvered melancholy of the night. The big trees looming out of the park-land seemed to him to be brooding like giant gods over the passionate entrancement of the scene. "'In such a night,'" he murmured, "'Troilus methinks mounted the Troyan walls, And sighed his soul towards the Grecian tents, Where Cressid lay that night.'"

He had sunk deep into his dreams, when all at once Isabel drew herself up and pointed across the lawn. "Look there!" she whispered.

He looked, and at the same instant his heart quickened its beat.

"I saw someone moving!" said Isabel. "There! Behind the mist!"

Lilian stared and slowly shook her head. "My dear, you were dreaming."

Hardly had she spoken, however, when, in a hollow across which the night-vapours were lying in level streaks, a human form became partially discernible.

"There! There!" the girl exclaimed with subdued excitement. "His head and shoulders . . . They are rising out of the whiteness!"

"Yes! You are right!"

"And he is coming straight towards us!"

In silence now, they watched the stranger's leisurely advance. Crossing a belt of darkness, where tall trees flung their shadow across the turf, he disappeared for a short time from view. Then again he became easily visible; and presently, as he emerged upon the open lawn, his whole outline was sharp and clear.

At a distance of about thirty paces he stopped. They could see that he had only just descried them. They felt the weight of his gaze, although, with the moon behind him, he was still no more than a dark and featureless image.

Nicholas, however, had made out who it was; and he realized that he had deferred his explanations too long. Glancing uncomfortably at Lilian, he observed that she was gazing at the enigmatic figure with intensity. Did she, too, recognise Allen? Her aspect disquieted him; there was a look in her eyes which seemed to put her infinitely aloof.

In a minute Allen moved forward again; and this time did not come to a halt, until he had reached the flight of stone steps, at the top of which they stood. With one foot upon the lowest step, he paused, looking up into Lilian's face questioningly.

"I haven't frightened you, have I?" he asked in a low voice.

She started, as if coming out of a dream. "No, I am not frightened,—only—I wasn't expecting you!"

"You were not?" And his glance turned upon Nicholas.

They were deep, soundless moments that followed. Still with his foot upon the lowest step, Allen seemed to meditate.

"Am I as unexpected as that?" he murmured. "I thought——" His voice fell to silence; then slowly he came up the stair.

Nicholas felt that speech had now become imperative; but he also felt less competent than ever to tender sufficing explanations. During the last few moments, while his eyes had been shifting between Lilian and Allen, he had plunged into a state of absolute mystification. Could it merely be owing to all its accidental circumstances of stage-effect that this meeting struck him with such wonderment? Or was he right in his persuasion that it contained elements that were completely outside his understanding, and that nothing he had to say would bear upon its deeper significance? Giving up, he stepped forward and embarked upon a recital which became more and more halting as he perceived that it was commanding but a superficial interest. Instead of turning to the speaker, Lilian kept her eyes fixed steadily upon Allen, as if referring everything to him. And Allen's answering looks seemed to justify her, his eyes promising, all the time, something more—something more and something other. . . . They made their promise, too, with a kind of half-acknowledged, half-dissembled fervour. This—this it was that clenched and sealed the mystery; and, for whatever reason, sent a chill creeping over Nicholas's heart.

It was not long before he found an opportunity to draw aside. And presently, with Isabel, he slipped away.

Chapter 4

Lilian Mayne sat in her room before the mirror. It was a pleasant room. She had taken it for her own after the storms of the two critical years of her life were over. It had no associations with John Mayne, nor yet with Charles Orisser. It was the harbour into which she had steered her bark at last. It was a refuge, a solitude, with which she must perforce be content.

Here she had recovered herself after much buffeting,—not the old self, but a new, which, alas! she did not like so well as the old. Still, she was wiser, she supposed. Two unfortunate marriages and leisure in which to consider them must count for something. It did not occur to her that Fate sometimes drives its lessons home too hard. She told herself she had done with romance; romance had died with Charles Orisser. John Mayne stood for reality; and, to be sure, she had done with that too. What remained? Really, she could not tell!

John Mayne never offered himself to her imagination as a subject for compassion. He had made mistakes from the first that put him beyond the pale.

The marriage ceremony was hardly over before she discerned in his eyes a light, which—in a flash of divination she knew it!—must often have appeared in them at the conclusion of a successful business deal. A cool sense of achievement seemed to permeate even his tenderness during those early days, a tenderness, to own the truth, which she would have shrunk from even without that,—for the simple reason that the man was physically repulsive to her.

Then, he had taken no pains to make his sphere of life less unattractive than it threatened to be. They were sojourning for a period in a series of huge hotels in which they usually occupied the "Royal Suite." What dreadful hours she spent in gorgeous sitting-rooms,—empty-minded and empty-handed,—with no alternative but to join the over-dressed crowd, beguiling a hideous leisure with second-rate music below. In the evening there would be long banquets at which each bulky guest represented something equally bulky in the realm of finance. The costliness, the dullness, the ugliness of it all! It was the revelation of an existence more barren than she had been able to imagine. The life would have been almost unbearable even without that perpetual sense of being shown off as a trophy—as a piece of bric-a-brac for her husband's friends to admire leeringly, as though they actually held her between finger and thumb. And the whiles she lay awake at night, she saw herself embedded in this existence like a currant in dough—like a currant in the rich, heavy slice of life that John Mayne and his peers went to make up.

In marrying John Mayne she had intended to get at least as much as she gave. She had expected to build up a tolerable life for herself and for Nicholas. She had imagined herself living amidst a circle of her own friends, little disturbed by John Mayne, who was sure to remain a slave to his old habit of constant work. It ought not to prove difficult to satisfy him. And at the end of the vista shone the happy day when Nicholas, grown to man's estate, would receive through her agency the secure possession of Eamor. That was to be her achievement; that, the justification of her present step.

But alas! she had not known herself well enough in those days! Terrible things in the meantime had befallen her! Terrible things had passed between her and John Mayne! How little they had either of them suspected what degradation two human beings can inflict upon one another! Through the gradual emergence of inexorable antipathies they saw their earlier calculations and resolves broken down and mocked. The deep volitions that lie at the unconscious depths of every human nature moved and shook the ground beneath their feet; life's surface was riven, disclosing abysses of humiliation, rage, and hate. Could John Mayne ever forget those reflections of himself which flashed upon him out of eyes set in a countenance cold and white with contempt? Could Lilian ever forget the shining desire in his eyes to wound and break the innermost spirit within her? How swiftly they grew to understand one another, those two! And how invariably each accretion of knowledge brought about an accretion of disgust! Was there any feeling, opinion, or taste, of his wife's that John Mayne did not feel injurious to his own? Was there anything she held in love or admiration which was not the object of his secret hostility and disdain? Much did they learn, and quickly, in those days! It seemed to them that they had been as little children until then. Man's fundamental unity in aspiration was a myth; the simple old saying that one man's meat is another man's poison was the first and last word in human philosophy.

The day arrived when Lilian felt that this lesson, so difficult in its simplicity, was really driven home. She fled back to Eamor, leaving a letter in which she implored her husband not to follow her. He did follow nevertheless, and since then there had been several attempts at reconciliation, but all in vain.

She was twenty-two when she settled down at Eamor for good and all, and John Mayne may well have reckoned that the tranquillity she was entreating would prove her own fittest punishment. Time assuredly—time and her mirror—would work for her despair. When has a woman ever been content to let her beauty bloom unseen? Was it likely that the cultivation of her garden and the education of Nicholas could satisfy her for very long? No, no! something would come to pass—something from which he would find means to draw profit. In the meanwhile he would let his magnanimity shine in the decision that she might serve her own sentence.

And now some seven years had passed and here she still was. Upon Charles Orisser's house and Charles Orisser's son all her love and pride had concentrated themselves. For them alone this evening, as on so many others, she had been adorning herself. For them, and for her own solitary heart, the entire grace with which she sought to invest the prison and the imprisonment. Presently she would go down to the terrace, and there she and Isabel and Nicholas would again be alone together,—alone, as they had been just a week ago,—that evening when Allen had appeared. But this was to be the last of such occasions for many a day. Perhaps for ever! Madeline was driving to the station to meet John Mayne and Walter, who were to arrive at Eamor that very night. John Mayne had not told her how long he meant to stay. . . . But her heart was full of apprehensions.

She had risen from before the mirror, and was on the point of pressing the bell for her maid, when Isabel knocked and entered.

"Ah! it's you!" There was eagerness in her tone. "Tell me, darling, has Nicholas been there again?"

"Yes, he was there all the afternoon."

"But Allen was there too?"

"I suppose so."

She sighed reflectively. "And Cosmo," she asked, "how is he?"

"No better, I think—and no worse!"

She sighed again, but this time with impatience. Cosmo's continued presence in the neighbourhood was torture to her; but the man was too ill to be moved. The day after his arrival he had sustained a kind of stroke. One side of his body was paralysed; he could hardly speak. Yet, for all this, there had developed between him and Nicholas a singular relation of understanding—almost of intimacy. This relation puzzled and distressed her. But whilst waiting for Cosmo to die, she was helpless.

The chain of accidents which had brought the two half-brothers together was extraordinary enough to inspire her with a species of superstitious dread. The rapid movement of recent events—Madeline's engagement, the advent of Allen and Cosmo, and John Mayne's return from abroad:—all these circumstances had combined to throw her spirit into a turmoil. Although during the past week life at Eamor had appeared to flow on its usual placid course, to her sense everything was changed. She thrilled with a deep, inward perturbation; her mind was fluttered by a thousand shadowy presentiments. In these conditions the person to whom she addressed herself with most comfort was Isabel. It was Isabel's very childlikeness that commended her. The touch of the girl's sympathy was light; she seemed to be set aloof from all possibility of personal concernment; and Lilian could not have brought herself to expose her agitations to anyone who was not incapable of sharing them.

For a space, while Isabel was fastening her dress, she brooded in the isolation of her own thoughts. Indeed, she almost started, when Isabel, in her turn, put a question.

"How long is John Mayne going to stay?"

"My dear, how can you ask! Of course, I have no notion."

"I was thinking," returned Isabel with tranquillity, "that he might have come here to die."

Lilian gave a little laugh and a shrug. "Well, perhaps he has!"

The girl went over to the window. "Are we having dinner on the terrace again?"

There was no reply. Lilian was moving aimlessly about the room. A full minute passed before she again spoke.

"Tell me, darling, has Madeline been down to the village lately?"

"I don't think so. She hardly ever goes there now, you know."

This was said in a manner of reassurance. It was very undesirable, as Isabel knew, that Madeline's attention should fall upon the occupants of the cottage. Cosmo was passing under the name which he had borne for the greater part of his life, the name of Richardson; and Lilian was quite determined that his identity should not become known, if she could help it. Alone, the village doctor, an old and trusted friend, had been let into the secret. And, having regard to Cosmo's actual disabilities, there was no obvious reason why the truth should ever spread itself farther afield.

She had not defined to herself very clearly all her motives for this reserve regarding Cosmo, but the fact that John Mayne was coming to Eamor did, unquestionably, occupy the foremost place among them. The old man had never showed signs of "taking to" Nicholas, and supposing Cosmo were to make a miraculous recovery, might not John Mayne be tempted to "take to" *him!* Regarded from one angle, the supposition was extravagant. Cosmo had amply forfeited his claims to be counted a member of the family; by all considerations of honour, propriety and justice he was debarred. But—John Mayne was ill, John Mayne was full of rancour. Might not John Mayne decide to accept Cosmo as a god-send, as the one person in the world through whose instrumentality he might elude an obligation that was odious?

This notion appeared now insubstantial as air, now heavy with probability. She constructed visions of John Mayne upon his death-bed, saw him calling for his pen, and by one stroke putting Cosmo into Nicholas's place. Such an act, although it would constitute an absolute breach of the spirit of his engagement to her, would involve no violation of the actual letter of his promise. Eamor he had said was to be saved for the Orissers. Well; Cosmo was Sir Charles's eldest son!

When she and Isabel went down to the terrace, they found Nicholas already there. He was reading, or so it seemed, although in the gathering twilight reading appeared hardly possible. As he did not look up at their approach, with linked arms they fell to pacing to and fro.

Since the evening of Allen's appearance the young man's relations with his step-mother had become constrained. Her disclosure to him of Cosmo's identity had indeed passed off simply enough, considering the nature of the information she had to present. After his first surprise, Nicholas had accepted the situation with what affected to be no more than a kind of ironical amusement. But she had not failed to discern that he was hiding a good deal of perturbation. And during the ensuing days his ostensible unconcern had been further belied by a moodiness which he could not dissimulate.

She was not slow to suspect, moreover, that his secret preoccupations did not cluster entirely around Cosmo, but in part around Allen and herself. Nor was she mistaken. The spectacle of her meeting with Allen had imprinted itself deeply upon the young man's mind. How far into the night their talk had lasted, or what its full import had been, he had no means of telling. But he was intimately persuaded that something significant had that night taken place. And despite the seeming frankness with which she had opened herself to him the next day, he retained the sense that he was being excluded from her innermost counsels.

With the development of his relations with Cosmo, this sense enlarged itself. Lilian, he saw, viewed that intercourse with disfavour. In fact he soon discovered, to his astonishment, that she actively disliked Cosmo. And as he, for his part, felt magnetically drawn towards him, a point of actual discord had arisen. He was gradually acquiring a sympathy for Cosmo which caused him to resent Lilian's and Allen's attitude towards that unhappy creature. He could not put his finger upon the centre of his objections, for neither Lilian nor Allen ever gave him the opportunity to enveigh against them, even in his own mind, for harshness or pettiness of intention; but he felt inclined to cry out: "Cosmo is one of us! And yet merely because he is dangerous, you think of nothing but how to be rid of him!"

As he sat there on the terrace with his book still open in his hands, his thoughts hovered unceasingly over that little cottage in the woods. It lay on the outskirts of the village, in a retired spot approached by a grassy lane. You went in through a wicket gate, you knocked at the door, and presently Allen appeared to usher you into the clean, bare room at the back of the house, where the paralytic was lying. The mere aspect of the man made a deep impression upon Nicholas. Cosmo's emaciation was such that his face appeared almost fleshless, and a contraction of the muscles held it fixed in a grin that was like the grin of a skull. Some times the words that issued from that ghastly mouth smote upon the youth's overstrained imagination with the weight of utterances from the other side of the grave.

Ever since his early boyhood Nicholas had suffered from a recurring sense that he had once known something so terrible that he had been compelled to forget it. And he was at once tantalized and repelled by that mystery—the unveiling of which would surely be fatal to him. There were occasions when he suffered under the impression that glances of pity and wonder were being directed upon him, as if others knew what it was he must not know. But no one had ever given him so deep and persistent a sense of contained powers of revelation—and of willingness to reveal—as Cosmo. Cosmo, he felt, knew not only *that* secret, but the secrets of all men; he knew the deepest things, the things that all men instinctively conspire together not to know. Therefore all men were in league against Cosmo—even Allen. They feared him for what he might bring out into the light of day.

Cosmo's body lay straight and stiff under the sheets like the form of a corpse. His head alone lived—lived with a concentrated and ferocious life of its own. The feverish light in Cosmo's eyes was the reflection of a brain working with abnormal intensity along forbidden lines, and consuming itself with its own fervour.

During dinner the young man was silent. Afterwards he withdrew again to his former seat. And there he sat in the dusk, whilst Lilian and Isabel again paced slowly up and down. Listening to the click of their heels upon the flags and to the murmur of their desultory speech, there fell upon him the phantasy that he was no more than a disembodied spirit, hanging restless, invisible, impotent, upon the dark, misty airs of the night.

Yet, as the hour of ten approached, he was drawn back into their world. He entered with them under the bondage of a single oppressive and unrelenting preoccupation. With them he strained his hearing to catch, upon the muffled stillness of the countryside, the hum of John Mayne's approaching car.

Chapter 5

It was four o'clock. John Mayne stood on the balcony of the room that he had been occupying for the last three weeks. Below Madeline and Walter were setting out on their usual afternoon ride. The sun struck upon the old man's grey, cropped head, red neck, and broad shoulders, which hung above the jessamine that poured in a thick tangle over the balcony railings.

"My dear, that mare won't wait much longer," he heard Walter say. "The dogs must have gone hunting again. Come, let's be off!"

Walter was impatient. The light and heat thrown up from the gravel and reflected from the walls of the house, were disagreeable to him. He felt ill at ease.

Madeline shook her head laughingly. She was one of those persons who are not irked by waiting; and the sultriness that troubled Walter did not trouble her; or, if it did, she found, maybe, compensation in a consciousness of the picture she presented. She looked her best on horseback, and the mare that carried her seemed to share her awareness of effect. Sidling and curvetting backwards, the animal scraped the ground with polished hoofs and champed noisily at the bit; at each movement its glossy coat caught some new sheen from the sun; at each toss of its head a multitude of white sparks flew out from the fittings of the bridle. And the girl, high in colour and vitality, tapped her teeth with the ivory handle of her whip, looked down at Walter through half-closed lids, and smiled.

"Madeline!" said Walter abruptly.

"Yes."

"Let us be off!"

Her companion spoke with a new note of decision. Truth to tell, he had for the last few minutes been unpleasantly aware that John Mayne was watching them from the balcony above—unpleasantly, because there was something in the old man's expression that he did not remember ever having seen there before; and he did not like that look.

"Come, Madeline!"

The tone of his voice caused the girl to give him a quick glance. "Very well, then!" said she.

They cantered off, and from his position above, John Mayne followed them with his eyes, until they were lost to view under the trees. Then, loosening his grip on the railing, he let his thick, powerful body fall back into a chair. His head dropped, the lids sank over his eyes, and thus he sat.

Sharply, for his inward vision, did the bright scene below recreate itself. With strange and bitter satisfaction he beheld, vivid in light and colour, vivid in movement and energy, blocked out in large bold masses against the dazzling ground, the forms of the man, the woman, and the two horses. In his mind those shapes stood forth as delineations of corporeal vigour and nothing more. In them he saw, albeit unwittingly, an expression of life's willingness to dispense with spiritual significance—nay more, in their fulness and perfection he recognised and greeted the tokens of her pleasure in living forms of mortuary emptiness. He saw in the haunches of the horses, in their nostrils, in the throat and bosom of the girl, in her hips, in her lips, in every line and feature of those carnally resplendent bodies, nothing but a brutal exposition of the self-sufficingness of the flesh; and at this spectacle of vitality without the spark, of life triumphantly dispensing with the spirit, he smiled, drawing down the corners of his mouth with scorn. Still smiling and muttering to himself, he rose and went back into his room.

For a few minutes he walked to and fro in agitated preoccupation. Then, his expression suddenly changing, he stood still, put a hand up to his chin, and stared, frowning, into vacancy. "That's how it is," he mumbled; "and it's all one . . . all one . . . but . . ." The words died on his lips, and he realized abruptly that he had lost the thread of his thought. The thoughts that passed through his brain nowadays were so incomplete, so rapid, so numerous that he could only arrest one in a thousand. Where were his old calmness, his assurance, his sense of mastery over life? A new and staggering conception of his mental condition swept over him as he stood there. Could it be that he was afraid—afraid? "My God!" he cried out to himself. "Oh, my God!"

He hurried to the door and locked it and, flinging himself down at his bedside, stumbled into prayer. The prayer which came had lost all significance long ago; it was the same that a tight-lipped, mournful congregation had droned forth every Sabbath of his childhood in a little, stone meeting-house on the bleak hillside. But, although it conveyed no meaning, his spirit was fortified. When he rose from his knees, he showed a firm face. The lines of his mouth and jaw were those that had made many men's hearts to sink.

Having filled his cigar-case, he went down to the terrace. It was his habit, while Madeline and Walter took their ride, to sit here and smoke. So now, pulling his chair out beyond the shade of the awning under which his wife was sitting with a book open on her lap, he selected a cigar, lighted it carefully, and settled himself. He was apt to feel cold these days, and liked to have the sun on his back. And thus, in attitudes of peaceful abstraction, these two would keep each other company, their hands idle, their gaze, for the most part, distant;—and all about them the fierce languor of the drought.

Thus they would sit, while the minutes piled themselves up into hours, and the shadows lengthened. Thus they had sat, nearly every day, throughout the past three weeks; and in the silence their thoughts moved like wild animals padding to and fro behind bars; and their hearts grew sick and sicker with fear and revolt, and the disgust of antipathy repressed. Outwardly, a part of the reposeful scene; inwardly, they were all fret and rage. Their senses, sharpened to a fine point of exasperation, allowed no dulling of the consciousness. The flapping of the canvas overhead, the skidding of a dry leaf against the flags, their own movements of respiration:—these were things that impinged on the taut nerve, and reverberated within.

From his earliest acquaintance with Lilian Orisser, when she was still unmarried, John Mayne had been troubled in his senses. And later, after he had made up his mind to marry her, and found that his suit did not progress, he was troubled in his pride. Pricked up to an acute perception of the contrasts between her manner of envisaging life and his, he felt his self-satisfaction beginning to ooze out of him drop by drop. Not that hitherto he had been entirely without an inkling of realms beyond his ken, but never before had he coveted access to them. This girl, however, was infinitely desirable in his eyes: and for her sake he must attain to mastery in a new sphere of taste and thought; he must penetrate the mystery of appreciations and antipathies that were foreign to him. It was not that he attached a personal value—or was even willing to concede an abstract value—to what Lilian Orisser possessed and he did not; but proficiency in her own little game was clearly necessary for the winning of her; and afterwards—well, it would be amusing to let her see how little her standards counted in the real game of life!

Her sudden marriage to Charles Orisser had shocked and angered him. He knew the man slightly, having met him in the City, where the latter's advantages as a man of culture, and incompetencies as a man of business, had earned him a kind of envious contempt. Partly by chance and partly because Sir Charles was Lilian's cousin he had followed the amateur financier with a more observant eye than most. At the time of the marriage he, better than anyone, knew the way affairs were drifting. He investigated, he watched, he waited; and when he had called upon the newly wedded couple in their country home, he had half expected an application for a loan.

On the morning when, scanning the newspaper, his eye had fallen upon the announcement of Sir Charles's death, the blood had gone surging to his head. "My God!" was his inward exclamation, "I should not wonder if . . .;" and, as we know, his surmise was correct. Not many days later he stepped out of the train at Eamor station, grim, outwardly self-possessed, but more reckless than he himself knew. At sight of the young woman, a sensual craving to dominate took redoubled force. She, on her side, already knew her man, and—well! what had to be had to be. Yet in his heart did not John Mayne know that he was playing the part of a fool? When a man counts on a reciprocation between material and spiritual values, when by mere weight of obligation he makes a bid for gratitude, when he calculates upon the worth of generosity in terms of affection, he is, of course, a fool, and a dangerous one. But John Mayne never stopped to pause on these things, until he woke up to find his whole life changed and embittered. His horny skin was actually being corroded. Tender places were forming, and they constituted so many inlets for perceptions which, instead of refining, corrupted his spirit. He began to lose that quality which is the saving grace of such men, their spiritual obtuseness. Hard externally, well equipped to face the world, he could offer no effective resistance to the subtle poison of self-hate once it had found its way into his veins.

And now a shattering blow had fallen upon him. Only a few days before his arrival at Eamor he had learnt with certainty that his life was doomed. He had an internal cancer. As he sat, in the inactivity of perfect hopelessness upon that glowing terrace, and waited,—for now he was uninterruptedly waiting,—the cold of the tomb seemed actually to strike up through the flags. It would catch him so wickedly that he was forced at times to set his jaw lest his teeth should chatter. He, who had lived all his life ignorant of physical infirmity, now found his body monstrous. Although he was hardly sensible of pain as yet, his thoughts were no longer free; the clay seemed to encompass them,—a damp, chilly cavern, in the dark of which they fluttered blindly, like sea-birds seeking a lost outlet. And the cavern was full of rumours and menaces, whose import was confirmed—at least so it seemed to his strained imagination—by the furtive or evasive looks of those who shared his secret. There was, indeed, something awesome about the man in these days. In bulk, and strength, and outward quietude, he suggested the image of a great rock buttress, standing out upon the coast, with sea below and sunshine over it,—a peaceful granite thing, out of the depths of which, nevertheless, there would rise at uncertain intervals a muffled booming and a roar.

Chapter 6

This was the man who had come to Eamor to die. A powerful intelligence, hitherto ridden masterfully through a world of hard externals, was drawn up short at last—flung back upon its haunches—before a sudden gaping of the ground. Henceforward John Mayne's part must be to sit and wait. He chafed at what he regarded as his inactivity. Yet probably at no time in his career had his brain worked with a more feverish energy. In broken fragments his life-history would recreate itself before his eyes; and day by day he sat in judgment over it. His standard had been, his standard still was, success. Memories of old turpitudes troubled him not at all; memories of unrequited injuries much. Old scores which he had been unable to pay off brought the blood up in a dusky flush under the yellow glaze of his disease; envies, jealousies, rivalries reproached him that his task was not yet done; and above all, illuminating all, like the hot sun that poured down upon this detested house and these detested woods, was his failure with this woman who sat beside him. These Orissers! It was a fatal mistake ever to have become aware of them; standing, as they did, for what life intended should be ignored, even this sense of contest against them ranked as a kind of defeat. He could not crush them, because they triumphed over him merely by occupying a place in his consciousness.

With these thoughts he would turn his gaze upon Lilian, and his eyes, grown small and piercing, would run over her figure surreptitiously, like two ferrets scenting in the dark. Still, as of old, there was a fascination for him in the very quality of her flesh. Its transparency, illustrated by subtle luminosities and shades around the modelling of the features; the firmness of it, as indicated by the clean, fine curves; the rare health of her—ah, that alone now had the power to fill him with a sort of aching wonder!

Resentful and contemptuous as he would have shown himself at any expression of sympathy, he found in her present inexpressiveness an intolerable offence. Did she, he wondered, suspect that the thought that she would outlive him was the very sting in death? A little while, he said to himself, a little while, and I shall be rotting, but those lips will still continue to move in speech and part smilingly; those white teeth will still gleam in laughter. I shall be rotting; but that mouth will remain fresh and red; that rounded neck will carry with a yet greater pride that small and shapely head. She will still know the coolness of water upon her skin, and the softness of silk and furs. That body will continue to exist warm, scented, lithe and living, in these sweet, upper airs. And she will enjoy all things the more for her new freedom; she will indulge all her senses and be a delight to herself and to others. He threw back his head and laughed aloud at the mockery and humiliation of it.

The sound went out harshly over the sultry lawns. His wife winced, threw a brief glance at him, and fell back into her seeming repose.

John Mayne leaned forward.

"My dear, what would you say: Is justice possible in this world between a man and a woman?"

His lips, drawn back in an unnatural smile, revealed his strong, blackened teeth. Mouth agape, he waited.

The other drew herself together with visible effort. "Justice? I don't know," she murmured.

"No, no! I must have an answer. Come! What do you say?"

She flushed, then as rapidly paled. Her eyes, darkly smouldering, wandered round to return to his at last in a kind of desperate defiance.

"Justice?" she breathed. "Poetic justice—yes!"

"Poetic!" he sneered. "Poetic!" And loudly he laughed, while seeking a rejoinder. "Well, there are some cases no doubt that would look better for a touch of poetry!"

She turned her face away, and he sank back in his seat. No more was said. A distant cawing of rooks, the spiteful note of a passing wasp, the rustle of a light, dry eddy in the leaves, filled an interval of silence.

Sundown was not far off. The light from the west, now slanting in beneath the awning, put a rosy glow upon Lilian's dress. She stirred a little, as if wishful to rise, yet lacking courage.

A distant cry came floating to them over the trees—a cry ringing with gaiety as though laughter went before and after it. Passing his hand over his brow, John Mayne lifted himself from his seat.

"Come," said he in his accustomed tones, "that must be Walter and Madeline. Let us go to meet them."

Together they descended the terrace steps, shading their eyes against the declining sun. The smooth slope of turf stretching down to the wood was no longer green, but mauve under the glare; upon the tree-trunks in front of them the light splashed ruddily; the interior of the thicket was filled with a rich, deep blackness.

When they had gone a little way John Mayne halted and gave a call; it was answered from somewhere behind a shrubbery that here made a barrier between the garden grounds and the untouched woodland beyond. There was no passage in this direction, nor any path for riders across the close-cropped lawn. This lawn had been brought by centuries of careful tending to the perfection of fineness and smoothness. It was therefore with a certain surprise and a dimly-defined misgiving that Lilian listened to sounds of approach from this quarter of the wood. The noise of trampling hoofs drew closer, however, and presently, amid a havoc of flying leaves and twigs, Madeline emerged, with a great leap of her mount, on to the open lawn. Close in her track followed Walter, but evidently against his will. His horse had taken the bit between its teeth; the rider was without control.

Thus for a space the two excited animals pranced and curveted upon the turf, the glare from the west playing upon their sweat-stained sides and shining on the flushed faces of the riders.

"Bravo!" shouted John Mayne with a gleam in his eyes. "Bravo!"

Dismounting at last and leading her horse, Madeline came up to slip a hand through her uncle's arm. "Oh, it has been a glorious ride!" she exclaimed, and pushed the hair back from her forehead. Her hat was somewhere there among the trees; Walter must get it for her.

Her companion, however, had other thoughts upon his mind. The fact now staring everyone in the face was that this lawn, in which no owner could but take a certain pride, had suffered unprecedented outrage. Walter's countenance expressed genuine distress. He had approached his hostess and was breaking out into apologies, when Madeline, running up with a little cry of dismay, thrust him impetuously aside.

"Oh, Lilian!" she exclaimed, "the poor, poor grass! Can you ever forgive me?"

A prettier picture of contrition could not possibly be imagined. To match it with one of equally graceful exoneration was no easy task. But Lilian rose with spirit to the occasion; and John Mayne, watching from a little distance, did honour to the double exhibition with a satirical grin.

A groom having arrived to lead away the horses, the whole group now moved up towards the house. Madeline was again hanging on her uncle's arm. "Uncle John," murmured she, when they had advanced out of earshot, "I should like to tell you something. Do you know I don't think I want to marry Walter just yet—not just yet!"

"Why not, my dear?"

"I don't know; but I don't want to. Not just yet."

The old man patted the hand which lay on his arm.

"Why should I?" she persisted.

"You'd better—before very long. I want to see you safely married before——"

"Hush!" She would not let him finish, making as though to put her hand over his lips. All the animation went suddenly out of her face.

They walked on in silence.

"Uncle John!" cried she all at once in a shocked voice, "why are you smiling like that?"

Again he patted her hand.

"Tell me!"

But he could not, even if he would. In his mind he kept a vision of her as she had leapt out upon the lawn, while Lilian looked on helpless and smiling. And then with what distressful accents the girl had expressed her regret! Verily, in Madeline he had found a perfect successor. "Vengeance is mine!" her femininity said. Yes, dim as the future was, he felt sure that Madeline's femininity and Walter's obtuseness would serve them both well. Happy creatures! To be young, healthy, and insensitive, what further could be prayed for or desired? Superbly, from their vantage-point, would they carry on the feud against the other kind, the enemy, and perhaps without ever clearly understanding what they were doing. Yes, there was the beauty of it! There was the triumph! Long might they preserve their innocence! To do that which you will, that which you are fashioned to do, in all innocence—there was the secret of life! As for him—he had been poisoned;—for him nothing but bitterness was possible; his old male hands were too clumsy for adequate revenge.

Lilian had strolled up to the house with Walter, who there left her and went indoors. Alone, she let herself drop on to a stone seat at the foot of the terrace and drifted into reverie. The stone felt warm to her open palms as she pressed them against it. She sat erect, with backward-tilted head; the last glow of evening fell upon her face; her lids drooped.

For the moment she was all weakness, and she was afraid of her weakness. She was afraid of the provocation in store. She was afraid of the insubordination of her own nature. But no! One could control oneself, she supposed, up to the very end—only how tiring!

The ruddy light of sunset faded; odours of damp uprose. She leant her head against the corner of the seat, and was happy to let the tears mount unchecked into her eyes. "This place is more dear to me than ever," she thought; "but how little Nicholas really cares for it! He is absorbed in himself. I pretend that it is for his sake that I struggle. But it is not for his sake, nor yet for my own. I struggle simply because my heart is set. I cannot help myself."

Thinking of Nicholas, she realized that she was waiting for his return from the village. As usual he had gone to see Cosmo; there was no doubt but that Cosmo, half mute as he was, exercised a strange fascination over him. And Nicholas had at last summoned the resolution to insist that they should be left to converse in private. What was Cosmo's design? Ah, that man was a demon! He was now attacking her through Nicholas.

In a little while she caught sight of the youth approaching over the lawn, Isabel by his side. They seemed to be walking in silence, and their movements, she thought, gave token of dejection. Fearing that they might pass her by, she called out to them.

They came and stood before her. She smiled wanly.

"What news of Cosmo, Nick?—as charming as ever?"

"Quite!"

"Aren't you tiring of him at last?"

"Not at all!" He paused. "Besides, Cosmo is much more entertaining by himself. Allen's presence was becoming irksome."

Lilian turned to Isabel. "What were *you* doing down there, my dear?"

"I just went down the wood-path a little way to meet him." She looked at her companion meditatively. "He's in a dismal temper."

"What about?"

"Everything."

Lilian laughed softly. "So am I. I feel like giving up the ghost—and a feeble, wretched, little ghost it will be."

"It seems to me," said Nicholas, "that in John Mayne's eyes we are all of us ghosts already. Thin, bodiless shades! The best we can do, for our own satisfaction, is to hover around him in mid-air for a while, gibing and mocking."

Lilian turned sharply. "Oh, you don't care about Eamor, Nick! What do you care about, I wonder!"

"*You* care—too much!"

"It is all I have!"

He was silent; she regarded him pensively.

"Things matter to me too much, maybe,—or, maybe, too little." She broke off. "Do you know, I have had another talk with Walter."

"Ah! he spoke to me, too, a few days ago."

"Nick, why didn't you tell me before?"

"Because there was nothing particular to tell. For half an hour he wavered round and about, and over and under, his subject; but never once had the courage fairly to alight upon it."

"What did he say then?"

Nicholas considered. "Well, he talked mainly about John Mayne's virtue and integrity. It was quite plain that he is beginning to feel uneasy—at last!"

"You mean——?"

"Oh! you know what I——"

The sentence remained unfinished. With a sudden rasping sound a window somewhere above them had been thrown open. The young man, who had given a start, emitted a short laugh.

"Our nerves are breaking down!" said he jestingly. "I must be off!—it is time to dress for dinner."

Turning, he sprang quickly up the steps. Lilian drew her brows together and bit her lip, then looked round for Isabel.

"Where are you, darling?"

"I am here." And the girl stepped forward. "How misty it is to-night. Don't you think we had better go in?"

She was looking at a nebulous beam of light that slanted out from Madeline's window above.

Lilian glanced up. "Yes. We must go in," said she.

Chapter 7

Whilst holding women in high esteem, Walter never thought he would marry; for not all men, he used to say, have the vocation. His estimate of himself once changed, however, he felt a certain exhilaration. In writing to his intimate friend, Henry Portman, he assured him that the alliance was "in every way suitable." And he went on: "You need have no fears for my future happiness, just as I, thank God, have no fear for Madeline's."

If he was acting under the spur of impulse, and he stated plainly that he was, the impulses of a man of forty were not, he reckoned, those of callow youth. "More dangerous!" some might reply; but to that he would make bold to answer by a smile.

The fact was that Walter felt he was putting a bright dash of colour to his life at a point where a bachelor's existence is apt to turn a trifle grey; and he doubted not that even Henry Portman, when he saw Madeline, would feel somewhere in his heart a touch of envy. After penning the words "in every way suitable", he had paused lengthily. He did not quite like the expression, and yet he could not erase it, for it meant a great deal. It meant more, indeed, than he was wholly aware of. It epitomized a large bulk of careful, anxious, private thought—thought so private that one might say he kept it from himself—thought, of which the slowly matured fruit alone was allowed to emerge into the full light of his consciousness. For it was the impulsive side of his action that he liked to dwell upon. Impulse is the gilt on life, and not to allow one's ginger bread some gilding is not to give it a fair chance. Prudence, nevertheless—sound, honest prudence (provided it can afterwards be forgotten)—is never out of place; and Walter had fairly envisaged the fact that Madeline was by many years his junior. He met this consideration, however, with the reflection that such a disparity was a danger or an advantage according to temperament, and he was convinced that Madeline inclined temperamentally to pleasures of the steadier sort. He could not see her falling a victim to catastrophic passion, or driven by her senses to demand of him greater expenditures in that direction than could comfortably be afforded. He needed reasonable assurance on this point because he had become of late a little suspicious of his own prolonged and easily maintained chastity; and now, while his senses affirmed that Madeline would afford the test to which they would most willingly submit, a secret instinct told him that she, on her side, would not make that test more exacting than it need be. So he had taken the plunge; and his first visit to Eamor as accepted suitor fortified his self-confidence. Madeline's attractiveness awakened in him a physical response which he noted as unquestionably adequate.

His phrase therefore comprised suitabilities other than the mundane, which last was so patent as to be almost inconvenient. But he trusted that only those who did not know him would look upon the contract as a mere *mariage de convenance*. By those worthy to be numbered among his friends, by those having some knowledge of his convictions and ideals, its felicities of circumstance would be seen, he made sure, in their proper proportion;—as accidents, added by that Providence of whom he had always been the signally favoured creature.

And Madeline, how amply did she by the sweetness and sincerity of her presence inculcate a true comprehension of the bond which united their two souls! With how strong, yet gentle, a light did her character shine out! Take, for instance, her greeting of him that morning when he had arrived at Eamor,—her first meeting with him as her future husband. Could any thing have been more gracious and womanly! And later, in the presence of the others, what ease and simplicity in a situation which her strained relations with her hostess indubitably made difficult.

His engagement was opening, for the rest, in sad circumstances. The days following John Mayne's arrival in Tornel had not only been painful;—that was inevitable;—but also unsatisfactory. The words, the looks, the bearing, that he had prepared for the occasion found no place in the interviews accorded him,—interviews in which John Mayne showed himself far less resigned to his fate than Walter had hoped. The old man indeed was quarrelsome and morose. He made no secret of grudging his subordinate the advancement which his own death would bring; and so made expressions of sympathy well nigh impossible. In fact it was only when Walter was by himself, that he was able to evoke the sentiments befitting the situation. Then only was he able to put aside the thought of his approaching accession to larger fortune and power, and to concentrate upon the pathos of his old chief's decline. A noble life John Mayne's had been! he would repeat to himself. Yes, a noble life—a life of service! Well might one say, gazing forth from this high office window: *Si monumenlum queeris, circumspice!** That hospital yonder, those public baths, this church, that crematorium in the distance and these spacious playing-fields in between, all were donations of John Mayne's to the community, and were to be maintained through his bounty, not for a lifetime only, but for ever! The good he had done was to endure; a great trust was being handed on to him, Walter Standish, and he was determined to prove worthy of it. "To scorn delight and live laborious days," he would then murmur, as he drew towards him his morning's correspondence. That should be his device—and Madeline's.

When John Mayne told him that he intended to make a stay at Eamor, Walter felt some misgivings. He stifled them, however, and even encouraged himself to hope that this visit, undertaken beneath the very shadow of death, might become the occasion for some sort of reconciliation. A new gentleness in Lilian Mayne was surely to be looked for. Worldly wisdom, if nothing else, would surely direct her along the proper path. She must be aware that she had gone far towards forfeiting what she once hoped to have securely won; her conduct had done much to convert a debt of honour into a mere question of personal feeling; and she must know that John Mayne was not the man to have the terms of his generosity dictated to him. Even if, inwardly, she stood upon the letter of her bond, she ought to have the grace to dissemble.

However, as he soon came to see, John Mayne, for his part, was not going to make it easy to strike just the right note. Anxiety gathered in Walter's mind, and gradually soured into disappointment and vexation. The occasion was being turned to evil, instead of to good, account. It became urgently desirable that John Mayne should leave Eamor and regain in a more wholesome atmosphere the impartiality and high sense of honour that were proper to him.

But unfortunately the old man showed no disposition to make a move. Although none of his previous arrangements pointed to his having intended to remain for long in the place, he allowed the days to go by without offering the smallest allusion to departure. And when Walter permitted himself to drop a few hints, the response was surly and indefinite. Indeed, it was becoming plain that he had fallen into a condition of mind which made it difficult for him to break away. With every day that passed he was sinking deeper and deeper under some spell. What spell? Ah! that was a painful question! A question that

---

* "If you seek his monument, look around you." — the epitaph of Sir Christopher Wren, in St Paul's Cathedral.

puzzled and disturbed Walter the more for his understanding that the fascination which Eamor exercised over John Mayne had long been operating on Madeline as well. Something attached them both to the place, and one could almost say that the bond was forged out of their very dislike.

Already, before his betrothal, Walter had discovered that the Orissers, and the difficulties of her life with them, provided the theme nearest to Madeline's heart. And at the present period, in their walks and rides together, he received daily evidence that her taste had not changed. For his part he was eager to awaken her interest in the wider life that was soon to become hers, and to engage her in discussions of his plans and ideals. It was not without chagrin that he came to realize the degree of her entanglement in the toils of Eamor.

Well; it now appeared that John Mayne was succumbing to a similar engrossment; and the moral consequences, in his case, threatened to be more serious. In the first place, abstraction from the world of men and affairs was unnatural to John Mayne; then, his perspectives, at the present day, all converged upon the narrow gate of death; and finally the atmosphere of Eamor was charged with baleful effluences, to which he, of all men, would be specially susceptible.

After Walter had been at Eamor four weeks, he suddenly decided to take a brief holiday. The situation was assuming a nightmarish quality. He felt the need to place himself at a certain remove. He was not accustomed to dealing with affairs in such closeness and particularity. He liked to transcribe every particular problem into general terms, and then treat it according to the rules laid down for the man of probity, who is also a man of the world. He apprehended that the problem at Eamor, viewed thus abstractly, would lose its baffling character, and that he would see how the ugly emotions with which he had to deal could be rendered docile to the injunctions of good sense and good will.

He would seek out Henry Portman, and see what suggestion that very capable civil servant had to make. He would also consult Percy Fellowes, a literary man, who was said to possess deep insight into the feminine composition. After a little conversation with these two, his mind would become clearer.

On the very day of his departure from Eamor, however, he was destined to have two conversations—one with Madeline and one with Lilian Mayne—which much complicated his projected confidences by emphasising the importance of just those elements which he felt some hesitation about disclosing. Madeline, in what was clearly an unguarded moment, let drop something which indicated beyond the shadow of a doubt that she was counting on John Mayne's delegating to her the act, *le beau geste*, of surrendering Eamor finally and definitely to the Orissers. The colloquy in which this came out was, perhaps fortunately, cut short; for Walter was quite at a loss how to treat so explicit an avowal.

His conversation with Lilian Mayne had been deliberately initiated by her. Most unaccountably, she had selected the moment when his car was driving round to the door, to unfold an amazing tale, which concluded with the information that Sir Charles's scapegrace son, Cosmo Orisser, was actually being housed by her in Eamor village! This piece of news affected him, although he hardly knew why, most unpleasantly. Why had not Allen, when he wrote to ask for leave of absence, made any mention of Cosmo? The whole business smacked of intrigue; he could not feel confident that Lilian was letting him get to the bottom of it. Thus, in danger of missing his train, he vacillated between instant departure and a recasting of his plans. Had he seen his way to cross-question his informant with any effect, he might have stayed; but Lilian's story was succinct and, in appearance at least, complete; so that, feeling that on the whole *he* rather than *she* stood in need of time for reflection, he abruptly held out his hand and dashed for his train, which he caught by no more than three seconds.

The next day he had his conversation with Henry Portman. He decided that, with certain reservations touching Madeline, and without dwelling too much upon the curious story of Cosmo and Allen, he might well put the whole case before him.

The interview was rather disappointing. He had expected to interest Henry, and was damped by finding that he did not. The characters and circumstances were too remote from his auditor's sphere. Henry's predominating sentiment was surprise at discovering his friend *dans cette galère.* If Walter had appeared before him in the character of a cattle-breeder, bringing a problem connected with pedigree cattle, or as a gambler, with suggestions for breaking the bank at Monte Carlo, Henry could hardly have been more taken aback or less ready with advice. "Extraordinary people!" he kept muttering, and then burst out: "Why the deuce don't you wash your hands of them? But," he added hastily, "I refer of course only to the Orissers. What does it matter to you whether John Mayne leaves them penniless or not?"

In this Walter saw a remarkable exemplification of the obtuseness which is apt to descend upon quite intelligent minds, when called upon to deal with matters outside the ordinary run of their activities. Gently he pointed out that he could not be indifferent to the case of Eamor for the following reasons. First, he was an ear-witness of John Mayne's promise to Lilian that she and Nicholas should eventually have free possession of the property (for that unquestionably was the signification which everyone present, including John Mayne, had attached to his words at the time); secondly, he, Walter, was John Mayne's appointed executor, whence it followed that the actual fulfilment or violation of the promise would devolve upon him in person; and thirdly, unless John Mayne took definite action and cancelled the mortgage before death came upon him, the probabilities were that Madeline, who was her uncle's residuary legatee, would be the beneficiary, and thus indirectly Walter himself.

Hardly had he finished speaking, however, when he regretted having stated the case so baldly, for he perceived that he had placed a very simple observation within Henry's reach. And Henry reached out to it at once. Miss Madeline, said he, would of course, in any case, "do the right thing," and the question whether Lilian obtained her release from John Mayne or his niece was surely unimportant.

Concealing a sentiment of inward irritation, Walter, after a moment's silence, murmured what might be taken as an acceptance of this view. He proceeded, however, to protest that the matter, all the same, was not quite so simple as that! For one thing, Lilian felt—and he could not help agreeing with her—that John Mayne was in honour bound to execute his promise himself. And then—well, there were difficulties! Yes, there were difficulties . . . which he had no time to go into. . . . Of course, everything would work out satisfactorily in the end, but . . . In this strain he wound up the interview; and, not altogether pleased at the way Henry looked down his nose, took his departure.

Wiser for this experience, he was careful, when discussing the case with Percy Fellowes on the following evening, not to suggest that the whole issue hinged upon Madeline. This time he dealt circumstantially with Allen and Cosmo. His sketch of the latter's life history, including Lilian's story of Cosmo's attempted suicide, of his rescue by Allen, and of his transportation to Eamor village, struck the imagination of his auditor as vividly as he had anticipated. Percy was a much more sympathetic counsellor than Henry. His eyes grew bright behind his tortoiseshell glasses, as he took in point after point with an attentive nod. The dramatic character of the situation appealed to him; and by the end of dinner—for they were dining together at Walter's club—he positively vibrated with interest. "I have my suspicions about that man, Allen," said he, tapping the table with his forefinger. "I deeply suspect him!"

"If you mean that you don't trust him," returned Walter, "I entirely agree with you. His long connection with Charles Orisser is, in the first place, by no means to his advantage. And then—well, what little I have seen of him has not prepossessed me in his favour. Quite the reverse!"

"I am not surprised," replied Percy impressively. "You may take my word for it! Between him and Mrs. Mayne there is some relation of—well, of connivance. And as for his——"

"My dear fellow," interrupted Walter deprecatingly, "don't let us turn this into a melodrama."

"Life *is* melodramatic!" asserted Percy, emptying his glass. "Very!"

Walter sighed. "Aren't we wandering rather from the main issue?"

"Well!" said Percy suddenly; and at once Walter saw that he was to be brought back to a problem from which he had glided uneasily at an early stage in their long and rambling discussion. "Well! the immediate question is, are you, or are you not, going to tell John Mayne that Cosmo is there,—in Eamor village?"

Walter stared uncomfortably. "I have no particular reason," said he, "to suppose that John Mayne would be interested in the news."

His tone was fretful; and when the other asked him whether Mrs. Mayne would agree with him on that point, he admitted that she would not. No; her desire—for she had already expressed it—that John Mayne should *not* be informed, rested, he was bound to admit, upon the apprehension that the latter might be far too much interested.

Percy broke into a laugh. "Come, come, my dear Walter!" said he. "Have you really any doubt in your mind that the only course is to lay the whole matter before the old gentleman at once! If you don't, you will never know where you are from moment to moment! Anything may happen where such persons as Allen and Cosmo are concerned. It is essential that John Mayne should not acquire knowledge of the situation from anyone but you;—otherwise you appear in the guise of Lilian Mayne's accomplice, her ally in a piece of deliberate concealment! And your motives would appear exactly the same as hers. Not very flattering to John Mayne,—if, as you say, his honour demands that Eamor should be made over to Lilian or Nicholas!"

Walter looked at his friend in silence for some instants, then sighed profoundly. Percy was echoing the voice of his own best judgment; and his respect for Percy was enhanced. He sighed, partly in regret, partly in relief. He believed he would now find strength to crush his deep-seated unwillingness to open the subject of Cosmo with John Mayne. This reluctance he had not explained to Percy. He did not fully understand it himself, and he certainly did not wish Percy to understand it.

As they made their way up to the smoking-room, the latter let it be seen that he was plunged in deep meditation.

"You say," he pronounced, after he had chosen a cigar, "you say that Mrs. Mayne is really and truly afraid that her husband might hand that mortgage over to Cosmo?"

"Well!" began Walter cautiously, and was embarking on a qualified assent, when his friend excitedly broke in:

"And your fiancée, if *she* knew about Cosmo, what would she think?"

Walter was dumb. Percy was displaying more astuteness than he liked.

"I don't know," he said at last, without much conviction.

"It's an important point," insisted Percy.

But Walter felt he simply could not give his mind to the subject any longer. Why did all roads lead to Madeline, whose character, desires, and intentions he simply could not discuss? Turning in his chair with a frown, he resolved, at all costs, to give the conversation a fresh departure. But the other was too quick for him.

"Look here!" said Percy, his forefinger raised for emphasis. "If *that's* the view of two clever women, it's my view, whatever you may say."

"What? Which?" asked Walter, confused.

"I hold that Cosmo is a real danger—and you ought to realise that you will vastly complicate the situation by informing John Mayne of his presence."

"You change your mind every two minutes," commented Walter sulkily. "Besides," he added, "Cosmo is on the point of death."

"Whose word have you for that?—Mrs. Mayne's!—and she will always say just what suits her. If she really believed Cosmo to be dying, she would hardly object to your revealing his existence to her husband. But she does object. And again, you have practically admitted that Miss Madeline, if she were aware of Cosmo's existence, would similarly object. Both these women have the same cause for objecting. Each—for reasons best known to herself—believes that *she* will get possession of that mortgage, and Cosmo therefore is to each—"

"My dear Percy," interrupted Walter with exasperation, "I know John Mayne better than either Madeline or Lilian do, and I refuse to believe for one moment that——"

"Oh, all right! All right!" interrupted the other, throwing up his hands. "You certainly ought to know John Mayne better than *I* do. I only give you my opinion for what it is worth. But—do you know whether the old man has made his will yet? If not, what is he doing about it? Some of these business men are very casual. They seem to like being casual. However"—and here a new light came to him—"if you marry Miss Madeline before her uncle dies, he may leave the whole matter in your hands. And that would be the best possible issue. Hurry up and marry her, my dear fellow!"

Walter smiled and blew out a cloud of smoke. He had thought of that. But he had also reflected that if John Mayne was surrendering to feelings of rancour, such a solution of the problem was not likely to strike him as being a solution at all.

After wondering for the moment whether it was worth while, he pointed this out to Percy. The latter was silent, then said dryly:

"Well, if John Mayne is as bitter as that, Miss Madeline will get—what she wants."

And the next minute, to Walter's annoyance, he actually went so far as to hint that Walter might not find it very easy to persuade Madeline—married or unmarried—"to give up any power she may get, over the woman she hates."

To this Walter made no direct reply, but observed rather stiffly that to his mind any apprehension of human affairs, which took no account of the moral sense, always struck him as rather cheap and as likely to lead into the vulgarest forms of error. "My mistrust of anything in the nature of cynicism," he explained, "springs from the head just as much as from the heart. I believe that few, very few, people act consciously from base motives. Madeline and John Mayne certainly would not. Madeline, I need hardly say, is not that type of woman at all; and as for John Mayne—well, a man does not change his character in an instant. John Mayne would not act in a manner which he could not justify to himself. His career proves it. He may be sorely tempted, but——"

Percy considered a minute, and then spoke hesitatingly:

"I don't wish to be offensive about your friend, my dear fellow; but what people very much want to do they generally find some high-minded reason for doing. And—well, I have heard John Mayne cited as a case in point."

"Ah, yes, of course!" and Walter had a gesture of impatience. "But haven't you noticed that nowadays a little cheap cynicism goes a long way among small men to reconcile them to the fact that there are others of bigger calibre? There's a lot of petty jealousy in the world, my dear Percy!"

"No doubt!" said Percy. "No doubt!" And they went on smoking for some time in silence.

Indeed, the moment had arrived when neither felt equal to exposing to the other the subtle ramifications of his thoughts. And, simultaneously, each began to doubt whether, in view of the other's inferior acumen, it was worth while trying.

As they were putting on their coats, however, Percy came up to Walter and tapped him on the arm.

"She's a dangerous woman!" he whispered. "Mrs. Mayne—she's a dangerous woman,—I feel it."

Walter smiled reassurance.

"If she can create a misunderstanding between you and Miss Madeline, she will," Percy went on huskily. "You remember that!"

The beam of his glasses was intense; Walter met it unflinchingly and nodded with kindly understanding. He was thinking that he might perhaps have used the words "a dangerous woman" himself; but in Percy's mouth they sounded rather ridiculous.

On the doorstep, as they shook hands, he promised to let his friend know how the affair turned out. "I shall feel my way," he said. "I am going back to Eamor to-morrow, and there I shall feel my way."

Chapter 8

Walter had come to know Madeline much better during his sojourn at Eamor, and better still during his absence at Tornel, when, at a certain remove, he was able to focus her with greater sharpness. Truth to tell, it seemed to him now that his understanding of her character had not been very close before his engagement. He saw many blemishes unsuspected before; but his attachment, become more binding by virtue of the hours and days they had spent together, helped him to make little of them.

Madeline had already let him see that, if by her surrender he gained certain privileges, he also incurred new obligations. He had to look upon himself henceforward as her confidant and defender. Not only must he listen untiringly to her accounts of what she had been obliged to endure at the hands of Lilian, but he must show promise of developing into a doughty champion.

Her pathetic and sometimes naive exposure of the feminine meannesses and cruelties of which she had been the victim during her four years' residence at Eamor, amazed almost as much as they pained him. He learned how an ostensible friendship could become falser and falser as the days went by, until in the end it existed merely as a cloak, under which every conceivable refinement of malice would be practised. And what specially confounded him was the pertinacity with which the combatants would ever labour to patch up the tattered, perished fabric of a duplicity which deceived neither. The fair-seeming veil, torn to shreds one day in a sudden turn of cynically disclosed animosity, would reappear the next, to be worn with unaltered composure.

And to think that this had been going on for four years! Sometimes, when he turned Madeline's confidences over in his mind, he had to struggle hard against feelings of veritable consternation. Into what an appalling *milieu* was he not introducing himself! He thanked heaven that, as a man of the world, he was not unacquainted with human nature and its weaknesses; nevertheless he could not but anticipate with a certain alarm the heavy calls which might at any moment be made, not only upon his tact and *savoir faire,* but upon his reserves of moral strength and manly authority. Madeline was so desperately determined he should understand that by confiding in him she was also, to her sense, equipping him for the fray. She was buckling on his armour, polishing his sword; she even seemed resolved upon arousing in his breast a battle-spirit as fiery as her own. To all this he felt he must put up a firm, yet gentle, opposition. He could well understand how deeply the unfortunate girl longed for a confidant and supporter; but he was equally convinced that she mistook the kind of assistance she needed. To put it mildly, she was prone to lose her sense of proportion; and he could not permit himself to endorse the errors of taste and judgment into which the impetuosity of her feelings ever threatened to betray her.

He was particularly anxious to take a detached view of the case. But he failed to realise that no amount of sagacity could make up for inadequate knowledge of the personalities and conditions involved. A clear statement of fact was not Madeline's strong point; and, for all her emotional expansiveness, there was a strong vein of reticence in her composition. He learnt all that she wished him to learn about the others, but about herself very little,—even when she gave the appearance of being most intimate. He learnt next to nothing, for example, about her existence before she came to Eamor.

The prettiest of a large family of sisters, Madeline had been John Mayne's favourite from her youngest childhood. She had lost her father, Richard Mayne, at the age of twelve; and unfortunately the latter, two years before his death, had become engaged in a bitter quarrel with his wealthy brother. He died, leaving his family in actual want; and although John had come to the rescue, his disapprobation continued to rest heavily upon the widow. In these circumstances Madeline was unofficially adopted by her uncle, and came to serve as intermediary for such bounties as the family received. The girl's relations with her mother and sisters was exceptional; if she was ruled by her uncle, she ruled them in turn. At home—and she spent half the year at home—she was absolute mistress. Robust, self-willed, active-minded, she learned at an early age both how to cajole and to domineer.

John Mayne's marriage to Lilian Orisser had been taken by Madeline and her family as nothing less than a disaster. But while they were still lamenting the darkness that had fallen over their future prospects, there came the joyful, almost incredible, news of the rupture between husband and wife. Lilian's folly was giving them another chance. Madeline made good her opportunity to return to her uncle's side. From this time forward her duty to herself and her family was in her eyes crystal-clear: she must cultivate her uncle's affections to the uttermost and spare no effort to prevent Lilian from re-entering into his good graces. Such was the situation, when the old man expressed the desire that she should live at Eamor. She was not pleased, but she dared not put up a refusal. Besides, if she could not be with John Mayne himself, the next best position, strategically, was in the enemy's camp.

John Mayne was actuated by motives mixed and obscure. In the first place he was becoming a little oppressed by Madeline's proximity,—her anxious attentions, her watchful devotion. Then, too, he was jealous; he did not like Lilian to live alone, unobserved, and at liberty to follow her own will. He had the intention of visiting Eamor himself occasionally, and wanted to find someone there whose presence would give him countenance. Lastly, he took a certain pleasure in exercising his prerogative as master and in punishing his wife; he had no desire that she should settle down contentedly at Eamor, and was shrewd enough to expect that Madeline would be a thorn in her side.

For her part, Lilian divined these motives well enough, and could, moreover, make a fair guess at the spirit in which the girl herself envisaged the situation. Her intuition was shaped principally by the fact that Madeline was a Mayne; but it had also been given consistency by the manner in which John Mayne had been wont to speak about her, and by certain letters received at the time of their marriage. It was in the nature of things that these letters should be insincere, but they seemed to her to go a good deal further in the way of insincerity than the occasion required. To her sense they were blatant. Indeed, John Mayne himself had smiled over them; but his amusement, if cynical, was quite untinged by any flavour of disgust; and she perceived, incidentally, that he was capable of relishing insincerity as a tribute to power.

At the epoch of Madeline's arrival at Eamor, Lilian still nourished some hopes of coming to rather better terms with her husband. She felt the danger of letting John Mayne's inclinations militate persistently and unreservedly against his sense of honour; and she made sure that Madeline's presence in the house would not make the path of reconciliation any easier.

So the two women secretly regarded each other from the first as enemies; but each in her own fashion was anxious to make the best of a difficult situation and to avoid, if possible, an open trial of strength.

It was an instinct in Madeline, although she had plenty of spirit, never to avow enmity until every other means had been tried. To please was her passion. She met no one but she was moved to captivate, to seduce, to charm. Male and female, old and young, rich and poor, were alike to her in this respect. And in those with whom she was brought into close contact, her aspiration was to arouse a yet deeper feeling; she was dissatisfied unless she obtained their absolute devotion—that is to say, complete domination over them.

It was accordingly in obedience not merely to policy but to her deepest instincts that she received Lilian's friendly welcome with more than equal friendliness. To all the inmates of Eamor she was as forthcoming as the circumstances would permit; and, encouraged by the manner of her reception, it seemed to her at first that her position would be less difficult than she had feared.

In entering this house, however, she was coming under conditions strikingly different from any she had hitherto met. In her own home there was a perpetual clash between a deep, subconscious family loyalty on the one side, and envy coupled with an arrogant egotism on the other. In private, manners were rough to the point of cynicism, habits were slipshod, slovenliness was accepted, and parsimony of the pettiest kind ruled in every department of life. But when, after careful preparation, a stranger was admitted within the gates, the whole face of things underwent a miraculous change. The creaking, jarring mechanism of the household suddenly gave the appearance of functioning with perfect smoothness; to all appearances familial affection reigned supreme; a spirit of mutual toleration and respect animated the entire community; frankness, ease, and good-humour, were the order of the day.

One of the consequences of this was that Madeline grew up in the belief that every household had its disreputable underneath, however admirable its outward aspect; and during the first week of her stay at Eamor she wondered rather ironically how long the present illusion would be kept up. She hoped in course of time to obtain confidences; to enter into little, private alliances with each member of the company against the others; to become "one of them" and to gain understanding, insight, influence, power. But the Orissers, she gradually discovered, were a strange race. They were cold; they did not, even among themselves, offer a spectacle of vivacity, fondness, or even of intimacy, in her understanding of these terms. Thus she began at last to modify her picture of what their hidden life must be, conceding that in many particulars it must differ from that of her own people. As this impression gained strength, she suffered considerable disappointment and perplexity, and finally had to set about explaining the fact in a manner which would render a comparison between her own home-life and that of the Orissers less injurious to her self-respect.

One palliating consideration was ready to hand. At Eamor there was no lack of money, and she very reasonably accounted money capable of smoothing over nine-tenths of the rough edges of life, and of saving a corresponding amount of wear and tear on the temper. But this tacit admission of a superior standard of manners at Eamor was not one under which, even so, she could rest content. After all, were orderliness, self control, and gentle behaviour, the highest virtues in man? Was there not something more valuable lacking at Eamor? Something of paramount worth, absent here, which you might find in the turbulent and slatternly domesticity of the Maynes?

Yes, indeed! More and more confidently, as time went on, did she assure herself that something at Eamor was wanting. More and more did she long for the opportunities for emotional exuberance and violent self expression which her own home afforded,—all the rough contacts and sturdy resistances which were in her view the essence of intimate intercourse. Life in this house, which at first had seemed so smooth and restful, soon began to appear sterile, colourless, empty. Moreover, it involved effort; for how could one resist "letting oneself go" without effort? And as a pretence, it argued a prodigious fund of obstinate hypocrisy.

But the chief reason why Madeline was dismayed by these conditions was that they baffled her. She wished to ingratiate herself; and the easiest way to approach people was of course through their little weaknesses. The one touch of nature for which she was ever on the look-out was an unlovely touch. And it was part of her method to exhibit with humorous frankness the same blemish. She would offer the appearance of "giving herself away," in order to induce others to give themselves away. On the same principle, too, it often served judiciously to "let oneself *go*"; but how on earth was one to make progress with persons to whom the satisfaction of letting oneself go did not seem to appeal? Was it all hypocrisy! No, not all. If the Orissers did not suffer overmuch from this strain of keeping up appearances, it was doubtless in great measure because they lacked heart, they lacked vitality, they lacked the abounding energy which demands a wider outlet than is offered by an over-fastidious conventionalism.

Her goal—more definitely than ever in this case—was personal ascendancy, power—the power to guide, direct and control the destiny of those with whom she came in contact. But the inmates of Eamor were like figures in a painted scene; she could not reach the human creature within them. Impervious to sympathy, so also they were resistant to the superior force of her personality. Yes, the amiable persons around her were eluding her grasp; she was making little progress in intimacy; she was not commanding increased affection or influence; she was not taking the place she desired. And what made this all the more galling was her certainty that in the eyes of the world she would appear by far the more brilliant figure. The trouble was that at Eamor there was no appeal to public judgment. Even her advantages over Lilian in youth and vivacity were lost.

In her resolute determination to make the most of every opportunity, she had not neglected at the outset to make herself agreeable to Nicholas. No one could be more unlike the smart, alert, intelligent boys with whom she was accustomed to be popular. But in a sombre and somewhat effeminate style he was good looking; and, as a young male, he should prove less difficult to manage than the others. However, she soon found that, if he did not really attract her, neither did she him; and it was in his regard that she soonest relaxed her efforts. It was not merely that he had no fun, no *entrain,* no *savoir-faire,* but, as she presently discovered, his character contained distinctly objectionable traits. While remaining singularly childish in many respects, he displayed in other directions an undesirable precocity, an insight which was unwholesome and repellent. "I don't know how clever he is at his books," she wrote to her sister Nina, "but he certainly thinks himself a very superior person. *I* should say he had a very petty mind; and I am quite certain he will never do anything in this world." Two years later her criticism followed the same lines, but was more severe. "As for Nicholas, he is utterly contemptible. He sees his own mean, little character reflected in everybody else. To live in the same house with such a creature is in itself a penance."

Soon after giving up Nicholas, Madeline turned her attention more particularly upon Isabel, who had come to live at Eamor not many months before. Isabel was then thirteen years old, and a great favourite of Lilian's. Madeline opened her advances with impetuosity. The fact was that she had already begun to feel starved for companionship. Hers was one of those natures that require that to all feeling there shall be contemporaneous expression. Unless she could manifest herself in voice and gesture before an appreciative auditor and thus obtain material confirmation of what she believed herself to feel and to be, she lost her sense of being truly alive, she became oppressed by a sentiment of personal nullity. A sound instinct told her that it is natural and healthful in human beings that emotion and expression should go hand in hand, each encouraging and interpreting the other, so that one need never be in doubt as to what one's emotion is, or find difficulty, when the occasion is over, in putting it behind one.

Well; with Isabel she could reasonably hope for swifter success than with Lilian, who was quite friendly, but appeared to ignore the true meaning of intimacy. Few children, she knew, could resist the little endearments, flatteries, and presents, of which she was prodigal. But this child, unsophisticated as she had seemed, showed herself to be already tainted with the Orisser taint. She was strangely inaccessible; she received blandishments with surprise rather than with gratification; she showed herself extraordinarily unready to deviate from her lonely, childish way. In the end, however, Madeline won her over, although not so completely as she could have wished. Isabel remained very reserved, and this did not suit Madeline, to whom the making and receiving of confidences was nothing less than a passion. She felt that a confidence gained was an accession of power; and if for this reason the making of a confidence was unwise, she compromised between inclination and prudence by letting her imagination rule her tongue—that is to say, by revealing a fictive rather than a real life and self.

The making of false confidences was, however, by no means an inexcusable self-indulgence on her part. It served an urgent requirement of her nature. For, while speaking, she lent a certain credence to what she said, and thus imparted a measure of solidity to the phantasies which sustained her through the experiences of real life, which were apt—as they are for most of us—to be disappointing and dispiriting.

After three or four weeks the intimacy between Madeline and Isabel appeared to be firmly established, if not yet very close. But one morning Isabel awoke with a sense of *malaise*; and, when she encountered Madeline, detestation sprang up in her heart. The fulness of Madeline's gestures, the round, rich tones of her voice, the scent of her hair, the whole fleshly bigness of her, were unbearable. Madeline was an encroachment; Madeline threatened her with a spiritual envelopment. She struggled away from Madeline's personality as from the rise of a sticky, cloying tide.

In a flash she turned upon Madeline; there was a scene short, cruel, and decisive. Madeline retired to her room and there wept.

So deeply was she wounded that for many months she concealed her hurt. She told herself that Lilian had poisoned the child's mind against her. To her calumniator, however, she breathed no word of reproach; she was still hopeful, at this period, of obtaining the woman's friendship; to quarrel with her over the child would have been folly.

It was significant that nearly all the entries in her diary treated of her relations with Lilian. Her scheme for gaining the position of superiority which she coveted, was based upon attaining an intimate knowledge of Lilian's character, and of the causes of her estrangement from John Mayne. Indeed, the subject of Lilian's past and present relations with her husband exercised over Madeline an intense fascination. It was beyond her comprehension how this woman, who had been clever enough to marry the old man, could subsequently be so silly as to jeopardise the fortune which she had secured. She suspected there must be some other man in the case. This would go far towards explaining Lilian's cautious reserve.

Meantime both women clung desperately to the fictions mitigating their position. If for Madeline the difference between appearance and reality was always immense, she was not thereby deterred from putting belief in appearance, when the occasion demanded it. Thus, when, at the arrival of a stranger, the Mayne household was transfigured, Madeline believed that the aspect presented was the true one. They were all then showing their better—indeed, their *true*—selves, (which, however, so soon as the visitor left, were discarded with a sigh of relief). Similarly, in her relations with Lilian, although capable of regarding the situation with an almost cynical acuity of vision, and whilst prepared on an emergency to act accordingly, Madeline was by no means willing to live with that depressing aspect of affairs constantly before her. This she would very justly have characterized as "morbid." On the front page of her diary was the dictum: "We must idealize, or we should cease to struggle."

The Orissers seemed to her depressingly empty of idealism, painfully deficient in aspiration. The kernel of mischief in the actual situation was, she saw clearly enough, the absence of love. But *she* longed for love; *she* craved for love; *she* pined both to give and to receive it. "I have been conscious from my earliest childhood," she wrote in her diary, "of a desire to help people. And how can one help people better than by loving them? I know that nothing makes *me* feel happier than to know that I am loved."

For a temperament of this kind Eamor was veritably a desert. "How I am wasted here!" she lamented at the end of her first year. "I can see that Lilian is unhappy, although her pride makes her try to conceal it. I know, too, why she is unhappy; and I believe I could help her. Why does she do her best to make an enemy of one who would be a friend!" And again: "Poor Lilian! why can't she see that it is her own paltry, personal pride that stands in the way of her happiness? She affects to despise the world, to despise religion, to despise everything! When I told her that every night I go down on my knees and pray to God to make me better, she smiled uncomfortably. I said I also prayed that she might be made happier. And I could see that she was annoyed. How petty!"

Chapter 9

So Madeline did not make very much headway; and yet it could not be said that she failed to make her presence powerfully felt. Lilian found that the defences upon which she had counted were quite inadequate, nor could she devise any other scheme of behaviour effective in keeping Madeline off. In spite of a certain clumsiness of attack,—indeed, by virtue of that very clumsiness,—Madeline forced her way through every obstacle. It was all very well for Lilian to decry the girl's methods as crude, those methods were successful; and how could one call her insensitive, when she displayed so much sensitiveness, and turned it to such good account? Her hardihood and persistence in exposing herself to rebuffs was only equalled by her skill in making capital out of them. She was an adept at offering and extracting explanations, from which she would emerge with the apparent advantage of having made a step forward towards mutual understanding and friendship.

Of course, these advances, in point of fact, were a regression in the opposite direction. But it was not in Madeline's nature to act differently, or to recognise the true motives and consequences of her behaviour. No! her idealism forbade her to admit to herself that she was developing a serious hatred of Lilian. To her thinking, hatred was an ignoble passion. She could not allow that such a weed had taken root in her being. Her assumption of a superior warmth of heart and breadth of feeling absolutely precluded any such admission. It would make her whole manner towards Lilian look not only hypocritical but absurd. In her diary there was many a passage like this: "In spite of all her faults and the great dissimilarity of our natures, I feel drawn towards Lilian. I have never met anyone before, whom I so much wanted to help. Poor Lilian! she finds life so difficult! She has such a complicated nature!—far more complicated than mine. She is always dissatisfied. But I have Faith to guide me! I wish I could show her what it is she really needs."

Alas! it was only too true that Madeline did "feel drawn towards" Lilian. Even had there been other persons at Eamor to whom she could turn, and no ulterior object at the back of her mind, she would have singled out Lilian for her attentions. For, do what she would, Lilian gave Madeline the feeling of being unfavourably criticised, and thus lured her fatally on to the attempt to impose a better opinion, or to obtain a position of superiority over her critic. Lilian saw this, and yet could not successfully dissemble. Temperament will out; prearranged schemes of behaviour are ill-executed, if executed only under pressure of the will. In reaction against Madeline's temperament, certain characteristics of Lilian's became exaggerated. She could not avoid displaying an ever greater fastidiousness and intolerance; and in measure as Madeline claimed greater liberty of self-expression, she, on her side, allowed a disdainful censure to become more and more apparent. Thus her latent criticism of Madeline's whole view of existence rose month by month nearer to the surface; and Madeline fell insensibly into the habit of taking periodical revenge.

She did this by creating a "scene." The scenes which she devised varied somewhat in character, but they generally began with reproaches, which, whether passionate or tearful, would develop into denunciations, and finally into threats. She would taunt Lilian with the mercenariness of her motives in marrying John Mayne, and with her actual position of financial servitude. And then presently, when her passion had risen to incandescent heat, she would vow to make herself the instrument of Lilian's chastisement and of the ruin of the corrupt family of Orisser.

But violent as these passages were, she contrived, as a rule, to bring the episode to a close upon a note of forgiveness and reconciliation—at least so far as she was concerned. She was not prepared to defy her uncle by leaving Eamor, nor willing to give Lilian the gratification of seeing her go. Besides, in a way, she enjoyed her battles, which, giving her a sense of intimacy with her antagonist, ministered to the fiction that she was gradually overcoming Lilian's hardness of heart, and making victorious progress towards a Christian friendship. The development of this fiction kept pace with the deep-seated hatred which it was designed to conceal. Never did she feel more "drawn towards" Lilian than after a scene of unusual violence; and nothing that the other could do or say was capable of impairing the illusion.

Before this extraordinary phenomenon Lilian realized, with profound consternation, that the sheer violence of Madeline's insincerity almost turned it into its opposite. It was, after all, true, in a sense, that Madeline did want to be friends, that Madeline did want to be sincere, and even that Madeline did want to love and be loved. But sincerity, as understood by Lilian, was psychologically impossible to Madeline.

When, in desperation, Lilian tried to explain the inescapable realities governing their relation, she found herself confronted with a determination equalling her own, and with a line of argument that her logic could not break. Madeline said that neither of them ought to give in to animosity and that, for her part, she never would. To understand, said Madeline, was to forgive; and forgiveness was the beginning of love. She quoted from St. Francis and the Bible. Never, never should one submit, or confess submission, to the dictates of one's lower nature. For her part, she was still full of hope. Why! their present conversation yielded inspiring evidence of their power to enter into spiritual communion with one another. They must go on striving, striving—always striving! And tears of exaltation would pour down her cheeks, whereas the moisture that gathered in Lilian's eyes was engendered by unutterable vexation and disgust.

At the root of Madeline's trouble was the immense discrepancy between her habits of mind and her ideals. Conscious of a vital need to idealize herself, she could not conceive that anyone should be willing to take himself for what he was; or she imagined that, if anyone did so, such a person must be an inhuman cynic. Lilian appeared to her monstrously materialistic, cynical, and even vicious. The girl really felt at times that contact with her and Nicholas was destroying her ideals and sapping the foundations of her moral being. "One must idealize or one will cease to struggle." But, gracious heavens! how was one to idealize with a Lilian Mayne as a companion?

"Dear God!" she wrote in her diary, "I feel I shall not be able to stand this life much longer! Lilian is really becoming impossible. Her coldness, hardness, pettiness, and malice, are beyond belief. What have I done to make her hate me so? It is inhuman. The more I force myself to be amiable, the more malicious and spiteful she becomes. God alone knows what efforts I have made to forgive her for her unspeakable conduct to me regarding Isabel! God alone knows what a torture it is to me in my utter loneliness to see that darling, who once cared for me, now treat me like a stranger! God, to whom I have prayed for the strength to endure all this in silence—God alone knows what I suffer! For I still love poor little Isabel! She is after all nothing but a child, and I often wonder whether, when she grows up, she will look back and understand how she has wronged me! I should like her to understand some day, although I would not wish her to suffer from remorse on my account."

Moments came at last when a sudden perception of the darkness closing about her, drove Madeline, in a frenzy of disgust, to seek escape from Eamor. Once or twice she composed letters to her uncle in which she declared outright that she would not stay. But never did such a letter reach the post-box. No; her will forbade it. She had gone to Eamor under the sternest and clearest injunctions from Providence to do her duty to herself and her family. These injunctions must be obeyed.

On her side, however, Lilian, as may be imagined, was ready to do everything in her power to secure Madeline's removal. She brought herself at last—though with little hope of success—to petition John Mayne. Endless explanations and recriminations followed; and in the end, as she had foreseen, John Mayne bade them each start afresh with a clean slate.

The most hopeful factor in the situation was Madeline's marriage-ableness. It was certain that she found life at Eamor extremely unsatis-fying. The scenes, which in the beginning she had initiated at will and guided to an appointed end, became a matter of physiological necessity; and during the course of them she would lose all self-control. Just as a tremendous explosion of heat and fury can be provoked in an Icelandic geyser by the stimulus of a clod of earth thrown into it, so there were times in Madeline's life when some trivial incident would provoke a quite disproportionate ebullition of wrath. The pent-up bitterness of weeks, of months, of years—for she had now been nearly four years at Eamor—would then come to light; and it seemed impossible that so vast a passion should deny itself a more satisfactory issue for much longer.

On his rare visits to Eamor John Mayne had brought Walter with him; and Lilian, seeing that the latter was attracted by Madeline, had not been slow to invite him on other occasions. Madeline's quick perception of what was hoped of her had of course militated against Walter; but in the end the forces of nature and circumstance had pre-vailed.

Lilian's satisfaction was great. She had begun to feel that Madeline was wearing her out. The scenes from which the girl emerged, physically a little tired perhaps, but spiritually refreshed, made a severe drain upon her opponent's vitality. What was to Madeline no more than a healthful psychical cathartic acted on Lilian's organisation with exhausting effect. It was true that Madeline often recorded: "Lilian tires me terribly!" but she was referring less to their passages-at-arms than to the intervals of strain in between times. She did not realise how exhausting her person-ality was to everyone with whom she was thrown for any length of time, and especially to those who were unable to accept, in all innocence, her presentment of herself. Such persons found themselves under the constant obligation to appear deceived,—an effort of simulation to which they would be prompted by considerations of kindness, tact, and self-protection alike. For Madeline's combative instinct was ready to start up at the first call of her *amour propre*, like a tigress at the whimper of her cub.

Nicholas used to declare half-humorously that she inspired him with a kind of terror. He was more justified in his feelings than he knew. Human beings have but a limited fund of psychical energy, and in the expenditure of this energy they unconsciously exercise a certain economy. By making constant calls upon the resources of those around her, Madeline, for all her apparent buoyancy, exerted in the long run a lowering influence; and commerce with her was specially costly to the Orissers, because they paid in currency of higher value than hers, and from stores which nature was less quick to replenish.

But Nicholas had not yet arrived at any clear understanding of this. Another aspect of that bitter clash of temperaments engrossed him. He was at the metaphysical age, and saw in the drama working itself out upon the puppet-stage of Eamor the semblance of a wider contest. Groping after universal characters of the human spirit, it seemed to him that in the person of Madeline he had before him an incarnation of the highest significance. From the very first he had but one word for her: she was *formidable*. "The better I understand her," he would say to Lilian, "the more she disgusts and terrifies me. It is all very well to call her crude and to laugh at her stupidities. They are modes of her strength. Madeline is strong and tenacious with the strength and tenacity of the forces whose instrument she is. All that we love, all that we admire, all that we are, is hated by Madeline. And the world is behind her. Yes; she is of the world, and the world is of her. Reveal her in her true colours, and still the world will sympathize with her rather than with us. The world does not want us, nor what we stand for. And in the end Madeline will down us."

Chapter 10

Madeline's feeling for Walter was one of genuine affection, and she respected him with the better side of her nature. He was to be considered a good match; especially as the connexion would consolidate her position in her uncle's favour. These were sound reasons for marrying him. If she had not yielded to his suit a year ago, it was chiefly because he had not succeeded in captivating her girlish imagination. Walter was not in her eyes a romantic figure. And she clung to her romanticism, as to her idealism, with a fervour that intercourse with the Orissers had imbued with a kind of desperation. Thus, marriage was not an affair in which she judged it proper to be guided by convenience. She cherished a conception of herself as the very type of warm, rich, generous maidenhood; she had a strong sense of the preciousness of her innocence, her virginity; the bestowal of herself was a holy matter, an event that very properly had to be solemnised by a sacrament; and a sacrament was the expression of a spiritual—not merely a utilitarian—sanction. So it was necessary that she should love Walter. And in the end she persuaded herself that she did love him. Walter, whatever the Orissers might think of him, was an important person in the eyes of the world; and her union to him, whatever the Orissers might think of that, would indeed and in truth be the beautiful thing she had always determined her marriage should be.

It was no small satisfaction to her to reach this conclusion. Once betrothed, her affection for Walter gathered force considerably. For one thing, it was a great comfort to have somebody at hand in whom one could confide and from whom one might expect support. She found, as time went on, however, that it was difficult to make a sufficient impression on him. It annoyed her to be told that it was beneath her dignity to throw the weight of her personal emotion so liberally into the scale against Lilian. When Walter said this, she would sigh and fall into a silence from which his conciliatory sallies did not easily rouse her; or else she would point out with reproach in her eyes that it was not on her own account that her feelings were so deeply stirred, but on behalf of her uncle.

Then Walter, on his side, would sigh and resign himself to silence. For how could he reprobate her loyal sympathies? For his own part, he knew John Mayne well enough as a business man and as a public man, but hitherto had hardly thought of him as the possessor of a private life. The picture she drew of the hard-working, self-willed old man, captured towards the end of his career by the implacable love-interest, was extraordinarily arresting. He was shown John Mayne's emotional simplicity, his want of insight where women were concerned, the inevitability of his falling into the trap which an unkind fate had placed across his path. Yes, a fate most signally unkind; for as his manly virtues had rendered him an easy prey, so did his masculine chivalry deny him the satisfaction of retributive justice. How insignificant, said Madeline, was what *she* had endured from Lilian Orisser compared to what *he* had endured! He was a man—more vulnerable! He loved—how bitter! He had given his all—what a sting! His money Lilian had taken without thanks; his affection she publicly rejected; his self regard she had made it her study to wound in every possible way. "And yet I am sorry for her!" Madeline would conclude with a sigh. "She has not had a happy life! For the wrongs she has done *me* I can forgive her. But the suffering she has inflicted upon uncle—that I don't think I shall ever be able to forgive!"

And Walter would knit his brows and nod gravely. She brought things home to him—he had to admit it. He could well understand her pain and indignation. But—and here he shook his head—the persistence of these feelings at fever-heat was, he feared, almost—well, almost morbid.

Deep in his heart was the uneasy sense that, although her presentment of the case might be just in the main, some of the things she said would have been better left unsaid, or at any rate said differently. In certain rather undisciplined, rather graceless, rather childishly cunning, and even unprincipled, turns of thought and language; in her behaviour as she herself described it during certain unfortunate episodes which might be called "scenes" he saw a characteristic that displeased him— yes, displeased him, although explicable as nothing worse than the vigorous reactions of an uncorrupted nature, protesting blindly against what it perceived as hard, cold, and ungenerous in its spiritual environment. Madeline was young; Eamor had done much to deviate into undesirable channels the flow of her emotional life; but he did not doubt that the intrinsic sweetness and sanity of her disposition were but thinly and temporarily obscured.

These were some of the thoughts which had lain at the back of his mind during his conversation with his friends at Tornel. In the train on his way back to Eamor he debated whether it would be wise to question her outspokenly regarding her expectations, her desires, her private intent. Why not invite her to set forth all her views about the Eamor property? What did she want exactly? Yes, why not ask her frankly; What did she ultimately want? One part of his brain urged him with impatience in this direction, but the other part made weighty objection. Did he not know well enough in his heart that Madeline was quite uncertain what she did want? Was it not clear enough that she was torn between two conflicting modes of feeling? And was there not a danger of raising her baser inclinations into a position of direct antagonism to himself? Had he not a letter in his pocket which showed that the girl's nerves were on edge? Was she not passing through a phase of hysterical mistrustfulness? Yes, indeed! Was she not ready, upon the smallest provocation, to inveigh against him as half-hearted, lukewarm, judicial to the point of priggishness, and even perhaps infected with secret sympathy for Lilian Mayne?

Moreover, if he invited her to be frank, he must not be failing in sincerity himself. In other words, it would be obligatory to introduce Cosmo to her as a factor in the situation. And Walter positively shuddered at the thought of the excitement into which that story would precipitate her. He felt sure that she was, on the whole, satisfied to let affairs drift along in their present direction, and that he would not be able to insist on laying the matter out before her uncle, without a serious quarrel. Nor were his own convictions on the subject entirely settled. The more closely he considered the situation, the more clearly he perceived that Cosmo's appearance on the stage at Eamor *would* produce tremendous complications. He wished to heaven that Lilian Mayne had abstained from telling him anything about Cosmo. If, as she affirmed, the man was on the point of death, she might at least have waited till he was dead. But every now and then he would have a dreadful foreboding that Cosmo was not going to die. And there was, to his sense, something positively sinister in the thought that Cosmo and Allen were actually in Eamor village. Cosmo, he imagined, was capable of anything; and as for Allen,—well! he could not forget that Allen had once intimated, in a most offensive manner, that he would hold him strictly to account as a guarantor of John Mayne's good faith towards Lilian, and had even hinted that he, Allen, would assuredly find means to make himself unpleasant in the event of matters turning out badly! Idle bluster, of course! For what, on the worst supposition, would the man be able to do? Nevertheless, Walter heartily wished that Allen as well as Cosmo were a thousand leagues away.

For the first few days after his return to Eamor he contented himself with watching and waiting. He was reconciled to this policy the more easily that, on his arrival, he was informed by Lilian that Cosmo's condition had much deteriorated and that the man's death might be expected any moment. In the matter of "feeling his way" he took action by having a talk with Nicholas. Not much came of the talk, it was true; but he hoped he had given the youth to understand how desirable it was that he should win John Mayne's good graces. Why should not the old man's feelings towards him become those of a father for his son? He dropped a hint that, if Nicholas awaited favours, it was his duty to render the bestowal of them as agreeable as possible, and that John Mayne's apparent intentions to prolong his sojourn at Eamor afforded opportunities of ingratiation which it would be folly to throw away.

With Madeline he remained cautious. The girl continued nervous and irritable in a degree which forbade the discussion of difficult subjects. During one of their afternoon rides, however, he made certain definite gains of understanding. She disclosed that in some of the scenes which had unfortunately taken place between her and Lilian, the question of Eamor had been quite cynically bandied about. This lack of scruple and taste shocked Walter considerably. And it was a distressing revelation of the low level which had on occasion been reached, to learn that Lilian had once roundly declared that, although John Mayne could act as he chose, never would she allow him to deceive himself into supposing that he could rely on his niece to carry out obligations *merely moral!* At this Walter marvelled, then put a question. Had Lilian, to Madeline's knowledge, actually discussed the question of Eamor with John Mayne? Madeline thought not; or at least only obliquely. Lilian, she surmised, was waiting. Walter uneasily wondered what for! Waiting! Why, that was what Madeline, too, was doing. Each evidently imagined that the tide was running in her favour. Which was right? It was extremely perplexing. But it confirmed him in his decision that he also would wait. And presently Madeline went on to explain how, "in the meantime," Lilian never lost an opportunity of injuring her in her uncle's eyes. The subtle work of defaming her, of undermining her uncle's love and trust, was never set aside; but, thank God, she concluded, the woman's efforts had so far been unavailing.

Chapter 11

It was remarkable that the only person from whose society Walter derived any pleasure, in this period of his perplexities, was Lilian Mayne. The other inmates of Eamor, allowing themselves to be engrossed by separate preoccupations, bestowed, as he thought, a quite insufficient attention to the ordinary amenities of social intercourse. Madeline, in particular, gave him too little consideration. But Lilian was consistently gracious; and, although he kept his distrust of her, he submitted gratefully enough to her charm.

There was occasion for him to spend a good deal of time with her over the accounts of the Eamor estate. John Mayne had recently called for statements and balance sheets. Lilian had been supposed to send accounts, every quarter, to the office at Tornel; but she had never done this with exactitude; and in the past, when Walter had reported the matter to John Mayne, the latter had simply shrugged. It now pleased him, however, to call for accurate figures; so Lilian had to bring into order the accumulated disorder of years. And Walter was giving her assistance.

Madeline did not altogether approve the closeting together of these two. She apprehended that Lilian would make the most of her opportunities for "getting round" Walter. The idea that the woman might be telling him things which would lead him to question the accuracy of some of her own statements, made her checks burn; while the bare supposition that he in answer might be saying things which he would not say to her, caught her spirit up in little gusts of anticipatory fury. Always prone to believe that secrets were being kept from her, she became even more watchful and suspicious than usual.

Walter was not without some inkling of what was passing in his fiancee's mind; and, although he felt that her uneasiness, or jealousy, was a just punishment for her neglect of him, he tried his hardest to allay it. But not with complete success. The fact that he was, in very sooth, sharing with Lilian a secret of no small importance, weighed upon his conscience and embarrassed his tongue. Every day his impatience to receive the news of Cosmo's death augmented. Great was his vexation, therefore, when, about a week after his return from Tornel, Lilian informed him that Cosmo's condition had taken a decided turn for the better, and that the doctor now said the man might possibly drag out a crippled existence for some months, or even years, more. This intelligence at once revived his dormant suspicions that Allen and Lilian between them might be playing with him; and in a sudden gust of resolution he declared that Cosmo's presence must no longer be kept secret. John Mayne must be informed forthwith.

He was sitting with his hostess in her boudoir, when this critical passage took place. The look of grief and reproach that swept over her countenance was no deeper than he had expected. In previous conversations she had hinted plainly enough that the surrender of Eamor to Cosmo would, in her opinion, offer irresistible attractions to John Mayne. For while it would satisfy his longing for revenge, it might at a pinch be held to satisfy honour as well. Walter at the time had summarily scouted the notion. And yet in his heart he had been considerably impressed. The decision, therefore, before which they now stood, seemed to him also to be truly momentous; but he still concealed his real feelings; and, while she went over her old arguments with redoubled persuasiveness, he permitted himself to interrupt her every now and then with an observation that sounded almost flippant.

The fact was that in their long colloquies over the Eamor accounts, he had fallen into a certain manner with her that he could not at once discard. He had responded to her appealing, feminine helplessness with an air of easy, masculine capability. With pretty women—and Lilian Mayne was unquestionably a very pretty woman—a slightly ponderous playfulness came naturally to him. It was a small, unconscious grievance of his against Madeline that she did not know how to lend herself to his badinage. But Lilian did; and this was a strong point in her favour.

When, therefore, she gave him her news about Cosmo with the same looks of distress and entreaty that she was accustomed to wear when presenting him with some tangle in her accounts, he instinctively responded with something like his habitual display of imperturbability. And such is the force of appearances that his deep, inward misgivings were actually mitigated by this superficial airiness.

"My dear lady!" said he, "Cosmo is a bogey, who, I regret to say, doesn't give me the smallest shudder! Your picture of John Mayne welcoming him with open arms, strikes me as positively comic."

"Oh, Walter, how can you say that! Surely——"

"No, no, surely not!"

But she failed to return his smile. And realizing, on his side, only too well that a greater seriousness was called for—

"I cannot," he protested, "I really cannot entertain your suppositions!"

"But why not?"

"Because I should be doing your husband a grave injustice."

Lilian bit her lip.

"And this idea that Cosmo is so hostile!—Why should he be? You have continued his allowance. And you admit that he is on the best of terms with Nicholas!"

"Come, come!" he went on, smiling into her woeful eyes. "Courage, my dear lady! Out with the whole story! You have nothing to be ashamed of. On the contrary. Your part—and Nicholas's—and Allen's— they all redound to your credit. No one could think otherwise!"

"Not Madeline?" asked Lilian, turning her head away.

"Certainly not!"

She kept her eyes averted. "Do you think that Madeline would wish her uncle to be told?"

Walter suppressed a wince. "I can't say what Madeline's views would be. I have abstained, at your particular request, from mentioning the matter to anyone—even to her."

Lilian sighed. "Well," said she, "you will give me a few days, Walter,—to think this over, won't you?"

He hesitated.

"You see," she went on, "Cosmo might decide—any moment—to go back to Mexico. And then——"

Walter permitted himself a shrewd, inward smile. "My dear Lilian, you must forgive me for observing that your accounts of Cosmo are rather mystifying. One day I hear he is on the point of death. The next day I am told he may live for years. By one report he came to this country with the express purpose of doing you mischief; yet now you tell me that he is quite ready to return peaceably to Mexico! I ask you, what am I to make of all this?"

During the ensuing pause, he smiled. But his smile was not an easy one. The conclusion that did, unhappily, offer itself was that Lilian had been simply playing for time; and again it came over him, in a wave of positive dread, that the risks she was inducing him to run were by no means inconsiderable. Chance might at any moment reveal to John Mayne the fact that Cosmo had been living at Eamor village for several weeks, during which period he, Walter, had conspired with Lilian to keep that fact secret.

Changing his position in the comfortable armchair which habit had made his, he looked round the little room and gave a profound sigh.

"My conscience," he went on with solemnity, "my conscience really will not permit me to withhold my information from John Mayne any longer. No!" And his voice grew stern. "I blame myself for having held my peace for so many days already. I think we have both acted unwisely. Every hour that passes makes the position more difficult."

Whilst he was speaking Lilian's face changed. It assumed an expression that he had almost forgotten it could wear. With a sinking of the heart he apprehended that she certainly had a will of her own.

She was silent for longer than he liked. Then she rose and went over to the bell. One finger on the button, she paused.

"If you wish it," she said, "I will send for Madeline."

"Why should I wish it?"

She opened her eyes. "You cannot tell John Mayne without first telling Madeline!"

A wave of annoyance swept over him. "Why not?" he asked.

She looked surprised. "Don't you want to tell Madeline? I assure you, she will have very strong views on the subject."

Walter's stare became glassy. A three-cornered interview did not commend itself to him. He scented danger. The woman meant mischief.

Suddenly, however, her hand dropped from the bell. Once again her face became reproachful and appealing. "Walter!" she cried with a catch of her breath.

"Must I?"

It sounded as if the pressure came from him, and this put him in a position to give a shrug of partial relentment.

"Sit yourself down again!" said he with a smile. "You go too fast, my dear lady! I have more to say to you—before we take others into our confidence."

Lilian reseated herself. "I was thinking," she added reflectively, "that we cannot, in any case, go to John Mayne to-day."

"Why not?"

Again she looked surprised. "Because he is much too unwell! Madeline would never allow it!"

John Mayne was in fact confined to his room. He was suffering from what was believed to be a temporary ailment, in no wise connected with his disease. Madeline was in attendance on him.

Walter entered upon weighty considerations. "Well," he murmured, as though addressing himself, "to-morrow—or the next day, maybe——"

Lilian lifted her eyes upon him with the most submissive of smiles. "Ah! But what would you say, if—when you next came to me about it—I were to tell you that Cosmo had gone!"

"Gone? Where?"

She laughed gently. "Back to Mexico, of course! I know you didn't believe me when I said it was possible. But it is! And I'll prove it!"

Walter made an odd sound, opened his mouth, and then closed it. "Allen would go with him?" he finally inquired.

She nodded. "Yes, Allen would take him."

Walter breathed heavily through his nostrils, frowned, and held up his well-trimmed finger-nails for scrutiny. He had to think. There was something here that puzzled him. After a moment he rose and, going over to the window, stared thoughtfully out over the sunlit garden. The idea that Allen as well as Cosmo might soon be got out of the way was very pleasing. But it was quite clear that Lilian's last manoeuvre had been dictated by sheer desperation. Could he take her suggestion with any seriousness? Of course, if Cosmo were really well enough to travel, the obvious thing to do was to ship him out of the country; but was he in truth well enough? And did he consent to go?

He turned presently to put her this last question.

She hesitated a moment, then very quietly replied:

"He will have to go!"

Pursing his lips, Walter again faced round towards the view. He could not say why it was, but the feeling had come to him that they were trenching on the region of the sinister. In dealing with Cosmo, he gloomily supposed, you inevitably descended into this murky atmosphere. Gazing out over the bright, peaceful garden, he was oppressed by a sense of contrast, of incongruity. Those two men were not in keeping here! If it could be contrived that they should take themselves away, what a blessing it would be! And why should he press an inquiry into the manner of their going?

"Tell me," he said at last, "is the secret of Cosmo's identity still secure?"

"Absolutely!" returned Lilian with eagerness. "You must remember that he remains partially paralysed. He is still almost speechless. Allen believes that his mind, too, is slightly affected. And then, he has had no opportunities of communication with anyone. There is no possibility——"

With a nod Walter cut her short and turned back to his contemplation of the prospect. It was Lilian who next broke the silence.

"Walter!"

Her voice was tremulous and low. At the sound of it, he knit his brows still more deeply.

"Walter!" she breathed again, and he heard her rise and take a few steps towards him. "You have your duty towards yourself, I know! And your duty towards John Mayne—which you will never forget! But you have a duty towards me, too, Walter!"

Slowly he moved round, his face all puckered with concern. At one moment his lips parted, but with a gesture he gave up.

She came and laid a hand on his arm. "Eight years ago, in this house, you and John Mayne, and Allen, and I, we were standing together in the library—oh! don't you remember it, Walter?—and John Mayne solemnly promised that Eamor should never be taken from us—from Nicholas and me! Walter, is that not true?"

A grave nod was his answer.

"And I—I relied upon his honour! I relied upon *your* honour. Was I deceived? Was I wrong?"

During an interval of pregnant silence her gaze plunged straight into his.

"I signed that deed!" she went on, "I signed it, because I believed in you! Oh, why, if you meant to turn away from me like this, why did you let me do it?"

She dropped her head, then lifted it to him again.

"Answer me, Walter!"

She was beautiful. And in that moment he saw her beauty as the veracious expression of her innermost self. He could not question her sincerity in the desperation of this final appeal. And if, in order to bend him to her purpose, she had been prone to make use of wiles, it was not, he felt, against his deepest sense of right that she exercised her woman's ingenuity, but against what, in the light of her present impassionment, appeared nothing more than a formal rectitude, made attractive to him by considerations of private expediency.

Yet he would not submit to these feelings without some kind of protest. What right had she to put upon *his* conscience and upon *his* honour a burden that properly rested on John Mayne's? And why, instead of pleading for a policy of concealment, did she not call upon him to declare his whole mind to John Mayne, and to challenge the old man to an open declaration of *his* intentions? As an ear-witness of John Mayne's early promise, and as the appointed instrument of its violation or discharge, he had the right to make such a challenge—and was even under the obligation of accompanying it with a statement that, unless the answer were satisfactory, he must decline any part in the execution of the will. What such a challenge as this would mean—what awful wrath it would arouse, and how ruinous the issue was likely to be for his career and all his hopes—Walter could foresee only too well. A complete breach with Madeline as well as with her uncle was quite a possible result. Visions of dreadful discord, culminating in disaster, floated before his eyes. Far be it from him, then, to inquire of Lilian why she did not make this call upon him; although before the spectacle of her present desperation he could not but speculate about her reasons for abstaining. Did she divine that she would call in vain? Or did she re-doubt, on her own account, the consequences of such a storm?

"My dear lady!" he groaned. "My dear lady——"

But she had turned away. Her hands clasped over her face, she did not seem to hear.

"It is true," she said in a muffled voice, "that I on my side have been ungenerous! But who can judge between John Mayne and me? Who can say that the whole blame is mine? And what of my long trial of patience? Eight long years at Eamor, Walter! Are those eight years going for nothing? Oh!" she cried, looking round at him with eyes that flashed fire, "can you doubt that there have been days when I would rather have been dead?—days when I should have preferred——"

"Hush, hush! Enough!" And with a resolute gesture Walter strode towards the door. "We have talked enough for this morning, Lilian. . . . For the present we will leave matters as they are."

Chapter 12

Nicholas sat in the library, reading. It was late in the afternoon; a thin, persistent rain had been falling all day; the house was very still. The stillness indeed seemed to him too deep; it inspired him with a vague unrest; his attention wandered.

He was glad when he heard a step in the passage and Isabel entered. Isabel was his refuge in these days. His thoughts raised a barrier between himself and Lilian; but Isabel stood between him and his thoughts. He took pleasure in her detachment, her unconcern, and her insight; all of which had a child like and—in his eyes—a fascinating quality. She was never perturbed about others, nor about herself. There was something exquisite in such irresponsibility.

For his part he was suffering from a deep depression of spirits. He was estranged from Lilian; he felt hostile to Allen; he had developed an intense hatred of John Mayne; and his sentiment for Cosmo was inexplicable even to himself. He was conscious of a perverse allegiance to Cosmo; he had the desire that Cosmo should rise up and triumph over the world. But alas, the only triumph that he could see for Cosmo was a triumph over Lilian. And in that triumph Nicholas Orisser would suffer as seriously as anyone else.

His first thought, when he saw Isabel, was to question her about Lilian. He still had the feeling that she and Allen were in league together and working towards an end of which he could not approve.

The girl had come in with the smiling, casual air that was characteristic of her. Seating herself on a sofa opposite, she regarded him in silence.

"Well?" said he.

"Well!"

Affecting to yawn, he made a general inquiry as to what was going on in the house.

She gave a little shrug. "Nothing particular!" Then after a pause: "But here am I—rather bored!"

He smiled faintly. "Why don't you help Lilian with those wretched accounts?"

"Why don't you?"

"Because she won't let me."

"Have you asked her?"

"No." And he lit a cigarette. "It wouldn't be any use. How beautifully Lilian and Walter seem to be getting on nowadays. Have you noticed it?"

"Yes! Madeline will soon be getting jealous."

"Lilian has always been marvellously polite to Walter," he continued reflectively; "and—well, so have I, for that matter. But one day, I know, I shall put out my tongue at him."

The girl smiled. "Lilian is polite to everyone."

"When I see her and Walter together," he went on, "I can picture exactly how she will appear before God Almighty, when she dies. I can see her murmuring something about having had a delightful time on earth; and passing on,—so polite, so scrupulously polite!"

At this sally they both laughed; but Nicholas abruptly broke off. Walking over to the window, he glanced up at the sky.

"I am going down to the village," he announced. "Will you come with me?"

Isabel looked reluctant. "Isn't it still raining?"

"No, it has just stopped. Will you come with me?"

She frowned. "I'm tired of going to the village, Nick!"

He took a turn down the room.

"They are planning to get Cosmo away. Did you know that?"

"Yes."

"Lilian told you?"

"Yes."

"When?"

"Yesterday." And then, after a pause, the girl added: "She sent me down yesterday afternoon with a message to Allen. He was to meet her in the usual place."

"In the old rose-garden, you mean?"

She nodded.

Nicholas fell silent. He knew that his step-mother had occasional meetings with Allen; and he knew that they met in the rose-garden instead of at the house, because they wished to reduce the likelihood of an encounter between Allen and John Mayne or Madeline. This old rose-garden was a secluded spot, surrounded by high, thick hedges of yew. It was rarely visited by anyone but Lilian; and, as it lay in a line between the village and the house, a person chancing to come upon them there, might well suppose that Allen had met her on this spot by accident, on his way up to the house. To give colour to this supposition Lilian always went to her rendezvous with a flower-basket and garden scissors.

"Nick," said Isabel after a pause, "why do you object to Cosmo's going away?"

"I don't object; I only resent not being told what is being arranged."

"I don't believe anything actually has been arranged yet. I am sure you know all there is to know. It is not an easy thing to arrange, is it? But Lilian had to say something definite to Walter in order to pacify him."

The young man continued to stare out of the window.

"I suppose you know," continued Isabel, "that you are puzzling her dreadfully."

"She is also puzzling me!"

"She asked me the other day whether you really thought Cosmo was your friend."

"He *is* my friend."

"Do you mean that, although he would like to hurt Lilian, he would be nice to you?"

Nicholas laughed contemptuously. "Of course, he wouldn't be nice to me! Why should he? Why should anyone be nice to anyone, if he doesn't feel so inclined? Besides, he couldn't hurt Lilian without hurting me."

Isabel sighed. "Then why—oh, why do you like him?"

"My dear child," exclaimed Nicholas, "you are being rather silly! I don't like or dislike people just because they are nice, or not nice, to me! I like people for what they stand for. And so do you! Otherwise"—and a malicious light came into his eyes—"why didn't you take to Madeline?"

Isabel blushed slightly. "Anyhow, I know I shouldn't like Cosmo!"

"Well, I do!" returned Nicholas with obstinacy. "Come!" he added a moment later. "It is getting late."

The sky, as they set out, was showing spaces of pale, rain-washed blue. It was three miles to the village by a narrow wood-path, which they took single-file, their steps falling noiselessly upon a brown carpet of leaves, which yielded up a moist, autumnal scent. Nicholas went fast; so it was not long before they came out from under the trees and stood on the edge of a narrow, steep-sided dell, at the bottom of which the little village lay. Beneath them the clustered roofs were already dim in the early close of that wet evening. Thin, blue films of smoke hung half-way up the slope, pale against the dark of the leafy hangar opposite. Long, purple clouds barred the sky beyond. The faint smell of the rising wood-smoke gave a sense of habitation, and the dell had comfortable suggestions of shelter. But over the whole scene there brooded too heavy a tranquillity; and the absence of any sound or movement other than the dripping of the trees and the lazy curling of the smoke-wreaths in mid-air—this stillness brought melancholy into the heart.

"I will wait for you here," sighed Isabel. "Only promise me you won't be too long."

He escorted her to a place where she could rest in comfort,—a sandy ledge protected by overhanging slabs of rock,—almost a cave. The approach to it was difficult with bramble and gorse; and, as he was helping her along, the present suddenly became vivid to him—intense, surcharged with an unnatural reality. The feel of her warm, moist fingers in his hand, her body's nearness, the damp scent of the gorse and honeysuckle, the glistening slabs of stone, the low, wet light—"I shall never forget these things," he said to himself, "never, so long as I live!"

For a moment, without speech, they stood side by side, looking out into the dusk; then with a nod he was off.

Alone, Isabel sank down, clasped her knees with her hands, and watched the brightness fading between the gaps in the dark foliage opposite. There crept into her dreaming a sense, not unpleasurable, of isolation. She felt herself small and frail and unafraid. With her hand caressing her ankles, her hair falling about her eyes, and her thin skirts clinging damply about her, she enjoyed the charm of her false fragility, gave herself up to melancholy, and secretly anticipated, as youth will, a deep measure of happiness.

Chapter 13

She started when the bushes behind her rustled and Nicholas re-appeared. He threw himself down at her side, and for a moment neither spoke. Then: "Well, that is the end!" he muttered. "And I know I shall never understand! But that is the end. . . . It is all settled. He is going away!"

Through the dusk her eyes questioned.

"What don't you understand?"

He made no reply.

She let the fine sand run through her fingers. "Of course he must go!"she said. "You know he must!"

"A woman down there," he broke out suddenly, "told me that yester-day evening he and Allen had a great argument. The window was open, and she could hear them talking far into the night. And this morning Cosmo was constantly on the look-out for me. He is now able to walk a little, as you know. Weak as he is, he stood about, near the gate, in the rain. He was in a state of high excitement—in a frenzy, she said—muttering to himself, biting his nails and grimacing."

The girl moved uneasily. "He is mad!" she said softly.

"No, he is not mad, although——"

"Well?"

"Although even Allen seems to be afraid of him at times. Those two appear to be fond of one another, and to understand one another; and yet there is fear on both sides! Allen, for all his authority, looks upon Cosmo with a kind of awe. He is sometimes quite humble before him."

With this Nicholas paused, and in the silence his companion sighed wearily. Her fingers were still playing with the sand; her head was turned away.

"You know," he continued after a moment, "for a long time Cosmo could not—or would not—speak. But now, when the fit seizes him he talks continuously—sometimes like a man in a delirium; yet I think he always knows what he is saying. Allen does not like me to be with him. For one thing, he is afraid lest I should understand how much we are alike. Ah! if I had been through the things that Cosmo has been through——" His voice shook and died out.

"Listen!" he went on abruptly, after another pause. "I will tell you about my first real talk with him—when Allen was not there. He had crawled to the end of the garden behind the cottage and was sitting in an arbour among some decaying hollyhocks. There was a large, tame rabbit in the path, which I nearly trod on. I was dazzled; puddles shone out everywhere reflecting the red evening sky. He greeted me with ironical politeness. I could see by the look in his eyes that he meant to talk. He began at once. He told me about his old hatred of the world, and how it had now suddenly turned into horror and fear. Oh, it is terrible, listening to Cosmo! How can I describe the effect it has upon one? Afterwards you hardly remember anything he has said; and yet you come away from him saturated as with heavy night dew. Allen, I know, has that feeling too. When he is there and Cosmo begins talking, I catch him looking at me furtively. He is uneasy on my account. If you ask me what is actually wrong with Cosmo, I cannot answer you. Is he mad? In some respects I think he is. He has hinted extraordinary things. . . . Perhaps he is touched with delusions of persecution. Why does human nature fall so readily into that fear? I found myself tainted by his fears even while I was listening with incredulity. But he is not really mad. No, he is only very human—human to the point of inhumanity! It seems as if he had overshot the mark—as if he had descended too deep into the primordial nature-stuff of humanity. . . . Yes, that has been his peculiar fate! For I must tell you that in old days he was not like this. He was born into this world a creature of another kind from us. He was thrown down amongst us, captive, restless, raging! His earliest feelings as a child were fury, disgust and hate! All things have come to him as injuries; all the circumstances of our life have outraged him. All kindnesses have been insults. You see, he was born clean, and with visions of perfection; our humanity was necessarily defilement to him. And the cold fire of his continuous rage was his protection up till now; he defended his innocence by scorn. All the makeshift happiness of this poor world, all man's low content, all his paltry self-adjustments to capricious imperfection, were an abomination to him. All our little charities and forbearances, engendered by misery, revolted him. For he brought down with him from his own paradise the memory of a perpetual transfiguration. His imagination was so violent that it opposed itself to every actuality here below; he lived in the bright, white glare of a continuous lightning, compared to which our sun's best light was tame.

Our feeble humanities have wrung from him howls of painful laughter. Ah! I know well how he felt! Poor Cosmo! But the world was bound to wear him down in the end. His body weakened. The bright, blue steel of his mind became engrained with dirt and grit; the fiery innocence of his spirit was quenched; he felt himself sinking into the slough of ordinary humanity. He knew it was time that he should die. He should have been allowed to drown in that river at Tornel; his resurrection to this abominable existence was a disaster. For, as he once soared in heaven, so now he grovels in hell. His is not the spirit to float on the surface of life and drift along under the sun. He is water-logged; he rolls helplessly in the deeps. And when you talk with him, he drags you down as well. Deeper you sink and deeper, until the light grows dim and panic seizes you; then like a drowning man you struggle for the surface; you struggle like a swimmer in the grip of a devil-fish, but you find him more powerful than yourself, more powerful if only in this—his profounder sincerity.

"It is strange how we all habitually succeed in ignoring the things that are dangerous to our mental health. There is a zealous porter at the doors of the consciousness, who is working for us night and day. All disreputable thoughts are turned away. He has a keen eye for undesirables, this porter; he is a safe, sound, honest fellow. And this is the man Cosmo has assassinated. The halls of his mind are filled with scarecrow figures, dancing and rioting to drown their fear. Yes, 'evil things in robes of sorrow' have assailed him. They pour out of his mind what he speaks, and the guardian of your own sanity quails before them.

"But you must not imagine that Cosmo is tragic in the ordinary way—nor even impressive! The tragedy of art is one thing, the tragedy of reality another. You are not purged by emotions of pity and terror, as you listen to Cosmo; but your heart's blood is gradually chilled by a gathering conviction of Truth! And you resist with defences very different from what might be imagined. For let me tell you this: the most efficient of all protective armours is inattention, lack of interest, boredom, ennui! At the outset the guardian of your sanity always presents what is dangerous as merely dull. You find Cosmo hard to listen to; if you persist your ennui becomes excruciating; it turns to acute discomfort, restlessness, and an ill-ease that is full of antagonism; you sicken with a secret nausea and disgust. I say secret, because you are not willing to admit to yourself that he has had so much power to affect you. Your pretence is that all that he has said is flat, stale, platitudinous. Surely, you protest to yourself, this is all to be taken for granted! This doesn't cut deep! No, no! What is interesting, what is inspiring, lies beyond!

"For have you not still a conquering certitude within you, an assurance, an inextinguishable light? And, if that light cannot altogether dispel the fogs and the darkness, does it not drive them back to a comfortable distance, leaving the path of your daily existence tolerably clear? And is not man's destiny, too, still as splendid as he has the faith to believe it?

"To be sure, you can afford to smile at Cosmo, at his hatreds, and his despairs! Yet, if you look into your heart, you will find, beneath your contemptuous pity, a hard, unacknowledged fear! You are still striving to misapprehend or falsify his meanings; you are still obstinate and irritable; you are even half-consciously hypocritical; you pretend that you are trying hard to do him justice, whilst in reality you are searching your mind for any verbal quibble which, ingenuously uttered, will serve as an effective retort. But Cosmo is not unaware of your manoeuvres, and steadily he tracks you down. He knows that your nature is blindly, intuitively, fighting against him. But he knows, too, that there is something within you which, once cornered, will surrender, because it must. He sees that you are like a mouse that has lost its hole, like a squirrel whose secret store is about to be discovered; he sees you as a man being robbed of the falsehoods upon which his happiness depends! And he laughs a little to himself, and he goes on."

Chapter 14

The way back through the forest was dark. The wet glimmer that filtered through the branches from the west soon faded out; and afterwards each step was through a close, leaf-hemmed obscurity, gloom receding into gloom, and the path at times only to be felt. Isabel went first. Her eyes open wide to the darkness, she sped along nimbly, diving under the boughs that dipped across the way. As she went, the discomfort with which she had listened to Nicholas, fell from her; willingly she yielded to the dark spell of the wood. And he—could he remain insensible to such enchantment? Unburdened by speech, and therefore lighter of heart, was he not yielding too? He was! He was! She could feel the magic working in him as he followed her; she could feel it in the soft, quick rustle of his feet on the moist, fallen leaves. The forest was drawing them together in its atmosphere of secrecy; and now he was thinking less of Cosmo than of the darkness, and of the mystery, and of her!

Ah, there was magic abroad! The moon—yes, suddenly through the boughs the waning moon appeared, and gave distorted bigness to the trees, and lit pale alleys down which they stopped to peer. How the moon glittered upon the rain-drenched foliage! How wide and deep the hush! Drip went the leaves—drip, drip! And in that multitudinous pattering of water-drops they heard an invisible army of gnomes upon the march. The night, they knew, was full of busy mystery.

On they went in a growing flush of enchantment. On, beneath the heavy, dragging boughs; and care lagged further behind them. With an ease that is only to be found in youth, and best in such youth as is by nature and natural prevision a little disabused of life, they had thrown off care and were gay. They had cast their unwelcome thoughts from them, not savage wise, but lightly, deftly, using a wisdom more subtle and expert than any in the gift of years. For it would seem that this, like all qualities based upon an innate sense of values, demands that one shall be on equal terms—not through the intelligence, but through instinct,—with death. Here is the panache of youth: that knowing not life outside itself, it has not the bitter severances of death to fear! And although youth is concentrated upon itself, its egoism is too passionate and disinterested to provoke aught but admiration and envy. Let the young demand happiness imperiously; and when the Fates deal out misery, and Dame Nature complacently declares: "Il vous faut tout de même vivre!";* with lightness, let them reply: "Je n'y vois aucune nécessité."†

With age it is different. Tough attachments of memory, affection, and habit, bind old people like old trees to the ground. They owe a sort of allegiance to life; they stand obstinately against the storm. Their limbs may be torn from them, but the trunk lives on, and time will cover the scars. Alas, then, for age! With this greater tenacity a sterner morality accords.

It was breathless and smiling, though with a half scared look over her shoulder, that Isabel came out first upon the lawn, and saw before her the house lights streaming through a faint mist. For some moments she halted to recover her breath; but she would not look round at Nicholas, when he came up close behind her. Secretly she was glad of the darkness, which hid the shine of her eyes and the pink of her cheeks and her bosom's rise and fall. For she had come out of the wood a startled thing, a creature quivering in every nerve, deliciously and yet fearfully alive; and the reason was that a moment ago there had been a touch, a stumbling together in the gloom, a clinging contact and a sudden, swift escape. On his side, Nicholas had a heart that was beating no less tumultuously than hers. He had strained to his breast a nymph that did not turn into a reed, a nymph that kept a body that was warm, a face and eyes that gleamed and shone in the moonlight, and a mouth with warm breath.

They approached the house over the turf that yielded spongily under their feet, and entered under the black shadow of the walls. The brightly-lit window of the Big Hall drew them like moths towards it; they came up within a few feet and looked in. The head and shoulders of John Mayne seated at his desk showed forth clear and hard under the lamplight. When he raised his eyes, his pupils stared out with an unseeing gaze that pierced through them into the darkness beyond. He wore the face of a man who believes himself alone; the muscles were lax in meditation; the face was heavy, haggard, portentous.

* "You still have to live!"
† "I don't see the need!"

For longer than they intended the two stood there. Then quietly they moved away. When they had turned the corner of the house they came out once more into the moonlight; and here by a common impulse they stopped and looked at one another.

They looked and said nothing.

But as they went up the steps to the door, the young man slipped his arm through Isabel's and drew her close. "After all," he whispered, "what does it matter!"

The door, thrown open, let the yellow lamplight stream upon her. For an instant their eyes met; then, half-smiling, she looked down and away. In spite of everything, their meeting eyes had declared, they might still be very happy. They might have their little day.

Thus, before entering once again the common life of the house, which had become so hateful, they formed a pact—they sealed the old conspiracy that two are constantly together making—to be happy.

Chapter 15

The following morning, on his way down through the wood to the village, Nicholas came across Allen, seated on a fallen tree-trunk a few yards from the path. Allen rose at once when he came in sight, leaving him in no doubt that the meeting was designed.

"I have come to bid you good-bye," said Allen.

Nicholas looked at him for a moment without speaking. "Here?" said he at last.

"Better here!" said Allen.

Nicholas frowned and looked away.

Not once since their conversation in Tornel had these two come together in any kind of familiarity. They had studied each other covertly, and each perhaps knew the other somewhat better than before; but none of this appeared on the surface, and the terms on which they stood had become, if anything, less easy.

Allen was the first to break the silence. "I want, before I go, to have a quiet talk with you."

He smiled as he said this, but his steady look showed that he meant to have his way. With an ill grace Nicholas followed him to the log where he had been sitting, and waited for the opening of speech.

Allen began by discussing John Mayne's physical and mental state. But, as he talked, Nicholas could see that this was not the subject uppermost in his mind. He fell to studying Allen with a greater attention than he ever bestowed upon him when Cosmo was of the company. He had the sense that a passage of some moment would take place between them, and he wondered in what aspect his companion would reveal himself.

The damp, still wood, now steaming under the sun, provided a background against which that compact, alert figure detached itself with a telling distinctness. His fancy placed Allen before him as a pioneer in tropical climes. The languid atmosphere, the leafy scents, the windless overhanging boughs, lent force to the illusion. Allen's bronzed face was the face of an adventurer. An adventurer! It pleased him to have lit upon the word. He was acutely sensible of the contrast in type between this man and himself; and unconsciously he pitted himself against him.

It was disagreeable to hear Allen speaking with such knowledge and incisiveness of matters about which he could only have gathered information from Lilian. "Upon my soul!" he exclaimed, breaking in with a laugh, "one would imagine, to hear you, that you are John Mayne's valet! The poor old gentleman has nothing hidden from you!"

The other stared, then smiled, as if confident that this was said without unamiable intention.

"Lilian and I," he returned with simplicity, "we have naturally been speculating pretty actively about what is passing in John Mayne's mind. And Lilian, as you know, has great powers of observation! Great in tuition!" Then after a pause he added: "But nothing that she has said has impressed me so much as what I myself have seen!"

Nicholas lifted his eyes in surprise. "What have you seen?"

"More than once, from the shelter of this wood, I have watched John Mayne pacing to and fro upon his favourite strip of lawn. And the look on his face has positively overawed me!"

"May I ask what you read there?"

"Oh! many things; but chiefly indecision—inward conflict!"

Nicholas was silent. He, too, had observed John Mayne. Like a beast in a cage, the old man would stump heavily to and fro, to and fro, along the verge of the wood. Eamor was the cage; and the great trees hemming it round were, seemingly, a barrier through which he could not break.

When Allen resumed, it was with a change of tone. John Mayne, he observed, would find himself constrained to come to some decision before very long, and consequently every day, every hour, that now passed was crucial. Lilian appeared to be still quite hopeful about the outcome; but, for his part, he was more than uneasy. He doubted whether John Mayne's sense of moral obligation would prove equal to the strain that was being put upon it.

"You know what human nature is!" he smiled. "One blurs the outline of one's dilemma; and then one takes what one presents to oneself as a middle course; but what is, in effect, a line parallel to the desired course, and equivalent to it."

A frown appeared on Nicholas's averted face. "This middle course at which you are hinting—what is it likely to be?"

"I cannot say!" returned Allen dryly. "But between the first extreme, which would be to leave you and Lilian in a position to live *independ-*

ently at Eamor, and the second extreme which would be to turn you both out, penniless, I can imagine various middle courses."

Nicholas turned upon him sharply. "There is a clean-cut distinction between dependence and independence. John Mayne can't get over that!"

"John Mayne——" began Allen, but was at once interrupted.

"Lilian claims independence—nothing less! Madeline demands power over her! Between those two, at least, the issue is as definite as you could wish!"

"My dear Nicholas!" rejoined Allen with half-humorous sententiousness. "For the moment we are only concerned with what is going on in John Mayne's mind. We are trying to conceive what compromise sophistical human nature will suggest to him. No issue is so clean-cut but that a man can obscure it. No chain of argument is so direct but that he can entangle it. Consequently the only question that interests me is: What are John Mayne's actual and possible loopholes?"

Nicholas twisted his lips into a smile. "Do you suppose I don't already see the point to which you are tactfully leading me? The middle course from which we must debar John Mayne, is represented by Cosmo! Your object is to impress upon me that danger."

Allen returned the young man's gaze without visible discomfiture.

"I want to discuss the whole matter calmly and openly; that's all."

"Very good! Let us discuss it!"

"You know as well as I do," commenced Allen with smoothness, "that Cosmo is not an easy person to deal with! And every day he is becoming more capable of mischief. It is, accordingly, high time we took him away. If he knew exactly what he wanted, or if he had any idea what our circumstances actually were, he would have done something disastrous before now!"

Nicholas sprang in sudden agitation to his feet.

"I can see one thing clearly enough—I can see that you are his enemy!"

"Only because he will have it so!"

"Then tell me this!" cried Nicholas. "Why is he afraid of you?"

Allen gave a movement resembling a wince. "He is afraid of everything and everybody, in a sense! And in another sense he is afraid of nothing! He longs for rest!"

Nicholas laughed. "Rest! I know what you mean."

He turned away as he spoke. From Allen's lips there came no immediate reply. His expression, as he gazed at the young man's half-averted face, was peculiar.

"At any rate," he resumed in an even tone, "Cosmo is now able and ready to go back to Tornel."

"Will it be possible to get him out of the country?"

"I think so."

Nicholas said nothing for a minute. Then:

"Tell me," he asked with greater quietude, "was it you or Lilian who decided that Walter must be let into our little secret?"

"It was I."

"I congratulate you."

"Is that sarcastic?"

"No, merely sardonic. Poor Walter!"

"Walter has been more troublesome than I expected," said Allen, smiling. "But I still think I was right! We had to insure, so far as we could, against the consequences of a discovery. Had the secret come out, and Walter not been in our counsel, he would have been able to join in the outcry against us. Madeline and John Mayne would have been free to put the worst possible construction on our motives. They would have represented us as holding Cosmo captive, concealed, maltreated. We should all have been made to look like criminals. And Walter would have had the opportunity of considering that we had forfeited his favour. But, with him in our secret, the affair takes on a totally different aspect. We creep in under the mantle of his respectability. Accusations levelled against us, are also levelled indirectly against him. In a word, Walter, who otherwise would have found an excuse for weakening in his support of Lilian, is now additionally committed to her defence."

Nicholas threw back his head and laughed.

"I feel pretty confident," continued Allen, "that when Cosmo has gone, Walter will settle down and hold his peace."

"When Cosmo has gone!" echoed Nicholas, paused, looking into Allen's face. "Gone to that undiscovered Mexico, from whose bourn he is extremely unlikely ever to return? Is that it?"

Allen's expression changed.

"For some time past," said he with deliberation, "I have been considerably puzzled by your attitude. The moment has come for you to explain it."

Nicholas, breathing deeply, turned himself away.

"This talk," he brought out at last, "this talk was not of my seeking! And I am more than ready to make an end to it! Let us say good-bye!"

"No!" returned Allen. "Not like this!"

There was a silence. For a space both stared hard at the ground beneath their feet.

"In my opinion," said Allen at last, "your view of Cosmo is a mistaken one. But that does not mean that I am unable to understand it. No! the fact is that for many years I myself made a hero of him! But now——"

Nicholas emitted a sound of bitter amusement. "Now you know better, I suppose?"

"I think so."

Nicholas smiled.

"In those days," continued Allen, "he was a splendid creature!"

Nicholas laughed. "Well, what is he now?"

"Hardly splendid!"

"No—hardly that!"

"Something—you think—more?"

Nicholas nodded.

"That," returned Allen, shaking his head, "that's where you are wrong! He has simply—failed!"

Nicholas's eyes glittered with scorn. "Whereas you—and Walter, too, we may say—have succeeded!"

The other laughed good-humouredly. "I maintain no more than that he has failed!"

"Allen," rejoined Nicholas after a short silence, "I believe that Cosmo has gained more than he has lost, whereas most men lose more than they gain.—You," he went on with subdued passion, "have certainly lost more! There are two kinds of understanding, and the lesser develops at the expense of the greater. I don't care a fig for the wisdom of this world! And that is all you have acquired! You have made friends with the Mammon of Unrighteousness. God help the world, if Cosmo's values are not finer than yours!"

He stood before Allen, looking down upon him heinously. "In my view," he added, "you are a renegade!"

The other laughed, but it was to be seen that his patience was wearing thin. "My good sir!" he exclaimed, "when all is said and done, what is it that you want of me?"

"Nothing!" replied Nicholas with violence. "And I have nothing left to say but this"—he paused with vicious deliberation—"the next time you try to kill Cosmo, I hope you will make a better job of it!"

Allen sprang to his feet and gripped the young man by the shoulder.

"What right have *you* to talk in that fashion?" He was livid with anger. "If you want to see Cosmo installed at Eamor, why have you not had the courage to say so?"

"I do now say so!"

"You young fool!" cried Allen, whose voice and aspect had in one moment become positively terrifying. "Do you suppose that I am going to sacrifice Lilian to your folly?"

Nicholas gazed at him, speechless. Allen's voice and Allen's eyes had a significance that pierced down to the depths of his spirit. He received a revelation, and that revelation was the more devastatingly complete for the reason that it gave him no knowledge that was not dormant in his heart already.

With an unconscious movement he wrenched himself free from Allen's grasp, and, taking a few steps away, stared blankly into the forest. There was no thought of resistance in his mind now; there was not even any hostility. His spirit lay submerged under a quiet, ironic sadness. Softly he laughed to himself. Lilian and Allen! Of course! Their love was no dim, uncertain possibility, but a vital, forceful fact. It dominated the whole situation. No wonder poor Allen had lost his patience!

And yet—there was Cosmo too! But Cosmo had become remote! Cosmo seemed to have lost his right to interfere. In this world of matter, and fleshly energies, and cravings for earthly happiness, Allen and Lilian alone counted. In this world they had heavy stakes, while Cosmo was just playing a game. His game was of course infinitely more important; but you couldn't in common decency let it override . . . No! not in a world where human beings took on an aspect as pathetic as that of dumb creatures, who crave warmth, food, freedom, the opportunity to enjoy!

This flow of feeling held him spellbound, until the sound of Allen's feet rustling in the leaves brought his mind back to actuality. He could guess that Allen was now suffering from a certain embarrassment. And he, too, felt embarrassed. Presently, without turning, he said:

"I am afraid I have been rather thoughtless of Lilian!"

Allen gave a short laugh. "Well, no matter!"

Nicholas faced round. "I see the position more clearly now." And in token of his change of mind he went back to his old place on the log.

There was a pause. Allen walked restlessly up and down; then suddenly halted, a dogged look upon his face.

"I want you to make sure of your own mind," said he. "I think you understand the situation fully. I propose to take Cosmo away with me to Tornel. Do you acquiesce, or do you not?"

Despite his efforts to subdue himself, his voice had a new ring, his eyes a new openness of determination. He did not look the same man as before. Gazing upon him, Nicholas marvelled at his success, up to this time, in the difficult art of self-effacement. He had known how to keep a veil drawn over his living personality. He had made himself colourless, characterless.

Allen had to repeat his question.

"Do you acquiesce?" he demanded.

"I do," replied Nicholas after another, but a shorter, pause.

Allen knit his brows as if still dissatisfied. "Let there be no mistake," said he with sternness, "our plans lie before you. Examine them well!"

"*Our* plans!" repeated Nicholas to himself with an inward smile of sadness. "Our plans!"

"I must tell you," continued Allen in a tone of forced and unwonted harshness, "I must warn you, that I regard Cosmo simply as a diseased degenerate, whose existence——"

"No, no!" said Nicholas quickly, but gently, breaking in. "You should say, 'I choose to regard.'"

"Very well, then!" Allen sombrely accepted the emendation. "I choose to regard Cosmo's present existence to be worthless." He paused. "Nevertheless, I mean to give him every chance!"

Nicholas turned his face away and gazed stilly into the wood. "I understand!" said he at last, uttering the words with a deep, inward breath. "And now—is that all?"

"Yes, that is all!" said Allen.

Nicholas rose. But, as if to postpone the actual moment of leave-taking, the other, his hands clasped behind his back, resumed his thoughtful pacing to and fro.

"You bear me no grudge?" he threw out.

Nicholas looked him full in the face. "Certainly not!"

It was evident that Allen wished to say more, but words seemingly failed him. Some moments went by in silence. Both men sank deep into their own thoughts. At last, with a sigh Allen came up and laid a hand on Nicholas's arm. "I shall do my best!" said he. "For your sake, in particular!"

As he moved slowly back along the path towards the house, Nicholas's reflections were bathed in an atmosphere of resignation which relieved them of much of their poignancy. Who was Cosmo, what was Cosmo, that he should stand between living creatures and their desire? What was his own devotion to Cosmo but an indulgence, a luxury, a conceit? The figure of Allen re created itself before him. There the man was, standing square on Mother Earth, and longing for the attainable! Why should he not have it? "Were I the Almighty," he said within himself with a smile, "I think I should abstain from pressing my ideas of morality upon mankind at the expense of so much deprivation and suffering. I should ask, 'Are those ideas worth it, or is mankind?'"

Allen was a good fellow. He liked Allen better than ever before. A few days ago Lilian had said that Allen's whole soul was in his work. He wondered what Allen's work consisted in, and reflected rather ironically upon the present interruption of it.

But while these thoughts floated through his mind, his heart ached; and that pain, he knew, would not quickly fade away. For his old relation with Lilian was dying or dead. So soon as John Mayne was in his grave she would marry Allen. Was she his mistress already? Even that was possible, although he could not force himself to believe it.

It seemed to him now that he had always respected Allen, although he had tried hard to think otherwise. He remembered how on more than one occasion he had been arrested by a singular gleam in the man's eyes—a speaking look of intelligence, capability—and imagination. Yes, Allen had sensibility and imagination! They shone out of him even when he chose, as recently, to obscure them. A renegade? Perhaps! but under the compulsion of his love! And not at heart a self-deceiver! Lilian—with a sigh he admitted it—was justified; her love was no self-derogation.

That love, however, which he could no longer doubt, still pained him as an infidelity. He felt it make him homeless. What was Eamor to him without her? And she had secretly taken herself away.

Well! he had one delight to fall back upon. Isabel! But Isabel represented something absolutely different. Lilian was understanding, intimacy, security. In Lilian he found himself. They were mirrors to each other,—mirrors, in the profound depths of which a single soul saw itself reflected, backwards, into the remote past of their breed. Compared with Lilian, Isabel was foreign. The charm the girl had for him was derived as much from her extraneousness as from her kinship. And deep in his heart was the sense that the lure of the external, the extraneous, was vulgar and delusive. All true wealth was elaborated within. Was there not infinite diversity, were there not infinite potentialities of exchange and fecundation, within? To maintain one's spiritual activity upon the minimum stimulus from without, not to be distracted from those recondite wonders by the transient excitements obtainable in the phenomenal world;—concentration, the development of the intrinsic,—that was his ideal! The quintessential alone had value, alone endured. The world of action and accident was a perpetual temptation to the dissipating of one's energies. That was a world of vain Becoming without the possibility of an issue in Being. But it was of the essence of spirit to strive towards the static, towards creation, towards Being, which meant the fixation of chosen elements in satisfying order, in significant form. Such schemes were those presented by science and art—and, pre-eminently, by philosophy. In action, in behaviour, intelligence could never find a mode of satisfaction.

Well! but how did all this accord with his present renouncement of Cosmo? Alas! that was a difficult question! Cosmo was not outside him; Cosmo was within; wherefore his renouncement of Cosmo was of the nature of a self-surrender, a self-betrayal.

Chapter 16

Lilian's assurance to Walter that Cosmo was about to leave Eamor village, received fulfilment within a week; and, after that, Walter's mind became much easier. The fact that Cosmo and Allen had ever been in the neighbourhood, at all lost a great part of its reality with their departure. And as for his participation in the affair, the reality of that, too, faded rapidly. He soon began to feel that should he at some future date be taxed with any kind of complicity with Lilian, he would be able to meet the charge with surprise and indignation. "Let me see!" he could hear himself saying, whilst frowning in the effort of reminiscence. "Let me think a moment!" And then he would come out with the assertion that to the best of his recollection he had not been apprised of Cosmo's whereabouts until just before the latter's departure for Mexico; and he would explain that during the interval John Mayne's health had stood in the way of communicating with him on the subject. Then, Cosmo once gone, the matter did not seem to call for mention; especially as he had no reason to suppose that John Mayne's interest went out in that direction.

That Cosmo had in truth returned to Mexico was a presumption that he considered himself fully entitled to make. Lilian had told him that the big car which had brought Cosmo to Eamor had as quickly and silently borne him away again; and she had added that he was being lodged at Allen's rooms at Tornel, and would be looked after by Allen, until they took ship together.

Although he would have been glad to learn that Cosmo had actually sailed, he did not care to risk further inquiries. Lilian's transactions with Cosmo were not, after all, his business.

John Mayne did not make his reappearance downstairs until some time after Cosmo's removal. His disease was now causing him a good deal of suffering, which reflected itself, as Walter soon discerned, in a weakening or coarsening of the fibres of character. Intercourse with him on the old terms had become impossible—a circumstance that Walter noted with sorrow, but also, it must be admitted, with a tincture of relief.

Leaning upon the doctor's support, Walter now made a resolute attempt to bring about John Mayne's departure from Eamor. But he discovered to his surprise and chagrin that Lilian was no more disposed to give him assistance than Madeline. In the end he was obliged to argue the point with John Mayne single-handed, and the experience was just as discouraging as he had feared it would be.

Indeed, he would not have made the essay but for his increasing uneasiness about Madeline. It seemed to him that the atmosphere of Eamor was not one whit less demoralising to Madeline than to her uncle; and each appeared to react upon the other, giving the baleful influence of the place a double effect. The girl's self-dedication to the service of the sufferer was admirable in spirit, but in practice decidedly pernicious. Not only did she isolate him from every one else by her ministrations, but those ministrations were of a nature to encourage the very tendencies that were to be deplored.

The medium of indulgent femininity in which she swathed him was relaxing, enervating, insidious. She teased, petted, coaxed and flattered him. Morning, noon and evening she was there, interposing her presence—and a gracious, radiant, caressing presence it certainly was!—between him and the outside world. That John Mayne himself struggled against this envelopment was obvious; but his struggles were intermittent, and on the whole unavailing. Each of his failures, too, was accompanied by a small but permanent loss of self-respect. He became more and more content to fall back upon his ease, and enjoy with a smile of cynical resignation the youthful freshness, the rich, warm femininity that were outpoured about him.

The manner in which he received the suggestion that he should leave Eamor was an unkind revelation to Walter of the little consideration the John Mayne of to-day was willing to accord him. And the bitterness of this discovery was intensified by a perception that Madeline's cavalier manner was not seldom a direct reflection of her uncle's temper. There were times, it was true, when she would be perfectly charming, and then he would charitably attribute her lapses to the strain of her duties as sick-nurse; but there were also times when her lack of consideration for him, her superciliousness, her singular want of respect for his feelings, opinions, and even his principles, forced him to doubt whether he had any trustworthy hold upon her affections. Yet even in these moments of misgiving, he felt that his censure of Madeline did little to make him the readier to give her up. No, it was incidental to the closeness of relationship into which they had been brought that he appreciated more keenly than ever before, her physical attractions. The contacts and caresses of which she was innocently prodigal—demonstrations legitimatized, as he constantly reminded himself, by their affianced state—had the power to soften the memory of her worst offences.

One evidence—a particularly vexatious one—of John Mayne's increasing demoralization and of Madeline's share in it, was provided when, inadvertently, the girl disclosed that she had no scruples about attempting to inveigle her uncle into a discussion of his will. That she had dared to do so, and had met with more or less success, when *he*, out of delicacy and prudence, was holding his hand,—this was extremely galling to Walter. Besides, it robbed him of all confidence in the sick man's powers of discretion; and the indispensable condition to a frank talk with John Mayne was the certainty that whatever might pass between them would be kept absolutely private. Madeline's disclosures showed that the delicate question of Eamor had been brought down from the high plane on which it ought to stand. Dreadful was the thought that it had already slipped some distance towards the quagmire of vulgar domestic intrigue. His luke-warm hopes that John Mayne might yet seek from the mouth of Walter Standish the counsels of his own better nature—these hopes were chilled to zero. And as for inter-vening without invitation, Madeline's revelations vastly increased his disrelish of the idea. Indeed, the question actually arose in his mind whether her words had been dropped with as little intention as it seemed. Was she conceivably *warning* him to stand clear?

In the course of the ensuing weeks, his sojourn at Eamor was broken by short visits to Tornel, rendered necessary by his participation in the public life of the town. He was sensible that he derived benefit from these absences. A man needs to correct his vision at intervals by new observations from the worldly standpoint. At Tornel Walter again met the two friends to whom he had already opened his mind. From Henry Portman he received no encouragement to continue his confidences, but Percy Fellowes questioned him with an avidity that Walter would have found more flattering, had he not known Percy to possess a hearty appetite for everything that held promise of sensation or scandal. All things considered, he was not inclined to gratify Percy. What he did say was said with quite another intention. "I think," he observed, "that my tendency hitherto has been to assume a heavier burden of responsibility than can in fairness be laid upon me. John Mayne and all the others concerned are, after all, free agents—persons over whose actions I can exert no effective control. I should deeply lament any failure on John Mayne's part to discharge his moral obligations, but the fact that they are wholly moral precludes me from being more than a spectator of his mental conflict. His illness has not materially affected his intellect, even if it has shaken his moral equilibrium. But here it would be presumption on my part to sit in judgment. I am inclined to think my views have been a little narrow. Madeline has her idea of justice as well as I; and although feminine conceptions are not precisely the same as ours, they rest on a broad human basis none the less. Do Madeline's passionate attachment to her uncle, and her resentment of his wife's past and present behaviour, really falsify her vision of the case? Is she at fault in maintaining that whatever Lilian Mayne's original rights may have been, she has actually forfeited them? Does not her claim, based as it is on *moral* considerations, wear an aspect of effrontery? These are delicate questions upon which I hardly feel entitled to speak—still less to pass judgment; but they are questions on which women—and loving kinswomen at that!—can scarcely fail to feel deeply."

"Do not think," he went on, "that Madeline wishes John Mayne to wreak vengeance on his wife by leaving her penniless. That would be a gross travesty of the truth. What Madeline resents is Mrs. Mayne's aspersions on her disinterestedness, her trustworthiness, her honour. What she desires from her uncle is a testimonial of his confidence, the opportunity to prove her possession of those qualities which her enemy denies her. She longs, in short, to vindicate her personal honour. It is not against Lilian's ultimate independence that she is set, but against the means which Lilian sees fit to employ to achieve that end. For we must not allow ourselves to be deceived as to the real nature of the issue. It is not so much material as spiritual! It is a contest of pride! Either Madeline's or Lilian's pride deserves to be humbled. And I have no doubt in my mind on which of the two humiliation ought to fall."

"It seems to me that you have slightly changed your point of view," said Percy.

"No, not really!" replied Walter, and brought the subject to a close.

The truly vital aspects of the question were precisely those upon which he was not desirous of enlarging; and what he would have taken a certain relief in expressing he found himself unable to express. "Do you not," he had once begun, "do you not find it almost incredible that the various personages involved in this little drama should in fact prefer to remain together rather than to draw apart? I confess I do—or rather I should, were I not myself plunged in among them. As it is——"

And there, with a gesture, he gave up.

How describe the intense concentration of the inmates of Eamor upon the web of their interlocking interests? How explain that such a life, unlike the loosely-knit life of wide social units, retracted by a natural and irresistible tendency upon itself, rarefying its essence and growing richer, deeper, and more subtle, as it became more self-absorbed. Eamor was a backwater, a pool severed by drought from the mainstream. Yes, it likened itself, in his imagination, to a small circular pool upon which he had once stumbled in the woods. At the sound of his approach the water had been stirred into intersecting ripples by creatures of shy and secret life, which were hiding themselves from his gaze. In a moment the surface was calm again, and as he peered into the dark, reedy recesses of the pool, he had been seized with a kind of repulsion at the diversity and exuberance of the life engendered in this stillness, in this sheltered stagnancy, which left each vital element, untroubled by the gross, physical commotions of the outside world, free to work out the laws of its own nature to their extremity. Walter would willingly have flushed out that pool with a fire-hydrant.

In striking contrast to the passivity in which he found himself held at Eamor, was the activity that characterised his affairs at Tornel. Rumours respecting the old man's health had flown abroad; every day Walter felt a new vigour in the upward tide which bore him along. This increasing consideration that he commanded was gratifying; but it threw into stronger relief the contrary movement at Eamor. Sitting like a monarch in his office, he brooded a good deal, in the intervals of business, over Madeline's attitude towards him. He could not recall certain of her outbreaks without deep resentment, although conceding that a native share in the fiery temper of the Maynes might be pleaded in her individual exoneration. His mind moved back and forth between domestic and worldly affairs with singular rapidity, and this concatenation of Madeline and business was no random process. Supposing—just supposing—he were to have some serious difference with Madeline, a difference which gave rise to an absolute breach between them; and supposing Madeline were to succeed in enlisting her uncle's sympathies on her side so ardently as to kindle in the latter a sentiment of positive unfriendliness—what would be his, Walter's, position then?

Well, the answer to that question was becoming each day more definite! Ruin was not the word—no, no! But his career—or in other words, his hopes, his designs, his prestige, his position in the world, the elaborate structure of his legitimate anticipations—would be brought to disaster! For it was in the natural order of things that at the present juncture he should take a line of conduct which was grounded on the assumption that so far from "letting him down" John Mayne would deal with him as a successor and a member of the family. The bare notion that matters might turn out otherwise struck Walter with a deadly chill, or rather, so would it have affected him, had he at any time consented seriously to entertain it.

Matters, however, had not, thank heaven, come anywhere near to that! He had no more than dim, hypothetical causes for alarm. Nor was he wholly unaware that his genius lay in inaction. All his life, on occasions when another would have leapt with the greatest vigour and determination to the doing of the wrong thing, Walter had been content to do nothing—greatly to his advantage. So now, gazing thoughtfully through his office window, he determined that his apprehensions should never drive him out of the ways of circumspection and self-restraint.

Chapter 17

His last hopes for the removal of John Mayne and Madeline from Eamor disappeared with the arrival of a number of large cases, despatched from John Mayne's offices abroad, and forwarded, in accordance with recent instructions, from Tornel. These cases, stuffed with papers, the accumulation of a lifetime, were set down in the Big Hall, a vast apartment, detached from the main body of the house, which John Mayne had chosen for his workroom. The thud with which they descended upon the polished floor rang in Walter's ears with a dreadful finality. John Mayne, he felt, was fastened to the spot for the remainder of his life.

The arrival of this expected material threw the old man into a feverish activity. Gathering the residue of his strength, he put Madeline away from him, discarded his invalidism, and fell to the task of examining and arranging the records of his past with a zeal that betrayed the sense that he was beginning none too soon.

For Walter the days immediately following were long and dreary. Madeline, thrown upon her own resources, showed greater and greater inequalities of temper. Minor embroilments with Lilian, in which she endeavoured to obtain Walter's co-operation, grew more frequent. When the suggestion came up that her sister Nina should be added to the community, Walter hastened to give it his warm support. Nina was six years older than Madeline, a widow, and, as he remembered her, of a quiet, self-controlled habit. He dared hope that her presence would relieve the existing tension. In any case, it would provide Madeline with feminine companionship, and, as Nina was presumably free of personal animus against Lilian, whom she had never met, her influence was likely to be good.

With Nina's advent Walter's happy expectations received some measure of fulfilment. Life at Eamor, to his sense, became easier. This impression, however, was no doubt partly attributable to the increasing occupation of his hours by work in the Big Hall. So busily engaged did John Mayne keep him that he found no time for the indulgence of his former frets and anxieties. Taking stock of this, he could not but pity less fortunate womenfolk, who have no opportunity of drowning their private concerns in the great tide of public affairs. Hard work, he reflected, was good for all men. The only drawback to his own work at the moment was that he had so direct an interest in many of the issues. The happiest man he knew was Henry Portman, who spent his life in the consciously capable and inflexible discharge of duties, which, since he was a public servant, were totally indifferent to him in their practical results.

The Big Hall in which he and John Mayne laboured together had been anciently a chapel, and it seemed to hold an atmosphere different from that which permeated the rest of the house. A real peace pervaded it. The house might be quiet, but reposeful never. Its silence seemed rather a veil drawn over intrigue, the breath of a conspiratorial hush. This quiet, moreover, was liable to be broken on the smallest occasion by sudden gusts of nervous excitement, on the wind of which Madeline, flushed and palpitating, would burst even into his bedchamber. Full of indignant declamations and tearful appeals, she would require skilful soothing; it was not without considerable expenditures of tact and patience that he could prevent these squalls from developing into storms.

But the Big Hall, additionally hallowed by John Mayne's presence there, was sanctuary. Besides, Madeline had now other facilities for emotional discharge. There was Nina. Nina, now duly established in the house, had made her appearance very quietly, and spent most of her time with Madeline in the wing occupied by the Maynes. A certain discourtesy which had been supposed to characterize Lilian's reception of her, had been explained as arising out of a misunderstanding. The two women had been profuse in exonerating each other of all blame, the error being tacitly recognised as Madeline's. And Madeline maintained the patient silence of an ironical scapegoat.

It was certainly a great solace to the girl to have her sister in the house. Nina possessed pre-eminently the qualities of self-reliance and self-control. Five years of married tribulation with a husband whom intemperance had ultimately removed, had done much to develop the sternly practical side of her nature. Life had few interests and no terrors for Nina. The sight of her handsome wooden face and stiff, untiring back, as she sat imperturbably knitting or stitching, inspired Madeline with courage and confidence. An inexpressiveness, which would sorely have exasperated her in Walter, did nothing, where Nina was concerned, to rouse her ire. Nina was of her own blood, and the blood-tie was strong in the Maynes. With Walter she could never be sure how much support she would get, but Nina would never hang back, excepting under the dictates of a more experienced wisdom.

"Oh, my dear!" she would cry out to her sister, how glad I am that you are come! You cannot imagine what my life in this house has been! Only after one has lived with these people day after day, month after month, as I have, can one begin to fathom the depths of their meanness, their pettiness, their baseness! Poor uncle! What he has suffered! Wherever he has been, the thought of Lilian has haunted him! The memory of her sneers, her treachery, her ingratitude, has pursued him through all his life! You cannot understand him without realizing these things. If he is now embittered, it is *her* doing! Sometimes he says things to wound me, speaking as if all women must be like Lilian. Am I like Lilian, Nina? If I thought I were, I should kill myself! But no! Uncle *shall* know me, and trust me! And he shall show *her* how he trusts me! Ah, if he only knew how I love and admire him! But I will make him know it—yes, in spite of that woman's lies and cunning! No one shall come be tween us!"

And Nina, her head bent peacefully over her needlework, would do no more than heave a long, deep sigh. But that sigh would satisfy Madeline. She knew what stuff Nina was made of.

Indeed, this was the beginning of happier times for Madeline. Very soon after Nina's arrival she became aware that somehow or other this added presence just tipped the scales of the social balance, and that she could now carry off what she could not have carried off before. Day by day she felt an increase in her power to be comfortably, and even at times aggressively, herself. When, in the old days, she would have been made to appear shallow, tasteless, and even vulgar, Lilian was now made to appear pinched and bloodless. By using their combined weight, she and Nina together could successfully oppose their codes and standards to those which had hitherto ruled at Eamor. Her opposition to Lilian, which in the past had never been more than insurrectionary, was now placed upon a permanent, organised basis.

This being the drift of affairs after Nina's arrival, Walter, who had at first welcomed her as a godsend, began in time to grow a little uneasy. Madeline could not resist letting him see that in her opinion Nina was succeeding where he had failed. When, humorously affectionate, she said to him, "You men are all such children, you know!" he apprehended pretty accurately what she meant. He began to understand how much better fitted a woman is than a man to impose upon a household, to pick up invisible reins of government, to appear without self-assertion to be the person in authority. And it was not only in a domestic capacity that Nina's influence exercised itself. She was working her way into John Mayne's good graces, a notable instance being provided by her intervention in the matter of the old man's autobiography. This manuscript, the existence of which had only just been revealed, was a source of great worry to Walter. He had read it with a consternation that he was unable wholly to dissimulate. When he told John Mayne that in his opinion it did not do justice to its author, and that certain passages, he feared, would be misunderstood, he had been careful to embed these criticisms in a mass of indeterminate praise. The effect, however, had been deplorable. John Mayne, his cigar in the corner of his mouth, had sat envisaging him in stony silence; not a word did he produce in reply. Walter saw that he had not avoided giving terrible offence. And then, a few days after, he learnt that all the business connected with the eventual publication of the book had been entrusted to Nina!

Yet he owed it to John Mayne to see that the book was not published in its present form—and more, he owed it to himself. He had walked in John Mayne's footsteps all his life, and his path after John Mayne's death must inevitably be a continuation of the old road. If this book put a weapon in the hands of John Mayne's detractors, the sharp edge would not be used against the bodiless ghost but against the living man. Those who found in John Mayne's book a more or less unconscious admission that his charities were the oil with which he lubricated the cogs of an iniquitous industrialism, those who saw in his paternalism slavery, those who mocked at his religion as that of the Old Testament with John Mayne in the place of Jehovah,—cynics of that stamp without wasting their time upon the dead lion, would turn their attention upon his unfortunate successor. And Walter, as a matter of fact, had already received some indication of the probable line of their attack. John Mayne, some people said, was a Tory of the old school, not ashamed to be raising barricades across the road to freedom; Walter was a Liberal of the new school, who only rode the chariot of reform in order surreptitiously to apply the brake. Walter was John Mayne's logical successor; but for Walter John Mayne would never have adopted the charity and philanthropy "stunt." John Mayne was the honest, Walter the dishonest, enemy. And for these diatribes John Mayne's own confessions would supply admirable texts.

Walter therefore felt very strongly that John Mayne's book would not do. He went straight to Nina and explained matters with frankness. Nina's good sense was equal to the occasion. She appreciated his points, and promised that, after John Mayne's death, he should revise the book as much as he pleased. Her attitude was admirable—so admirable that Walter took leave of her with a comforting sense of her sagacity—a feeling that went some way towards allaying his other misgivings on account of her rising influence in the house.

Yet although, when challenged upon a definite issue, Nina was able to make herself eminently pliant, as time went on, Walter did not fail to detect a deep vein of stubbornness and arrogance beneath her quiet demeanour. She knew well enough that her handsome countenance, her statuesque placidity, were attractive to John Mayne's augmenting feebleness, and that when the invalid found Madeline tiring and Walter tiresome, he could put up with her. Very soon her position in the house became paramount; and Walter's annoyance thereat unconsciously revived his sympathies for Lilian. He could not but admire the way in which his hostess managed to keep up her dignity under very trying conditions. With no more than the raising of an eyebrow, or the flicker of a smile, she succeeded in deflecting slights and taunts, which, especially when they came from Madeline, were too palpable to be ignored. Whence came this strength? It was almost as if she possessed some undiscovered chamber of the mind—or of the heart—to which she could repair. Walter pondered. And with the notion, perhaps, of profiting by a chance ray of light from outside, he made a determined attempt to improve his acquaintance with Nicholas. It was his duty, he told himself, not to leave untried any soil in which the seed of goodwill might germinate. Nicholas, however, disappointed him, his advances meeting almost at once with a puzzling check.

The occasion was a talk in the library. He had decided to make a direct appeal to the young man's confidence. "I do wish," said he with great earnestness, "I do wish, my dear Nicholas, that you would join with me in the attempt to introduce a better tone of feeling into the house! I need your help. It is so necessary that we two should pull together. You and I, as the two men in the household—for John Mayne, alas, now occupies a position by himself!—you and I ought to stand shoulder to shoulder in the difficult times that lie ahead of us. We must recognise that it is for us to set the tone, to lay down the standard, that shall prevail; and for this we shall need all the judgment and authority, all the mutual confidence and tact that between us we can muster."

For some time he continued in this strain, only desisting when he observed that Nicholas's first embarrassment was changing into some deeper emotion. He was surprised and inclined to be gratified. Had Nicholas's better feelings really been touched at last? Was the isolation in which the youth had been living—for Walter had observed that his relations with his step-mother had been distant of late—was this spiritual isolation beginning to tell? It seemed so. It seemed that his appeal was well timed; and its success, he apprehended, would mark an important advance. With Nina figuring as a moderate on the one side, and Nicholas on the other, pourparlers between the Maynes and the Orissers might be established. With a coadjutor in each citadel, he, Walter, would be in a position to bring his tact and diplomacy into play.

As a matter of fact, Walter was not entirely mistaken in his diagnosis of Nicholas's condition. The young man recognised beneath Walter's phrases a spirit of good intention, a quality that came so near to sincerity that one could not properly ignore it. But was Walter's belief in his own sincerity justified? Was Walter really and truly prepared to plunge to the very heart of the problem? Would he be willing to follow his interlocutor down the path of conjecture, until they stood face to face with the starkest alternatives that the future could present? And would Walter consent to regard these alternatives with unblinking eyes, and declare himself upon them?

Great was the temptation to put the matter to the proof. Walter's prolixity had given him time to prepare just what *he* had to say. His imagination had run forward to construct the scene in advance. He could see himself passionately expounding, explaining, and, finally, challenging! He could see, too, Walter's face as he listened! And, alas! by no stretch of fancy could he picture upon that benign countenance any look that was not the mask of a secret annoyance and dismay. In how puzzled a manner would Walter knit his brows! How kindly he would try to understand, and how satisfactorily he would fail! How urbanely he would evade! How superciliously, at a pinch, he would brush the awkward point away! To put the issue before Walter's eyes in all its nakedness—to corner him with it—why, it couldn't be done! And he foresaw only too well how all these manoeuvres—that glassy look of defensive non-comprehension in particular—would madden him! He would go too far, and so give Walter the opportunity of rejecting the whole of what he said as extravagant and unseemly.

Indeed, the case was hopeless! Never could Walter, while remaining Walter, yield a satisfactory response! Although there was nothing, in pure abstract, to render it impossible; practically, and having regard for the character of each, an understanding was flatly out of the question.

And the rage with which the young man registered this conclusion was not mitigated but infused with despair, when he reflected that Walter's foregone recalcitrancy might be largely excused as a resistance against his own exorbitance. Were there many men who, when so challenged, would reveal a different temper? Were there many, who, when presented with hypothetical cases, would consent to step up onto the scales, weigh themselves and declare the result? His questions, Nicholas saw, would amount to this: Given the opportunity of abandoning the Orissers without too much loss of self-respect, would Walter do it? Or, more briefly: How much, in any and every conjecturable event, could one expect of him?

No, decidedly it was too much to ask! A man likes to give himself the benefit of every doubt, and likes, moreover, to leave the point of dubiety unformulated, both in the hope that the test may be spared him, and with the secret knowledge that, if it does come, his best chance of rising to it lies in the courage of the moment, in a sudden invigoration of character that premeditation would only impede.

"But if," thought Nicholas, "I have no right to force Walter to anticipate the future, what right has he to challenge me to do so by inviting my confidence? What right has he, who at bottom does not trust himself, to ask me to trust him?" With these reflections a bitter scorn of Walter awoke in his heart. Understanding little how to spare the secret weaknesses, or to encourage the secret fineness, of human nature in himself, he resented the obligation to treat others differently. Placed in Walter's situation, would he not, long ere now, have laid his whole inner mechanism bare before his own eyes? He swore he would! And although he might not have scorned to abandon Lilian, he would assuredly have scorned to place himself in the position which Walter was occupying with such complacency at this moment. Did the man really ignore that, among his many gifts, the gift of saving his face was pre-eminent? Walter was what passed in the world for an honourable man; but he saw to it that honour should not lie along too difficult a road. It was fortunate, indeed, for the Orissers that his honour and their financial emancipation were so closely linked. The real point of interest was: Did a disentanglement lie beyond the scope of Walter's unconscious art? Who could say? That benign countenance of his, upon which there still lingered an expression of dignified appeal, furnished no reassuring answer.

But there the man was, still intermittently throwing out a phrase meant to inspire sympathy and confidence! There he stood, waiting! What in heaven's name was to be replied? Alas! there was nothing to reply! Absolutely nothing!

So Nicholas stared, and continued to stare, until his sense of frustration, anger, and disgust, reached a climax. Then at last, muttering words of unintelligible apology, he made for the door. Walter was left alone, wide-eyed with astonishment.

Chapter 18

The summer was passing away. Little change was taking place in the conditions at Eamor. Since Cosmo's departure Nicholas had held aloof from every one save Isabel. A species of disgust at the whole tenor of life within and around prompted him to cultivate carelessness and indifference—a mood, in the indulgence of which no one could offer him better partnership than she. It irked him to consider how important a place was taken up in Lilian's mind by concern for *his* future. Especially, as he made no doubt that, in her passionate attachment to the idea that he should inherit Eamor, she was losing sight of every other condition of his, or of her own, happiness. But he saw no means of bringing this home to her, or of gathering the courage to take his fate into his own hands. What could he do, short of shaking the dust of Eamor off his feet and going out alone into the world? And would that act, which she would certainly regard as a heartless betrayal, really be the fine gesture it would pretend to be? He doubted it. If the present conflict was repugnant to his taste, if the weapons and the tactics were not to his liking, was that a reason for slinking out of the fight, and leaving Lilian stabbed with disappointment at his departure? Could he say to Lilian that he was ashamed to stand by her side now, but would not be too proud to enjoy the fruits of her victory, if she conquered? And how could he abjure those uncertain fruits beforehand without robbing her straightway of all that she was fighting for?

No, no! The little she asked of him—his passive acquiescence—he must give her! He wished to heaven she would ask for more! He even reproached himself for not attempting to curry favour with John Mayne, although that seemed to go against every fibre of his nature. He had early developed a quite personal antipathy for the old man, and was sure that his feelings were reciprocated. The memory of one particular evening, following shortly after John Mayne's arrival, was conclusive. Walter was absent in Tornel; the hour was late; the womenfolk had retired; and he had felt obliged to keep John Mayne company upon the terrace during the smoking of a last cigar.

The night was dark, warm, cloudy; the air without a stir. They were sitting together in a silence that he, for his part, felt helpless to break. Of his companion he could discern no more than the general bulk, and the waxing glow of his cigar-stump, when he sucked it. Yet his sense of the man's proximity, his sense of the whole working of that large, coarse organism, and of the congruous spirit animating it,—this sense became so oppressive that he was drawn into a veritable trance. He was drawn by a kind of physical empathy into the very centre of the being from which his spirit strained convulsively away. In his imagination he not only beheld the decay-blackened teeth, but could taste the taste of the mouth containing them; he not only beheld the big bullet-head attached to the body without any visible space of neck, but could sway that head from side to side; and that thick trunk inflating and deflating in respiration was moved by a breath that seemed to be his own. And he felt that the corporeal was a similitude of the psychical form. To his sense the night was suffused with a thousand evil irradiations; the trees in their hushed stillness stood around as creatures of sinister intention; and in the centre of this gross witchery sat John Mayne, squat, like a toad, in his chair.

At last John Mayne heaved a sigh. The wicker framework of his chair creaked, as, slowly, he pulled himself to his feet; slowly he walked over to the balustrade; and slowly expectorated on to the flowers below.

"My young friend," said he, returning, "one of these days you and I must have a talk!"

"Yes," said Nicholas, rising in turn.

John Mayne moved towards the house with heavy tread.

"Good night!" said he.

"Good night!"

That threatened talk had not yet been held, and Nicholas dared hope that John Mayne would decide against it. What was there to say? Did not their reciprocal antipathies speak plainly enough? And if, in spite of everything, the old man succeeded in forcing himself into the *rôle* of benefactor, need there be any assumption of good grace on his side, or a pretence of gratitude on the other?

His increasing detestation of John Mayne gave substance to his compassion for Lilian. To stand in the relation of wife to such a being— how terrible! How had she ever persuaded herself into the marriage? For the sake of Eamor? For his own sake? For his father's sake? Alas! the consequences declared loudly that not all these incentives combined made up a justification.

This being his disposition, and in view of the further difficulties produced by her relations with Allen on the one hand, and Cosmo on the other, it was not surprising that his intercourse with his step-mother had become scanty and constrained. There were still some rare moments, it was true, when they got back to something like the amity of their old footing; but they were never able to return to plain speaking, and as a rule the barrier of what lay unexpressed between them was more than he could even pretend to surmount. Her beauty in particular now harassed him. He studied her covertly and wondered. Had Allen kissed that lovely mouth? Were those two really sworn to one another in a secret alliance of love? If this were so, then he, Nicholas, was reduced to little more than a shadow, and the smiles that she still gave him must be more than half made up of pity.

One day, as he and Isabel were on their way down to the woods, they came upon her, standing in the arched opening of the yew hedge that encircled her rose-plot—hers, because already haunted by her for so many summers,—for long before it had become her trysting-place with Allen. That morning had the freshness of autumn in its air. The sky was astir with flocks of cloud. Bridal-white and gay as birds, they scudded over the forest; and the forest itself was in perpetual movement, showering down leaves, nipped by the first hard frost of the year. On coming out under the breezy heaven, Nicholas had felt the sunshine strike down into his heart. His spirits went up with a bound. He left the house and the heavy shadow of the house behind him. Joyously with Isabel he came racing down the lawn. But Lilian's solitary figure gave them both pause. They faltered uneasily, and knew that their faltering had been perceived.

Lilian was equipped with basket and scissors. Smilingly she exhibited the blossoms she had picked. They followed her through the portals of evergreen because they felt they could not do otherwise. And when she went back to her task, they stood by. She made a radiant figure against the sombre wall of yew; rime lay within the shadows on the turf.

In a minute, straightening herself, she gave a small cry and put to her mouth a finger pricked by a thorn.

"I've forgotten my gloves," she murmured, examining the hurt.

"Darling," said Isabel, "let me get them!"

For a while after the girl had gone, Lilian remained silent. Then with a sigh she said:

"Nick! I have been meaning for some time to talk to you—about Cosmo."

At the mention of that name Nicholas frowned and looked away.

"Won't you listen to me?" she asked rather wistfully.

He wore an air of constraint. "Not unless you really wish it." And then, as her eyes continued to rest upon him: "You see," he added with evident reluctance, "I——"

She waited.

"I have finished with him," he brought out at last; "I have given him up!"

She stood very still whilst he was speaking, and continued in the same posture for some moments after. His face had darkened to the point of sullenness. He was still looking away.

At last, and with a certain abruptness, she resumed:

"Allen writes that the situation in Tornel is becoming impossible. Think of it! They have been living there together now for two whole months! Cosmo still refuses to leave the country. And his condition grows neither better nor worse."

Her low voice thrilled with feeling, but the nature of that feeling was obscure to him. He shot a glance at her. "What do you want me to say?" he muttered.

She gave no immediate reply; and he had just formed the suspicion that she was keying herself up to some painful disclosure, when, drawing out a postcard which had been hidden in the folds of her dress, "Nick," said she, "look at that!"

He took the card quickly and read: "No more Mexico for me, thank you! Send Nicholas here. I have something to say to him. Yours, as the spirit moves me, Cosmo."

The young man flushed, then uttered a short laugh. "Is that all?"

She hesitated; but his eyes rested on the ground, and he did not notice it.

"Well, I shall refuse to go!" he cried with a kind of dull anger.

"That postcard came about two weeks ago," she avowed beneath her breath.

He threw her a brief smile. "What does it matter? I have no wish to see him. I refuse to see him, unless——"

"What?"

He laughed again. "Unless you insist!"

She turned away. He saw her look up into the sky.

She seemed to meditate. The wind rustled in the trees behind them. Absently she twisted into her hair a whisp that had blown loose.

"I don't insist!" she said.

He handed the card back to her.

She regarded it ruefully. "For all I know," she observed, "Madeline may have seen this!"

"How dreadful!" said Nicholas dryly.

"Yes," she chid him, "it *is* dreadful!"

"Can't Allen prevent that sort of thing?"

"My dear!" she exclaimed impulsively, then stopped short; and it was in quite another voice that she went on: "Ah, my dear, you don't understand! Allen is doing all that man can do! But—I *must* tell you!—the position is becoming desperate!"

With this a silence descended. She was looking straight out before her with sadder eyes than he had ever yet seen in her face. Following the direction of her gaze, his own eyes fell upon an ancient mulberry tree that grew at the other end of the enclosure. Its trunk was encircled by a wooden seat; and it was there, as he knew, that she and Allen used to meet.

Again turning towards him, "Oh, Nick!" she cried. "As the days go by, and I think of those two together in Tornel, I feel I shall go mad! God knows what Allen must be enduring!"

Her accents brought a rush of blood into Nicholas's cheeks; he lifted his head, gazed at her with shining eyes, impetuously caught up her hand. "And you, Lilian dear, what about you!"

Her eyes swam; she gave a little shrug and a head-shake. He pressed her fingers against his lips.

"As for me," he went on bitterly, "I am shirking everything!"

"No, no! What is there for you to do?—nothing!"

He laughed, self-scornful.

"Nothing, my dear!" she tenderly protested. "Nothing!"

He dropped her hand, and with a hopeless gesture turned his face away. "These Maynes! Give me the word to murder them—and I'll do it!"

She smiled, but her lids were wet.

"Not yet!" said she. "Not yet!" Then, looking round: "Here's Isabel!" she added.

The girl had just entered the enclosure, and was sauntering towards them, a pair of gauntlet gloves in her hand.

"Thank you, my darling!" said Lilian. "And now—be off—both of you! The morning is already half gone."

Chapter 19

Making little account of time, Nicholas and Isabel that day wandered far. It was their habit to walk fast on the whole, but with childish inconsequences, of pace and direction; and it amused them, when they could, to lose their way. On this forenoon they quickly abandoned the trodden paths, plunging in amongst the smooth, rounded trunks of the beeches, where the sunlight entered flickeringly, or was tempered to a golden glow. There was little undergrowth in these parts, so that they could go forward, for the most part, unimpeded. It was only under gaps in the leafy roof that clumps of bramble and thorn appeared; these, red with berries and implicated in the rough, brittle tangle of autumn, were obstacles round which one had to skirt; and, in doing so, it was not difficult to lose one's sense of direction.

By midday their wanderings had brought them to the brink of a small ravine, a gully that Nicholas fancied they had never been to before. Peering through the trees that clung to its steep bank, they heard, but scarce could see, a stream running below. To have reached a hitherto unvisited spot was in itself an excitement. Regardless of the hour, they determined to push on.

Skirting the ravine as closely as they could, they presently came out onto open ground. Before them stretched a wide, grassy slope, dotted with junipers and yew-trees lit by coral berries that shone in the sun. Nicholas stood still and looked before him wonderingly. The scene had a remote, seductive quality, a charm resembling that of landscapes beheld in dream. In the centre of the smooth expanse of turf there rose a clump of lean ash trees, whose arms upheld a meagre foliage. To these they advanced, and found, clustered among the snaky roots of the trees, raffish tribes of toadstools,—sticky discs of orange, and white, and red. Light airs whispered furtively in the branches overhead; all around was silence; the effluence of the spot was delicately derisive.

"Isabel," said Nicholas suddenly, "we have been here before!"

"Do you think so?" And she moved carelessly away. His eyes followed her with a peculiar look. A smile hovered about his mouth.

"Isabel, don't you remember anything?"

"Ah, yes!" she cried, and straightway bounded forward. "I remember a waterfall! A little further on, we shall find that lovely waterfall! Come along, Nick! Come along!"

Thoughtful, he followed. A memory had come back to him. Yes, they had been here once before as children. And did she recollect all that he did of that day, of that exquisite, barbarous day? There she was—the same! Slender in her clinging frock, she looked, and moved, the same elfish being now as then! She had not changed! No! and if not, what of the impudence, the naive animalism, of the little maiden of that time? Was she not to-day the identical creature, artful, inquisitive, secretly rejoicing in her treasures of instinct, and innocence, and guile? Was her mischievous effrontery all gone, replaced by the doleful dignity of womanhood? No, no! She was Isabel still! Life had not yet mistaught her! Wonderful gift of unteachableness! To be natively sceptical of the world's adult values, to be impervious to accredited notions—not by effort, but by grace!

He followed her to the head of the gully, which was no great distance away. And here at last they saw the stream that had hitherto been invisible, toppling over a ledge of rock, and falling in a glassy column as clear and straight as the stem of a crystal vase, through fifteen feet of air. Foaming among the stones below, the water dashed headlong into a lower pool, above which blew an iridescent water-dust, feeding the dark mosses and ferns at the base of the cliff.

The slope at the top of which they stood was not easy to climb down. Its tufty grass had made scant root, and came away in the hand. But Isabel in a moment had made the descent; and she it was who first reached the foot of the fall. One hand against the wall of rock, she swayed tip-toe towards the sparkling shaft; laughing, she shattered its swift and rushing smoothness, her rosy fingers the centre of an explosion of coruscating drops.

"Look!" she cried. "Look!"

But Nicholas was already looking. She was, he thought, a wonderfully lovely thing. Wonderful, too, were the freshness and fulness of that autumnal noon, glittering upon the rapid water, and shimmering amid the golden trees. Wonderful was the air still quivering with the hum of summer, and the keen light falling out of a dappled sky.

But those clouds up there, for whatever reason, reminded him of the rose-garden—and of Lilian. What was Lilian doing now,—what, in her solitude, thinking?

Again he regarded Isabel. "You pretty thing!" he said to himself, "you lovely thing! compared with *her*, how little you signify to me!" Lilian was a communicating intelligence. He and she did not need to unite. Spirits cannot unite. The spirit is a conscious isolation. Spirits communicate without uniting; the flesh unites without communicating. The world and circumstance might part Lilian from him; but he and she would always reflect each other's innermost spirit. "She lives—*I* live," he said, "whereas all this"—he looked at the eager girl, and the hovering dragon-flies, and the hurrying water—"all this is dead. Yes, either the life by which I live, or the life by which this lives, is unworthy to go by the name of life. And how, in the deep, the vibrant, the detached self-consciousness of my self-conscious mind, can I doubt that it is I who am truly alive? The rest is not life but mere existence."

"All," he continued within himself, "all that which flows along in the stream of mere existence, be it animate or inanimate, is devoid of life. To be alive is to offer resistance to the flux, to contract out of the general fluidity into a hard discreteness, to curdle into independent self-consciousness. And yet it is true that self-consciousness turns living into a mummery. Mine is a case in point. I escort myself through life with a humour like to that of a rich man who takes a beggar into his house and sets him at table for the amusement of seeing him gorge. Shall I say that my intelligence is mated to a small heart, which is unworthy of it; and that my intelligence for that reason is trying to kill my heart? But what's a heart? What's the heart of a man, that has no counterpart in the universe, no ensample in the breast of a God?"

While he was thus communing with himself, his eyes rested upon Isabel, and his imagination worked in the service of a growing desire. It was no wish of his that she should ever enter into the sphere of his thought. The plane upon which he would have them meet should be the gay, careless plane of juvenility. He said in his heart: "All that lies between animalism and pure intelligence is rubbish. Man's twofold error is this: that while contemning the child and the animal in himself, he is yet afraid of the intellect's hegemony. Manhood's ideal of itself is sentimental, weak, and not a little vulgar! Manhood! Let us leave that to Walter with his fine, civic seriousness! And Womanhood to Madeline, drawing herself up, all bust and self-respect! 'We are neither children nor gods,' says Walter, 'but men in a world of men.' Well, so let those worthies be! But in my eyes the world of men includes all childishness and lacks all child hood's charm. Mine be the higher wisdom which makes itself the plaything of a puerile, gracious folly!"

Thus thinking, he watched Isabel turn and idly pick her way over the boulders towards him. Her arms were bared; her skirt kilted; like a fawn she poised and sprang. Presently she alighted upon the warm rock at his side; and there they stretched themselves out and lay shoulder to shoulder, looking down into the water, while the sun beat upon their backs. They were thirsty, and they drank, scooping up the cool water in their hands. His excitement had concentrated into a hard, small kernel of resolve. Through the rest of his being there spread somnolence and peace. Taking a long strand of her hair that was hanging over her ears, he pressed it against his check and lips. One half smiling glance she gave him, while her fingers played with the water.

When the time came to go home, their fancy took them along the narrow margin of the stream, at the foot of the high banks. They went this way until they reached a place where the gully made a decided turn in the wrong direction, and here they paused to consider. The banks on either hand rose higher and yet more steeply above them; but the side which they had to climb was not too difficult; for young trees had spread a network of roots over the earth, and these offered a fair foothold right up to the top.

Isabel started first on the ascent, her companion standing and watching her. Slim and small did she look against the wide, brown earth, with the columns of the young alders rising about her. Half-way up she stopped and glanced down. Her eyes encountered his. Was it a challenge? Like one awakening from a dream, he sprang forward. She turned as if in flight. He gained upon her. In a short while the sound of his quick breathing came to her ears; already he was close behind; with a little gasp she gave up, faced round, and stood still.

At that moment a puff of wind swept down the gully and set the whole landscape rocking. Above the topmost tiers of trees clouds raced over; the foliage rustled, the branches whistled, and all the air was a flurry of yellow leaves. Shrinking against the bank, she felt Nicholas beside her. His face was near to hers; she opened her eyes, eyes so deeply blue as to be almost black. Now they were timorous, defiant, secret. Deep in those wells her soul like a treasure was hidden, and he could peer and peer, and learn nothing. But what matter? for he could press his lips to hers and feel her bosom rise and fall. The warmth of her limbs and the smell of her hair penetrated him; all the warmth and fragrance of her body came to him on the breath of the damp earth and the crushed leaves. How her heart beat! And now her head fell back and her eye-lids flickered down. And her lips parted; and again he kissed them. She seemed to die. "Isabel!" he whispered. Her mouth quivered, her eyes opened, piteous, protesting. "Isabel! Isabel!" he pleaded, and unclasped and made her free. For a moment she remained, panting; then took her freedom as with a spread of wing. This time he gave no chase, but watched, then followed slowly. On the way home she was a child offended, and although he was suppliant she would hardly speak.

Chapter 20

The Big Hall in which John Mayne and Walter worked, had retained its ecclesiastical character. It kept its ancient vaulted roof, wooden panels running half-way up the stone walls, and narrow mullioned windows, untouched save on one side, where they had been extended downward for additional light. It was before one of these windows, in a corner of the hall, that John Mayne had caused his writing-desk to be placed; flanking it, on the one hand, with an unsightly and immense filing cabinet of his own recent purchase; and, on the other, with two of the newly arrived chests, which contained the most private of the papers that he had to overlook.

In the mechanical part of his work, in the simple docketing and laying by of the sifted material, he let himself be helped by Madeline, who from the beginning had pressed her services upon him with great eagerness. She proved herself intelligent and methodical. Yet so firmly rooted was his instinct for secrecy in his affairs, that he was restless all the time she was there; and on some days, in an access of jealous irritation, he would incontinently send her away.

One corner of the chest beside his chair contained his old correspondence with his wife. It was there in its entirety; for beside her letters he had kept copies of his own. To have that long and bitter record so close beneath his hand was a torment to him. He feared to study it, and yet he knew he would. Those lines, penned with such gall upon his side, and with such desperate fluctuations of entreaty and resentment upon hers—how would they strike him at this day? He feared equally to rouse his old sense of outrage, and to discover, perchance, new and disconcerting aspects of the case—blemishes of character, errors of taste on his part, which, perceived now for the first time, would bring the hot flush to his cheeks. Why read those letters at all? Yet he could not forbear. Whenever he found the courage to dare, or lacked the strength to resist, he would draw forth a packet, and with throbbing temples scan two or three sheets. Rarely did he peruse more. For his mind under the impetus of those faded lines would go off on journeys of its own. Memories, speculations, dreams, led him along in a kind of feverish stupor, out of which only the fear of interruption and discovery could rouse him.

On the day of Nicholas's wanderings with Isabel in the wood, and late in the afternoon of that day, while the naked globe of the westering sun slanted its rays across his desk in such a fashion that, had he tried to read the written page beneath his hand, he would assuredly have been dazzled—on this afternoon John Mayne sat, hunched in his established seat, with head down-hung and the lids drooping over his eyes. Madeline was late. He hoped she would not come at all. He had almost ceased to expect her, when at last her step sounded in the uncarpeted passage-way. It startled him guiltily back out of regions of secret thought; he scowled, and with a furtive gesture covered over the letter that was lying before him.

Without turning his head, he listened to the rustle of the girl's movement across the room. At his side she dropped down upon her knees, and with smiling eagerness launched forth into explanations.

"Uncle dear, I have been saying good-bye to Walter! He promises he'll be back in a day or two.—I know I'm dreadfully late. But you'll forgive me, won't you?"

Her brilliant regard was lifted upward to the old man's face. He returned the look stonily. A stare of such heavy irresponsiveness might well have crushed the light and life out of any countenance upon which it was directed. Forgive her for not coming before! He declared more plainly than by any speech that he only wished she had never come at all! That he only wished she would never come! But if his looks failed even momentarily to becloud her radiance, it could be seen that he did not expect them to do so. Oh, no! He had good knowledge of her endurance. And now, in truth, she was doing more than endure. She challenged! The late light, glinting in her hair and glowing on the robust curve of her cheek, lent fire to her resolute audacity. "Uncle John!" she cried, "Uncle John, say that you have missed me!"

She pitted her feminine freshness and vivacity against him—and she carried off the victory. A kind of contemptuous leniency crept into the old man's eyes. "Missed you? Well, well!" And he pinched her chin. "I don't know but what I did."

Tilting her face up to him with his hand, he eyed her again, this time with ogreish tenderness. He sought in the enjoyment of this broad offering of beauty, forgetfulness of the *other*. Was this not better?

His fingers fondled her cheek and throat. For a minute the girl let it be; then jumped to her feet. His arm went round her hips; slowly, smilingly, she made herself free.

"Is this all you have ready?" cried she, pointing to a pile of papers on a table behind. "Oh, Uncle John, you've been lazy!"

Yes, he had been lazy! All the afternoon he had been sitting before one time-faded letter, which at this moment lay hidden beneath the sheets of his blotter. He said nothing, and she turned away. As she moved to her own appointed table in the background, her face was dark and scornful. Oh, she knew well enough what ailed him! She knew what poison it was he had in his veins! Could she not guess what lay beneath the blotting-paper?

In the ensuing silence, whilst he, relying upon the breadth of his back, slipped the letter before him into its packet, and the packet into the drawer of his desk, and whilst her busy fingers tied up, sealed, and docketed the papers committed to her care,—in this heavy, dissembling silence her heart cried out: "Burn those miserable letters! Burn them, old fool, and despise *her!* What is Lilian—body, soul, and spirit—for a man to fret about? A faded, lifeless woman—past thirty—old, old!" She fumed at his male subjection, and in her anger poured a cynical contempt upon the whole feminine lure. After all, what's in a woman? How little, a woman only could know! Ah! could he but see Lilian through *her* eyes! And as for punishment, did he not hold her in the hollow of his hand? Masculine passions! Masculine scruples! What gratuitous foolishness! Poor, poor Uncle John! She pitied, admired, loved and scorned him.

A little later the old man rose from his place. Madeline, too, had finished her task. She linked her arm in his, and together they passed slowly out of the hall; the *portière* fell behind them; their footsteps receded down the passage.

A frosty sunset was closing the day. The last of its crimson gleams struck through the window on to the writing-desk, glittered upon the silver of John Mayne's inkstand, and put a dying flush upon the panelling of the embrasure. Motes floating in the shafts of light hung visible like constellations in the sky. Immensities of space, millennial revolutions, silences, flux of time—imagination here could watch and spy upon them!

High overhead, shifting, and fading, and reviving again among the rafters, the red rays played for a moment and then died away. The spaces of the vaulted roofing changed from a rich umber into the velvety blackness of night.

The inmates of Eamor had, however, formed the recent habit of spending the evening in this apartment, which John Mayne preferred to any other. After a while, accordingly, a servant entered, struck a match, and moving to the large, open fireplace which had been built into the centre of the opposite wall, kindled the firing already laid upon the hearth. Here, before a blaze of logs, John Mayne would presently sit, for the most part in silence, staring at the flames and sucking at his cigar. Sometimes Walter, or perhaps Madeline, would read aloud. Nicholas would play chess, if either Lilian or Isabel could be persuaded to give him a game. And occasionally, accompanied by Isabel on the piano, Madeline would sing.

That evening, as they drifted into the room, an ill-omened hush fell upon the little group. During dinner Walter's absence had already made itself painfully felt. He it was who, with Nina's tacit support, did most to impart to the evening gathering at least a semblance of sociality. But how valuable his presence was, they did not fully realise till now. The last sparks of their laboured animation were quenched by the gloom and chill of these vast quarters. Although the curtains had been drawn, the fire built up high, and lamps set here and there against the darkness, the Big Hall was still funereal enough; they would be hard put to it to hold their own against the established silence that hung about its walls.

Having desired the others to pass on before him, John Mayne was the last to enter. As he stumped heavily to his chair—a figure of squat and forbidding uncouthness—the desultory talk faltered away. Slowly he let himself sink into his seat, slowly pulled forth a tobacco-pouch, and, while stuffing his pipe, shifted his small eyes this way and that with an air of lowering disfavour.

"Stir the logs!" he ordered.

It was done. The flames leapt up with a stronger roar; the shadows of the company danced upon the walls.

Stiff and motionless, the old man stared into the heart of the glow. "It wants more than that," said he, "to make this old barn look gay. Why!" he cried, suddenly pointing into the dimness of the vaulting, "what do I see there? Bats, eh? Bats?"

There was a moment of uneasiness. Lilian went through the form of scrutiny.

"No. There are no bats!" she replied.

John Mayne looked at her, then threw back his head, while his mouth opened in a soundless laugh.

"Sure?"

It was a jest, seemingly. The amusement lay in discovering to what extent they questioned his mental soundness, and how far they were prepared to humour him. During dinner he had already played upon them in like manner. Lilian flushed slightly and turned her eyes away.

"Uncle John," said Madeline, coming forward, "shall I read to you? What would you care for to-night?"

She received no answer. John Mayne had settled down into that appalling stolidity which they had learnt to know. His eyes, half shadowed by their heavy lids, were fixed upon the flames without blinking. A massive weariness was exhaled from him. Like a savage and morose beast, he sat. Weary he was; weary of himself, of them, of everything!

At last the light of reviving consciousness of his surroundings flickered back into his eyes; this way and that he slowly turned his head; mouth agape, he seemed to quest after the evil that tormented him; or, since he knew that evil was within, to seek an object upon which to vent some fraction of his baffled rancour.

"Lilian," he cried, and struck the chair-arm with his fist, "why must we sit in darkness? Why not more light? This hall is black as hell. More light, I say!" And he lapsed into inarticulate muttering.

Taken aback by this outbreak, Lilian flinched, then rose from her seat.

"What shall I do?" she murmured.

"Do? Light the candles!" and he pointed to the big chandeliers. "Do you grudge me the price of a few candles, eh?"

Lilian looked up. It was true, the candles were there,—old, dusty candles, which, on some festive occasion of long ago, had been only half consumed.

Her eyes came back to him doubtfully. "They can be lit, if you wish it," said she.

"Light them all!" he mumbled, his pipe once more between his teeth. "Light them all!"

At this Nicholas rose, kindled a taper at the hearth, and started on a round of the room, visiting each bracket and chandelier. On his passage point after point of flame struggled into brilliance; and, as the illumination proceeded, the others, watching in silence, were moved to astonishment at the effect. It was singular how complete a transformation the old hall underwent. The shine of the candles, as they gained strength, dyed its ancient, timeworn features with a flush as from a transfusion of blood. Proudly it enlarged itself; its confines widened; its faded colours revived; the long, crimson curtains, the dark panelling, the dusky portraits, the bookshelves and the books—all, up to the very apex of the vaulting, smouldered in a rich glow.

John Mayne turned in his chair, then struggled to his feet and advanced to the centre of the room.

"Ha! Is that not better?" said he. "And now, I declare, we ought to have a dance! A dance, ladies! What do you say?"

His eyes travelled over their faces, as he spoke; he smiled, but not so as to relieve their constraint.

"Madeline"—and a violent laugh burst from his mouth—"give us a dance, my child! You know how to do it, I'll swear!"

The girl compressed her lips. "You are joking, uncle; I could not dance—not here—not now!"

"Not for my head on a charger?" put in Nicholas beneath his breath.

She flung him a look of scorn. But John Mayne, who had caught the words, threw up his chin and once again laughed out loud.

"Well, if you won't dance, my dear, perhaps you will sing?"

"Certainly, uncle, if you wish it," returned Madeline with dignity. "Isabel, will you accompany me?"

They went over to the piano. John Mayne, who stood with his eyes fixed upon Lilian, rubbed his chin, and a look of secret amusement gathered upon his face. When she had seated herself, he drew his chair close to hers. There was that in his regard which augured no good. From a corner Nicholas watched, glowering. Nina picked up her needlework.

After the song was over, John Mayne clapped his hands.

"Bravo!" cried he. "And now—give us something a little different—a warm-blooded song—a song of the south! Here, bring me your songbooks! I'll find you what I want!"

With an unwonted gleam in his eyes he turned, leering, to his wife. "You know what it is! I warrant you'll remember it, my dear . . . a song full of memories. . ."

He leaned towards her; and, although she did not move, her very frame seemed to shrink.

"Oh! you'll remember it, my dear! Very well—very well! A song charged with tender memories!" He gloated. "It was sung outside our window, one evening, on our honeymoon! Come, don't you remember?"

Madeline was standing before him, but he did not heed her. He saw no one but his wife. Lips parted, eyes bloodshot, he thrust at her a face both shining and dark—a face lit with the black light of hate. She blanched and stiffened. She remained without movement, save for the rise and fall of her breast. For a few seconds no one stirred. The smile and snarl upon John Mayne's visage seemed fixed beyond his power to break them. In the end, however, his victim thrust back her chair, and with a convulsive effort rose to her feet.

"What!" cried he. "Our bridal song! And you fly from it! What! are you leaving us? Are you put to flight?" Flinging himself backward in his seat, he tilted his face up, and laughter rattled in his throat. The sound of that abominable hilarity pursued her down the passage as she fled.

"Well," said John Mayne presently, when he had recovered himself, "that's enough music for this evening—or so it appears!"

He pulled out his handkerchief and wiped his face. "By God, this room is hot! Nicholas, open the window!"

Madeline bent over him with troubled look, "Uncle dear, it's getting late——"

He waved her impatiently aside.

A sigh came from Nina, who was methodically rolling up her needlework. "Indeed, Uncle John," said she, "it is time for us all——"

"No!" He made shift to pull his chair round so as to face the window. The casement was now open, and the curtains had been drawn aside. "Ha! that's better, that's better," cried he, as the cold air, together with a frosty blue moonlight, streamed into the room. "Now then, gather round, all of you! Madeline, come! Where two or three are gathered together, there should be a little gaiety, eh?"

Then, addressing the young man: "Well, Master Nicholas, why so glum?"

The latter was leaning against the window-frame; his pale face was blanched on one side by the bright moon. He fixed John Mayne and kept silent.

"Tell us what you were doing in Tornel the other day," the old man went on; "seeing life, I take it?"

"Seeing life, no doubt!" he continued banteringly. "And that means running after the girls. Tell me, have you ever done an honest day's work, sonny?"

"Work?" Nicholas laughed gently. "That depends on what you mean by work!"

"By work I mean—work!"

"You have worked all your life, I suppose?"

"Yes!"

"And what good has that work done the world—or you?"

The smile departed from John Mayne's face. His eyes blazed. Forestalling his speech, or his attempt at speech,—for rage seemed to choke him,—Madeline interposed.

"Nicholas intends to be impertinent, uncle," said she quietly. "And it's not very difficult to be merely impertinent." She paused, her bosom heaving with suppressed passion. "Nor is it difficult to be an idler,—if others will support you!"

John Mayne still glared; but gradually he recovered his smile. "Young man!" said he, whilst he fingered the loose flesh beneath his chin, "you know mighty little about Life. But very soon you'll know more."

With a smile and a shrug the other averted his face; he appeared to lose himself in contemplation of the night.

John Mayne's countenance darkened again. "What you need, my young friend—what you need——"

"Is charity!" put in Nicholas with a mocking glance directed at Madeline. "Charity!"

"Eh?"

"I said charity."

"And faith and hope as well!" murmured Madeline beneath her breath. "You need them all!"

"Experience!" brought out John Mayne with a shout. "Experience of life! Experience to teach you what it is to struggle for your daily bread!"

"Why struggle?"

"Eh?"

"Isn't it a question of what one considers worth while?" He paused for a smile of insolent suavity. "You, I know, have always been ready for life on any terms—for life at any price; but after all——" And he ended with a shrug.

"Aha! that's it, is it? A man might just as well cut his throat! Very well! Very well then! Do it!" A look of savage amusement came into John Mayne's face. "Do it," said he, "if you dare!" He waited, then struck the arm of his chair. "But you won't! Oh, no! Not you, young man, not you! Day and night, night and day, you would toil and scheme and sweat—rather than that! Starvation, exhaustion, pain—you would bear them all! You don't blackmail me with suicide talk! No, no! Your wretched little body and your wretched little soul—you would sell them both, but you would go on! Anything to live! Aye!" he cried in a voice ringing with desperate exultation, "men cling to life even with a cancer

194

gnawing at their vitals! And they do well!"

Madeline rose, her lips twitching.

"Uncle," said she huskily, "it's late—very late! Come!"

"Give me my whisky!"

She turned hurriedly and handed him his customary dram.

Still without removing his gaze from Nicholas's face, John Mayne took the glass. It seemed as though he were about to break into speech again; the next moment, however, he tossed the liquor off, and then pulled himself to his feet.

He took a few uncertain steps.

"Do you feel less well to-night?" whispered Madeline. "Uncle, take my arm! Please!"

He accepted her support. Followed by Nina, the two progressed slowly across the room and disappeared into the curtained passage-way.

Left alone together, Nicholas and Isabel exchanged a long, unfathomable look. At last the young man came forward a little, but almost immediately turned back to the window; and there stood staring out at the moonlit landscape.

"Nick," the whisper came to him, "why did you do it?"

"How could I help myself?"

Silence again followed. Then he heard the rustle of her movement, uncertain and reluctant, towards the door.

All at once he faced round. "Are you going?"

"I must go and see Lilian."

"Isabel, I want to talk to you—to-night! I must! I must!"

She looked over her shoulder, saw him very pale. Her steps faltered.

"Come back in a little while!" he entreated. "Will you?"

She hesitated; she considered him with big, serious eyes; then slowly she went on.

Would she return or would she not? His gaze followed her with anguish. He remained motionless, listening to her footfalls, until they had completely died away.

Chapter 21

He thought: "If she does not come back, my God!—what shall I do? But she will! She will! And then let the heavens crack! Let John Mayne do his worst! Yes, even to Lilian;—for she is strong. And has she not got her Allen? As for me, I want Isabel—nothing more! Let John Mayne pitch us out into misery, if he will! Ah! he knows what poverty is. 'And that,' says he, 'that's what I want for them!' Well, let him do his worst, and die!"

He had advanced into the centre of the room. A continuous tremor shook his frame; but he felt endued with an unnatural physical and mental vitality. He had a sense of divine self-dominion. He was no longer subject to the coercions of ordinary mortality. "For," he declared within himself, "the whip with which men are driven along the road of their fate is, in the last resort, only the fear of death. After the commands of duty have become no more than an empty bluster, after the voice of conscience rings hollow, and the appeal of the affections has become vain; the sibilation of that fear continues—an ever-ready serpent-hiss in the darkness of the heart. But let that fear be strangled by your defiance, let it be crushed under an insensate resolve; and straightway you become free! Slave-driving Nature is disarmed; the goad, the whip, the spur, fall from her! She regards you in glowering impotence, and can do nothing."

Never before had he felt such plenitude of self-mastery. Yet even whilst rejoicing, he took thought to examine whether his exultation was in truth anything other than a delusive drunkenness playing upon the shallower elements of the mind. Could he be sure that he had won to a strength that the future would not reveal as illusory? Circumspectly he estimated the physical factors in his condition. A reaction, he reflected, was bound to step in. Sooner or later, and not once but often again, he would sink back into a sick and flinching debility. "But," he asked, "shall I then need to accuse myself of having been befooled? Shall I not by an effort be able to recall the authoritativeness of this present revelation? And will not the memory of it enable me to recover some portion of my present strength?"

He pondered. The answer was dubious. But why, after all, should the question trouble him? The miserable wretch that Nicholas Orisser had been, and would be again—that wretch was of little account. Let it suffice that through him the divine Ego in man had raised itself for an instant to godhead! "Let it suffice," he said, "that I, as I stand here, at this moment, profess myself, in my complete self-consciousness, content!"

He was smiling. A vision of his material form—an insignificant figure standing in the centre of the room—projected itself upon his mind. He could even see the strained, ecstatic smile upon the puppet's face. Poor, small fragment of humanity! Around it the candles shone; about it the silence pressed deep. In the glorious impassivity of lifeless things the great hall glowed with a dim and dusky grandeur.

Time! Time pulsed through it all! Time, the mocker! Time, that would inevitably cast him down! Already the touches of Time's ghostly fingers were settling chillingly upon his heart. Yes, the old chill of mortality ran through him. His spirit shuddered. His spirit shrivelled and shrank within him; his spirit drooped and sank.

Late! It was late! And Isabel had not yet come! Would she not come at all?

Down went the tide of his valiance, until it had dropped to the lowest ebb of life. His very soul became weary, and old, and grey. Vanity of vanities! All was deception and vanity!

His eyes wandered about the precincts of the hall. The air had lost its radiance; the candles glared; memories of old weaknesses and failures thrust scornful visages through the curtains; out of every corner there was watching and sneering. The place had become demonic. Loneliness came forth and spat in his face.

But presently his anguish by its intensity defeated itself. Presently he became numb.

What did he care for the world, for himself, for anything! As for Isabel? Foolishness! Sex was the vulgarest of all the vulgar lures in life's whole bag of tricks. . . .

Yet he suffered; and his suffering humiliated him; for it was still the suffering of suspense. Isabel might yet come! Life had but to whistle, and up he would run like a dog!

Yes, he would obey—although it was already too late. The virtue had gone out of him! He had been withered and sucked dry. Should she come now, she would find a spiritless loon;—abject, with a hanging head!

Light footfalls sounded in the passage. His heart dropped a beat; a shudder ran over him. He sprang to the window; he could not endure to let his face be seen.

The moon had risen high in the heavens. An immense calm, an immense, sardonic beauty, lay upon the silvered face of earth. He looked up into the blue tranquillities overhead; he inhaled deeply, and slowly there gathered upon his lips a smile of self-derision.

He heard Isabel advance half-way across the room. But still he made no movement. He waited, whilst she paused, hesitating.

"Nick!" she murmured. "Still here!"

Of a sudden he faced round, and at the sight of her his spirit quailed again. His desire appalled him. That girl, he felt, had it at her option to fill him with delight or to cast him into a pit of misery. But he would be cunning, subtle, ruthless. So now, exploiting the involuntary strangeness of his air, he kept his eyes fixed stonily upon her, and said nothing.

She was puzzled; she studied him wonderingly.

"Nick," she breathed, "what is the matter? What has happened?"

"My God," he said within himself, "how fatally I am caught! And how she will play with me, if I but give her a chance! She will demand sentiment, lovers' confidences, quarrels, and reconciliations! She will want marriage—even children! But above all, sentiment! Her elfishness is but a lure. The woman lurks beneath."

O threadbare ironies of sex! He would seduce her, would he? Seduce! What cant lay in that word! Behold the pretty thing! What other path than that of sex had she to follow? Seduce? No, no! It was he, that had been seduced . . . for his true life lay elsewhere.

Thus thinking, he kept silent; and, as if some faint effluence of his thoughts were reaching her, Isabel for a moment turned her head away.

Her next words came more coldly. "What do you want with me?" she asked. "It is late. I must go."

And still he remained mute. In truth he scarcely apprehended what she said. He was thinking: "I will take her in my arms and kiss her. If she protests, I will smile. I will assume that she has already surrendered. I will meet resistance with astonishment—with pained reproach. I will mystify her. At all costs she must be mystified. What a comedy!"

Uplifted on a wave of confidence, he advanced.

"Isabel!"

His voice rang with a note of triumph. He could see that she knew not what to make of him. Following a sudden inspiration, he took her hand and led her up to the window.

"Look!" he commanded exultantly; and she obeyed him. Her gaze went out over the still, bright scene with mingled perplexity and awe. She stared for a while in silence, then questioningly raised her eyes to his.

Smiling inscrutably, he drew her to him. His air proclaimed him the possessor of some ineffable secret. "Listen!" he said. And she listened.

The unclouded moon hanging above seemed to radiate silence as well as light. Silence enveloped the world. Life was entranced. She gazed and listened; he felt her spirit yielding to the spell of the night. Beside her, like a grand initiator, he stood. He seemed to be pausing on the verge of a stupendous revelation.

"Isabel!"

She lifted a face dreamy with expectation. He bent and kissed her on the mouth. For a moment she was inert, then passionately she struggled against him. He held her fast, frowning down with sternness. And all at once she became still. Flushed, with averted face and parted lips, she held herself passive within his arms—passive, yet taut. Her gaze went out wildly through the open window into the shining spaces of the night. He could feel her will ebbing away. "One moment more and she is mine," he said to himself, "one moment more . . ."

But—God in heaven!—what was that?

Issuing from they knew not where, a long-drawn groan fell upon their ears. It petrified their immobility. Each faculty strained to the uttermost, they waited. In a minute the sound rose again.

Rage entered Nicholas's heart. What was this thing that came to thrust itself between him and his triumph? Swiftly he apprehended that those groans must have emanated from the upper storey of the house—from John Mayne's room, one window of which overlooked the roof of the hall. He clasped Isabel tighter in his arms. She was trembling; her limbs had lost their rigidity; he felt her yield completely. Why! the good John Mayne had actually lent him assistance! The battle was won. Yes! he could now relax, even as she. The last barriers between them were broken down; antagonists no longer, they clung to one another. And he was lapped in an exquisite peace. Let the mysterious night yield what it would of horror, of beauty, and of unreality! There was nothing in the world but would serve to conjoin them more closely still. This startled hush was deeper surely than any natural silence; this sublunary land-scape more bright and cold and dead than any prospect of the natural earth. They were not in the world;—all was well!

But the groan was repeated—and more horribly. It sent a tremor over the liquid surface of their dream. And again! And again! A note, the human agony of which could not be withstood. Tearing herself away, the girl put her hand up to her ears. Her bosom was shaken by sobbing breaths.

He took her hand, and she suffered him to lead her away from the window; she let herself fall upon a couch and hid her face.

The house was still without a stir. It seemed to be sunk in a monstrous torpor of indifference. Long minutes passed before the bustle of assistance came to their ears. But John Mayne's agony had not yet reached its term. Once more, and again at shorter intervals, the night air was torn by that sound of horror, which rose in the end to a shrieking pitch and died down in a series of inhuman grunts.

Isabel lay back among the cushions and did not move. Her companion, heedless of her at last, turned away and cursed God in his heart. Much as he hated John Mayne, he hated this thing more. Well could he picture the scene in the room above: the four-poster with the fire's glow upon the coverlet, the movements of a big body writhing beneath it, a face distorted and glistening with sweat. And that tortured flesh called unto his flesh; the deeps of animal nature were communicant. He could feel how the man's teeth were grinding together, and how his muscles were stretching and straining. It was proclaimed to him how, gradually, all in her own good time, the Flesh had assumed unqualified dominion, he saw the human spirit beaten down at last into the mire of sheer animality.

When all was over and silence had returned, he sat down beside Isabel and rested his head in his hands. The girl was still outstretched in an attitude of prostration; her lids were sunk as in sleep.

Chapter 22

Unreckoned, the minutes slipped by. A kind of listlessness descended upon them both. They stared into vacancy and dreamed.

There arose before Nicholas's eyes an imaginary landscape that had been one of the visions of his childhood. Across the plains of that impossible world it had been his habit, while awaiting sleep, to set out on curious wanderings. The ground underfoot consisted of smooth, polished slabs of rock, in the interstices of which coloured flowers like anemones were growing. There was a milk-white radiance over everything, an ecstatic peace. And insatiable was the sense of wonder that ever drew him on. From the plains he would ascend to the mountains, and find himself in a region of ledges and pointed crags—places all precipice and ravine, where the landscape was vertical. By overhanging paths and by tunnels he visited platforms where painted kiosques were mirrored in wells of stillest water, and frail trees, springing out of aridity, blossomed redly over the featureless dark. What marvels of sudden colour discovered round an angle of grey stone! What silence everywhere! What immobility! Some joyful, incommunicable secret hung in the air.

From this phantasy he was aroused by a sudden movement on the part of his companion. With a little moan she cried out: "I cannot stay in this house any longer! I must go! I must go!"

He gazed down at her for a moment in silence. "Isabel," he said, "there is nowhere to go."

Raising herself upon one elbow, she gave him a long, deep look. "Not for you, perhaps!"

And sombrely he replied: "Nor for you."

Her lips parted, but no sound came, and presently she turned her face away.

His eyes roved round the apartment. The world had grown haggard about them. Of the candles on the walls many had burnt themselves out; the remainder were flickering, guttering, dropping long beards of wax. He sighed, and she echoed his sigh.

Foolish child! he thought. Where did she dream of flying to? Did she not know that the outside world was all of a piece? Whither could one escape but inwards? To escape one must create. The spirit to find satisfaction must go forth over lands of its own imagining. But, alas! in those paradisal lands each spirit was alone!

When he again turned in her direction he found to his surprise that her eyes were fixed half mockingly upon him.

"Are you laughing at me?" he asked.

"Why should I?"

"But you are!"

Faintly smiling, she lowered her lids. "You look so terribly gloomy."

He was silent, at a loss for an answer.

"You have no right to look gloomy!" she went on.

"Haven't I?"

"No!" and she lifted a face, the expression of which was mysterious to him. "Not if you love me!"

He was discountenanced; his visage returned no light.

"Perhaps," he replied, as if the syllables were forced out of him, "perhaps I love no one but myself. Perhaps I do not even love myself!"

Whatever impression these words may have produced, she gave no sign of disconcertment. Indeed, the gleam in her eyes was now discernibly malicious.

"Poor Nick!" said she teasingly. "How you do hate the word love!"

With a laugh the young man strove to make an escape from his embarrassment. "Isabel, darling," he cried with a playfully exaggerated rapturousness, "I swear—as there is a God in heaven—I adore you!"

Her reply to this was a small grimace. Whereupon, to cut the passage short, he jumped to his feet.

"Don't you think it is time we found out . . ."

She shuddered and said nothing, but continued to look at him.

"I wonder," he pursued beneath his breath, "I wonder whether the old man is dead?"

She gave a sigh and, bending her head, began playing with the sash of her dress. Standing before her, he seemed to fall into a muse. The silence was full of unuttered things. His eyes rested heavily upon her, and she knew that he was thinking less of John Mayne than of her.

After a minute he said: "I want you to wait here, whilst I find out how it is."

He was trying to speak unconcernedly. But his inward agitation was not hidden from her. She understood that he was eager to ascertain whether their tarrying in the Big Hall had been discovered, whether the time was still theirs....

"Will you—will you wait for me, Isabel?"

For a few seconds more she held him in suspense; then, lifting eyes that kept her secrets well concealed, she gave a little nod.

Left alone, she sank back upon the cushions and lay still. Her gaze travelled upwards into the golden, smoky radiance of the vaulting, and she smiled. But her smile was different from those which she had given Nicholas. It was touched with an intimate sadness. It was the smile that one gives only to oneself.

In a little while, however, she stirred. Springing to her feet, she ran over to the tall mirror that stood at the further end of the room. There from head to foot she surveyed her girlish figure; and, as she looked, her face was reanimated by the glow of self-confidence and youth. Seemingly the companionship of her outward self was able to do for her what the companionship of the inward could not do. "Who could be prettier than I?" were the words spoken by that delightful image. And, turning about, with glances darted over her shoulder, she gave it the most joyous of replies.

But in a minute, while she was still thus engaged, there came over her the sense that her privacy had been impaired. She had the feeling that she was no longer by herself.

Wheeling round and stiffening into immobility, she sent her gaze round into every corner of the apartment. Was not the heavy curtain still hanging unmoved before the passage-way? Was not her solitude complete? Was not everything just as it had been, before her back was turned?

Ah, no! Her body quivered. A wave of dismay swept over her. Someone was at the window! A man! A stranger! And what was the meaning of his ominous smile?

The face that held her eyes fixed upon it in wide affright was one that she had never seen before, unless in some half-forgotten picture-book or in an evil dream. It was protruding itself at her through the window; its expression was wicked; and—she never doubted it—the face was Cosmo's. Who else would look at her so hatefully? Who else could be so heartless as to importune her in this precious, fateful hour?

Uncanny and abominable haunter! Why had he come back? How had he escaped? And again, why that contemptuous amusement in his eyes?

Well! she would return his mockery. Her unspoken message should be no less eloquent of disdain than his! She was given courage by the certitude that he could not reach her. His head and hunched shoulders were thrust forward over the narrow sill, but further he could hardly press. Slowly, answering stare with stare, she stepped forward. Heroically impudent, she strove to pass off as the effect of inward merriment the tremulousness of her advance.

But Cosmo's smile, if it altered at all, altered only to express an ironic appraisal of her audacity. She was charming, to be sure, quite charming! That air of defiant timidity well became her! How Nicholas would appreciate it on his return!

O fatal wretch! Was it Nicholas he was waiting for? Had he come back to nip their happiness in the bud? Yes, she divined him! He had come to tear and destroy the enchantment by which her lover was bound. She could see how Nicholas would start and blench on beholding him. This hour, that was theirs, would be snatched away from them. Had she not already knowledge of his ascendancy over Nicholas? Alas! his apparition was like a stroke of doom!

What was the secret of his power—of that life-sapping power, beneath which she herself was now impotently writhing? Why did her pride, her spirit, her courage, wilt beneath his smile? Where now was her confidence in her beauty, her hidden faith in love, her belief in her strength to teach the truth of love? What was left of her? what was left to her—beneath that corrupting smile? Passionate protest surged up within her heart; she would, she could, rise to the height of defiance and give him the lie.

But no! Nicholas at any moment might reappear! Intolerable suspense! She must entreat; she must submit; she must confess! She would abase herself before him. Gladly would she avow: "I am no more than you count me! Love is no more than you count it! Only go! Go, and leave me some little value in my lover's eyes!"

But with the curl of his lips Cosmo was already answering her: "If love be such a petty thing as that, why should I spare it? My claim is greater, my purpose is deeper, than yours."

And in response to this, although she had no words to utter, there welled up in her bosom a flood of inchoate supplication. Her hands were clasped, her mouth had opened; but ere any sound could come forth, something had happened, something had taken place the nature of which was at first incomprehensible to her. The aspect of Cosmo's face had changed. Its hard-set, steely surface had been flawed as by a wind. His eyes, whilst remaining fixed, no longer saw her. He was listening—yes, and hearing some sound that had not, as yet, reached her ears. He twisted to look behind him; his eyeballs rolled like those of a creature trapped. There was a stir and a rustle among the dark bushes in the rear. The head and shoulders of another figure became visible at his back. Then she saw Cosmo grasped by strong hands. She rushed up to within a few feet of the window. "Take him, take him!" was the prayer that issued sobbingly from her lips. For an instant Allen's face came forward into the candle light; she saw a resolute mouth and deeply-knit brows; she discerned in that countenance a purpose that answered to the desire of her heart.

Then for a space there was confusion in her senses. But the perception of a struggle came to her; she saw straining arms and heard panting breath. During these seconds her principal concern was lest Cosmo should shriek aloud. Obeying a sudden inspiration, she tore off her sash and held it out. Allen rapidly snatched it; and the next instant, formed into a noose, it had fallen around Cosmo's neck. In another minute the window was empty.

A little later, when Nicholas reappeared, she was standing once more in the neighbourhood of the mirror. In silence she followed him with her eyes, as he advanced across the room. The tranquility of his demeanour reassured her. She could see that he was wholly occupied with the tidings that he brought. His unsuspiciousness affected her with a kind of hysterical amusement.

Irresistibly her gaze vibrated between his figure and the still open window. Each step of his was bringing him nearer to that sinister spot. This so engrossed her that she could hardly apprehend what he was saying; but she gathered that although John Mayne's seizure had been critical, it had not ended fatally. The old man was now well out of danger; Lilian had not been roused; quiet once more reigned over the entire house.

She noticed that he kept his eyes darkly fixed upon her, whilst speaking. Did he observe something singular in her appearance? The mirror, to which she had resorted for assurance on this score, had shown her nothing strange—no change, save the loss of a sash! Was it likely that Nicholas would notice such a trifle as that? No, no! His gaze had a significance of another order; and the woman in her knew what it was.

Yet, as she stood before him, tense, quivering, and alert, she conceived, against all reason, that he was hovering on the brink of discovery. She could not trust her voice to reply to him, and he, on his side, disconcerted by her muteness, turned his eyes away. Wandering, his regard came round to the window; whereupon, giving a shiver, he stepped towards the casement with the evident intention of closing it.

A small cry broke from Isabel.

He wheeled round in astonishment. "Why! What is the matter?"

"Nothing! Nothing!"

Perplexed, he came towards her. She backed away from him, shaking with a painful and unnatural merriment.

"But what is it?" he persisted, in accents now tinged with alarm.

"Nothing!" she gasped. "Only—while you were away—I was frightened."

"By what?"

"At being alone—that's all."

He continued to stare; but, as she seemed to be laughing, turned once more, with a frown of non comprehension, towards the open window.

"It is cold," said he. "Do you mind——"

"No, no!" she cried. "Shut it! Shut it—for pity's sake!"

With immeasurable relief she watched the casement swing to, and heard it fasten with a click. "Draw the curtain," she begged, and he complied.

Deeply, tremulously, she drew in her breath. The shutting out of the cruel, fantastic night brought back her courage. The Big Hall fell once more into the focus of her normal vision. Its familiar character was restored, and simultaneously came the restoration of her familiar self. Now, indeed, it seemed to her that she could deny to what had gone before, the validity of reality. All was the same as before! No change, no loss—save the loss of a sash!

Rejoicingly she entered into possession of her own life again. Nicholas was there; and as much hers as ever he had been. She was happy. She was reckless. She awaited his approach.

"Come, Isabel!" And his voice was husky and low. "Come! It is late."

Thus speaking, he lit a candle for their passage through the darkened house. In the high spaces of the hall, above their heads, the gloom had been rapidly thickening. The few remaining candles were failing and guttering out; long, greasy smoke-ribbons hung in the air.

But she dallied. She drank the homage of his constraint. Brilliant were her eyes, as she stood maliciously away from him.

"Come, Isabel!" he entreated.

And then, gaily, she went.

Was it innocence or effrontery that shone out of her? Of a truth, who can tell!

Slipping past him, she sped down the passage. She reached the foot of the stairs, and up them nimbly she darted. But at the corner, where the corridor branched aside to her room, she stopped and looked behind her. Finger on lip, she cautioned him to tread softly. Pale, he followed her.

Part Three

Chapter 1

A fortnight had passed since the foregoing occurrences, when, on a dull November forenoon, Allen mounted the steps of the Museum at Tornel and betook himself to his private room at the back of the building. After dropping with a sigh into his desk-chair, he looked reflectively about him. Yes, it was actually three months since he had given thought to his work. A long interruption!

Yet he was without the sense of having wandered far. When he had abandoned his routine, he had abandoned little else. The garments of mind which he had stepped into were neither strange nor new; they were the vesture that he had folded up eight years ago, at the epoch when the Orissers had withdrawn out of his life.

Egypt and the Orissers were still, in his imagination, intimately connected. In was in Egypt, to be sure, and under the influence of Sir Charles that his adolescent energies had taken their determinative bent. And, later, his sentiment for Lilian Orisser had given a romantic furtherance to the association. It even pleased him to trace in the cast of Lilian's features a similarity to the features of a certain princess in antiquity. For years he had gathered from an effigy in the Museum aspects of the living woman's charm; just as in older days her face had put him in mind of beauty immortalised by an artist, who must have been his own ancestor in the spirit.

Fancies such as these had kept her image vital in his memory, even whilst his common sense was urging him to forget her. Cosmo's appearance upon the scene had been more than enough to cause all his old recollections to wax brighter; and then, with the prospect of renewed relations with her, they waxed brighter still, but were also curiously changed. Quite suddenly he brought into activity faculties which he had not till then had any incentive to exercise. Lilian was transformed from a princess in an antique remoteness to a woman of the modern world, a woman of flesh and blood, whose accessibility was a challenge. His sense of opportunity was in especial aroused by the news that John Mayne was ailing. What hold had John Mayne ever taken upon her affections—or how much longer was he to remain upon earth—to stand in any man's way? Eight years ago, when John Mayne and he had confronted one another as rivals, the spectre of Sir Charles had pointed sardonically to the man of wealth. But now it was different. And unless she had frozen her heart by dint of hugging to it the cold phantom of an old-time love, there was a chance for a new suitor.

Much did he ponder over Sir Charles's early influence upon her character. Without doubt she had loved her first husband very deeply. But that love had been the sentiment of a girl for a man who much outdistanced her in years and in intellect. Important regions of his nature had been hidden from her whilst he was alive, and in his death he had presented an appalling enigma. His suicide had left trenchant alternatives. She must either repudiate him as a heartless egoist, or, valiantly ignoring her own hurt, range herself with him, in defiance of the world, whose condemnation he had earned. It was quite plain what course she had chosen. After her flight to Eamor, she had taken Charles Orisser and John Mayne as type and anti-type of everything she cherished in life. Short and infrequent as Allen's visits to Eamor had been, they had afforded him clear indication of this, and revealed the main features of the cult to which, in her retirement, she had vowed herself. All that was left to her of Sir Charles was Eamor and Nicholas. And Nicholas at that time was no more than a child. The potent and continuous influence upon her disposition was that which emanated from Eamor. The antiquity of those grey walls and the repose which they contained, the seclusion of those close-cropped lawns hemmed in by beech and oak, the spaciousness and silence within doors and without,—how easy it was to identify the spirit which they exhaled with the spirit of him she had lost! How tempting to accept the suggestions breathed out by the Genius of the Place as the promptings of the dead!

The greater its sensitiveness to locality the more amenable is the mind to the sausions of a visual self-consciousness. There is a satisfaction in making the natural and human elements in any scene coalesce in the expression—as perfect as may be—of a single appropriate sentiment. At Eamor Lilian was placed in a setting powerfully fitted to concentrate her attention upon those arts—and upon those alone—which go to make the passage through life resemble the performance of an elegant ritual. Living as a recluse in such surroundings, she had found little inducement to attend to any but the pictorial aspects of existence. In her recoil from the mentality of modern barbarism, as exemplified by John Mayne, she had been ready to stiffen herself in whatever attitude of counter-assertion came most easily. John Mayne had given token not merely of deficiency in the qualities she valued, but of a hostility towards those values themselves. At Eamor she could retaliate by offering him a spectacle, which, while doing honour to the memory of the man she loved, reflected injuriously upon the tastes, the codes, the whole way of life, distinctive of his odious successor. Thus had she slipped imperceptibly under the sway of appearances, forcing herself to rest content with the construction of a particular effect. In spite of the emptiness and sterility of such a dedication, she sought, while life flowed past her, to imprison her ideals in the unchanging determination that within a world proceeding unconcernedly from ugliness to ugliness, here at any rate, in the domain of the Orissers, there should be something of beauty achieved.

Then, too, Nicholas was at her side to give a more human colouring to her scheme. Her stagnating existence, viewed in conjunction with his future, might be seen in a redemptive and sacrificial light. She drew strength to endure the arrest of her own life-movement from the idea that she was not only handing on a tradition, but purchasing the conditions necessary for its continuance.

With a new insight, born of his new sense of opportunity, Allen apprehended that this idea might prove an enduring barrier to her freedom. And yet . . . and yet was it conceivable that one so young still and so lovely—a woman with the memory of romantic episodes behind her—should resign herself to an existence empty of love? Deeply had he revolved this question in the car that bore him and Cosmo towards Eamor, on the day following the latter's rescue from the muddy Tornel river. His imagination had run forward from one fantasy to another, in all of which he attained at last to the fulfilment of his hopes. Destiny, he told himself, was in an indulgent mood. Whatever might be the outcome of recent events, a chance was being offered. . . After the drive to Eamor village and the installation of Cosmo in the little lonely cottage, he had set forth on his walk through the moon-dappled woods up to the house. In that hour his heart was keyed up to the highest pitch of anticipation. The scene was laid in circumstances of pure romance! Wonderful was the moment, when, emerging into the open, he descried the silver-grey facade shining out against a dark, night sky. For a space he halted there, while his spirit sailed forth in a rapturous flight. The mist, lying in streaks over the parkland; the massive blackness of the scattered trees; the abysses of shadow slanting out across the turf;—this scene, enveloped in the warm, windless silence of the summer air, breathed out a magic which not merely corroborated, but engulfed, the diminutive exaltation of the mortal heart. Awe-struck, he lost all consciousness of self, except as an initiate into mysteries. In his advance towards the lightless, gleaming house, he inhaled a legendary air. And when the figure of Lilian outlined itself before his eyes, her apparition was no more than he had expected. Of course, she was there!—waiting—waiting beneath the same bewitching moon, and under an enchantment not dissimilar to his. She, too, had recognised the hand of Fate. She, too, felt that these hours held her destiny.

Chapter 2

That night remained marvellous in his memory for ever after. It held the gift of an emotional experience which time could not depreciate; although in some of his later moods he made it the subject of reflections that were amusedly ironic. Who dared affirm that the great god Pan was dead? Who but Pan could have provided the inspiration of those hours? Who else could have been responsible for the perfect appointment of the *décor*? Unquestionably the most effective protection to social propriety was that given by the simple laws of chance. Those puritanical laws provide that impulse and favouring circumstance shall very seldom meet. Has any of us aught else to thank for escape from a number of terrible imprudences? And again, what are imprudences after all? What, but the pleasures and excitements that stand waiting beyond—and so often only just beyond—the frontiers of a caution that fluctuates hour by hour? And what is that caution's veritable worth? Prudence, caution, cautiousness, pusillanimity!—the different flavours of these words illustrate the uncertainty of our opinion. May it not be that human attributes, when abstracted from particular personalities, lack any determinable value? Does not the tone and colour of any portion of a picture derive its value from its relation to the whole? May we not compare a quality, or its expression in conduct, with a given tint, which will be pleasing upon one canvas but displeasing upon the next? If this be so, it follows that a proper understanding of any character will depend upon a fine, critical sense of what is becoming in that particular character. The critic must bring a delicate sensibility into play; and the severest test of this sensibility will arise, when his subject presents him with a novel, and perhaps a startling, manifestation.

Allen had not expected, but fortunately was not incapable of understanding aright, the liberty of action that Lilian extended to herself on that night. Her mind, as he justly conceived, had reversed—suddenly, but not arbitrarily—its judgment upon the sterile policy of so many self-denying years. The change had been no light caprice. The accumulated testimony of those years had already been carefully examined; she had balanced incentive against incentive, scruple against scruple; and the long unacknowledged conclusion which had at last imposed itself, was that self-respect enjoined rather than forbade the casting off of restraint. In an instant of time she confessed to herself that she could not honour as self-control or fastidiousness the inhibitions which sought to hold her back. And this, while recognising that, although she was not indifferent to Allen, she did not actually love him. No; she could not plead that passion was sweeping her off her feet. But, if not passion, neither was it anything she needed to explain or excuse. She had acted under the stress of an emotion that required no justification; she had acted with her nature's deepest sanction.

Yet it was true that after Allen had gone, a reflux of disestablished ideas clamorously assailed her. And in the ensuing days moments came, when her whole being was drawn up to a sudden standstill, aghast at what she had done. Although she knew those regrets to be simply the angry voices of outraged habit, she could neither smile, nor shrug, nor turn a deaf ear to them. So it often happened that she would become angry, and grow angrier still at being so. Allen was destined to become unhappily acquainted with these backward eddies of feeling. Uncertain as yet whether he was interpreting her surrender aright, she lost few opportunities of belittling the significance which a male fatuity might attach to it. She was ingenious to demonstrate that in spite of everything, she had known how to keep back her heart. At their subsequent meetings, which were in the rose-garden, her manner towards him was apt to be cold, satirical, and even bitter. What had passed between them she ignored, or, worse, her distant allusions to it would be made with an affectation of carelessness. And while Allen was not so dull as entirely to misinterpret this demeanour, he suffered from it little the less. He even wondered occasionally whether she had taken a dislike to him. His good fortune had fallen upon him with a suddenness and fulness that made it seem precarious and unreal. It still lacked important elements of the happiness he had dreamed.

All this, however, he was tactful to dissimulate; and it was well, perhaps, that their brief, clandestine meetings were packed with so much matter demanding impersonal discussion. The heavy problem of Cosmo was always there before them—a problem which John Mayne's arrival in the house made doubly urgent.

A stone's throw from the rose-garden, and within view of Lilian's bedroom window, there was an oriental summer-house, which was unfrequented and had fallen into disrepair. One of its shutters, the catch of which was broken, was wont to stand open or shut according to the direction of the wind. It was easy to arrange that when this shutter stood open, a meeting was in request; and the hour of the rendezvous would be pencilled lightly on the rough wood of the frame. At first it was always Allen who made the demand. But the comfort which Lilian derived from seeing him gradually wore down her pride. Her mind came to dwell more and more reposefully upon the consciousness of his devotion. His love irradiated her existence. It was an inward hearth at which she could warm her heart, when it was aching from the cold of her life at Eamor. Then, too, Allen's very discretion finished by stimulating her desire for emotional excitement. The presence of John Mayne in the house acted as an incentive rather than as a deterrent. Allen, who would have perished sooner than be the cause of her undoing, was resigned to every abstinence, every sacrifice. But she, on her side, presently developed a love of risk for risk's sake. She it was who furnished him with a pretext for another meeting in the house at night. And, on this occasion, as well as on later ones, she was gay, passionate, at moments almost tender. She enthralled and tormented him. Yet she would not confess to love; nor could he be sure, even now, that she was completely won.

Chapter 3

Such was the strain which these conditions imposed, that, when he removed himself with Cosmo to Tornel, the pain of the separation was mitigated by a considerable relief. Yet he hated to withdraw from her the solace of his companionship in this period of bitter trial. Indeed, the sacrifices to expediency to which he and she were constrained, moved him at times to fury. But how could he ask her to abandon the goal which she had kept before her for so many years? If only out of consideration for Nicholas, a renunciation of Eamor was out of the question.

His relations with Nicholas during this period were by no means easy. At first he was strongly inclined to take the young man completely into his confidence—at least so far as Cosmo was concerned. He had not found it difficult to make a full confession to Lilian. The whole history of the comfortless days he had spent with Cosmo at Tornel, had been detailed to her. He had even—when dealing with the final episode—gone as far as to expose his secret intentions at the critical moment—intentions that could not have been proved against him—not even by Cosmo himself. His words had been as follows: "After Cosmo struck me, I decided that he should at all costs be brought to book. And it was with this furious determination—but without any definite plan—that I set out in his footsteps and followed him to the edge of the river which was some five hundred yards away. There I again parleyed with him, but to no purpose. In fact I only aggravated his insane rage. And in the end—probably with the idea of scaring me off—he levelled his revolver at me and pulled the trigger. I think he intended the bullet to whistle just over my head. But when he pulled the trigger, there was just a click—nothing more! Well! when I heard that click, I determined to take my chance. I rushed in, and coming to grips with him, contrived to fling myself and him off the bank into the river. This fall of ours might have been an accident. Cosmo can never be sure that it was not. But I will confess to you that it was no accident, and that my intention was to drown Cosmo. I felt justified. I saw no other solution of the difficulty. And that solution seemed to be a safe one, as it would afford excellent opportunities for representing that he had committed suicide, and that my part had been that of a gallant, but unsuccessful, rescuer. Unfortunately, however, the arrival of genuine rescuers upon the spot gave the affair a different finish. Then Nicholas intervened. And—well, you know the rest!"

Lilian had received this statement with remarkable composure. But when he had proposed to make an equally frank disclosure to Nicholas, she had objected. Whether or no he should have overruled her objections remained a moot point; but certain it was that the circumstances rapidly became less favourable. A sympathy had speedily developed between the two half-brothers, and concurrently a coldness between Nicholas and himself. Although he was strongly tempted to combat Cosmo's influence, prudence bade him stand aside. Self-effacement was the wisest policy, for it was essential that he should keep his hands free.

When, however, the moment for Cosmo's removal came, the position had become so strained and the future looked so black, that he felt he could not leave Eamor without coming to some sort of terms with the young man. The conversation which he forced upon Nicholas in the wood was the outcome of this decision. It passed off about as well as he expected, but not nearly so well as he hoped. It left him deeply regretful that he had allowed Cosmo such a free field for the exercise of his peculiar powers, whilst he himself had remained in silence and in shadow. These regrets were accentuated by a sentiment of affection for Nicholas. He would have liked to occupy Cosmo's place in the youth's imagination. He would have liked to substitute his own philosophy of life for Cosmo's perverse and blighting ideology. Whether he would have succeeded was another matter; for between the half brothers there was, without question, a temperamental affinity. But, after all, Nicholas was only nineteen—a mere child! What had happened was a pity!

So, for Nicholas's sake, as well as on other considerations, he was glad to be able to take Cosmo away. At Tornel, however, as the weeks went dragging by, he was brought to realise how little he had gained by the change. The path to the goal which he and Lilian had in view seemed to grow stonier and more perilous as they went on.

The alterations in Cosmo's physical state—the bouts of racking pain, the long periods of apathy or stupor, the short hours of comparative well-being,—these changes followed no discoverable law and appeared to have no term set to them. If the sufferer did not himself make an end to his miseries, it was mainly, Allen reckoned, because his spirit rebelled against the tameness of such a conclusion. A comfortable suicide, of set intent, was not consonant with anything in the man's nature. It was conjecturable, moreover, that he was supported by the demon of a cruel perversity, who bade him extend his ordeal in order to extend the ordeal of others. But the point which Allen's imagination failed sufficiently to impress upon him was that Cosmo might also be planning to utilize a temporary recrudescence of strength in some desperate escapade, which should furnish a fitting climax to his career.

The business of watching over him was intolerably harassing. His guardian lived in the daily hope that he would die, or grow certifiably insane, or become able and willing to set out, by himself, for foreign parts. In the meantime there was nothing for it but to watch and endure. After a few weeks, however, the position became so difficult that he probably would have thrown up his task, but for Lilian's reiterated assurances that John Mayne could not last much longer. Nevertheless he judged it only fair to give her warning of the small extent to which he could be held accountable for his charge. Not only were minor pranks, such as the despatch of undesirable postcards, difficult to keep out of Cosmo's reach, but the avoidance of some serious disaster depended ultimately upon the man's physical capacities, upon the amount of energy and cunning that he might be able to put to the service of his sardonic humour.

Sardonic was positively the word. Yes, for Cosmo's savagest intentions were coloured by a kind of grim playfulness. Rancour and desperation were there; but they had ceased to take themselves seriously. Idealism was there too; but it had become nihilistic. It was a temper perhaps not altogether rare, but one certainly about which the general world was likely to remain for ever uninformed. Society, Allen reflected, is better pleased to suppress than to understand any disposition which is not common to all its members. That man must be wicked or mad who does not feel like the common herd. No instinct is truly commendable or sane which is not directed to the solid material benefit of the individual himself or of his community.

Allen abstained from arguing with Cosmo, but was always ready to listen to him; and so obtained strange glimpses into the mystery of human impulse and desire. Had it been necessary to persuade him that the social ideals of a utilitarian age were totally inadequate to satisfy the unconscious energies of mankind, Cosmo's feverish soliloquies would have sufficed.

Thus did the weeks pass by, and with the abatement of the autumn heat Cosmo's health began to gain a somewhat greater stability. Then, too, it became evident that he was resolved to bring about some change in his conditions. One day, after a long and intimate colloquy, in which he displayed a greater reasonableness than ever before, a solemn pact was concluded. Allen was able to write to Lilian: "*At last he has actually signified his readiness to leave the country—and without me!*" But he had to add that one condition had been laid down; and he was uncomfortably aware that that condition, though seemingly unimportant, had a decidedly fanciful character. Cosmo insisted upon it that he should visit the home of his fathers once again, and be granted a farewell interview with Lilian. He hinted that what he had to say to her bore reference to passages which had occurred between them in Spain—that misconceptions had there arisen, which he had it on his mind to clear up.

Although very impatient, and not a little suspicious, of these representations, Allen finally promised to do his best to obtain Lilian's consent. He did not give his promise, however, until he had endeavoured to evade the concessions by every means at his disposal, and at the cost of throwing his companion into a dangerous fury. The utmost he could accomplish was to arrange that the meeting should take place in the rose-garden instead of at the house, that he himself should be present, and that Cosmo should return to Tornel the moment the interview was over.

All this he explained to Lilian with great fulness; and then applied himself to overcoming the objections he well knew she would raise. "I admit," he wrote, "that Cosmo may be half hoping that the occasion will offer an opportunity for some mischievous stroke; but this at least is certain, he will not attempt to trick me again without full knowledge of what the consequences are likely to be. Moreover, I am convinced that there is no alternative to treating him as if we were assured of his good faith. Should we refuse him at this juncture, he would, I truly believe, embark on a course bound to end in a general catastrophe. He would endeavour—and I could scarcely prevent him—to publish his identity and raise a scandal. Although he is ignorant of the actual position of affairs at Eamor, he realizes that he might greatly embarrass us merely by making his identity known. We cannot rely for ever upon his hatred and mistrust of the machinery of civilization, to deter him from resorting to publicity. Pride, suspiciousness, and an ingrained sense of his own outlawry, have hitherto prompted him to pursue his own peculiar ends in his own peculiar fashion; but we cannot count upon his continuing to reject the most obvious means of causing us annoyance. He has threatened more than once of late to raise a public clamour—to bring accusations against me—and even against you—which would provide a fine sensation for the daily Press. As I have told you already, I suspect him of having divined the nature of the tie which binds us. So in more ways than one he could contrive, if once he set about it, to make our position extremely unpleasant. I have kept him in bounds until now largely by playing upon his morbid aversion from civilization,—its spirit as well as its forms. I have met his threats with bluff. I have told him that if he gives trouble, we shall find no difficulty in getting him imprisoned in a lunatic asylum. I have represented you as firmly entrenched behind the ramparts of the law, secure in the favour of the powers that be, invulnerable by slander, and well able to turn his weapons against him. But in spite of this, I say, he is now ready to put the matter to the proof.

"I do not profess to understand why he so violently insists on seeing you, or what he can have to say. Perhaps you are better able to guess than I. In any case, a man in his condition is liable to whims that others cannot comprehend. To sum up, I do not see what harm can come from the interview under the conditions arranged; and I cannot answer for what may happen, if we refuse him."

Lilian's reply was disappointing to Allen. He knew how extreme her antipathy for Cosmo was, but it seemed to him that the circumstances pointed overwhelmingly to compliance. Yet she resisted. She protested that she could conceive no better than he why Cosmo sought the interview, and that she could not imagine how any good could come of it. She therefore begged Allen to essay once again whether he could not persuade Cosmo to remit his demands.

Allen acted accordingly; but the other remained obdurate. And at last, after a further exchange of letters, she yielded.

Her deep reluctance to meet Cosmo impressed Allen afresh with the singularity of the feelings that, existed between the two. It was beyond his power to imagine what species of memory that could be, which retained its vitality after so long a lapse of time. Baffled and even slightly irritated, he assured himself that the secret, whatever its nature, could hardly be of an importance proportionate to the emotions attached to it. Not until later did he obtain the whole story from Lilian's own lips. But, as it assists to an understanding of Cosmo's behaviour in the rose-garden, the narration of it cannot properly be deferred.

Chapter 4

In the innocence of her eighteen years Lilian Orisser had conceived a romantic passion for Cosmo almost as soon as she set eyes upon him. His reputation had prepared the ground; his apparition before her on the Castilian plain struck her dramatic sense; and, finally, the propinquity into which they were thrown as fellow-travellers—a propinquity of which Cosmo, to her pique, took no advantage—achieved her infatuation. She was provoked into making hidden advances; and the day came when the other suddenly responded to them. He responded, indeed, with a suddenness and violence that gave her alarm. A tempestuous scene took place, at the climax of which she felt herself obliged to give Cosmo a definite repulse. Wounded in his pride, he thenceforward held himself sulkily aloof. But in point of fact his feelings were now involved at least as deeply as hers.

Such was the position when the party reached Tangiers, and the end of their associated wanderings was in sight. In the meantime, however, Lilian had been asking herself whether in repelling Cosmo she had not made an exhibition of timid, schoolgirlish prudery. No doubt an unconfessed ambition to regenerate the reprobate went for something in the shaping of her regrets. And it must be believed that Cosmo did really lie under the influence of a sentiment more idealistic than he cared to recognize. But while he, on his side, remained stubborn in his *morgue,* Lilian's pride urged her to demonstrate by some striking action how little trammelled she was by ordinary conventionalities. Cosmo, she vowed, should not be left the comfort of a small opinion of her.

She found her opportunity at the Moroccan Villa. The building was encircled by a verandah, to which the principal bedrooms had access through wide glass doors. Some time after the company had retired for the night, the girl went along the verandah to Cosmo's room, in which she saw a light still burning. She had designed to startle him by her appearance, to mock his sullen temper, and to show by her nonchalant demeanour how little she recked of him, or of the conventions, or of their near parting. But what if Cosmo should lay aside his ill-humour?

Ah well! in that case, perhaps, the parting need not be for ever.

The doors to Cosmo's room were closed, and a light curtain drawn over the glass, while admitting the passage of light, precluded the viewing of the interior. For a few moments she hesitated, then pressed against the glass to see whether the doors had only swung to or were actually latched. The pressure she exerted seemed at first to show that the fastening was up, but all at once something gave way, and the two heavy sheets of glass swung back, carrying the light fabric of the curtain with them.

For some instants, while she lacked the power to take herself away, a full view of the interior of the room was presented. Then she turned and fled. In a few seconds she was back in her own apartment, all entrances to which she at once locked; then she turned out the light and scrambled into bed. Her heart was beating with oppressive force, her limbs trembled, and upon her eyeballs there seemed to be stamped a permanent image of the scene she had just witnessed.

The subsequent events of that night—the Count's outcry when attacked, the confusion and general alarm which followed the discovery of his wounded condition;—these happenings had no power further to disturb her. Nor was she interested in the interpretation of them. Her sole desire was to forget. She was thankful to leave the Villa at an early hour the next day and to put Morocco behind her for ever. She made no confession to anyone of her part in the night's occurrences, and by making a tremendous effort of will, she almost succeeded in driving the whole matter out of her conscious mind.

With the assistance of these particulars—when, ultimately, he got them—Allen found little difficulty in putting together an explanation of Cosmo's murderous behaviour. He conceived that there had always been two antagonistic sets of elements in the man's composition, and that the new and wholesome attraction under which he had fallen tended to bring about a redistribution of the forces warring within. A chance had momentarily arisen that Cosmo's idealism might, by a sudden change, describable as a reform, have placed itself at the head of the impulses which he had hitherto kept in subjection. Without doubt his sentiment for Lilian was linked up with aspirations towards a general spiritual rebirth. And he must have been at once enamoured and distrustful of the new existence which his imagination painted for him. When the girl repulsed him, his pride was no doubt deeply wounded; but, until the final catastrophe, his fate was probably hanging in the balance. One must believe, indeed, that his hopes of establishing his life on a new basis were not dead even on that fatal evening. How otherwise could one account for his sudden violence? But if it be granted that he was still more or less under the spell of Lilian's charm, the extreme of shame and rage becomes intelligible. In one instant of time the unfortunate man saw the whole edifice of his dreams go crashing into the abyss. What an inrush of disappointment and humiliation! Lilian, his father, his whole future—all were irretrievably lost!—lost through an accident! Thus had ironic Fate decreed that he should remain an outcast for ever.

As for the abrupt change which transformed Cosmo from a homicidal lunatic into a devoted nurse—that second revulsion of feeling was explicable on the same line of conjecture. At the sight of his victim's blood his fury had faded almost as quickly as it had flamed up. Standing over the Count's unconscious body, he doubtless asked himself: "For what, or for whom, have I done this to the man whom I but lately held to be my friend? Which of my two selves is the true one—the self he knows, the self which has represented me in all my actual life, or that projected, unrealized self, of which I have vainly dreamed? Is it to the Cosmo of my imagination, the insipid regenerate, that my allegiance is really due? Have I not rather been duped, enticed into treachery to the veritable genius within me? Have I not been lured by the Woman into attempting a pact with Mammon, with Ease, with all the powers of Cowardice and Self-deceit?"

Such was Allen's subsequent understanding of the case; and if much pondering could avail to extract the truth, his interpretation was a true one. Lilian's narrative interested him as much for the light it threw upon her character as for the elucidation of Cosmo's. Not only her peculiar dread of Cosmo, but certain other idiosyncrasies, became intelligible. And although he was far from depreciating the depth and beauty of the sentiment which had bound her to Charles Orisser, he was inclined to suspect that the grounds for that sentiment had been prepared, and the sentiment itself fostered, by a number of obscure emotions and counter-emotions which had their origin in her experience at Tangiers.

Much did he afterwards regret that his knowledge had not come to him earlier. It would have caused him to think again before forcing upon her the interview to which she looked with such abhorrence.

Chapter 5

The morning appointed for the dreaded meeting was that upon which Lilian had intercepted Nicholas and Isabel upon their way down to the wood. In his last letter Allen had urged that Nicholas should be present for part of the time; not because Cosmo had expressed any such wish, but because he considered it desirable that the occasion, in so far as it was to be reckoned a leave-taking, should be made as conclusive as possible. And Lilian had almost given her word that Nicholas should be there. Only, as often as she screwed herself up to the point of speaking to him about it, her courage suddenly failed her. The conduct of an interview with Cosmo, Allen, and Nicholas, all together, was more than she had the heart to undertake. Her last attempt to fulfil her promise had yielded to the excuse which Nicholas's attitude in regard to Cosmo had afforded.

After Isabel and her companion had gone on their way, she seated herself on the bench under the mulberry tree, and allowed her mind to go off on a long train of dreamy speculation. The breeze was rustling in the adjoining wood; a little spring that welled out of a bank on one side of the enclosure emitted a constant murmur. Although her thoughts were absent, her senses were sharply on the alert. There were two narrow openings in the high wall of yew surrounding her retreat; the one gave passage on to the lawn that sloped up to the house; the other—and it was to this that her gaze perpetually reverted—led into a forest path which came out upon the lane down to Eamor village.

She could not have said how long she had to wait; but after a while her cars caught the sound of footsteps advancing along the track through the trees. A minute later Cosmo, closely followed by Allen, appeared under the arch of yew. A narrow grass alley ran between the rose-plots to the place where she was sitting. She heard Allen say "There she is!" and at the same instant she advanced to the encounter.

As he, on his side, came forward, Cosmo kept his eyes levelled boldly at hers. There was a challenge in his looks. His manner seemed to her to be marked by a savage, yet uncertain, bravado.

"Well, Lilian!" cried he. "So we meet again at last!"

"Yes, Cosmo, at last!" And she took his extended hand.

His gaze was still fixed insistently upon her. "My God!" he ejaculated with a bitter laugh. "How little you have changed!"

"Ah, no, we are both older! And as for me," she added, smiling, "I am certainly twice as wise now as I was then!"

For a space Cosmo said nothing. Then: "I not!" he returned sombrely. And she saw that his countenance had darkened.

Indeed, in the silence that followed his last words she became aware that a dull wrath was mounting within him. And his eyes betrayed the secret of that wrath. While she stood there beneath his lowering scrutiny, the blood was rising slowly to her face, producing a flush that rested with particular attractiveness upon cheeks usually without much colour. In contrast to Cosmo she gave an impression of physical and spiritual well-being that was vivid to the point of cruelty.

"I not!" said Cosmo again; and his tone had the effect of bringing them under a renewed spell of silence.

Allen, from his position behind, was unable to obtain a view of the speaker's face: but the hue of Lilian's cheeks, and the fine, resistant steadfastness of her regard, told him all too clearly the nature of her ordeal. In truth a common intelligence had enveloped them—as irrecusable as the air they breathed. And he could see that a mute avowal of her participation in this special consciousness was being extorted from her. With that ruthlessness which he was wont to use so fatally against himself no less than against others, Cosmo was drawing forth, into cynical prominence, the deep, unhappy verity with which the moment was charged. Little did he reck that his most lamentable victim was himself. It was his will that there should arise before the eyes of all three a vision of his ruin, a panorama of his frustrate life. It was his pleasure to contrast their destiny with his, to make Lilian's beauty say: "This is what you have lost!" and to wring from the silent presence of the man behind, the confession: "That is what I have won!"

At last, and with a perceptible effort, Lilian detached her gaze. "Your journey must have been tiring," she said in a low voice, and invited him by a gesture towards the bench.

"No, I am not tired!" replied Cosmo hoarsely. And he remained where he was.

"I would willingly have visited you in Tornel," Lilian went on, her eyes now fixed upon the ground. "Only Allen told me that you wished to see Eamor once again, before—before you went away."

"Yes. I meant to come."

Obviously afraid of any silence between them, Lilian went hurriedly on: "I chose this spot for our meeting, because my husband is at present staying in the house, and with him several others—strangers to you. Here, at any rate, we are not so likely to be disturbed."

Cosmo made no reply. It seemed to Allen that his vitality had begun to ebb away from him. His head had sunk forward upon his breast; his shoulders sagged; he appeared scarcely able to heed what was said.

Lilian raised her eyes, and a look of compassion came into her face.

"Cosmo," she began softly, "I want you to believe——"

The other cut her short. "When last I saw Eamor," he pronounced with gloomy deliberation, "I was fourteen years old—no more! I made my appearance at the house one day in rags. My father sent me back to France, post-haste. I did him no credit."

Allen touched his companion on the arm. "Do you see that bench under the mulberry tree? We shall be better there."

Cosmo advanced a few paces, then halted again.

"Dear step-mother!" he cried out, all at once, with something like his original manner, "what if I implore you to take in the prodigal son? What if I entreat you to let me spend my last days under my father's roof? Would you have the heart to refuse me?"

Lilian winced, then gathered her composure.

"It shall be as you please, Cosmo!"

The other broke into a short laugh. "I think," said he, "I think you lie! You are far from intending that it shall be as I please."

A silence followed, at the deepest moment of which, putting Cosmo aside, Allen stepped in between the two. A glance at the man's white, twitching face set his heart beating with anxiety. From his pocket he drew forth a brandy-flask, and hastily unscrewed the stopper. Filling the metal cup half full, he thrust it into Cosmo's hand.

"Here!" said he, "take this and drink!" And, as Cosmo, now again gazing upon Lilian, appeared not to hear him: "For God's sake!" he continued in an undertone. "Remember your promise!"

Cosmo drew in a long, deep breath; then slowly dropped his eyes, and bent his face to Allen's. "You pretty pair!" he brought out in a whisper that was like a hiss. "Ah, you pretty pair!"

Allen turned his head away and spoke no word. Unaccountably, and yet most patently, did the truth, and the whole truth, regarding his relations with Lilian lie uncovered. Cosmo straightened himself to emit a dreadful laugh.

"Drink!" cried Allen sternly. "Drink, man, unless you want to collapse!"

Either from emotion or weakness Cosmo was, in fact, tottering. Yet, looking down at the cup that shook in his tremulous grasp, he appeared to hesitate.

"I want water," he muttered; and his gaze went down a little transverse path, at the end of which was a spring. "Not this,—water!"

"Water!" echoed Allen with impatience. "Why water now?"

Cosmo looked before him unseeingly.

"No matter!" said he at last; and in one gulp, as was his wont, he tossed off the contents of the cup.

This time, however, the liquor seemed to choke him. A terrible coughing shook his entire frame. "My God!" he gasped. "Water! Water!" and, thrusting the cup into Allen's hand, clutched at his distorted face.

For one second Allen stood irresolute. Although his mind did not entertain any definite suspicion that Cosmo might be playing him a trick, yet he was reluctant to put between himself and the two others even the few yards that separated him from the spring. But this dim reluctance was effaced by the apparent necessities of the case; and, the next instant, he hurried down the path. As he was stooping to dip the beaker in the water, however, some impulse moved him to take a rapid glance over his shoulder.

The effect of that glance was stunning. There had been no sound, no cry, while his back was turned, to warn him that anything untoward was taking place; yet what was now instantaneously presented to his eyes was the spectacle of Lilian, tightly clasped in Cosmo's arms. Both figurants in this extraordinary scene had their faces turned towards him, and each was gazing at him in a different species of tranced expectation. Lilian's eyes were wide with terror and appeal; Cosmo's were agleam with a triumphant and dangerous alertness.

For a moment there was complete immobility on both sides. Then, while Allen was drawing himself up, Cosmo disengaged one hand, and, with fingers curved like talons, made a gesture illustrative of tearing his victim's eyes out.

Into Allen's mind there flashed the memory of tales of similar mutilation wrought upon their attendants by asylum inmates; and simultaneously he recollected that Cosmo himself was wont to tell the story of how once, when attacked by a jaguar, he had overcome the beast, without weapons, by recourse to the same horrible device. He saw, too, that Lilian's arms were pinned against her sides in a manner that deprived her of any power of self-defence.

Had this remained the exact position of the two, he would scarcely have found the courage to stir. But Cosmo, after eyeing him for a further space with an expression of indescribable malignity, lowered his head, his manifest intention being to kiss his prisoner upon the lips. This gave Allen his chance. Springing forward with amazing swiftness, he was within reach far sooner than the other had deemed possible. Lilian, too, who up to this moment had remained entirely passive, suddenly put forth all her strength. Confused by this concerted action, Cosmo found time only to fling the woman from him and dash away. Allen, seeing that Lilian was unhurt, followed the impulse of his rage and dashed after him.

For the next minute the two men were dodging each other, like schoolboys, round the mulberry-tree and its circular seat. It did not appear possible that Cosmo would postpone his capture for many seconds; but, unluckily, Lilian's gardening scissors had been left lying on the seat beside her basket; and Cosmo had bethought him to snatch this weapon up. So it fell out that just as Allen's hand was closing upon him, he had the means to deliver a vicious blow at his pursuer's head. By good fortune the point of the scissors struck slantingly and did not penetrate the skull. The lunge, however, was a vigorous one; Allen reeled, stumbled, and sank down, half-stunned, upon the edge of the seat. At this evidence of his prowess Cosmo sounded a triumphant yell; then made for a weak spot in the surrounding hedge, forced a passage through it, and disappeared.

Allen's collapse awakened Lilian from the stupefaction in which she had witnessed the foregoing proceedings. Hastening to his side, she caught him in her arms and made a tremulous examination of his hurt. A scalp wound stretched from above the temple to the crown of the head. It was not long before she had washed it with water from the spring, and bandaged it with his handkerchief. Nor did many minutes elapse before Allen came out of his bedazed condition; whereupon, as soon as he could sit up, he besought her to return to the house, leaving him free to go in pursuit of the runaway.

His pale face and hectic manner bespoke him not only physically shaken but burning with anger and self-reproach. Thrusting her almost roughly away, "Go back at once!" he cried. "But no! I had better accompany you. I must make sure *he* is not there! He did not start off in that direction, but he may have doubled back. Quick!"

Instead of obeying, however, she remained seated and looked up into his eyes with a smile that he could not understand. So widely did its tranquillity, its radiance, and its tenderness, remove it from the sphere of his own excitement, that he could not give credence to what it seemed to say. Still frantic, still quivering, he continued to stammer out his adjurations. Did she not understand that these moments were critical? that Cosmo, even now, might be raising dire confusion at Eamor? Did she not realize——?

His voice fell to silence, so quietly, so smilingly, did her eyes answer him. And as, gradually, the import of her looks penetrated, his heart was flooded with light. The flush of a new joy, still tinted with bewilderment, spread over the whole of his mental prospect. Could this really be what he had longed for and missed in their past communions? Was she at last ready——?

"Lilian!" he ejaculated beneath his breath. "Lilian!"

"Yes! Nothing matters now!" Tenderness rayed from her. "Come, sit here again!" And she lifted her arm to make a resting-place for his head.

The half-hour that followed was perhaps the happiest in his life. By an exquisite caprice of temperament his companion was prompted to interfuse her tenderness with a veritable gaiety. All her shackles had in one instant dropped from her. It sufficed that her lover had not taken fatal hurt, that the sunshine and the breeze were playing joyously about them, and that a united life lay ahead. It was this new sense of liberty that gave the finishing touch to their exhilaration; they came to the point of laughing over their recent discomfiture.

Practical counsel, however, had to be taken at last. Upon deeper consideration Allen rejected the idea that Cosmo had, then and there, made his way up to the house. Knowledge of the man's physical condition suggested it as much more probable that his access of frenzy had been immediately followed by a period of complete exhaustion. The likeliest supposition was that he was now lying outstretched upon the bracken in some sunny hollow of the woods, and there sleeping the sleep of the just. But what would he do when he awoke? Without a doubt he intended this escapade to be his last. He would attempt some outrageous feat which should form his climax.

On these assumptions it was to be expected that sooner or later he *would*, make a raid upon Eamor; and it followed that Allen could not do better than to mount guard in the vicinity. Accordingly, at Lilian's suggestion, he established himself in the summer-house nearby, from one window of which a fair view of the general premises was to be obtained. This post, too, had the further advantage that Lilian could signal to it, and thus bring him quickly to her side in case of need. A code of communication was arranged; and, a short while after she left him, a handkerchief, fluttered from her window, informed him that nothing so far had been seen or heard of the enemy.

Chapter 6

Early in the afternoon she came back to him, bringing some food in a garden basket. After making a light meal, he questioned whether he ought not to go out in search of the runaway. But the surrounding woods offered such numerous facilities for concealment, and he was so loath to leave her unprotected, that he gave up the idea.

Almost irresistible, too, was the attraction, which a new-born sense of comradeship gave to their intercourse. Holding her there before his eyes in the quiet and seclusion of their rustic hiding-place, he enjoyed a special sense of remoteness, of intimacy, and even of leisure. The precariousness of their tranquillity only enhanced its charm. Seated in an angle of a bench which ran round three sides of the room, she watched him, whilst he was eating, with that half-smile which was so familiar to him in his memories of her. The sun, striking through the shutters, put thin, bright bars of light upon the wooden floor; and this light was reflected up onto the silver-grey walls, filling the whole of the cool, dusky interior with an even radiance. Her face and hands seemed self-luminous; a thousand delicate shadows nested in the pale fabric of her dress.

"Aren't you going to light a cigarette?" she asked.

He considered. "No, better not. Anyone passing near by would see the smoke drifting out through the shutters. And it would be a surprise to find you sitting here with me."

She gave a soft laugh. "What does it matter? For all we know, Cosmo may be sitting with John Mayne at this moment. Smoke, Allen! I wish it!"

He shook his head.

"Haven't we decided to give up all worry?"

"All worry, yes! But not all precautions. And certainly not all hope!"

She opened her lips to speak, then desisted; and the faint anxiety which had prompted his last words, deepened. Was there, in the depths of her heart, an unavowed disappointment and regret?

"Lilian!"—and he gave her a long look—"I am feeling troubled about you."

Again she laughed softly. "I knew it, and I thought to myself: how silly!"

Never had she appeared to him more attractive than at this moment. Her heart was his; he did not doubt it. But in her mind there was something unconfessed.

While he was still considering his words, she suddenly took up speech.

"Hadn't it occurred to you"—and she looked down and away—"that *I* might be feeling troubled about *you?*"

He made a gesture of impatience.

"I have interrupted your work. I have broken into your life. I have plunged you——"

"My dear, I have heard all this before. Your letters——"

"Yes. But—oh, they were half-hearted!"

"And this is not?" he inquired lightly.

"No—this is not."

He was silent for a minute. "In any case, it's rubbish."

She sighed. "Coming as late as this, it does sound rather rubbish, I admit." Her gaze went out into vacancy. "I suppose I have waited on purpose until it was—too late."

"Yes," returned Allen, "you have!"

"Not altogether."

His brow clouded. "What do you mean?"

She drew a deep breath and bit upon her lip. There was pain in the clear depths of her eyes.

"Do you propose that I should give you up?" he inquired with sarcasm.

"Not quite—no!" and she threw him a brief smile. "But I think we must give Eamor up."

"Oh!" he rejoined quickly. "I don't agree with that."

"Listen!" she went on. "In the rose-garden, a little while ago, I told myself that nothing mattered but—but our being together. I was ready to renounce Eamor then and there. Well! I renounce it now. There is nothing to prevent me from going away with you to-night . . . I must not let Nicholas stand in our way. I must go . . . I *will go*, if you care to take me!"

For a minute, while he stood regarding her in silence, he gave himself up to a deep, inward joy. What beauty, what heavenly beauty, there was in the world! His heart sounded paeans of gladness; but his voice was both husky and harsh, when he said:

"You are pledged to me, in any case—come what may! Is that not so?"

She bent her head. "Yes, that is so."

He was ravished. He could have dropped on his knees before her. In order to retain the remnants of his self-control, he turned himself away.

"Very well!" said he. "The question of Eamor is to be judged separately—on its own merits."

She saw his emotion, and smiled; but with tears upon her lashes. "Yes," she replied, "coldly, critically—on its own merits!"

He collected himself for speech; but, suddenly, an impulse moved her. She leaned forward, and in a low strained voice she said:

"Allen dear, this is the way I look at my position. When I married John Mayne I entered into a bargain with him; and I have not kept my side of the bargain. I have given him nothing. On the contrary, I have caused him a great deal of suffering. That was not entirely my fault perhaps! But there have been times when I could not resist the temptation to give him pain. I have made him bitter. One might say"—and her face took on the semblance of a smile—"one might say that I have 'spoiled his character.' And yet I have been living on his charity all this while! Look at me now! I am still trading upon scruples, which he would certainly not have, if he knew the truth. I am struggling to keep alive in him the feeling that he is morally bound to give up Eamor to me. Yes, that is my aim, even now, when"—and she smiled again—"when I am not even being 'faithful' to him! That is how we stand to one another, he and I!"

A silence followed this speech. Then he gave a short laugh.

"Very well put!" he dryly commented. "I say what each of us knows, and knows that the other knows?"

"I say it because I feel it must be said."

He frowned. "Well, you have said it."

"And now," continued Lilian, "I am going to act on it. I ask you to take me away—to-night—now!" Allen stepped slowly up to her.

"My dear," said he with a deep, smiling tenderness, "I think you are a very wily woman!"

She opened her eyes. "Am I?"

"Yes. But I think I see through you.

She shook her head and sighed. "There is nothing to see—behind what I say."

"Isn't there? Aren't you being a little influenced by a fear of what may come to pass between Cosmo and me?"

She gave him a long look. "Perhaps. But isn't it right that should influence me?"

He laughed. "Quite! But, you see, I refuse to be the cause of your giving up Eamor."

Rising to her feet, she laid her hands upon his shoulders. "Allen——"

"Lilian, you *must not* be afraid. I have already vowed to myself that I will do nothing rash. For your sake, as well as for mine, I am going to be very circumspect—very cautious!"

"Very cautious!" she echoed with a look of anguish. "My poor darling! *That* you always are, aren't you!"

He made a gesture of entreaty. "No—seriously—you must trust me. I cannot let you renounce Eamor simply from the fear that I may make a fool of myself."

"But I want to renounce it," she almost wailed.

He stood away from her and shook his head. "Remember," he objected after a silence, "you have Nicholas to think of!"

She could not restrain a slight wince. Taking off her hat, she flung it on to the bench.

"However poor we may be," she murmured beseechingly, "you will help me to look after Nicholas, won't you?"

"Of course! But"—and his tone had a certain grimness—"Nicholas is not a person who can afford to dispense with any of fortune's favours. In that respect his estimate of himself is correct."

A gleam of resentment came into her eyes. "Nicholas has more spirit than you imagine!"

Allen took a minute to frame his reply. "He has spirit—yes! But it is turned back upon itself. He has no energy to apply to battling with the world, because all his energies are consumed in conflict with himself."

She said nothing to this; but after a moment, with a sigh, returned to her earlier point.

"I owe it to myself, and to John Mayne, and to you, to give up and go away."

Her voice was so low that her words almost failed to reach him. He frowned.

"Do you really *want* to give up Eamor?"

"Yes."

He shook his head. "That's not true."

She was silent.

"What am I to say to you?" he appealed.

She gave him an obstinate look. "I don't know what you can say to me, Allen."

"I can say, for one thing, that you are not speaking the truth!"

"Of course, in a sense, it isn't the truth, But, in another sense, it is."

The shadow of pain and perplexity deepened over her companion's face. She came up to him; put her arms round his neck; and regarded him with a deep, melancholy fondness. After a moment he drew her to the window, and, by raising a section of the shutter, made an opening through which they could look out. There, side by side, they stood, gazing over the lawn at the front of the sunlit house. It was a sunset the magnificence of which put him in mind of many an evening in Egypt.

Memories gathered about him. In particular, a memory of Sir Charles's last summer at Eamor. He felt himself standing once more by the casement in the hall, and listening to the ominous silence of the house behind. Was it possible that Lilian's mind was not flooded with similar recollections?

But he was not disquieted. Time had fulfilled its function. At this hour the shade of Charles Orisser would send her no looks of reproach. No! nothing but a faint, ironic smile of approval and benediction.

Deeply, and more deeply still, did the fading skies dye the prospect before him. Thoughts of John Mayne floated up into his consciousness. He had no actual knowledge of it, but John Mayne, too, was brooding over the past. He had no actual vision of it, but the same light which was colouring the lawn before him and setting the walls and chimneys of the house aflame against the cold, blue profundities of the north— that same light was pouring over the writing-desk in the Big Hall, and glowing upon the red flesh of John Mayne's ponderous hand. And that hand lay upon the pages of a letter, written by Lilian seven years ago.

This, indeed, was outside Allen's ken. Yet his sense of the old man's personality enlarged itself, until at last his whole heart lay under the shadow of that unseen presence. With a clouded face he drew away from his companion and stepped back into the dusk behind. For her part, she remained without movement. Her eyes were still fastened upon the house, and they were the eyes of an exile, who watches his native shores fade away. After a moment of silent observation, he fell to pacing to and fro. He had come to a definite resolve. Not if he could help it, should she make her intended sacrifice.

When next he addressed her, his voice had a different ring.

"Lilian, I have been considering what you said a little while ago about your position in regard to John Mayne." He paused, giving her time to face round. "What I have to reply is this: if you feel the position to be offensive to your pride, then of course we have no choice. No, in that case, we must give up. But"—and here he stepped forward and looked her hard in the face—"but can you honestly tell me that your pride *is* offended? I want the truth, Lilian!"

She knit her brows. For a minute she seemed to be struggling with herself. Then in a dull, flat voice she said:

"No, I don't feel that."

"Ha!—you don't?"

Her eyes had a wondering limpidity. "No. Perhaps it's odd—but I don't. I feel no shame—none at all."

He drew himself up and inhaled a deep breath.

"Splendid!" and he caught at her hand. "Superb! I knew as much!"

She took her hand gently away, and examined her fingers, as if his grasp had hurt them. She stood before him with bowed head.

"You feel no shame!" he repeated exultantly. "And you are right!"

She remained dumb; but he could see her bosom rise and fall.

"You feel no shame!" he said again. "Well! nor do I. It may seem odd,"—and he gave a low laugh—"but my feelings are the same as yours."

Her eyes were still fixed upon the ground. "What then?" she murmured with a catch of the breath.

"My dear," he replied, "you may be ready to give Eamor up, but I am not."

She seemed to tremble. There seemed to be a smile hovering about her mouth. Her fingers were twisting and untwisting.

All at once he grasped her by the arm and drew her, a second time, to the window. "That place is yours!" said he, pointing to the house. "It may be taken from us,—but we will never voluntarily give it up!"

A deeper, mellower radiance was falling from the heavens; a deeper, mellower flush rested upon the darkening landscape. In immobility they looked out before them; and the whiles he stood there, his desire and resolve received their final confirmation. That house, those lawns, those woods, that sky now fusing the whole into one peaceful, breathing entity,—that little island in the world, which Time had encrusted with its own particular memories,—it had a value, a sanctity of its own; it offered an incentive, which he was no longer minded to belittle or deny. In the past he had thought bitterly of Eamor as the cause of too much heart-burning, of too much sacrifice, of too great an expense of spirit. For as long as Lilian had been unready to renounce it, he had fretted against its domination. But at last she had won her freedom. And now he recognised that in common with all the objects of this world that have inspired human effort and absorbed human devotion, Eamor had its own ideal worth. Neither he nor she could ever voluntarily abandon it without inflicting upon themselves a spiritual impoverishment. Should they do so, their looks, in days to come, would steal backwards, and Eamor would glimmer forth out of the dusky past with a reproachful luminescence;—it would glimmer with an after-light derived from the warm sunshine of effort and hope which they themselves had once shed upon it.

The rest of the time they spent together was given over to a survey of their decision. She, though overborne, still resisted. Her companion was forced to expend himself for some while yet in argument and entreaty. "Lilian," said he, "between John Mayne and us there is no spiritual connexion. We come under no common law of mind or of heart. We give allegiance to no common ideal. Were it otherwise, you would not be unashamed. Have confidence in your shamelessness! Seven years ago you deserted John Mayne; you betrayed yourself to him; you exposed yourself to his vengeance. And never once since then have you made an appeal to his affections—nor to his pity! If he resigns Eamor, it will not be out of any regard for you, but out of regard for himself. The matter lies between him and his ideals, which are as private and particular to him as ours are to us."

Whilst Allen thus spoke, she looked at him and wondered. One half of her mind was occupied by musings of her own. She knew she lacked the strength to resist him; for her deepest instincts and desires went to his support. If she was afraid of the risks which lay before them, in her heart she believed that those risks should be affronted. She believed that he was in the right. And she saw that he, too, genuinely believed that he was in the right.

Chapter 7

Towards nightfall he paid a hurried visit to the village both to make inquiries and to give out a discreet account of what had occurred. He learnt that Cosmo had appeared at the inn early in the afternoon, and, after buying a bottle of brandy, had taken himself off again. Half-hearted offers were made to assist in a search; but he discouraged them on the ground that the light was already failing, and that a systematic beating of the woods was less likely to result in the poor lunatic's capture than in driving him farther away from the haunts of his fellow-men. It was to be hoped that some remaining flicker of reason would prompt him to seek shelter from the frosty air of night; for if not, he would be in peril of taking his death from exposure.

Leaving matters in this position, Allen returned; and a little later, under cover of darkness, took up a regular patrol of the grounds about the house.

The subsequent events of that night are in part already known. What remains to be told is that a labourer on his way to work the next morning came upon a man lying stark and stiff in the narrow country lane a mile and a half from the village, and a little less distance from Eamor. The body showed no marks of injury, excepting a bruise at the back of the head, such as might have been caused by a heavy fall upon the road, which at that point was steep and had been made slippery by frost. The villagers quickly recognised the dead man as Richardson; and the doctor who had attended him during his residence at the village confirmed vulgar conjecture by ascribing the death to cerebral hæmorrhage following the contusion caused by a fall. Richardson was lucky, he considered, to have found a manner of death so much easier than many of the others that imminently threatened him. Add to which, diseased as he had been, the man was better dead.

Allen, who had been admitted to the village inn in the early hours of the morning, in a state of exhaustion manifestly caused by his anxieties and exertions on Richardson's account, was naturally one of the first to be given the news. He showed great distress, but no more than was expected, for his devoted care of Richardson earlier in the summer had not escaped remark. It was evident that he took the affair deeply to heart, reproaching himself for having allowed his charge to escape. But his protestations that nothing in Richardson's demeanour, up to the moment of his flight, had given the slightest indication of such intention, won him sympathetic exoneration from all. He explained that the man's mental condition had seemed so much better of late that Mrs. Mayne, whose charitable interest had been engaged, was endeavouring to find him some occupation suited to his restricted capacities; and he added that it was in order that they might all discuss this subject together that Richardson had been brought down to Eamor.

The stir which the occurrence would at ordinary times have created among the village folk was considerably reduced by the almost simultaneous receipt of news of far greater moment. Tidings came from Eamor House that John Mayne's illness had taken an alarming turn and that his life hung in the balance. Here was intelligence to make a commotion not merely at Eamor, but throughout the whole country! The truth touching the great man's condition, hitherto suppressed, now became public. During the next few days local interest was focussed upon the events passing up at the house. The inquest on Richardson, which was held in a barn, not far from the place of the body's discovery, constituted a formality that concerned no one very greatly. Concluded without distinguishing incident, it was barely noticed even in the county Press; whilst every paper, great and small, contained ample, if inaccurate, information regarding the condition of the munificent millionaire.

Late in the day, however, on which Cosmo, under the name of Richardson, was committed to the earth, a train steamed off from Eamor station bearing one person at least in whose thoughts John Mayne occupied a place second to Cosmo's. Allen had been living through some very anxious hours. It was all very well for him to assure himself that his part in the events of that tragic night lay impenetrably concealed from the world's eye. A cold comfort at best is that which reason has to offer to the imagination pricked by uncertain fears. Until the inquest was over he could find no peace. There was a possibility that the doctor's evidence might not be so satisfactory as it seemed likely to be. There was a chance, too, that someone besides himself and Cosmo had been abroad in Eamor Park that night. What if some villager should come forward with a thing or two to say pertinent to the finding of Cosmo's body on that country lane outside the palings of the park? And then, again—but no! Of remote suppositions there was of course no end. It ought to suffice that those suppositions were all so very remote.

The inquest once closed, moreover, and Richardson duly buried, the point around which his worst apprehensions had been congregating, no longer offered itself as a danger centre. An exposure of Cosmo's identity was all that he had henceforward to fear. Gossip, for all he knew, might be busy already. Idle tongues might be wagging in the village, in the servants' hall at Eamor, or even at Tornel. But after all, what could gossip now do? It would be unpleasant no doubt, if the secret of Cosmo's identity were to leak out; but the disclosure, unless exploited by persons of hostility—by the Maynes, for instance—was not likely to have any important practical consequences, nor even to bring under serious censure those whose only delinquency would appear to have been that they had allowed Cosmo to be buried under an assumed name.

No; there was no one but Madeline or Nina who would care to make a scandal of the matter; and, as the object of John Mayne's two nieces would be simply to furnish their uncle with another pretext for repudiating his obligation towards his wife, at the old man's death their main incentive would drop. And John Mayne could not last much longer.

For all this, nevertheless, the tone of Allen's mind, as he travelled back to Tornel, was still that of an invalid. His convalescence, it was true, had begun; in his innermost heart he felt that he was safe; but his nerves were still aching and strained. The knowledge that during the last three days Lilian had been suffering under an anxiety no less cruel than his, afflicted him with bitter pangs of self-reproach. "Would to heaven," he cried within himself, "that I had done earlier what eventually had to be done! How much better it would have been for Cosmo as well as for her and for me! I verily believe that during the whole of the past month Cosmo was looking to me for his death,—sometimes in hope, sometimes in fear, and sometimes—for he discerned my weakness and despised my scruples—in bitter, contemptuous malice. How easily I could have contrived that he should give himself an overdose of some narcotic! Did I stay my hand from conscience or from cowardice? Can it have been cowardice, when the risk was practically nil? Yet I believe that cowardice it was! I could not bring myself to act in cold blood. I was frightened by the word murder. Time and again the mere mental pronunciation of that word was enough to check the sequence of my thoughts, converting what had argued itself a justifiable homicide into a vulgar police court brutality."

Thus did Allen commune with himself; and the mental detachment of which he made play did some thing, perhaps, to restore his spirit. But he was weary, very weary. And after a while the movement of the train lulled him into a profound sleep. Nor did he awake until his journey was ended.

That sleep was what he had required. His mind came back to reality with a fund of fresh confidence. He was no longer tormented by the irrational fear that Lilian had ceased to love him. Their ordeal had drawn them together as nothing else could have done. Cosmo had vanished for good and all. The future was much simplified. A little patience, and all would be well.

The train which carried Allen away from Eamor had Walter also as a passenger. And Allen was not unaware of this. At the little country station he had not been so deeply absorbed in his thoughts as to over-look Walter among the other persons on the platform; and he had noticed, too, that Walter, after scrutinizing him for a moment through the gathering dusk, had quietly withdrawn to the other end of the station.

John Mayne's seizure had been the cause of Walter's hasty recall to Eamor; and in spite of a great pressure of business he had remained there until it became evident that the old man's immediate demise was no longer to be apprehended. He had consequently been at Eamor while the inquiry into the death of Richardson was taking place in the village; and that incident, as was only natural, had come up as a topic in the house. Allusion to it, however, had been cursory; for John Mayne's nieces were occupied with other matters, which ranked quite otherwise in their minds.

A mention of the occurrence, casually thrown out by Madeline at the dinner-table, had, however, sunk deeply into Walter's consciousness; and his glimpse of Allen's figure on the platform caused his thoughts to hark back to it with extreme disquiet. He wished he had not seen Allen, and hoped that Allen was not aware that he had seen him. For the last two months he had considered himself entitled to the serviceable supposition that Allen had actually taken Cosmo abroad. But if the man glimpsed on the platform really was Allen, that supposition must, he supposed, be discarded ...

Then, again, Allen had not been up at the house; or, if he had, his visit must have been more or less clandestine. What in heaven's name had brought Allen into the neighbourhood just at this time when an inquest on a person named Richardson was being held in the village? Richardson? Richardson? Walter felt himself invited—nay, constrained—to enter upon a series of extremely distasteful cogitations. Was it a fact that Richardson was the name under which Cosmo had been known to the world? Had he reason to *know* that it was so? *Must* he know? Was anyone aware that he did know?

Hidden away in a secret chamber of Walter's mind, there had lain, for some time past, certain items of knowledge which he had judiciously consigned to oblivion. Every man alive is, after all, busy ignoring and forgetting so long as life lasts; and there was nothing remarkable in Walter's putting away those particular items of knowledge, excepting perhaps the care and deliberation he had exercised in so doing. The human consciousness is selective. As in our houses we dispose of our possessions according to their usefulness and the promptings of our taste, so in arranging the dwelling-house of consciousness we place some objects in conspicuous positions, and relegate others to dark corners; whilst not a few, because we judge them ugly and useless, we hide away altogether. Further more, persons of delicate moral sensibility are of necessity more ruthless in their rejections than others. They cannot bear to keep in the living-rooms of the mind anything that is not to their liking; and, as life, unfortunately, is an undiscriminating donor, these persons have their lumber-rooms and cellars crammed to bursting. Walter's taste was fastidious; and, living as he did, in the full stress of public life, the busy chambers of his mind would soon have become encumbered with unserviceable and distressing objects, had he not been firm in his rejections.

Like all true idealists, too, Walter was a practical man. Accordingly, the problem now before him did not define itself in the question, "Was the individual found dead outside Eamor Park in truth Cosmo Orisser?" but rather in the question, "Is anyone in a position to show that I have good grounds for conjecturing that that individual was Cosmo Orisser?" A little reflection will suffice to show that, from Walter's standpoint, this was all that mattered. After all, wherein did Cosmo's death, or the manner of his death, concern Walter Standish, save in the degree to which the latter could be proved to have been privy to it? We all are aware that this world is full of evil, but—heaven be praised!—we can generally lay claim to astonishment and indignation, when this or that particle of it receives exposure. And this immunity we owe to our ignorances. Indeed, every man possesses not merely the right, but the duty, to maintain such ignorance in himself as is the pre-requisite of his blamelessness; and the touchstone of blamelessness is public opinion and common law. Never in his life had Walter committed any action of which he could not render honourable account by showing that he had acted according to his lights. Nor was anything more distressing to him, as an honourable man, than to see his lights questioned—to see impugned those proud, simple-minded ignorances which were the very substructure of his honour and self-respect.

It was a wise instinct, then, that had rendered him, from the very first, chary of contact with such a person as Allen, and apprehensive of even so much as the sound of Cosmo's name. It was not consonant with what he knew of himself—and still less with what the world knew of him—that he should be concerned with, or even cognizant of, such persons' affairs. His spiritual compeers were men of a different stamp. Take Henry Portman, for instance! Ah, there was a man of wisdom! How jealously did Henry guard himself against evil communications! Was it possible that the time might come when Henry would turn a cold shoulder upon him?

The journey from Eamor to Tornel provided time enough for Walter to make a very careful survey of his situation. Whilst Allen slumbered, he pondered deeply. But the result in each case was the same. Like Allen, he alighted at the terminus with a mind brought into a state of comparative tranquillity. The answer to the great question, "How much, in any event, can I be proved to have known?" had worked itself out, on the whole, satisfactorily. He had brought himself up before an imaginary tribunal of accusers; he had anticipated their questions and rehearsed his replies; he had sifted all the evidence; and he had found it quite inadequate for a conviction. Indeed, he had come out of a self-applied cross-examination with great dignity; he could leave the court without a stain on his character. As he stepped out of the railway carriage at Tornel he squared his shoulders; he felt he could look even Henry Portman full in the face.

Chapter 8

After his seizure John Mayne's appearances downstairs became short and infrequent, and presently ceased altogether. Little by little a completely invalid existence was forced upon him; and with his growing disabilities the sentiment that Madeline nourished for him developed into a positively gluttonous tenderness. She had always taken pleasure in ministering to old and sick persons, and to young children. She knew how to look up or to look down, but had no capacity for dealing with people on equal terms. It was natural for her to seek out those whose dependent condition enabled her to assert herself over them without expense of effort. She took comfort in the sense that they were not competitors with her in the production of effect. If they flattered her, she was well pleased; if they slighted her, it was easy to put that down to the peevishness of their years or of their infirmities. Great was her happiness, when her uncle, instead of forcefully motioning her aside, as he had been wont to do, was constrained to accept with submission, if not with gratitude, the attentions she thrust upon him. In her solicitude she swathed him; and if he sometimes looked up at her out of his swaddling clothes with ferocity and despair, she knew that the rebellious mood would pass, and that he could neither escape her nor dispense with her.

In these circumstances the whole train of life at Eamor underwent a gradual but profound alteration. The ferment of excitement which the presence of serious malady always engenders spread itself over the entire household. The wing occupied by the Maynes, while tending to become a separate establishment, increasingly engrossed the attention and vital energies of everyone about the place. Lilian, excluded from all participation in the care of the invalid, fell into a position of deeply anxious, but helpless, inactivity.

It was not long before symptoms of nervous strain became manifest in all. The signs in Madeline were an almost hysterical self-devotion to the service of the sufferer, combined with irritability and jealousy. She fell a prey to an all-embracing suspiciousness. It was seldom that Lilian had verbal intercourse with John Mayne,—indeed, it would have been deemed an outrage had she set foot in the Mayne's wing of the house without a summons,—but husband and wife still kept up some communication by means of notes. And Madeline came to see in this exchange an opening for intrigue, a device for obtaining greater secrecy than would otherwise have been possible. For her uncle's room was separated from its antechamber by a very thin partition; it was easy to overhear every word spoken at the bedside. The idea, then, that John Mayne and Lilian might be patching up some kind of understanding, without her knowledge, became an obsession to her; especially as she apprehended that the mental enfeeblement which might incline him towards forgiveness would also make him extremely desirous of keeping his forgiveness secret. He would realise well enough that the tranquillity and comfort of his remaining days would be forfeit, should his nieces discover his perfidy.

This, then, was the most constant of Madeline's fears, but it was by no means the only one. Minor panics and agitations were perpetually sweeping over her spirit. For instance, one day the key to John Mayne's filing-cabinet mysteriously disappeared. This key had been, supposedly, in the old man's personal keeping. When he wanted certain papers from downstairs he would give Nina the key and send her down to get them. But now, either her uncle had mislaid the key, or Lilian had induced one of the maids to steal it for her, or—well, or Nina herself was up to some trickery!

It was illustrative of Madeline's condition at this time that she was ready to entertain—or to pretend to entertain—even this last supposition. Her own room she never quitted without locking the door behind her. Fear of eavesdropping prevented her from holding any private conversation with Nina above a whisper; and in order to make sure that Lilian did not make nocturnal expeditions to the Big Hall, she herself took to prowling about the house at night.

The desirability of precautionary measures such as these was, possibly, suggested by certain activities of her own. None of the papers in Lilian's boudoir, excepting those securely under lock and key, kept any secrets from her. Through the medium of a maid, with whom she had reached very confidential terms, she had early become aware that Lilian was receiving sealed letters from Tornel that were burnt on the day they were received. As for Cosmo's postcard, an accurate copy of it had been brought to her on the very morning Lilian received the original. And it was her habit to pass on to Nina all the information thus gathered. By a kind of tacit agreement Madeline was the purveyor, and Nina the scrutinizer, of the material obtained.

Cosmo's postcard, when put before Nina, had caused her to lay down her needlework for several moments in order to subject it to a profound and pensive scrutiny. And when with a sigh she returned to her occupation, her looks remained deeply meditative. Madeline, for her part, was too busy, too agitated, too engrossed in the details of her routine, to spend much time, either then or later, in pondering those cryptic lines. If the thread were worth following, Nina would be sure to follow it.

Thus the days and weeks went by. Lilian, had she not been sustained by the sense that the real treasure of her life could not be taken from her, would not improbably have sunk into despair. She could not doubt that the seclusion in which John Mayne was being kept was taking fatal effect upon him. Whatsoever the feelings which her presence might arouse in the old man, the mere sight of her would do much, she felt sure, to keep alive his consciousness of what self-respect demanded. She and Walter were the sole medium through which he could remain in touch with the world; theirs were the only presences by which he might be reminded of his ancient standards and his ancient promise. Subtly, indirectly, less by speech than through the impalpable infections of their characters and ever-pressing desires, his two nieces were urging surrender to the vindictive rancour that tormented him. Daily they were parading revenge before his eyes—revenge dressed up in the guise of retributive justice.

For this reason Walter's tendency to remain away from Eamor became very distressing to her. She was constrained at last to address a plain-spoken appeal to him. But he put her off with excuses. His instinct at this period was to keep a certain distance between the inmates of Eamor and himself. With Lilian he was ever on tenterhooks lest she should favour him with unwelcome confidences regarding Cosmo; then, too, he apprehended that his reabsorption into the household would vastly increase the chances of an embroilment with Madeline; and, finally, he was now quite sure that the less he saw of John Mayne the better.

At Tornel he was figuring more and more eminently in the public eye. The mantle of John Mayne had descended upon his shoulders; he was becoming a very considerable personage. The resolution which he had formed, not to allow the mystery surrounding Allen and Cosmo to weigh upon his mind, was assisted by the variety of his social and political engrossments. And yet, as the days went by, that unpleasant subject continued to obtrude itself. Curiously enough, all paths ultimately brought him back to it. The closeness of his business connexion with John Mayne constantly forced him into speculation regarding the degree of confidence and amity which the old man's will was likely to exhibit. And the terms upon which he stood with John Mayne were largely dependent upon his position in Madeline's regard. And this position, again, was liable to be severely deranged by any disclosure which chance or human malice might bring about in regard to Cosmo. That matter, so different in character from the complications to which he was accustomed, impressed itself at times quite luridly upon his imagination. It was true that, on the path of life, he had been confronted, before now, with the danger of implication in questionable affairs; and it was true that in the past he had always managed to slip quickly and discreetly round those awkward corners, where scandal hung, like a potential avalanche, overhead. Yes, and the avalanche, when it did come down, had overwhelmed (for a moral avalanche must always find a victim) another less wary than he. But the present case comprised persons and circumstances that did not accommodate themselves within any of the categories of his experience; its ambiguities were not of his own devising; they did not raise doubts of which it would be easy for him to claim the benefit.

And then, was it not outrageous that a man of his stamp, a man of consequence, of influence, of responsibility, should suffer from such vulgar harassment? Was it not outrageous that he, Walter Standish, should in moments of reverie surprise himself rehearsing scenes of self-exoneration, like any petty shop assistant with a till robbery on his conscience? What a picture was that which his uneasy imagination presented—a scene in which John Mayne and Madeline were sitting over him as judges, whilst he stood rubbing shoulders with that rascal, Allen, in the dock! It was positively comic, and yet he could not entirely shake off his sense of danger.

He did not like to confess to himself how largely his feeling of insecurity was attributable to a want of confidence in the steadiness of Madeline's heart and mind. Fortunately her letters at this time began to be less unsatisfactory. They ceased to treat of nothing but the infamy of Lilian; and he was able to make his replies less exhortatory in tone. On his short visits to Eamor, too, he detected an improvement. He had gained prestige by absence. He was able to command greater consideration than before. It seemed to him that by maintaining a certain aloofness he was playing a wise hand.

There was, however, another side of the matter. In abstracting himself from the current of life at Eamor he was avoiding one danger only to court another. Eamor would have to be reckoned with in the end. And although a wise man will sometimes elect to live in a fool's paradise for a term, he must be ever on his guard against becoming set in the intellectual habits of its regular inhabitants. Walter would have done wisely to speculate whether the improvement in Madeline's exterior reflected any real improvement in her inward temper, or whether she was not merely revealing herself to him with less candour than before. He might have questioned, too, whether his earlier letters had not, possibly, produced in her much the same feeling of helpless annoyance that hers had produced in him. As a matter of fact, Madeline would have found it quite easy to address him, from the first, in just the style he approved. But she had wanted to see how unalterably Walter would remain Walter. She had been putting him, in her fashion, to a test.

There are few experiences more irritating than failure to arouse in one's friend a hatred of one's enemy. It is such a little thing to ask of a friend! To hate costs nothing. Refusal is a mark of lukewarmness; it sets a narrow limit to one's friend's affection. Walter had puzzled Madeline from the first by his apathy. So simple-minded a person should have been easy to rouse. Because his insight was of a different quality from hers, she hardly credited him with any insight at all. Moreover, she failed to comprehend that he was constitutionally incapable of bitter hatred, just as he was incapable of passionate love; or, indeed, of any passionate feeling whatsoever.

With forebodings of strife ahead, she had been anxious to determine how far it would be possible to bend Walter to the service of her purposes. Until recently her desires with regard to Earner had been moderate, her intentions, in her own estimation, generous. She had not contemplated—and she did not, even now, contemplate—turning her enemy adrift upon the world without a penny; what she desired was to make Lilian the recipient of her bounty. She craved to be in the position to heap coals of fire upon Lilian's head, while retaining, however, "some hold over her." And, as her hatred deepened, her notions regarding the tightness and permanence of that hold developed in proportion.

Thus the conflict, begun for purely material ends, had become, as even Walter realized, a spiritual conflict. What he failed to perceive was, that if, in material conflicts, compromise is usually possible, enemies in the spirit demand that there shall be a conqueror and a conquered.

Chapter 9

In the meantime Nicholas's intrigue with Isabel was running its pre-destined course. The tone of his mind, from the beginning, had been unpropitious to the unfolding of a true love sentiment. The present was nothing more to him than a reprieve in which to snatch at pleasures which the jealous gods were planning soon to put beyond his utmost reach. Moreover, the happy, but superficial, consonance of feeling that existed between him and her, constituted, in his view, an obstacle rather than a stepping-stone to the relation upon which his desires were now bent. "*Ne pas aux choses d'amour mêler l'honêteté*"* was a maxim which he had taken deeply to heart. His sensuality, so far from idealizing itself or its object, caused him to question with added sharpness the likelihood of its introducing a higher or more enduring connexion.

Up to this time his amours had been venal in all but two cases. And those two episodes were the only ones in his sexual career of which he was ashamed. He judged them to have been indulgences of vanity rather than of inclination. During the first he had persuaded himself for a brief space that he was in love; but on the second occasion he had been unable to rise, even temporarily, to such an illusion. Wherefore, since his lady's self-respect demanded it, he had been obliged to act a part which he considered inept and was conscious of acting badly.

Before embarking on his adventure with Isabel, he had asked himself more than once whether the game was going to be worth the candle. But these misgivings he hastened to repress. Life, he imagined, held very few games that were worth the candle. Here was one, however, the rejection of which would seem to convict him of a want of confidence in his interpretation of life, or in the powers given him by his understanding of life, to defeat her unaccepted purposes. Was he afraid that proverbial morality would contrive to make an example of him? Did he fear lest Dame Nature should discover a means of avenging the attempted affront?

Such doubts were slighting to Isabel and himself alike. Of himself,

---

* "Do not mix honesty with things of love."

to tell the truth, he felt tolerably sure; but as for his companion—well, while smiling at his fatuity he could not but speculate whether her sentiments might not lose their happy, careless quality, and turn into the sick, heavy obsession of love. Such, he sagely apprehended, was the feminine tendency; and, although he had not yet observed in her any predisposition to this weakness, he saw the wisdom of considering the situation in its general aspect. Life, he told himself, had an ironical way of dealing with those who rely upon their idiosyncrasies to make their case exceptional.

Conscience, then, or prudence counselled him to let the quality of his love stand tolerably manifest from the beginning. And yet in this very procedure he found another point of scruple. For such honesty was not wholly unlike a precautionary measure of self-insurance against responsibility. He would be delicately warning her that, if her feelings betrayed her into unhappiness, the fault would be entirely hers. And then—another point—would he not, by this attitude, be daring her, as it were, to take the risk?

The fashion in which the affair was to come to an end also weighed upon his mind. The rapidity with which he "got through" his experiences was a characteristic of his with which he had early learned to reckon. Isabel, on her side, ought to reckon with it. Was it too much to hope that she would keep pace with him? If she did not, there would be an awkward interval, during which the waning of his ardour would be a source of irritation and disappointment to her.

Well, well! provided her feelings remained within those bounds, he would have nothing to regret. A deeper hurt she must not experience. For that would convict both him and her of being their own dupes. Yes, *his* position then, in particular, would be one of ignominy. By making herself piteous, Isabel would be making him—in his own eyes at least—more piteous than she. She would have thrown him into the position of a conventional Lothario, and created a situation upon which he would be forced to give a judgment similar to that which the world (if it knew) would delight to give. The kind of comment which a censorious Walter, or a scandalized Madeline, would bestow, would not be out of place. Artificial, callow, weak in their naive intellectualism, would his notions then have proved themselves; and the collapse of his spiritual habitation would compel him, either to accept another ready-made, or to set about an appallingly arduous task of reconstruction.

These misgivings beset him in full force after his walk with Isabel in the wood. But a few hours later, impassioned by his passage-at-arms with John Mayne, he suffered excitement to carry him away. That excitement, however, which accompanied him upstairs to Isabel's room, there, of a sudden, dropped. He found himself face to face with an actuality that confounded him. At one critical instant a glaciating self-consciousness threatened its worst, The next instant it met with conspicuous defeat. And the completeness of his victory over the dismal, inhibitory demon that had attacked him, became evident in a lightsomeness and jubilation such as he had rarely known before.

What he achieved, in fact, was a casting off of the sense of precedence. Nothing more, and nothing less, than this was required. For it is chiefly a sense of precedence that hampers us in our manifestations. Each one of us has a fixed, unconscious notion of what constitutes his character, and is prevented from carrying into effect the behests of his imagination, by an irrational, but compelling instinct to conform with that accepted idea of himself. This compulsion is strongest when intimates are present. The unfortunate ego, partly in deference to the suggestion of others, and partly in self-protection against them, has encrusted itself in a hard shell. It has made public profession of a certain "character," which its manner and behaviour are constrained to illustrate. This is its response to a need to exhibit a definite outline, by which its fellow-creatures shall recognize it; but it is also—and, alas, more urgently still!—a response to its own need to possess a form by which it shall recognize itself.

In the conduct of everyday life each one of us likes to refer to some fairly well-defined conception of his own character in order to decide without trouble what to do, what to say, and even what to think. We require some rule of thumb in our current self-manifestations; for a perpetual effort of choice would be an intolerable burden. Do we not all habitually repose with a sense of satisfaction upon what we take to be our fixed characteristics—upon the supposedly fatal element within us? And of those *given* characteristics are not even the most trifling our pride? "Yes," we reflect with complacency, "I'm like that. It is strange; but that's what I always am." What pride in discovering in the malleable substance of ourselves some streak supposedly resistant—something irresponsible, something demonic, something which the reason cannot coerce, nor the consciousness incorporate, something genuine, in fact— in the sense of being spontaneous, self-existent, and inevitable—when all the rest of the poor little personality is a make-up, in which the only inevitabilities are those imposed by helplessness.

Man, then, assumes a character, and, having done so, can let the character-part play itself. But this sacrifice of variability has its disadvantages. The character develops at the expense of the perceptions and of the imagination. The young man is apt to feel at times that he is investing himself in habiliments which cramp him. He would fain throw them off; but almost irresistible is the force of precedent; that is, the force of interior and exterior expectation. Besides it is only in moments of unusual excitation that the ego gathers the energy to rebel. For the most part it prefers to take its ease in an inert illustration of the public personality, which has, indeed, become "a second nature."

In pre-visualizing his relation with Isabel, Nicholas had dreaded the absence of that freedom of self manifestation which he had found obtainable in commerce with persons from whom he was separated by wide differences, social, temperamental, and intellectual. Such a gulf corresponded conveniently with that other gulf, to his sense so profound, between the flesh and the spirit; and precluded the necessity of pretending to span the latter with a bridge of sentiment. Among men and women at large an emotion, self-judged sublime, was wont, as he knew, to supply a kind of natural arch over the chasm; and the world generally saw nothing strange in the fact that this emotion found its expression and satisfaction in acts which every impartial clement of mind could only regard as absurdly incongruous. This never ceased to be a source of wonder to him. Surely, men, as creatures of the flesh, would do better to repose, confessedly, upon animal nature, whilst enjoying the pleasures of the flesh? Surely the recourse to high sentiment was silly and self-deceptive? Why refuse to discriminate between the things renderable unto Caesar and the things renderable unto God? Lust was a thing to be recognised, licensed, prized, and despised. The confusion of spiritual motives and sanctions with material motives and sanctions resulted—the evidence was everywhere around him—in a general falsification of values.

It was for this reason that he liked to find in his partner a kind of tacit admission of the actualities governing the behaviour of both; and disliked intercourse with "self-respecting" women, whose sentiment was, to his sense, not merely ridiculous but positively repellant; being nurtured upon assumptions destructive of true self-respect.

His position, accordingly, in regard to Isabel was difficult. He could hardly believe that she had formulated views on these matters similar to his, nor was it practicable to submit her to a course of lectures, as a preliminary to action. But if she appeared untouched by solemn thought, that did not mean, he hoped, that her nature was less intuitive of the truth than his. No; the trouble lay rather in the fact that he and she had a relation already and that there was a difficult passage to be made from the old relation to the new. It was desirable—it was indeed necessary—that the old relation should survive for every-day use. The new must be super-added and kept strictly separate.

Everything depended upon how this fresh relation was initiated. Nothing less than an entirely fresh start was required. And by extraordinary good fortune he did actually achieve the rebirth that was necessary, when with a supreme effort he threw off the husk of his old character and emerged, like a winged insect, into the freedom of a novel state.

It so happened, too, that he was ready to take the lead just when Isabel shewed signs of faltering. He was able to catch her up in the flow of his vital spirits, and to sweep her off into a sphere where the enactment of his sensual phantasies was possible.

When he left her, the intoxication of delight was still upon him. For a long time, lying awake on his own bed, he gave himself exquisite satisfaction in recalling the details of the two past hours. And, night after night, on returning from Isabel's room, the same satisfaction was renewed. It was a delight irradiated with a sense of triumph at the capture of such intense pleasure in a world where pleasure was so elusive—especially for such as he;—and, as a rule, so imperfect. Never, he vowed, never again would he allow intellectual conceit to persuade him that for a young man the pleasures of the senses are not, after all, the best.

This feeling of pride and elation continued in full strength for three or four weeks; and for as long as it lasted nothing that happened outside the precincts of his private kingdom had the power seriously to disturb him. On the morning when Lilian briefly informed him that Cosmo was dead, his mind was still wandering in its own hidden paradise. To her astonishment and relief he asked no questions; but, after regarding her fixedly for a minute, murmured some thing about the inevitable, and turned himself away. Dully he marvelled at his own insensibility. Some day, he apprehended, he might well fall a prey to sorrow and self-reproach. But that day was not yet. And all trouble that could be postponed was premature.

At that time his infatuation with Isabel was actually at its height. She was amazing him by being far more delightful than he had dared hope she would be. For he had prepared, according to his fashion, for disappointments. He had envisaged beforehand all the snares and stumbling-blocks, physical as well as psychical, which, notoriously, lie in the path of two civilized human beings who set out to perform the antics of primitive nature. But he was soon to laugh at his fears. Isabel played her part with a happy aptitude which was a lesson to him not only on the faculty, proper to a healthy young animal, of appreciating the good gifts of its senses, but also on the exercise of that more delicate instinct, by which a creature, inculcated, but not too deeply, with a feeling for the conventions, may put to use the whole background of accepted morality as a set-off to its pleasure. No one, he realized, can taste the joys of libertinism completely, who has not some Puritan strain in his composition. Isabel's hesitances were delicious, as was also the amused consciousness of wrong-doing which gleamed from beneath her eye-lids, as those hesitancies were vanquished one by one. She offered to her companion's greater expertise all the satisfactions which the master can hope to obtain from the lively docility of a novice; she permitted a full and leisurely enjoyment of every step upon a path of dalliance which he had never expected to follow outside day-dreams.

During this period he lived entirely in the present. A golden mist enclosed him: the past and the future were blotted out. "The present," he remembered quoting, "the present is nothing but as it appertains to what is past and what is to come." Well! that dictum was exactly false. The present to be really good must be complete in itself; it must dazzle you with the timeless wonder and delight which comes to the child with a new toy, the lover with a new mistress, or the convert with a new God.

With such reflections as these did his happiness gradually wane. Gradually did the golden mist rise up, and the long, dark horizons of Time unfold themselves in front and behind. The old sense of flux, of attrition, of incompleteness, crept over him. He had expected it only too well; and, when it came, he recognized it only too well.

Presently, a haunting dread of detection was added to his gathering unrest. He confessed to Isabel that the fear lest Lilian should discover their secret was constantly at his side. "You used not to feel like that in the beginning," she answered; and to this he had nothing to reply.

As a solace in dejection he dwelt upon the thought, how largely, in this gamble for pleasure, he had already won. Had he not, time and again, caught himself up in the midst of his delight, to take stock of it and store it up in his memory? Had he not bidden himself remember for ever afterwards that he had been able to say: "*Verweile doch, du bist so* *schön!*"* Yes, while the gods were napping, he had snatched a treasure which they could not take back. Let him not pander to their vengefulness by slipping into weak regret.

Isabel's simple acceptance of the pleasures which they had discovered, had been a marvel to him from the first. It now became a source of misgiving as well. He could not make up his mind whether to regard it as an individual characteristic or as an illustration of a universal affinity between the child and the woman. What was at the back of that unspeculativeness? Innocence or innate knowledge? Her smile, as she looked up at him from the pillow, would seem at times to mock his wonder.

Be this as it might, her nonchalance alarmed him. And that smile of hers awakened, without his knowing why, a twinge of his earlier fear lest she should exhibit a foundation of nature similar to Madeline's. Although she had shewn herself, so far, most reassuringly true to his conception of her type, by enlarging that conception she had somewhat obscured its outlines. He was perpetually induced to draw comparisons between her and Madeline, in order to convince himself of the contrasts. But those very contrasts, viewed in another connexion, were disquieting. If Isabel was allied to Madeline in fundamental womanhood that was bad; but it was bad, too, to be unlike Madeline in being without the sentimental insensitiveness, the coarse-fibred vitality, and the crude cunning, which, after all, were the best equipment for life.

Isabel not only lacked the qualities which make for self-preservation, but seemed to be deficient in the instinct itself. She was careless of her destiny. She threatened to be a charge upon him. The burden of his own unfitness he could endure, but not hers as well. The thought that he had, perhaps, done something to dissociate her still further from the world, added to his uneasiness. He had nothing useful to give her. His inner life was not one that she could profitably understand or share.

He had a suspicion that she divined a good deal of what was passing in his mind at this time. But she said nothing. She revealed nothing. If her heart was gradually being infected by the sadness in his, she was successful in concealing the change. To judge from appearances, the affair was gliding to an undisastrous close. Much had been enjoyed, and no harm done. The reaction was no deeper than he had expected—or so he tried to think. And in the prodigious lassitude of his spirit, he murmured to himself that all was well.

* "Beautiful moment, do not pass away!" — Goethe, *Faust* Part 1.

257

Chapter 10

To break the chain of his relations with Isabel he began taking short absences from Eamor. His usual pretexts were good enough, their very slenderness serving to show how lightly he was bound.

Upon the occasion of his first visit to Tornel, Lilian, he could see, suspected that his intention was to have a talk with Allen. Without doubt she had been puzzled by his apparent lack of concern in regard to Cosmo's death, and was now inclined to ascribe to a suppressed fretting the moodiness that was visibly gaining upon him. One day she asked point-blank whether the matter was preying upon his mind. And he, answering honestly, said "No." Honestly, but perhaps not quite truthfully, for afterwards he realised that Cosmo was in fact haunting him. And the influence of that ghost was one that he could not appraise.

At Tornel he spent many hours in the libraries, attended lectures given by a distinguished foreign savant, and made considerable purchases of books. It pleased him to imagine that he had done with the excitements of sex, and that he would be content henceforth to give his desires a periodic and passionless satisfaction that would not distract him from intellectual pursuits.

All his appetite for books had returned. In them he was able to forget himself; and that, he was now only too ready to do. Yes, he vowed, he honoured the ostrich above all other beasts. Are not all wise men ostriches before those two pursuers, Self and Death? And where is finer sand to be found than in a good, dry book? Thank God! he could not yet say: "*Et j'ai lu tous les livres.*"*

Each time he went to Tornel he was seized with the impulse to call upon Allen. But a strong counter force held him back. One morning, however, he found himself mounting the steps of the Egyptian Museum. During a wakeful night thoughts of Allen had occupied his mind. "But what have I to say?" he still objected within himself. "For I am determined that not a word about Isabel—or Cosmo—shall pass my lips."

* "And I have all the books." — Mallarmé, "Brise marine"

Having pushed through the double barrier of swing-doors, he moved slowly down the broad, unpeopled gallery. Pleasant was the cessation of the street's uproar. Pleasant the inanimation of the place, its vast, slumberous detachment from contemporaneity. Cathedrals had less dignity. They made an appeal to the living. But these gods of black basalt were dumb. They expected no worship.

Almost at once he sank into a deep abstraction; and the desire to see Allen melted away. He dropped upon a seat. Opposite was an effigy of the lion-headed goddess, Sekhet. It filled him with wonder and peace.

When, after a while, he came back to himself, it was with the sense that someone was watching him. He looked over his shoulder and saw Allen standing a little way off. Their eyes met, and the other forthwith approached.

"Did you come to see *me?*" asked Allen. "Or *these?*" And his gesture took in the gods and ancient Pharaohs that stood on either side.

"Both," returned Nicholas after a moment's hesitation. "But having got as far as this. . . ."

"Exactly!" replied Allen, still smiling. "I am not surprised."

There was a pause, during which Nicholas looked upon the ground. Allen's coming annoyed him. He had almost made up his mind to leave the place without seeing him.

"Were you on your way out?" he asked.

"No. I'm not going yet."

This answer further exasperated him. He felt himself caught. "Allen intends to have it out with me," he thought. "Why on earth did I walk into his parlour? I suppose he has a fancy for excusing himself,—the murderer! He killed my half-brother, that is certain. And now he wants my sympathy."

A functionary approached, touched his cap to Allen and murmured a few words. Allen nodded, and the man withdrew.

"On Thursdays," said he, "we close at this hour. But of course you can stay."

Nicholas rose. "I don't think I want to stay," he answered doubtfully.

Allen said nothing, and together they moved slowly towards the exit.

Here and there they stopped to examine some object under glass. But Nicholas's interest had vanished. The atmosphere of the place was changed. The exhibits, so carefully "laid out," were like bodies in a morgue. Blankly dead, classified and catalogued into a perfect inexpressiveness they now inspired him with nothing but irritation.

He bent over a case pretending to study bangles, beads, rings, toilet-instruments, and toys.

"You take your humanity at a fair remove," he commented, looking up with an ambiguous smile. "And very wise too!"

Allen stood silent for a moment before answering.

"These dead help one to bear with the living, I find. It seems foolish," he added thoughtfully, "to take less interest in the living, merely because they are one's contemporaries."

"Yet there is a difference!" replied Nicholas, turning his head away. "And Time is what does the trick."

Yes! he could love this dead folk. He could love them with a godlike indulgence, with a pity that was not fatuous in himself, nor derogatory to them. Time had ennobled them. They were so grandly and remotely dead.

"The present," he continued aloud, "the present is always destitute, beggarly. To-day gains a little when it turns into yesterday. When it has become three thousand years ago. . . ."

Allen was looking at him curiously. "I admit that Time helps," he replied. "And if you need the glamour of Time, you should throw your spirit three thousand years forward and view the present from there! Why be the slave of the immediate?"

"Because we are its slaves. I can't ignore—and I won't pretend to ignore—what is actually presented. The wilful idealization of what exists is cant. It leads straight into every vice of mind. Idealization is the bane of the Ideal."

"The Ideal that is not discoverable beneath the forms of the Actual is a chimera," returned Allen. "There, outside, in the street——"

Nicholas interrupted him with a harsh laugh. "Are gobbets of coughed-up phlegm. Grey mud. Hand-bills. Threadbare, scurfy shoulders. Politicians. Public houses. Sweaty armpits. Reek. Lice. Pox. Horseplay. And always the old, old jests! The old, brief swagger of being alive!" He laughed again. "You think well of it?"

"It was the same in Thebes!"

"It was. But nothing of that remains, Thebes has been winnowed. The chaff has gone; we inherit the grain."

"By my soul!" cried Allen; "if I couldn't find in Thebes what I value in Tornel, I would let the past go hang."

Nicholas mused. "That enthusiasm for humanity as such, that loyalty to life, that determination to find a mystical value in mere living,—whence does it spring?"

"Can you tell me?" asked Allen, smiling.

"Well!" And the young man looked up. "Doesn't it sometimes occur to you that it might simply be a fashion of saving one's face?"

Allen frowned. "You mean?" said he.

"I mean that men must either call life good or admit themselves to be fools for living."

Allen gave a short laugh. "When did that idea occur to you?"

"At the age of twelve, I think." He paused. "When I was told about God, and a future life, and goodness being the important thing, I felt in my heart of hearts that my dear, kind teachers were simply making the best of a bad business. I felt that they did believe what they said; but simply because they wanted to so much that they had to. So out of pity I, too, pretended to believe."

Allen shrugged. Instinctively they had turned, and were now retracing their steps up the gallery.

"One begins by demanding good of the whole. One learns to be satisfied with the compensations one can pick up. Besides, how can one expect the universe to suit the idiosyncrasies of one's own particular taste?—God has so many tastes to cater for," Allen added flippantly.

It was Nicholas's turn to shrug. "I should have thought that an autocrat might have avoided the vices of a demagogue. But no matter."

"I am taking you to my private room," said Allen. "I have one or two things there which I want to show you."

"Showman!" thought Nicholas. "He feels monarch of all he surveys. His private room! I can see it from here. Big windows looking out upon a quiet court; leather chairs; shiny mahogany; card indexes; bulky volumes in the bookcase; and, next door, an obsequious secretary. There he sits, lording it over ancient Egypt!"

The reality, however, was different. The room into which Allen ushered him was more like a workshop than an office. It was dusty, untidy, littered with relics, both large and small. A carpenter's bench ran along under the unwashed windows; at right angles to it, was an enormous desk covered by a welter of papers.

Allen took him up to the window and removed a cover from several objects of wood and ivory. "Look at these!" said he. "They are worth it."

Upon a sheet of pale green glass lay a number of small ointment boxes carved in human and animal shapes. The one that Nicholas's attention fastened upon represented a wild duck swimming. Behind the duck, and clinging to it with outstretched arms, was a diminutive maiden, whose slender form, as she was towed along, made a handle to the receptacle. The colours of the painted wood, although partially effaced, were clear and bright. The lines were of a toylike simplicity. The little object had the gaiety of a toy; but it was perfect.

As Nicholas gazed, he felt tears mounting into his eyes. Over their unrippling pond of glass the maiden and her duck were moving down eternity. In conventionalizing the forms the artist had extracted from Nature, and distilled into art, all the charm that those forms, in all their natural associations, had to offer. They expressed dreams, atavistic nostalgias, memories of never-ending recurrences of spring—dreams of rushes, water-lilies, long pipy stems of water-weeds and water flowers; dreams of soft, sheeny-feathered birds, bird calls at dawn; dreams, too, of virginal slimness, of girlish bodies, sliding through green waters under a vaporous, rose-flushed sky.

And through the young man's heart there shot a stab of pain. "Isabel!" he cried within himself. "Isabel!"

Chapter 11

Allen had moved across to his desk and was signing some type-written letters.

"Well? Do they please you?"

"They do."

"What do you think of the girl and duck?"

Nicholas said nothing.

"It was discovered by your father," continued Allen. "It ought to be in the museum by rights. But I am so fond of it that I keep it here."

As he spoke, he offered his guest a cigarette. Nicholas took one and sat down.

"Whenever Walter comes into this room," Allen went on, "he looks at those specimens gloomily. You see, nearly five years have gone by since a place for them was fixed upon in the North gallery. But here they still are." And he chuckled.

Nicholas smiled. He was wondering what Walter thought of this curator, and of his untidy room, and of the duck. Most probably he gave them very little thought. He understood well enough that they didn't count for much in life. They were an insignificant little side-show. He could afford to be tolerant.

After a moment he said—

"Walter could get you dismissed to-morrow, if he chose."

"True enough!" replied Allen.

"Walter and Madeline," continued Nicholas thoughtfully; "they are our masters. We take our revenge by laughing at them. It is all we can do."

"On the contrary," rejoined Allen, "they are our servants. They run the world—a thankless, tedious task;—they are the Marthas, and we the Marys."

Nicholas shook his head. "We take refuge in art and philosophy, because we are slaves elsewhere. Even Cosmo, in the end, recognized that he was a slave."

Allen's face became grave. He leaned forward in his chair. "I have long wanted to ask you this: What Cosmo stands for in your ideology?"

Nicholas gave him a long, scowling look. "I will tell you what Madeline and Walter stand for—and what you stand for,—if you like?"

Allen nodded. "Yes. Tell me!"

After a moment's hesitation the young man drew a roll of foolscap out of his pocket. "As a matter of fact, I set it down on paper, only yesterday. Have you time to listen?"

Allen nodded again.

"My thesis," said Nicholas after another pause, "is this: we are entering upon an age of materialism; and the new materialism is coming, like anti-Christ, in the semblance of its opposite. It offers us a pseudo idealism, which is typified, in its male and female aspects, by Madeline and Walter. 'He for God only, she for God in him'—that is Madeline's device; but, in truth, she is sex personified,—that and nothing more.—Yes!" he went on, now reading from his manuscript. "A diffuse, unrecognized sexuality permeates every corner of her psychic being and finds a disguised expression in her every feeling, thought, and act. She is not self-conscious—that is, does not look into her mind,— but she is intensely and constantly aware of her body. Her appearance, and the effect her appearance produces on others, occupy her unceasingly; while her moral, aesthetic, and intellectual tastes, in so far as she can be said to have any, are sexually conditioned; inasmuch as her tastes are assumed, like her garments and the postures of her body, with an eye to enhancing her attractiveness. Naturally, however, it is essential to her self-respect that she should not be aware of this. Sexuality in its direct and primitive crudity is incapable of holding the attention of men. The appetite of the male, abruptly satisfied, leaves him free to devote himself disinterestedly to aesthetic or intellectual aims. The sexual subconsciousness of all women (and many men) is in consequence jealously occupied in hindering a divorce between the sensual and the intellectual; and time-honoured links between the two are to be found in the popular conceptions of art and ethics.

"It is a commonplace that art is constantly pressed into the service of sentimentality, whilst it is equally, if not quite so obviously, true that the function of vulgar 'morality' is the dignifying of sex. This is achieved by calling the sexual act a sacrament, by connecting it with religion, and by surrounding it with sanctions and prohibitions. Thus, dignified by morality as a thing of awe and wonder, or tricked out by art in robes of romance, sexuality in its various disguises, penetrates into every department of the mind, and, largely through the instrumentality of womankind, attempts to make subservient to its own ends every activity of man."

"Wait a moment!" said Allen, breaking in. "It appears to me that you are heading straight away from the truth. There is an innate propensity in man to dam up the direct flow of his sexuality in order that the stream may spread in a fructifying flood over the whole superficies of his nature. The highest creative powers probably derive——"

"Bah!" interjected Nicholas. "I know those ideas. And how lax they are! The theory of the sublimation of an undifferentiated, pre-sexual or proto-sexual life energy has been vulgarized into a supposition that the sexual instinct, in its fully developed character, is susceptible of sublimation. But, has any psychologist ever distinguished between an insecure, make-believe, makeshift substitution and true sublimation? I think not. In fact I deny that the higher intellectual faculties owe anything to sexuality proper. They derive their energy from the life-force which lies behind sex as well as behind mind."

Allen shrugged. "I will reserve my comments," said he. "I want to see how you go on."

"I admit," continued Nicholas argumentatively, "that the sex-ridden may obtain relief by distraction. We see them everywhere swelling the ranks of the social service brigade. They also write books and paint pictures. But they remain inwardly dissatisfied. And are their books and pictures good? Emphatically, they are not. I have no time to drive my point home with illustrations; but I think I could convince you that the popular, bad book is at the same time popular and bad just because it should have been a baby. What suppressed sexuality creates, suppressed sexuality will enjoy. But the great creations of the mind are neither indirect nor substitute."

After a pause he returned to his manuscript. "Sex is jealous. It grasps, and clings, and clogs. The Great Mother cannot bear to see her children venture forth into the regions of the intellect. Disinterestedness is her bane. Analysis, her mortal enemy. She will not have her children know themselves, for in so doing they learn to know her. In Madeline she finds a daughter after her own heart. Whatever solid elements of character that girl might conceivably have utilized in the building up of an individuality, are infiltrated and undermined by an uncanalised sexuality. She is intelligent, but has no intellectual interests; she is full of energy, but she neither achieves, nor desires to achieve, anything for its own sake. She has perceptions, but no tastes. She has thoughts, but no opinions, still less ideas.

"Indeed, as we watch her, we discover this active intelligence perpetually engaged in decorating itself with spurious enthusiasms and interests. Just as anxious to delude herself as to deceive others, she makes her mind the scene of a constant arrangement of stage properties. The latest tastes and ideas have to be acquired and displayed to their best advantage there. The fashion has to be followed.

"The fashion! Yes, alas! woman has created one thing, fashion! Fashion is change without progression; activity without achievement; variety without novelty. The impulse of the intellect is to move directly forward towards an intuited goal—towards creation. The use of fashion is to deflect that impetus and to produce movement in a circle. For innate preference, for individual taste, fashion would substitute public opinion and snobbery. In every age, moral, aesthetic, and intellectual, snobs set the tone; and three-fourths of those snobs are women."

"Hear! hear!" said Allen, smiling, with that I agree."

"Well! Now," proceeded Nicholas, "let us examine Walter. The Walters of this world are the instruments of the Madelines. Just as Madeline is representative of generative Nature, whose sole end is the perpetuation of the species, so Walter is representative of the semi conscious, but impersonal, spirit of the community, whose end is the perfection of the social machine.

"Like Madeline, Walter is not introspective; he does not look into his mind; but he is intensely and constantly aware of the communal mind. Just as Madeline is always preoccupied with the effect which her physical being will produce on others, so Walter refers all his thoughts and emotions to the tribunal of public opinion and dares entertain none which would not, in his estimation, receive the common sanction. Walter is the spirit of formalism, of institutionalism, of recognised authority. Walter feels that Life, when she allowed intelligence to develop into self-consciousness, took a dangerous step. Intelligence is useful in servitude, but dangerous when free. That is to say, intelligence, applied to the end of helping man to adapt himself to his environment by adapting his environment to him, is of immense utility; but intelligence has a way of going sick after a whole host of idealisms. Notions not merely subversive of order and comfort, but positively inimical to the preservation and continuation of the race, spring into being; and it is only by a falsification and distortion of these notions, such as will render them sterile, that life manages to prevent the thinking portion of mankind from hurrying the whole body-politic to its destruction. For the intelligence is always thwarted in the end. The natural man is far more subtle than the intellectual man. And the new materialism is the subtlest the world has yet seen. Its scheme is to invest society with all the dignity and authority of religion. But what, in heaven's name, is that religion, if not simply the deification of the instinct to develop, after the fashion of the social insects, a social automatism? Free intelligence is kept in being only by the friction between the individual and his society. As one philosopher has aptly put it: 'By the time we are all perfectly good, we shall, also, all be perfectly idiotic.' In the Walters of this world we witness the first stages of man's degeneration. Walter is the tame duck whose business is to decoy its free brethren into the net. Intelligence is being progressively brought under the shackles of convention, custom, and the social instinct. In the future millions and millions of Walters, in happy collaboration with their Madelines, and animated by nothing but an overpowering instinct for self-perpetuation and comfort, will apply themselves, undisturbed, to the soulless task of ordered, social living. Saturated through and through with the spirit of the Hive, the Walters will dignify their crass materialism with the title of Humanism, apt name for a religion as proper to despiritualised man as Apianism to bees and Porcinism to pigs.

"How, I ask you, in the absence of any extra-mundane faith or vision, how can we hope to prevent the gradual ossification of the intelligence into social instinct? The young men of our time, ensnared through love of justice into the dismal business of redressing social inequalities, thrust on towards their material Utopia, until their energies are spent, and they have lost the power of conceiving spiritual ends. Will *one* occasionally be found, in future days, to hover above the Hive on uneasy wing; and, looking down upon the busy, orderly multitude of his brethren, feel within him the tiny, stinging spark of an idealism condemned and outworn? Perhaps! But if he betray himself, he will surely die. He is not only a traitor, but a heretic. The God of the Hive is a jealous God. Mystical utilitarianism, which is the line of least resistance between the religious and the scientific spirits, will not tolerate any deviation from its own devious compromise. What does it matter if in serving your fellow-creature you are serving no child of God, or of truth, but only a replica of your own disinherited, degraded self? From reciprocal back-scratching merit mysteriously accrues. Humanity has no need for a belief in anything outside itself, because the service of itself, through a system of vicarious hedonism, is the highest good. Let the Hive hum and the honey of virtue accumulate in the cells!"

"Bravo!" cried Allen. "Admirable rhetoric!"

"It's more than rhetoric," rejoined Nicholas with fierceness.

"Yes. Perhaps it is," said Allen, and regarded him contemplatively. "But all the same...."

Nicholas laughed and got up. "You've got a hobby," said he. "You're all right. It's what all the doctors prescribe."

"There are hobbies and hobbies," said Allen.

Nicholas gave him a contemptuous look. "Personally, I should put stamp-collecting at the top."

"I don't feel that you have expressed your deepest thoughts," said Allen after a pause.

"You mean my most personal thoughts—or concerns," returned Nicholas, smiling disagreeably. "Why should I?"

Allen knit his brows.

"You are like a woman," said Nicholas, "who never reflects upon the truth of what one says, but only upon one's reason for saying it."

"It's a method that helps," replied Allen vaguely. "And now," he added after a pause, "will you proceed to translate *me* into abstract terms?—And, after me, Cosmo?"

"No!" said Nicholas. "Not now."

"Why not?—I have time."

"But I haven't."

Allen smiled incredulously. "Come and lunch with me!" said he, rising.

A hunted look came into Nicholas's face. It was obvious that he was searching for some excuse. "I am afraid——" he began lamely.

A sharp ring of the telephone-bell interrupted him.

"*I* have listened to *you*," said Allen with decision. "During lunch I shall want *you* to listen to me."

As he spoke he picked up the telephone from his desk and held the receiver to his ear. The conversation that ensued was short, and, on Allen's side, extremely laconic. "Very good!" were his last words. "You can expect me round to-morrow at noon."

Having put the instrument down, he walked over to the window and stood there for a few moments, presenting his back. "Well!" said he at last. "Are you ready?"

"No!" replied Nicholas. "I haven't time. I am going back to Eamor by the next train."

Allen stared at him in surprise. It was quite obvious that the decision was capricious, and had been formed on the spur of the moment.

At first he looked as though he were going to combat it; but, after an instant's reflection, he made a gesture of acquiescence.

Chapter 12

It was while Nicholas was away at Tornel that the end, which the inmates of Eamor had been awaiting for so long, came into sight at last. The appearance of a new symptom, diagnosed by the doctor in residence as critical, led to the summons of Tornel's leading specialist; and the latter, after a brief examination of his patient, returned to John Mayne's nieces in an adjoining room, and bade them prepare themselves for the closing scene. Although there had been no sudden decline in their uncle's physical and mental capacities, yet, said he, a certain culmination was now being reached; so that it could be predicted with certainty that death would take place within the next three or four days. Furthermore, he had not considered himself justified in withholding the truth from the dying man, whose surmises had already brought him very close to it.

With this, pleading urgent engagements elsewhere, he took a hurried leave; but not before requesting that the intelligence should be conveyed to Mrs. Mayne, who yet remained to be informed.

As soon as he had gone, the two sisters repaired to Madeline's bedroom, and there set themselves to collect their thoughts. The news came unexpectedly for having been expected so long. So sluggishly had the stream of events been flowing during the past weeks, that, although it was certain the rapids could not be far ahead, they had almost given up listening for the distant roar. The doctor's words, by disclosing the swiftness of the current now sucking at their keel, filled them with a species of awe. Was everything really shipshape? Were they as well prepared as they ought to be?

Sitting together in abstraction, they revolved their separate thoughts. It had occurred to both that, in one consideration at least, a longer forewarning would have been convenient. For many weeks past Nina had been busy with an intricate problem; and the solution was now tolerably clear. But only recently had she decided upon action. It was only two days ago that she had betaken herself, at a late hour, to her sister's bedroom, and there, with the directness that was customary between them, had gone straight to the heart of her subject. "Do you remember," she had said, "the post-card addressed to Lilian by one who signed himself 'Yours, as the spirit moves me, Cosmo?'" Madeline, a little taken aback, had looked up and nodded assent. "Very well!" Nina had continued; and that had been the beginning of an earnest confabulation that had lasted far into the night.

The next day a letter had been posted to Walter. It was a letter that Nina had composed with great care during the course of the proceeding week; and it had been her intention to give her uncle identical information immediately after sending it to the post. Her idea was that John Mayne would thus be unable to prevent the communication of her story to Walter (should he by any chance conceive the desire to do so), whilst Walter's almost certain supplication that she should keep her news from John Mayne, would come into her hands too late. Such had been her design; but a sudden turn in the old man's condition had caused the resident doctor to deny her admittance to the sick-chamber; and now it might appear—indeed, they felt sure that to Walter's sense it would appear—unbecoming in them to burden the dying man with intelligence of so disturbing a nature. Nevertheless in their opinion it was only right that their uncle should be informed. They felt it their duty to place him in possession of every fact which might assist him to a true estimation of Lilian's character. The occasion was falling unpropitiously, but that was no fault of theirs.

Nor had Nina any cause to reproach herself for an earlier want of initiative. When she had first read the name Cosmo on the post-card, it had awakened in her mind a memory so dim as to be no more than the shadow of a memory. "Cosmo? Cosmo?" Might it not be merely her fancy that she had once heard something about Sir Charles Orisser's having had a son of that name? And, surely, that son had died long ago? Yet here was a Cosmo, living in Tornel, who strangely subscribed himself "Yours, as the spirit moves me!" It was odd. The matter might be worth looking into; and the first and simplest step, since Madeline was no better informed than she, was to question John Mayne.

This she did; but, obedient to an innate secretiveness, abstained from making mention of the post-card. At the pronouncement of the name Cosmo, her uncle had looked up at her meditatively. "Cosmo?" he in turn had echoed with the air of one searching amid old recollections; "Cosmo Orisser?" Yes! Unless his memory was playing him false, he had once heard of the existence of such a one. "Cosmo! . . . ." And with that he had fallen, unexpectedly, into so deep a vein of musing that Nina had been moved to uneasiness. Casual as she had made herself appear, mere mention of the name had, seemingly, started the old man off on some novel track of thought. Was she mistaken, or did his rumination betoken the dawning of a new idea? Had she, in fine, presented poor Madeline with a competitor for Eamor?

After a while John Mayne came out of his abstraction to inform her with a certain curtness that such a man as Cosmo had undoubtedly existed. This Cosmo, he added, had always been ill-famed. Like his father before him he had been a scoundrel. What had become of him was a mystery. In all probability he was dead.

Nina nodded indifferently and passed on to another topic.

Various were the indications by which she ultimately penetrated the enigma. After her experience with John Mayne, she was fearful of questioning Walter about Cosmo; but, having frequently come across Allen's name among her uncle's old papers, it occurred to her to enquire of Walter who this Allen was; and then it struck her that if Allen had been Sir Charles's secretary and associate, he was more likely than anyone else to be able to tell her what had become of Sir Charles's eldest son. She was wondering how she might get into communication with Allen, when she chanced to hear that a person of that name had been staying not so very long ago at the village. Next, by dint of pushing her inquiries in that direction, she discovered that Lilian was taking precautions to keep secret the fact that she was corresponding with this same Allen, who was now residing in Tornel. And, finally, she conceived that these mysterious circumstances might possibly link themselves up with the puzzle of the post-card. From this time onwards her investigations moved forward with a livelier tread. In the imagination of the village folk a certain fantastical interest had attached itself to the persons of Allen and "Richardson." She found busybodies to relate to her the gossip of the cottagers and the tittle-tattle of the servants' hall at Eamor. Here, there, and everywhere, she gleaned scraps of information, which, strung together on the thread of one bold surmisal, presented her at last with a connected sequence of events.

In unfolding her tale to Madeline she had enjoyed a small triumph. For the latter, slightly jealous of her sister's acumen, had long preserved an attitude of scepticism. When all the evidence had been spread out before her, however, Madeline's agitation knew no bounds. Heaven be her witness! she cried, she had never entertained many illusions about Lilian; but this—this went beyond anything she had ever imagined. It brought the woman under suspicion of veritable criminality.

Exultant had she been at the time; but now, as she sat brooding over

272

the dark and difficult days that would precede her uncle's death, her excitement was of less sanguine a hue. Who could tell what wiles Lilian would not resort to in her extremity? Who could gauge the depths of her unscrupulousness? Even Nina was ill at ease. The very bigness of their secret made them nervous of disclosing it to John Mayne. They felt unequal to conceiving its effect upon him, or to imagining the outcome of the scene it might occasion between him and Lilian. A cloud of gloom and anxiety settled down over their spirits. To both the hour seemed dreary and ominous. The dull light of the damp, winter day fell palely upon their faces; their eyes were large and heavy with speculation. They dreaded the strain and the conflict that lay before them. Although tolerably confident of a victory, they could take no pleasure in the anticipation of it. Vainly did Madeline tell herself that this mood was no more than a passing distemper of the mind; the whole of life presented itself to her as a joyless struggle—a succession of petty harassments and deceptions. Her uncle, she said to herself, was the least unfortunate of them all. He was nearing his release. Before him lay peace—peace in the lap of God! Oh yes! she envied him! For him no more contending against the malice of enemies or the misunderstanding of friends. God did not misjudge one! When she stifled her sorrow in order to attend to the practical issues of the day, Nina, inwardly, might sneer; but God would not. Unlike Nina—unlike dear Walter even—God understood! He knew that, in her heart of hearts, all she longed for was peace—and love.

After a while, rising impulsively from her seat, she flung herself down upon her knees beside Nina's chair.

"Poor, poor uncle!" she sobbed; and buried her face in her hands. "To watch him dying here, in this house,—it is too dreadful! I cannot bear it! Why was it not granted us to have him to ourselves in some peaceful spot,—where he could forget everything except our love. What would I not give to be able to keep this horrible story from him? Is it really impossible? Would it really be unwise or wrong?"

A sick look of impatience came over Nina's face, but she continued to pass her hand caressingly over her sister's hair.

Madeline lifted her head to stare mournfully before her. "All his life he has hated concealments. If we were to keep this back, should we not be haunted by the thought that we had been insincere with him upon his death-bed? Oh, Nina! I feel we *must* tell him! I feel that he would wish to know. It may be that he is still troubled by the fear that he is treating Lilian with harshness. It may be that this revelation is the one thing capable of putting his mind at rest."

With a deep sigh she brushed her hair back from her forehead and rose slowly to her feet.

"What shadows I have under my eyes!" she murmured, after glancing at her mirror. "And you too, Nina! You look utterly exhausted."

Nina seemed not to hear. But, after a minute, she, too, sighed and said:—

"I wish you would give up wandering about the house at night, my dear. It tires you out."

Madeline's face darkened. "How can I help it? *He* lies awake for hours at a time. And I know it comforts him to see me."

Nina rose from her chair.

"Well!" said she, throwing her shoulders back and straightening her waistband. "I think we have settled everything. I will have that talk with Uncle John as soon as I get an opportunity." She paused. "The telegram to Walter has already been sent off. And as for giving Lilian the doctor's message, I will do that, too, if you like?"

Madeline turned away. "There is no immediate hurry," she pronounced after a silence. "Have you considered what you are going to say?"

Nina uttered a short, dry laugh. "It is simple enough—what I have to say."

"Nothing is simple!" retorted Madeline with energy. "Nothing!" And she gave Nina a look of anger.

"If you prefer to tell Lilian, yourself, say so!" answered Nina coldly.

"Very well!" returned Madeline with sombre vehemence. "I will."

As Nina suspected, Madeline had a private reason for wishing to be newsbearer to Lilian. Two or three days ago she had made a discovery— a discovery, which, to her sense, was hardly less monstrous than Nina's. Late one night, chancing to roam down the corridor that led to Isabel's room, she had noticed a ray of light escaping from under the door. It seemed odd that Isabel should be astir at this hour; and when, on listening outside, she heard sounds of low converse and a little burst of laughter, her curiosity was fully aroused. Laughter! Laughter among the Orissers, even now—when the day of judgment was so near! This in itself was enough to bring the hot blood to her cheek.

Holding her breath and straining her ears, she remained upon the spot for a full ten minutes. Not until she had attained to an absolute certainty of the abominable truth, did she regain her room. Her face was burning; her whole body shook with indignation. Repressing an impulse to burst in upon Nina and scatter her slumbers with the atrocity of the revelation, she fell to pacing distractedly to and fro before her own hearth. Nina, after all, was so phlegmatic that there would be little pleasure in telling her. Besides, it would be wiser, she felt, not to exhibit, even to Nina, the full extent of her present disarray. Yet surely there was warranty for the fullest measure of anger and disgust! It did not argue one a prude to resent such a thing as this—at such a time as now! Nevertheless, she was dimly sensible of a need to justify to herself the particular quality of her agitation; nor did she rest satisfied until she had explained it as wholly attributable to the insult offered—the insult, first, to herself as a pure girl dwelling beneath the selfsame roof, and secondly, to her uncle, who at least might claim the respect due to one lying under the deepest shadow of death. These reflections, by lending a more dignified tone to her excitement, helped her to desist from dwelling imaginatively upon the scene, which, although her eyes had not actually witnessed it, had betrayed itself to her ear in sounds to which visual images easily fitted themselves.

Having regained some degree of self-possession, she seated herself in a chair before the fire and fell deep into thought. Yes; she was glad that she had not gone to Nina. A manner of scornful and disabused composure would be much more effective, when she did impart the news. Similarly, when she came to tell Walter. A brief statement of fact, made in a level voice, would, she fancied, startle Walter pretty effectively. Hitherto Walter had always pooh-poohed her exposition of the innate viciousness of the Orisser character, but now. . . And a sad little smile would be her only comment on the *naiveté* of his previous incredulity.

It pleased her to have made the discovery herself; for Nina, in her quiet way, had always been inclined to take the foremost place. It was significant that for some weeks past, Lilian, when she had some communication to make, had addressed herself to Nina rather than to her. And then, Nina had taken to writing long letters to Walter, as if the whole conduct of affairs at Eamor were in her hands. Once or twice lately the thought had flashed across Madeline's mind that she must be careful lest Nina should usurp her place in John Mayne's consideration—or even in Walter's!

A glance at the mirror would, however, restore her confidence in regard to the two men. But she desired no less ardently to retain the first place in Lilian's consideration. Indeed, the loss of Lilian's hatred would have been more wounding to her pride than the loss of Walter's love. To see Nina fighting her battles for her; to see Nina and Lilian matching themselves against one another in the field as the protagonists, while she looked on, was a prospect she could not bear to envisage. Her own peculiar relations with Lilian were sacred to her.

It was consequently by a natural progression of thought that she presently asked herself why she should say anything at all to Nina about her recent discovery. Why not—especially as that would be the more generous course—let this matter be private to herself and Lilian alone? The longer she reflected upon this line of action, the more highly did it commend itself. Such conduct could hardly fail to kindle some flicker of admiration and gratitude in Lilian's heart. Before that woman, who had always denied her every vestige of nobility, she would present herself as superbly magnanimous. It was a wonderful idea! As her imagination leapt to a construction of the scene, her heart beat hard with excitement. How true it was, she reflected, that gentleness went with strength. Her hatred of Lilian was already beginning to melt away.

From that moment onward she nursed her idea with tenderness. The problem, to her sense, had always been how to get in an effective appeal to Lilian's better nature; and now at last it really looked as though Providence were expressly furnishing her with a key for unlocking the woman's heart. She had early perceived how important a place Nicholas occupied in Lilian's affections; and, as she was ignorant of Allen's entry into Lilian's life, she was inclined to over—rather than under—estimate the hurt that Lilian would receive. Not that she wished to be cruel; but she had a duty to perform. The Almighty had singled her out as the instrument by which Lilian's pride was to be humbled. She was equipped for an encounter such as she had often rehearsed in daydream, but the like of which had seemed remote from reality. And the beauty of it was that no one could say that the step she premeditated was uncalled for. It was *a duty* to tell Lilian what was going on in her house. No painful duty! Lilian would sneeringly surmise. But she would have an answer to that. For what would the woman say when she learnt that, her informant had not imparted—and did not mean to impart—the shocking news to anyone else—not even to Nina! That, she fancied, would fairly stagger Lilian. What! Not tell John Mayne, when in the present condition of affairs, so little would suffice to tip the scale against her! There was magnanimity indeed! For Lilian could hardly doubt that the old man would feel this latest manifestation of Orisser cynicism to be the last straw under which the backbone of his forbearance might legitimately crack.

Many hours did Madeline give to revolving in her mind the conduct of this tremendous interview. And such was the virtue instilled into her by her gathering sense of power, that unsuspected springs of compassion welled up within her heart. She fancied that her enemy had been looking weary and discouraged of late. No doubt her hopes were running low. What, then, would be her feelings on receiving the double announcement! Surely her pride would unfreeze, and her spirit turn to water? Was it unreasonable to suppose that she would break down and weep? And, upon that, with what exquisite gentleness and mercy would she, Madeline, bend towards her and comfort her! "Lilian! Lilian!" she could hear herself say; "Put away your fears! Do you really imagine I would deprive you of anything you love? Oh, my dear, how cruelly you have misjudged me! But now—your eyes are opened! Is it not so? Ah yes! I see it in your face! At last you trust me!"

Pleasant were these phantasies. And much time did Madeline spend in their elaboration. Yet certain obscure points continued to escape her study. She never made out exactly what the solid substance of her assurances to Lilian should be. At moments, when on the crest of an emotional wave, it seemed to her that she would be prepared to resign all "hold" over her former adversary; but—that was uncertain. That was not a question she cared to go into very deeply. Her practical decisions must depend, she felt, upon the degree of Lilian's contriteness and submission.

As to the wisdom of promising not to inform her uncle of the scandal, that renunciation did not greatly trouble her. At the back of her mind was the thought that the dreadful things Nina had to disclose were, by themselves, quite enough. The tragedy of Cosmo should be amply sufficient to protect Uncle John against the weakness of a death-bed relentment.

It would be hard to resist the temptation of informing Nina and Walter. But against this she could set up the satisfaction that she would derive from the exhibition of a mysterious ascendancy over Lilian. How astonished both Nina and Walter would be by the change in Lilian's whole manner towards her. They would rightly account it a great tribute to her personality.

Chapter 13

Early in the afternoon Madeline left her room, and proceeded slowly, but resolutely, down the stairs to the boudoir, where she knew she would find Lilian.

For a few moments, after opening the door, she stood erect and still upon the threshold. It was a long time—many months to be sure—since she had entered here. She knew that her apparition would take Lilian aback; and it was consequently her intention to indicate, at the outset, by her expression and bearing, that her present visit had a purpose which fully matched its unexpectedness. Yes, Lilian was to see that it had nothing in common with the passionate, unconsidered intrusions of old days.

Alas! these four walls had witnessed some of their most terrible encounters. This little room had associations that caused her instinctively to shun it. And now, even while her will was strong enough to stifle the memories which it evoked, its terribly familiar aspect, and the faintly distinctive perfume of its air, elicited from her physical being an uncontrollable response. Her mind she could command; but, as she stood there, her heart forthwith took charge and beat with a weightier throb.

The opening of the door had revealed Lilian seated at her desk, her profile sharply defined against the dull glare of the window opposite. The next moment, however, the woman lifted her head, and, having seen who her visitor was, faced round and stiffened into a pose of startled expectancy.

The room was grey with the harsh light of the December day. Madeline felt rather than descried the dark pupils directed upon her. White-faced she knew herself to be; but it was without a quiver that she supported that searching, unreturnable scrutiny. After a sufficient pause, she closed the door behind her; then advanced, and seated herself beside the desk. Now, beneath its mask of steady interrogation, she could discern in Lilian's face resistance, apprehension—perhaps even, fear. On her side, inly she trembled—not from fear, not from rage, but from some primordial emotion, parent of both. Yet, if this deep interior tremor was straining the foundations of the purpose she had builded up, she was as yet unconscious of any moral damage. She felt valiant to resist the effect which her surroundings sought to impose upon her. She scorned her perturbation as purely physical. The body shudders at the first shock of immersion into cold water; but, as the swimmer strikes out and makes way to his appointed goal, the flesh adjusts itself to its medium; the blood regains its glow. Even so did Madeline strike out. She broke the silence on the very instant she willed, and found that she was word-perfect; she had at her command not only the phrases she had prepared, but every look and tone, down to the flicker of an eyelid or the sudden catch of a breath. Only—it distracted her to feel within her bosom this tumult that so ill accorded with her words and her demeanour. She was giving voice to feelings that were true,—to feelings that were deeply cherished, and had been with her but a few instants ago. Why had they thus treacherously fled? Why was she made false to herself in the hour of trial? Why was she condemned to give, even hiddenly, a false justific-ation to this cold, sneering woman's interpretation of her? The unfair-ness of it made her heart boil. Anger came to aggravate the seethe and surge of the nameless passion within.

Her speech was of her uncle. The words that she had prepared dropped one by one into the heavy, inhospitable silence of the little room. They dropped into the rebutting silence, and were lost. Their staleness was dreadful. How many, many times had they not sounded already in her ears! But *then* they had been alive with something better than this mock-life.

Although, in its appearance at least, the scene had hardly, as yet, falsified her imagination of it, something was terribly amiss. If ever it had lain within her power to develop the situation as she had intended, that power had utterly abandoned her. This she perceived; and her heart began to sicken with a bitter prescience of defeat. Whither were fled the strength and the sweetness that, an hour ago, had belonged to her?—the strength to enforce the conviction of her sincerity upon the mean and frigid spirit of the woman who opposed her; the sweetness that would neutralize the acridity of the heart that resisted her. Was this the fashion in which the spirit of Christ served its votaries? Or by what art did her enemy contrive to reduce others to her own level, and make nobility seem nothing but a sham?

Why was it, too, that even while she was thus denouncing Lilian in her heart, an odious, involuntary interchange of understanding was going on between them? What was that cynical interchange which each was striving to disavow—that understanding, the vain repudiation of which carried them both deeper and deeper into a hated complicity? Was it the sense that she, Madeline, was playing a comedy? Was it that? But—as there was a God in heaven, that was not true! Or, at any rate, it was no more than a lying truth. What right had Lilian to think that she saw through her? For Lilian did think so; although she was pretending that she did not. And she, Madeline, was in turn pretending that Lilian's pretence took her in. Degrading duplicities! by which neither was deceived.

But the guilt and the shame were Lilian's. What right has cynicism to justify itself by creating the insincerities in which it believes? By what iniquitous decree of nature does cynicism possess that blighting power? "Why?" cried Madeline within herself, "why am I unable to impose my own truer conception of myself upon my enemy? Why am I unable even to break off this odious, unspoken communion between us—this running commentary too profound for any words?"

And how was it all to end? To what conclusion was the ignoble farce to run? Bitterly did she repent her of her enterprise which had seemed so fresh and full of hope! In a devastating flash of insight she perceived that nothing here was new. No; it had always been thus. Always the same misleading anticipations, the same desperate trial, the same blasting deception! Why had she not remembered? She had been mad, mad, mad!

But there was no turning back. From the subject of John Mayne she had drifted into an impassioned apologia of her own life and mind, involving an equally impassioned, if less direct, denunciation of Lilian's character. It was to this that the unconscious forces of nature and habit invariably drove her—even when, as now, she intended something different. For this occasion she had designed something far more dignified, and, at the same time, far more humanly appealing—something that would prepare the ground for the revelation of Nicholas's wrongdoing. That revelation was now overdue. But Lilian had not given her any of the cues she needed; and, being all rage and chaos within, she was obliged to yield to the force and volume of a spontaneous, almost automatic, eloquence, in order to keep her head above water at all. Unfortunately, however, that eloquence carried her in a circle. She was revolving in a frothy whirlpool of fervour that swept her, not forwards, but down into the depths. John Mayne, unhappy man! who lay dying in the room above! Lilian, his wife, and her own sister in Christ! Herself, poor girl, whose heart was overflowing with compassion and grief! Alas! was there no love—no faith in God, no trust in man—to be found under the roof of Eamor? No grace to save them from the evil under which they groaned? Was there to be no mutual forgiveness even under the shadow of death?

Thus, round and round, she eddied; and while her lips thus spoke, an anguished, and yet exultant, ferocity peeped out through the eyelets of her mask. At last her heart was making confession unto itself. Forgiveness, generosity, love—they were excellent no doubt in their place and season. But the hour, sometime, might strike, when reality must come by its own. Here, then, was the real Madeline!—and again for an instant the truth gleamed out from behind her eyes. Aye, that was she, naked and unashamed!

She rejoices in the horror which she excites. She sees Lilian—silenced, fascinated, revulsed—shrink uncontrollably away. Good! 'Tis good! Lilian doubted the other, the saintly Madeline, did she not? Lilian deemed the saintly Madeline no better than a hypocrite? Well! why then does she shrink back, when the real Madeline offers to appear? Why is she afraid of the only reality she knows? Is she affrighted by the creature of her own evocation? What does she find to dread? Does she, perchance, guess that there is one gesture, and one only, by which the real Madeline might express herself? Does she apprehend that the real Madeline might rise, and, putting forth a giant's strength, smite her detested face with open palm?

But no! That must not be! So at last, lest temptation should overcome her, she sinks into silence and covers her eyes with her hand. After all, she has a counterpart for the physical blow. The tale of Nicholas and Isabel remains to be told. The farce—since farce it is—shall be played to the very end.

Yes! the quaver in her voice, produced by hate, shall still be pressed into lending pathos to words of charity. The hate that imparts a terrible lividity to her face, a terrible intensity to the wide gaze of her eyes,—that hate shall still pass off its signs as signs of pity and love.

Wherefore, drawing a long, shuddering breath, she raises her head once more, and plunges her regard deep into her enemy's eyes.

"Lilian! I came here in the hope that your heart, at the eleventh hour, would be softened, and that you would allow me to tell you what I now have to tell you—as a friend speaking to a friend!"

She paused. Was it merely her fancy that Lilian's clenched hand had tightened, and that the chill of a new fear had intensified the pallor of her face?

She protracted her pause. She savoured her victim's suspense.

"Oh!" cried she, "I can hardly bring myself to speak it. Lilian! it reveals deceit in those whom you have trusted and loved. Yet I have no choice but to speak. This is your house. And in this house where one near to you—if not dear to you, alas!—lies dying—"

She broke off. She had heard footsteps in the passage outside. And the next instant the door opened, and Nicholas walked into the room.

She stared at him, speechless with disgust. The young man was not due to return until the morrow. Her disgust ripened into fury. Her lips quivered; her face crimsoned: she half rose from her seat.

As for Nicholas, his rapid, careless entry had carried him well into the apartment. There, before them, he stood; his whole posture was one of astonished interrogation.

For a few moments no one spoke. It was to be seen that Lilian did not intend to attempt any explanation. Her chill regard bade the newcomer draw his own inferences from the scene.

At last, with an inarticulate sound—a murmur addressed to himself—the young man made as though to withdraw. But the movement was undecided. Something—a supplementary glimmer of light—seemed to hold him back. His stare at Madeline became charged with suspicion.

The fact was that the girl's demeanour had already done much to betray her. And this she herself now perceived. She could see that Nicholas's guilty conscience had been quick to divine the significance of her own guilty and defiant looks. She could see his suspicions gathering strength every instant. And she knew not what countenance to give herself. He still hung there, a terribly expressive figure. And, alas, the light of a new intelligence was also dawning in Lilian's eyes.

Her last stroke had failed. She could not doubt it. In very truth, she felt herself to be actually standing at bay. Those two were ready to combine and attack her. Nothing that she could now say would carry home. Nothing would be allowed to count, excepting the fact that she stood before them as a common tell-tale, a vulgar mischief-maker balked of her mischief. Indescribable was her rage, when, after deliberately closing the door, Nicholas came and placed himself before her.

"Well?" said he.

"Well!"

"Have you, by any chance, been talking about me?"

"You!" Her eyes blazed. "No!"

Disconcerted, but not convinced, the young man continued sullenly to stare. Taking advantage of his set-back, Madeline rose from her seat. She meant to leave the room then and there.

"You were beginning to tell me something, when Nicholas came in." Lilian's voice was low and clear. "Don't let his presence hinder you. Say what you were meaning to say."

For a few moments of blind indecision Madeline stood without speech; then——

"Very well!" she cried in a voice loud with scorn. "This is what I have to say:—That contemptible little cur——"

"Ah, ha!" broke in Nicholas with a laugh. "So I was right after all."

Her visage congested by passion, Madeline advanced upon him.

"Let me pass!" she shouted. "I sicken at the very sight of you. Let me pass or——"

For a few instants, while the young man continued to bar her passage, it seemed possible that an act of physical violence might take place. In reality, however, it was not upon Nicholas that the main blast of her wrath was turned. A moment ago her glance had fallen upon Lilian's face, and there she had read a comment that expressed itself in no more than a faint, cool smile.

With tingling flesh and a roaring in the ears, with limbs weak as water and eyes that could scarcely see, Madeline made her exit from the room. Outside in the corridor she stumbled, and feared she might fall dead in a stroke. Still tranced, she dragged her quaking body up the stairs; and in the awful, sardonic silence of her own chamber sat, for over an hour, stiff and still as death.

Chapter 14

It was a sharp gust of longing for the tranquil, leather-scented library at Eamor that had transported Nicholas home twenty-four hours before he was expected, and introduced him into a scene for which he was singularly ill-disposed. After the door had closed upon Madeline, after the tornado had swept by, his mind, reacting from the tension of the previous moments, lapsed into a temporary condition of stupor. Barely ten minutes ago he had been indulging in anticipations of a comfortable seclusion in company with his new books. The contrast was stunning. He needed breathing space—an interval for recuperation. But none was allowed. The silence into which the little room had suddenly dropped, contained an urgent summons. Lilian was sitting quite still and looking down at the carpet. The ticking clock arraigned him. Time, instead of going forward, thickened and deepened over his head.

At length, moving to the window, he fell to drumming nervously with his finger-tips upon the pane. Beneath him was a shallow flight of steps leading down to an Italian garden. Moss-grown statues and pedestalled busts of fauns stood out at intervals against a hedge of clipped evergreens. In the centre was a fountain, now silent. The wind had dropped; the clouds were massing for rain.

"Well, Nick?" said Lilian in a colourless voice.

"Well!" he muttered. "I think you understand. She had come to tell you about Isabel and me."

With surprise he noted how little true emotion he was feeling. Whilst staring at the dull, wet garden, he had received indifference like a fog over his spirit.

"What brought you back to-day?" she asked. And then, as he was slow in answering: "Did you see Allen?"

"Yes. I saw him this morning. I don't know why I came back. However"—and he uttered a sound of dreary amusement—"I'm glad I came."

She said nothing to this; and presently he took courage to face round. Avoiding her eyes, which were fixed steadfastly upon him, he approached and let himself sink into a chair beside her desk. Already his alleviation was considerable. The thing was out. Perhaps the worst moments were over. Or must there be explanations, discussions, arrangements? Good God! what arrangements? He frowned moodily.

With a suddenness that startled him, Lilian sprang up from her seat and moved to the centre of the room. Her hands were clenched, her eyes dark with anger. Staring at the door through which Madeline had departed, she murmured indistinguishable words beneath her breath.

Never before had Nicholas seen her so deeply roused.

His heart once more began to thud against his breast.

After a moment she rounded upon him; but still she was without speech.

"Tell me!" said he, in an attempt to lend himself countenance. "Had Madeline been with you long?"

She disdained to reply. She continued to fix him with dark, contemptuous eyes. At last, most unexpectedly, she said:

"John Mayne is dying."

"Dying? Really dying?"

"He can only last a few days more."

The young man drew a deep breath. Here, at any rate, was a new topic. He racked his brains for some appropriate comment, but could find nothing. She was singularly beautiful in her anger; her anger and her scorn together robbed him of all his resources.

"That," she added with a chilling smile, "that was Madeline's first item."

He could manage no more than a nod.

"No doubt," she continued, "Madeline is with her uncle at this moment—telling him about you."

He cleared his throat. "Mercifully," he observed, "I don't count for much."

"No," she agreed. "But any stick is good enough——"

The young man uttered a sound between a laugh and a groan, and then turned his head away. For a minute she stood surveying him in silence; and although his eyes were elsewhere, he could tell that she was relenting.

"Heavens!" she cried. "How foolish you are, my poor Nick!"

"I am."

"And it hasn't taken you long to see it."

"No." He paused. "Seeing it—that's always the worst part of one's folly."

"Poor little Isabel! Is she unhappy?"

"Oh, no!"

"Not yet?"

"Why ever?"

"And you?"

"Certainly not!" He sighed. "Frankly, I don't consider I have been more foolish in this than in everything I do."

"Nonsense!" she impatiently returned. "Nonsense!"

With another groan he rose and, going over to the French window, threw it open and stepped outside. A moment later she followed, and stood by his side on the broad, stone stair. As they stood there in the hush of the coming rain, another surge of indifference enveloped him. An immense resignation emanated from the moist, passive earth. The damp air came to him with that peculiar sweetness which is appreciable for the first few inspirations only. And there followed the thought: "So it is with everything—everything!"

But his indifference was ever trembling on the verge of anguish. Anguish, indifference; indifference, anguish; he knew not which he felt! How hopeless was the earth under the heavy, stagnant sky! Did she feel it too? He glanced at her. Ah! what loveliness did she not embody—she with her clear eyes that remained so intelligent even when, as now, she was dreaming!

"Lilian," he cried with more courage than he knew he possessed, "I shall never really care about anyone but you! That's the truth." And he let his head sink.

A deep stillness continued after he had spoken. He felt her by his side and dared not move; and anguish was again uppermost in his heart. But after a minute she raised her arm and passed it round his neck. For an instant her check touched his, and he stood wrapped in a hopeless, poignant bliss.

Big, slow drops of rain were now splashing upon the steps beside them, and dimpling the water in the basin of the fountain. Patient was the face of the earth before winter's oncoming sadness. Nature brooded in resignation, stilling the memory of other days in which had been mingled marvel and expectation, and presentiment and hope.

Looking up, each with a sigh, they moved a little apart.

The raindrops thickened; a gust swept round the corner of the house. Scudding down a path before the wind, Isabel came into sight. Lilian stepped indoors; and Nicholas, perceiving that the girl had not yet noticed them, was tempted to step back too. But a kind of shame prevented him. Standing his ground, he watched the approaching figure with a distant, speculative wonder. She was intensely familiar, yet equally alien; he was fond, yet indifferent; he could pity, if need be; but he certainly could not love.

Her skirts blown out before her, wisps of hair flying across her face, she came on before the wind, and was now but a few paces distant. The next moment she looked up and saw him. Her smile, in its unconsciousness, made him feel weary and old. Darting up the steps, she brushed past and swept into the room upon a swirl of raindrops and driven leaves.

Himself entering, he made it something of a business to fasten the doors behind them. His self-consciousness was acute. The vulgarity of his nature astonished him. For what had been his first thought, as Isabel went in? It had been simply this, that before Lilian he need not be ashamed of her! So he prized her charm mainly as a protection to his conceit! Her prettiness did him credit,—the fatuous Don Juan! Bah! For all his would-be self-knowledge, was he not in truth as much the fabricator, dupe, and slave, of tasteless vanities as Madeline herself? Was his whole philosophy of life anything more but a pretentious monument raised to self-esteem?

Turning, he listened to the conversation of the two others with a pretended carelessness. Isabel had thrown off her cloak and hat. Poised on the arm of a chair, she gave no sign of apprehending any change beneath the surface presented. There was no symptom of a troubled consciousness in the sweet, high timbre of her voice, or in her easy pose. His discomfort, however, momentarily deepened; and he was already edging towards the door, when Isabel jumped to her feet with an exclamation, and, searching in the pocket of her discarded cloak, produced a telegram for Lilian. She explained that she had just taken it from the messenger on his way up to the house.

His eyes fixed upon his step-mother, Nicholas waited, while she tore open the envelope.

"It is from Allen," she said.

Her voice was expressionless—too expressionless, he thought. Looking at her hard, he waited for more.

She seemed to hesitate. "Allen says that Walter wants to see him to-morrow morning. After the interview he will come down here."

"Who? Allen?"

"Yes."

"Has he, then, already had news of John Mayne's condition?"

She reflected a moment. "I suppose Walter has just received a telegram from Madeline about John Mayne. I suppose Walter has told Allen. That would explain everything."

Nicholas emitted a murmur of doubt; his hands thrust deep in his pockets, he paced to and fro before the door.

"There was another telegram—one for Nina," said Isabel. "But I left that for the messenger to deliver."

"For Nina?" Nicholas looked up. "Why does Walter telegraph to Nina instead of to Madeline?"

Lilian answered his gloomy stare with a shrug of impatience.

"How should I know? I see nothing unnatural in it. Anyhow," she added after a pause, "we shall be wiser to-morrow—when Allen arrives."

"To-morrow. . ." muttered Nicholas. "Yes."

He knew not why, but his discomfort and disquietude had assumed overwhelming proportions. Isabel's presence irked him. His brain was heavy; his eyes ached. He wanted to question Lilian; but he could not even see her face properly; heavy rain-clouds had plunged the room into semi-darkness, and the dull glare from the window was in his eyes.

At length Isabel bent down, picked up her hat and cloak, and moved slowly towards the door. When she had gone, he breathed a sigh of relief. Going over to Lilian, he stood before her with a look of silent interrogation.

She returned a steady, impenetrable regard. He knew that she had thoughts which she was unwilling to disclose. With a quick movement of anger he turned away.

A minute later the abrupt opening of the door caused them both to start. It was Isabel who appeared upon the threshold.

"John Mayne has come down from his room," she breathlessly announced. "He is now in the Big Hall."

They stared at her without speaking. Then Nicholas brought out a sound resembling a laugh.

"Wonder upon wonder!" he exclaimed. "The dying man suddenly rises from his bed!"

Glancing apprehensively over her shoulder, Isabel closed the door.

"Yes! he is there!" she repeated, "in the Big Hall!"

Nicholas laughed again. "And the question for us now to resolve is: What, in the devil's name, has roused him?"

Leaning back against the door, Isabel stood silent, still watching the effect of her announcement.

"How do you know he is there?" asked Lilian in a low voice.

"I was at the foot of the stairs—and—I heard him."

"But how could you hear him down all the length of the passage? It's impossible."

Isabel shook her head. "No, no! I heard him! He"—and her voice sank almost to a whisper—"he was shouting!"

At this Lilian got up. "Shouting? What do you mean?"

"Well, it sounded as if he was very angry."

Lilian stood still, then turned her head towards Nicholas. "I see," she said quietly.

"What was he shouting about?" inquired Nicholas huskily. "Could you make out any of the words?"

"No."

Again silence fell,—a silence that was the more profound in that the rain, which had been beating against the window, suddenly ceased.

At last Nicholas seemed to come to a resolution. Muttering something about going out to investigate, he made a rapid move to the door. Before Lilian could say anything, he was gone.

Chapter 15

Halting at the foot of the stairs, the young man stood for several minutes in a deep abstraction. When he came to himself, it was to realize that he was listening with all his ears for some sound from the Big Hall. After a few moments he advanced to the entrance of the passage and peered down it, and listened again with intentness. He could hear absolutely nothing.

Turning away, he fell to ranging to and fro across the open floor. His tread was silent; his eyes travelled nervously about him. Through a small casement upon the west there slanted a ray of watery light that flickered upon the dark panelling. He moved towards it, and stood staring out over the damp woods.

Reviewing the movements of his spirit during the past weeks, he marvelled at himself. Insane in their compellent quality did his impulses appear, and equally insane his attempts to rationalize them. But "*L'homme,*" he remembered Pascal to have said, "*l'homme est si nécessairement fou que ce serait être fou d'un autre tour de folie de ne pas être fou.*"* Yes! that was the very soul of truth! To be alive was to be under the sway of instincts and desires which the reason proclaimed to be vain; yet, bereft of those impulses, you lost all motive for living. The reason, however, was generally in abeyance. You became aware of your irrationality only after excess; and then, as a rule, you resorted to the device of calling the *excess* irrational in order to absolve the impulses themselves. An error! Excess was of course unwise; but the irrationality of the instincts and desires of Life was independent of any intemperance in gratifying them.

He sighed and smiled. It comforted him, as he could see, to give a universal application to the philosophizings which his own little character and circumstances suggested. That again was human nature—vain, vain, vain!

Breaking off, he again crossed over to the entrance of the passage leading to the Big Hall. The passage was dark; its mouth was like the

---

* "Men are so necessarily mad that not to be mad would amount to another form of madness." — Pascal, *Pensées*, 414.

mouth of a cave. And all at once a memory, which had lurked at the back of his mind throughout the day, emerged into the light. It was the memory of a dream, or of a phantasy falling within the category of dreams; for he must have been less than half awake when he had fashioned it. It had seemed to him that he was sitting with John Mayne in a lofty cavern far underground, and prodigiously removed from the world of men. They were deep in talk, and it seemed that their colloquy had already lasted for untold ages. A crushing weariness oppressed him, notwithstanding which his attention was still anxiously engaged by what John Mayne was saying. "You see, my dear boy, you have been utterly mistaken. And it is because you have never really tried to understand me, that you cannot grasp what a kindly, simple soul I am. My trouble—if only you could believe it!—is that I am too soft, too impressionable,—in a word, too human. Yes, alas, too human, whilst you"—the old man sighed, shook his head, and looked at his companion reproachfully—"you are hard and inhuman!"

Utterly confounded, Nicholas remained silent. Whereupon John Mayne plucked him by the sleeve and in an earnest undertone resumed: "Nicholas, my boy, you are hard! And I will make use of an analogy to illustrate what I mean. You know, in the wrestling profession men use special exercises, and an artificial regime, to bring the body to its highest state of fitness. Well, it has been proved that a man can easily abuse of these means. Big, balled muscles that look very fine and feel like iron, are often quite valueless in a contest. There will be no quickness in them, no elasticity; and very soon they will tire. Now, so it is with the training of the mind. Life, for all our artifice, remains a very *natural* business, and is best transacted by natural means. A man ought to guard and preserve his spontaneity, his primitive, animal innocence, as his most valuable asset. The intelligence with its powers of reason may profitably interest itself in what goes on outside one, but not in what goes on inside. There are a thousand useful, though contradictory, impulses, ebulliences, attractions, reticences, withdrawals, and repulsions, in the natural man, which the reason should overlook. A man should not alienate himself from his own nature, nor look at his emotions to become their judge. Is it not through one's emotions alone that one can effectually reach one's fellow-men? And is it not true that one has to reach their emotions, be it to win their love, or to make use of them?"

Increasingly confused and ill at case, Nicholas again kept silence. He was longing to make his escape. It had come into his mind that the old man must be mad.

"My friend," continued John Mayne in a confidential whisper, while he gripped him by the arm and drew him closer yet, "my friend, look at me! Look at my life! I have never been a hypocrite in any admissible sense of the word, and yet—what have I done? I have gone my way through the world, pitiless, yet ever compassionating; blind to the sufferings that followed my footsteps, yet always ready to sympathize with grief. Let not your right hand know what your left hand doeth. Well! I have followed that precept and found it good. Whilst busily using one hand to encompass the good of others, I have let the other work instinctively, unconsciously, to my own advantage. While serving myself not too ill, I have left my heart free to expand with noble generosity, to swell with sympathy, to flutter with fond, disinterested hopes. I have clung to the mistiest and most puerile of idealisms, dreamt of universal brotherhood, sighed after friendship, and spent many a night in tears over the sternness of what I called necessity. We men of character, you know, are all alike." He smiled complacently. "Have you never read the self-revelations of the world's doughtiest bullies? No? Well, you should. There you will find what human tenderness was at the core of the iron will. I assure you, my dear Nicholas, you will read things that will touch you deeply! Such moving traits of sensibility! Such a sense of being misunderstood! Such a yearning for sympathy! In a word, so much *human nature!*

"Much better, too, will you apprehend the cruel injustice of calling me a hypocrite. Had I been a hypocrite, I should never have had the strength to live as I have lived. Hypocrisy weakens. Even the fear of hypocrisy is paralysing. But we, the simple, robust children of the earth, never question ourselves nor suspect our emotions. Pity, tenderness, remorse, even self-pity, gush up freely within us to purge and to invigorate. Our free emotionalism is our secret—the great secret of our vitality. We sin, as we call it, and repent, and sin again; and that is the way of nature. Hypocrisy is never more than a sorry attempt to do for yourself what nature, if you leave her alone, will do for you. *C'est son métier!* Nature tells a man what it is good to think and not to think, to remember and not to remember, to believe and not to believe, to know and not to know. Nature will keep you sleek, my dear boy, if you will only let her.

"Consider the immense range of reflection possible at any given moment to any human being! And consider what proportion of those thoughts constitute a wholesome food for the mind! Why, then, does man not exist in a semi-poisoned and miserable state? Simply because nature selects! Although embedded in a soil saturated with evil, the healthy human creature draws up into his system only the juices salutary to him. Our roots, governed in the dark of earth by Mother Nature, are for most of us, fortunately, almost outside our control. The healthy are well content if a healthful sap rises within them; or, if they turn their thoughts in dangerous directions, it is only to play with the perils there;—it is merely for the sake of a little exercise, at once academic and sentimental. It is only for the sake of being able to bring back the report that the terrors of darkness, boldly envisaged, resolve themselves into nothing!

"I, personally, however, prefer a simpler way of being. Do you remember Madeline's favourite lines:

> 'She holds her little thoughts in sight,
>   Though gay they run and leap.
> She is so circumspect and right;
>   She has her soul to keep.
> She walks—the lady of my delight—
>   A Shepherdess of Sheep.'*

"Now that embodies the spirit I most approve. Such a one is capable of maintaining her innocence under almost any conditions. Such a one could do, quite happily, all manner of things that you, my poor friend, could not do without grave self-reproach. That shepherdess is Nature's child. Her candid gaze does not pry beneath the sunny surface of her being. She has religion and morality, which you secretly envy her. But how can you hope to possess either religion or morality, when you have cut yourself off from Nature? Religion springs straight from Nature, and morality is Nature's shrewdest invention. Convictions and prejudices introduce into the tapestry of life all its brightest colours. Believe me, there is nothing like a little simple morality for lending zest to life! Life dotes on variety; she loves to see the play and counter-play of mimic forces within herself—plenty of movement, plenty of scope for the emotions, plenty of what is commonly called 'action 'and character'; and—here's the fun of it, my dear boy!—the saint, the moralist, and the ascetic, in their liveries of other-worldliness, are among her most vivid, telling figures. Yes, my dear Nicholas," chuckled the old man, "it's a brave show! and its purpose of course is—Come now, what is its purpose?—Why! to distract us from the real conflict, to be sure!—the conflict that no one talks about, that no one thinks about, if he can help

* From "The Lady of the Lambs" by Alice Meynell.

it—the conflict between life on the one side and, on the other, Boredom, Disgust, and Fear! Yes, those are Death's true names, those are Death's true characters! And those are what overtake the man whose attention is seduced from the mimic stage, to the moaning and wailing in the wings. That struggle—the everlasting struggle of the illusionist to maintain illusion—is petty and depressing. No one can regard it for long as either fine or funny. Irony soon grows weary of itself; pity appears a mutual derogation. And that is why, for you and your like, life is nothing but death-in-life. You are the small and sickly child, against which Mother Nature turns in disgust! She persecutes it, because it is moved to traduce her. You are Life's antipathy! You are one of those who radiate darkness and disease! Where you go a blight runs before you; colours fade; sounds are deadened; the earth is corroded; the sky tarnished; and the chill of sickness is communicated to living, human hearts!"

Nicholas, who had been looking into the old man's countenance as he spoke these last words, perceived that his eyes were now flaming with an undisguised hatred. Making a desperate effort, he tore himself out of John Mayne's grasp.

"What are you," he cried, trembling, "but *one of us,* since you know these things?"

"One of you!" And the old man, rising in his turn, thrust at him a face of heinous contempt. "One of you! No, no! I, in my time, have eaten the lion's share of life, and now—I eat the jackal's too!"

Nicholas turned and fled.

In terror he rushed along the dark passages of the cave, uncertain whether he heard the steps of John Mayne behind him. But to his joy he beheld, before very long, a distant glimmer. At the end of the tunnel he came out into a space, like a theatre, illuminated at one end by the lights of a stage. He slipped into a seat, taking his place amongst a large, silent assembly. A sound of music pulsed through the air—low, vibrant, splendid, but—as he presently perceived—indescribably menacing. Never before had he heard music like this, so harsh and brazen in tone, so significant of malignancy, deliberate and triumphant. While it gathered in volume the whole throng sat motionless and expectant. All eyes were fixed upon the stage, down which, stark naked, tall, and lean, and corpse-like, Cosmo was now slowly advancing. His body, obscenely daubed with paint, glistened as he stalked into the glare of the foot-lights; his face wore a smile of cruel meaning, and from his lips there issued a chant. The spectacle impressed Nicholas with unutterable horror. His whole being revolted against the felt, but uncomprehended, meaning of what he heard and saw. The music rose to a paean of frenzied jubilation. Starting up in his seat, he perceived for the first time that the gloating audience were fiends.

While recalling this phantasy, the young man had moved back to his position by the window. His grasp upon the dream had at first been slight, the memory of it threatening to depart should his mind stray for one instant out of the required key. But he had been determined to recapture the whole intensity of the experience; and he succeeded so well that, in the end, he became seized with panic lest the way back to reality should be lost.

So now, turning sharply round, he fixed his eyes once more upon the entrance to the passage and once more listened attentively. Was it possible that Isabel's imagination had played her false? Should he venture down the passage to see?

Just as he was about to put this idea into execution, a sound, the origin of which he at once recognized, came to his ears. Someone had drawn the curtain back from over the doorway to the Big Hall. And now someone was moving with an unusual, shuttling slowness of gait down the passage towards him.

For a moment he hung irresolute. It was at his option to glide away into the dark of the opposite corridor, in the direction of Lilian's room. But curiosity, or some sentiment akin to it, urged him to stand his ground. The dusk had thickened; the hall was now obscure. If he were to hold himself motionless against the curtain, John Mayne quite possibly would pass by without seeing him ...

Ah! but, to be sure, John Mayne would not be alone! No, he was not alone! The muffled sound of his speech came travelling down the passage; and the answer was in a woman's voice. That voice must be Madeline's.

It was many weeks since the old man had made his last public appearance—many weeks since Nicholas had last seen him. He waited, trembling. And when at last that well-remembered figure emerged into the hall, his eyes fastened upon it with a rapt, and yet shrinking, eagerness. Notwithstanding the gloom, he was able to discern how pitilessly these last weeks of suffering had ravaged their still defiant victim. John Mayne's broad form was crushed and bowed beneath his enormous, but invisible, burden. John Mayne's whole visage was written over with the sentence of his oncoming doom. It had not shrunk into emaciation, but was swollen into a fulness that his disease made pendulous and grey. Yet his eyes still burned, and the lines of his mouth were still expressive of unconquerable truculence. Life had not diminished within him; no! life had increased and insurrected inside that bloated shape. He fought for his existence against the insubordinate energies of his own flesh. Would that the foe had been outside, then might he have overpowered him. His eyes, staring and questing, seemed to hunger for a visible antagonist; his clutching hands were eager to grapple with an evil that he could seize and hold. Leaning forward from the hips, he dragged heavily upon the arm supporting him. And Nicholas perceived that, contrary to his expectations, John Mayne's attendant was not Madeline, but Nina.

Toilsomely did the two make their journey from the passage to the foot of the stairs. It seemed not unlikely that, in their labour, neither one nor the other would notice the form of their observer, who, standing rigid against the curtain, shifted only his head and eyes to follow their onward movement.

Step by step, with gaze fixed upon the ground, they crawled along before him, until at last John Mayne reached the bannisters, and there made a pause to gather strength for the ascent. Beside him stood Nina; and Nicholas heard her beg permission to send for a carrying-chair. But the sick man would not have it. Having dropped his niece's arm, he leaned ponderously against the oaken pillar, a heavy, sagging monument of decrepitude and despair.

Nina's eyes dwelt upon him for some while, dark and expressionless. Then with a sigh she lifted her head and let her gaze wander in gloomy abstraction about the hall. Twice did her unseeing regard pass over the still watcher by the window, without informing her of his presence. But, the third time, her vision was arrested and remained fixed. With knitted brows she peered. Nicholas and she exchanged through the obscurity a long, blank stare.

The young man was the first to turn his face away. He seemed to be resuming a meditative contemplation of the landscape. The silence continued for a minute longer; then there came to his hearing the murmur of Nina's voice, as she spoke something into her companion's ear.

John Mayne's feet shuffled round upon the polished floor. And, as the old man's gaze fell upon his back, it seemed to Nicholas that his heart started and shook under the blow.

Then Nina spoke again; and John Mayne stirred once more. The stair-boards creaked; the sound of laboured breathing announced that the ascent had begun.

Nicholas looked over his shoulder. The two figures were disappearing into the brown-black obscurity of the stairway. Another minute and they had faded out of sight. But he could still hear the heavy tread of John Mayne's feet, and the groaning and gasping that issued from his mouth. Then those noises, too, died away; and there followed the sharp, decisive closing of a door.

Chapter 16

The letter about Cosmo, upon which Nina had expended so much time and trouble, lay for some hours, unopened, on Walter's writing-table. A public meeting of no small importance had kept him up late the evening before. He was launching himself at last upon the troubled waters of political life. Nor had his prospects been dimmed by patient delay. On the contrary, he was sliding off the stocks with a much fuller majesty than he could have commanded before John Mayne's eclipse.

The meeting had been eminently successful; so it was in a good and comfortable humour that he sat himself down to a perusal of his morning's correspondence. As usual during the last fortnight, his first act was to run his eye over the whole stack of his envelopes in search of a letter from his old chief. Not that he wished to find one; but he had some reason for expecting one; and the non-appearance of the familiar handwriting never failed to call forth a small sigh of relief.

The fact was that he had taken courage at last to approach John Mayne upon the subject of Eamor. A fortnight ago he had written him a letter containing a statement of his views. It was a letter nicely calculated to provide testimony that he had done all that could properly be expected of him,—a letter that would afford protection against any censure that might be directed against him in the future; and yet it was not, he profoundly hoped, couched in so challenging a tone as to provoke the old man (or Madeline, who in all probability would see it) to unforgiving anger.

The step had been a bold one, fraught with hazardous consequences. And yet it did not explain the whole secret of Walter's daily thrill upon the arrival of the post. By a curious coincidence his letter had crossed one from John Mayne,—a bombshell of a letter; for it had actually contained the question whether he knew what had become of Cosmo Orisser. It will easily be conceived that this question had plunged Walter into the profoundest consternation. Everything pointed to an immediate crisis. But he had kept his head. He noticed that John Mayne made his inquiry in a manner which suggested that he had little hope of its bringing him any information. The question came, too, in the middle of a long, rambling disquisition on other topics. It was very unlike the letters which his chief used to write in the old days. It was distinctively the letter of a man who has lost the power of coming to grips with his subject.

These observations had renewed Walter's courage and helped him to decide how to meet the emergency. Undoubtedly the right thing to do was to ignore the awkward question altogether. Let John Mayne, first, reply to the letter which had been addressed to *him!* Deep in his heart, he cherished the belief that John Mayne would make no reply. And with an equal optimism he dared hope that the subject of Cosmo would also be allowed to drop. His correspondent, he reflected, was too infirm to persevere—especially against a passive obstruction. He lacked the necessary strength of purpose. Negative opposition would suffice to quench his initiative.

Upon assuring himself, then, that there was no letter from John Mayne among his correspondence, Walter settled down to his day's work with just the small pat of reassurance that he needed. Indeed, he would have been perfectly satisfied with his budget, had he not come upon Nina's upright, expressionless script. The latter, having perceived that Walter liked to feel that he was exercising supervision over affairs at Eamor, had taken to sending him what she rightly imagined he would conceive to be sober, accurate reports. But, unfortunately, the day had come, when she had overreached herself, by re-echoing with too masterly a fidelity her correspondent's manner and tone. One morning, as he was scanning her neat pages, Walter's complacent smile had changed into a puzzled frown. It had dawned upon him that what he was reading was a pastiche. And ever since then her missives, so far from gratifying him, had been a source of steadily increasing vexation.

This particular letter of hers offended him by its bulkiness alone. It bespoke pretentiousness in the writer that she should set out to engage the attention of a busy man with at least eight closely-written sheets. Nothing, he surmised, had occurred at Eamor that might not be succinctly related in a page and a half. Nina's verbiage was really becoming insufferable! After one cursory glance, he was on the point of casting the letter aside, when, however, it struck him that its tone was, after all, rather unusual. The woman had never yet presented herself as a mystery-monger; but here she seemed to be leading up to something dark and sensational. He accordingly let his eyes skim over the next page, and half-way down it, to his sudden horror, he came upon the name Cosmo

Orisser.

At once his expression changed. He read on with all his attention; and, as he read, his face grew ruddier and ruddier. Very soon it was glistening with countless, minute points of perspiration. He could not drink in Nina's words fast enough. The cant phrases and stereotypes, in which her meaning lay embedded, made it desperately slow work following her. She was "greatly troubled and perplexed"; she had been "convinced at first that there must be some mistake"; of course, she was "the last person in the world to think evil of anyone"; and yet, very soon, she had been "unable to resist the conclusion that something was wrong." Walter groaned with impatience and plodded on. It appeared that, next, Nina had "made a number of most disconcerting and painful discoveries," until at last she "could no longer refuse to admit that the worst suspicions were justified"; and so on—confound her!—until she had made the most of everything that she had been able to ferret out.

Her facts were bad enough, too: Cosmo's secret sojourn with Allen at Eamor village under an assumed name, his removal to Tornel, his mysterious postcard, his return to Eamor, his flight from Allen, the discovery of a dead body (which undoubtedly was his) in a lane near the house, the perfunctory inquest, and his burial without revelation of his identity; these facts constituted a tale ugly enough in all conscience!

After he had finished, Walter cast the letter from him with a gesture of the profoundest disgust, got up from his chair, and took several agitated turns about the room. When he reflected that Nina had probably imparted her information to John Mayne as well as to Madeline; and that John Mayne had probably called upon Lilian for explanations; and that Lilian, in that case, would indubitably have sheltered herself as far as possible behind *him*;—when he reflected upon these things, his heart turned to gall and he cursed Nina for the most evil-wishing and hypocritical busybody the world had ever seen.

The more deeply he considered her letter, the more he disliked its underlying tone. He, who had written so many careful letters in his life, could appreciate just how clumsily careful it was. Although she made a show of perturbation and distress, he was ready to swear that, when she penned those lines, her feelings had already settled down into a frigid, wily, vindictive satisfaction.

Her concealments and omissions he found extremely significant. For instance, the manner in which she had obtained her information, and how much of it was established by good evidence, remained, for all her eight pages, a matter for conjecture. She was successful, too, in leaving him to wonder whether she was not still keeping a thing or two up her sleeve. Then, again, not to state outright whether she had already informed John Mayne or not! . . . Oh! her disingenuousness was complete!

His first impulse was to take the next train down to Eamor, in the forlorn hope that he might be in time to put a curb on her mischievous tongue. But further consideration banished that hope as altogether vain. Moreover, precipitate action was foreign to him; and his mind had jumped to the thought that it would be wise to send for Allen, before doing anything else. After a talk with Allen he would be better equipped for coping with the situation at Eamor. So he would send Nina a telegram bidding her expect him at Eamor by the afternoon train on the morrow,—not before that. It would be just as well not to give any appearance of excessive perturbation. And his telegram might as well contain instructions that she was to keep her own counsel pending his arrival.

He was still gloomily deliberating, when Madeline's telegram, transmitting the verdict of the specialist, was put into his hands. This development he could not but welcome as enormously simplifying the problem. It seemed reasonable to suppose that John Mayne was in a condition which precluded him from giving sustained attention to Nina's news,—assuming that he had received it; and, if he was still ignorant, Nina could now hardly take it upon herself to disturb his ignorance. The whole question of Cosmo was therefore thrown into a subordinate position; it was shelved; it would have to wait; and with John Mayne's death it would lose more than half its portentousness. That he could see quite clearly . . . Yes! The prospect was not so threatening after all.

The next matter to consider was his coming talk with Allen. That interview would naturally be a difficult one; but he was in no uncertainty as to what line to take. First of all, Allen must be conciliated; he must be brought into a reasonable and friendly frame of mind; he must be made to understand that his interlocutor was no less desirous than he that justice should be done to Lilian Mayne. And the way to accomplish this would be to treat him on terms of equality, to speak as one man of the world to another, and to let him know that he, Walter Standish, had already, on his own initiative, made strong representations to John Mayne concerning the future of the Eamor estate.

Having thus prepared the ground, he would pass from the subject of

John Mayne's now imminent demise to his other, more difficult, subject. He would produce Nina's letter and say that, while questioning the accuracy of her information, and believing that the actual facts were susceptible of an interpretation very different from hers; yet he could not deny that the affair retained a distinctly unpleasing aspect; and he would beg to be put in a position to show her that her imputations were quite unjustifiable, quite baseless.

It seemed to Walter that Allen could hardly fail to accept this offer with thankfulness. The more so, that Nina's accusations and innuendoes would assuredly have thrown him into very considerable perturbation, No man can listen to a charge of—well! of homicide—with indifference, nor be without gratitude to a ready and influential defender.

But if Walter meant to be kind, he also meant to be firm. His visitor should not take leave of him before acquiring a proper sense of dependence and obligation. Eight years ago, Walter remembered, Allen had used a most undesirable tone in discussing the future of the Eamor Estate. That tone must not be heard again—not in any circumstances.

Chapter 17

At noon, the next day, when Allen was announced, Walter rose from his writing-table with friendly alacrity, pushed two easy-chairs towards the fire-place, and offered his guest a cigarette.

In due accordance with his plan, John Mayne's approaching death formed the subject of his opening discourse. But he was careful not to enlarge too much upon his grief over the event; he forced himself to proceed with all admissible haste to the vexed question of Eamor. Leaning forward with the air of one deciding upon a confidence—

"I must tell you," he said "that I have gone so far as to make a frank statement of my views to John Mayne himself! It was not an easy thing to do; but I felt it to be a duty . . . Or perhaps I should say that my feelings outweighed my scruples. I simply could not forbear!—I declared that it was for him to do justice to Mrs. Mayne—for him to take action in his own person. I deprecated any delegation of discretion or of powers.—I did not say this of course out of any fear that Mrs. Mayne would otherwise run the risk of not receiving justice at all; I said it simply because I considered that the promises given her at the time of her marriage required no less direct and unequivocal a fulfilment."

He paused. He was convinced that Allen was very favourably impressed. But, so far, most of the talking had been on his side, and he would have welcomed clearer indications of his guest's approval.

"My object in putting these things before you," he earnestly continued, "is to make it plain that your sentiments and mine are essentially the same.—I seem to remember certain interviews in the past, in which, quite unaccountably, the appearance arose that we were at variance! It would be sad, if misapprehensions of that kind were to continue. For one thing, should it prove desirable, or possible, to make further representations to John Mayne, those representations ought to proceed equally from us both. They ought to have the weight of our perfect unanimity behind them."

Again he paused; and was glad to receive a response of a more satisfactory warmth. Encouraged, he resumed:—

"It is so important, my dear Allen, that we should pull together! In certain quarters, unhappily, an appreciable amount of ill-feeling and mistrust already exists. It must be our business to remove it.—And this brings me to a rather difficult part of my subject—to a matter which I am obliged to raise now (untimely as the moment is), because, in its present aspect, it permits reflections to be cast upon your conduct and upon Mrs. Mayne's. We must clear those ambiguities away at once, if we are to institute mutual confidence and good-will."

His sentence ended with a sigh. After a glance at Allen he fixed his eyes thoughtfully upon the fire.

"In the summer," said he, "you applied to the Museum Board for a holiday, giving us to understand that you wished to go abroad for reasons of health. Since then we have not heard from you; but I did subsequently become aware, through Mrs. Mayne, that you were still in this country, and devoting yourself to the care of that unfortunate creature, Cosmo Orisser."

He broke off. Allen looking steadily at him, nodded.

"Next," continued Walter, "I was given to understand that you and Cosmo had left the country. But a few weeks ago—quite suddenly—you put in your appearance at the Museum.—Now . . ."

Scrutinizing his finger-nails with a frowning perplexity, he appeared to be searching for a continuation. As a matter of fact, however, he had finished. He was waiting for his lead to be taken up.

It was fully a minute before Allen made any response. And during that minute Walter began to question whether all his previous amiability had not been entirely wasted. For, the moment Cosmo's name was pronounced, Allen's face changed; a strange gleam came into his eyes,— a gleam which, astonishingly enough, seemed to betoken a kind of elated hostility.

"My dear Standish!" said he at last, "I must ask you to explain outright what you are driving at."

Walter lifted his eyebrows in dumb surprise. And he was still more surprised, when Allen answered the look with a short laugh, and said:

"As you can well imagine, Cosmo kept me pretty busy—until two months ago."

"Until two months ago?" echoed Walter in a hollow voice.

"Yes!" Allen's eyes dwelt steadily upon him. "And for a short time after that I took a well-earned holiday."

This tone was profoundly disconcerting. Indeed Walter was uncertain whether he had not reason to be more than disconcerted. Obviously

304

the next thing to ask was: What had become of Cosmo? But this he did not feel at all inclined to do—at any rate, just yet. He must first take his bearings.

"No one doubts that your holiday was well-earned!" said he. "Indeed I can't help thinking that you misconceive the spirit of my enquiries."

"Not at all!" returned Allen. "I am sure the spirit is friendly. But I still have to learn exactly what it is you want to know."

Walter gave a patient sigh. "My dear Allen! You *are*, I see, disposed to think me intrusive. Well! perhaps I should have done better by showing you, at the start, that I have a good excuse for inviting your confidence."

With much gravity he rose and fetched Nina's letter from his writing-table.

"I have here," he continued, "a communication of an unusual character . . . This letter, which I received yesterday—"

"Aha!" exclaimed Allen, and that unpleasant gleam again lit up his eyes. "A letter!—About Cosmo?"

Walter stationed himself before the hearth and looked down at his interlocutor with great seriousness.

"Yes!—About Cosmo!"

"Good!" said Allen laconically. "Let me see it!"

Walter was not well pleased. "What is here written was certainly not meant for your eyes; and I am by no means sure——"

Allen interrupted him by breaking out into a laugh. "Look here, Standish! Don't let's waste time. If you want news of Cosmo, say so! But—for fear lest I should tell you *more* than you want to know—I suggest that you begin by laying all your cards out on the table, without further ado."

Walter gazed at the speaker with an anger and astonishment that was by no means feigned. This tone increasingly bewildered him. It rang with the fearlessness of innocence; although the words themselves were quite otherwise suggestive. All he could yet see clearly was that Allen intended to be truculent. But why? To what purpose? His perplexity increased his annoyance. He was greatly tempted to adopt his most crushing manner,—to make the fellow understand, before he went any further, that this was not a trial of cunning, and that the language of the tavern—"cards up your sleeve," "laying your cards out on the table," and so forth—was not appropriate. No! all discussions to which Walter Standish was a party, were conducted as between gentlemen—gentlemen taking counsel together in the interests of justice and expediency.

Prudence, however, restrained him from expressing any more of this than was conveyable by means of a very frigid stare. Then, with the utmost deliberation he faced about, threw a piece of wood on to the fire, and went back to his seat.

"As I was saying, this letter was certainly not intended for your eyes; but, as it is not marked private, and as I am convinced that the writer would be the first to wish that you should have a speedy opportunity of—well! of clearing yourself,—I have little hesitation in reading you certain extracts."

Again he made a pause; he still hoped to discover tokens of uneasiness. But the same hard light, as of inimical amusement, was shining in Allen's eyes. So without another word he began. With breaks and hesitations, intended to conceal the fact that he knew the letter almost by heart, he read aloud practically every word. Having finished, he folded the sheets together again, settled himself down in his chair, and waited.

Allen's expression was peculiar. His thinking mind seemed to have retreated very far behind the outward mask. Its activity was betrayed only by the eyes. His eyes looked at you as might the eyes of a wild animal—a tiger, Walter mentally commented—staring out from the furthest corner of a darkened lair. The remainder of his features were fixed in a peculiar smile.

"Well!" said he, after a silence. "What do you think of Mrs. Pomeroy? A clever woman? Eh?"

Walter disdained to give this any acknowledgement.

Allen's grin ended with a short, sudden laugh. After which, abruptly, he looked away, and fell—or so it seemed—into deep meditation.

A minute later he drew out his watch.

"I am going down to Eamor by the fast train this afternoon. Are you, by any chance, taking the same train?"

"I am," said Walter, concealing his annoyance.

"Good!" returned Allen cheerfully. "In an empty first-class compartment we shall have every opportunity to thrash this matter out!"

And with that he rose, nodded, and made his departure.

Chapter 18

Alone, Walter paced up and down the room. "I don't like this at all!" said he to himself. "I don't like this at all!"

Not only was the journey before him most unpleasant to contemplate, but Eamor at the end of it—at the best an unattractive prospect—was rendered doubly uninviting by the knowledge that Allen would be there. All his plans were thrown into confusion; there was absolutely no telling how the man would conduct himself. His attitude so far was simply inexplicable. . . . "No! I don't like this at all!" said Walter.

A couple of hours later he found himself seated opposite his unwelcome travelling companion in a compartment of which they were the sole occupants. During the interval he had not ceased from anxious thought. But no fresh ideas had emerged. It merely seemed to him more urgent than ever that he should bring Allen into a friendly, reasonable frame of mind. He had to suppose, in default of any other explanation, that Allen's truculence was the effect of an excessive nervous agitation. In which case—and, indeed, in any case—the only thing to do was to show him that Nina's mode of envisaging the affair was by no means the necessary nor the proper one. No! certainly not! In fact the construction which she put upon the behaviour of those concerned was outrageous.

Accordingly, he brought all his urbanity once more into play. While they were settling themselves, he made light talk; and was ready, as soon as the train had moved out of the station, to glide into a good-humoured, but destructive, analysis of Nina's letter. It was easy to see, he observed with a laugh, that the poor, dear lady had wrought herself up into a dreadful state of nerves! And what a mare's nest she had discovered! Fortunately, it should not prove difficult to restore her peace of mind.

In this fashion he quickly got under way, and was soon giving a finished exhibition of his forensic ability. Nina's glooms and ambiguities were one by one visited with the torch of reason; sweetness and light were gradually shed over the entire scene; Lilian's supposed duplicity was revealed as prudence and discretion; the action which Nina had imputed to a callous self concern was shown to be the fine flower of charitableness. Allen's part similarly was transformed. No one in his senses could have anything but praise for the devotion with which the latter had applied himself to the service of Cosmo. The whole story from beginning to end reflected the highest credit upon both Lilian and Allen. Was it conceivable that John Mayne would take any other view? Hardly! The John Mayne of former days would certainly have dismissed Nina's phantasies with a broad laugh. And if one could not speak with such certainty of the John Mayne of to-day, there was no question but that a calm, succinct exposition of the facts—issuing from the mouth of a disinterested party—would achieve the desired result.

At this point Allen's face showed a smile, which Walter took to be expressive of dubiety.

"My dear sir!" he exclaimed, "is it possible that you are still troubled by misgivings?" And then, as Allen remained silent—" Can it be that the suppression of Cosmo's name at the inquest is weighing upon your conscience? I certainly cannot think of anything else that should do so! And as for that!" Whereupon he proceeded to argue that the inquest had been, quite naturally, no more than a formality: and if Allen's silence had been censurable technically, from every other point of view it was nothing short of commendable. Surely there would have been something heartless in betraying—over Cosmo's dead body—the secret which some spark of family pride had prompted that unhappy creature to preserve up to the very end? It would be strange if he, Walter Standish, should fail to make John Mayne appreciate this.

"I understand," said Allen reflectively, "that you are proposing to act as my advocate?"

"Well, yes!" replied Walter in judicial tones. "I think it really almost amounts to that. I feel it my duty not to let this empty scandal influence Mr. Mayne against his wife. And it is fairly obvious that the person best qualified to approach him is myself. The mere fact that I am so ready to defend you, will at once put a different colour on the affair. My representations, being manifestly disinterested, will carry a quite particular weight. In short, assuming that you and Mrs. Mayne agree to commit yourselves to me—and that you do not attempt to approach John Mayne directly—I can almost guarantee that this unfortunate complication shall not be allowed any evil consequences whatever."

At the conclusion of this discourse, which, from beginning to end, had lasted nearly an hour, Walter sank back into his seat with a sigh. His eyes, however, continued to rest upon Allen with a grave persuasiveness.

"All that I am now inviting you to do," he appended, "is to put me in possession of such further particulars as may assist me to dispel Mrs. Pomeroy's illusions."

Allen pursed his lips. "Mrs. Pomeroy's illusions!" he echoed; and emitted a dubious sound.

"Yes!" said Walter with great firmness. "The sooner her mind is cleared the better."

Allen was silent awhile; then, in turn, leant forward.

"You are assuming that John Mayne has not already called upon his wife for explanations?"

Walter nodded. "I can hardly say why, but I don't think that is likely to have taken place And even if it has . . ."

"You would still prefer to take the whole matter upon your own shoulders—to deal with it single-handed?"

"Yes! That, I am confident, would be best for everyone concerned."

"Mrs. Mayne and I would hold ourselves entirely aloof? And you would bring us reports on your progress?"

"Exactly!"

A smile spread over Allen's face. He shook his head slowly from side to side. "Oh! my dear Standish!" said he.

"Eh?" Walter's expression was one of rather indignant interrogation.

Again Allen shook his head. "Would it be fair to let you assume all this responsibility? Just think! the fate of Eamor is hanging in the balance! Supposing you were to give us to understand that all was well; and then, when John Mayne's will came to be read—disaster! How awkward for you!"

Wrathful as he was, Walter chose to ignore the ironic element in this speech.

"Although I should do my utmost for Mrs. Mayne, I should not, of course, hold myself responsible for any decision of her husband's in regard to Eamor. The most I could promise would be that everything should be done to prevent the question of Cosmo from prejudicing Mr. Mayne against her."

"Ah yes!" murmured Allen. "You would have done your best! Your conscience, in any event, would be at rest." And he nodded understandingly.

Walter turned his head and looked out of the window. Darkness was descending over the wet country-side. The flying landscape struck him as exceedingly dreary. A few moments ago he had been persuaded that

Allen was beginning to see reason; but now he had grave doubts. Anger and disappointment welled up in his heart.

After the silence had continued for some minutes, he shifted his position and studied his companion covertly. Allen had the face of a man wrestling with a heavy problem; but at last he looked up and said:

"Standish! What do you think of Mrs. Mayne's chances?"

"I think they are good," returned Walter with an effort.

Allen gave a short laugh. "You do, do you? Well! I am sorry to say that Mrs. Mayne doesn't agree with you. She was very optimistic at first. But the conclusion has been gradually forced upon her that her case is desperate."

Walter frowned up at the gas-light overhead and sighed deeply. "That's bad! That's bad! I can only hope—indeed I still believe—that she is mistaken."

He would have continued in this strain, had not the look in Allen's face checked him. He perceived that nothing he had to say would be sufficiently placating.

"Standish!" said Allen leaning forward and speaking with emphatic distinctness. "Measures very much stronger than any you at present contemplate are necessary! And I will tell you what they are." He paused. "You must be ready to present yourself before John Mayne *with me*. And you must not shrink from plain speaking. I consider it essential that you should bring the utmost pressure to bear upon him. Yes!" he went on, crushing an attempt at interruption; "You must disregard his anger completely. You will be within your rights, if you tell him that you cannot act as his executor unless he releases Mrs. Mayne, immediately, from all her obligations. You must make him feel that a refusal on his part will cause an absolute breach. He counts on you for the continuation of his life's work. You stand in command of the industrial, social, and philanthropic, machines which he has taken a life-time to construct. There is no one at hand to take your place. He has come to regard you as a member of his family; he takes pleasure in the prospect of your marriage with his niece. You are in the position to make a hard threat. And that threat you must make. He must see that you are in earnest."

During this speech Walter's face had assumed a more and more scandalized expression. At the end he continued to fix Allen with a glassy stare. How did the fellow presume? Whence came the audacity? From one in his situation it was monstrous! It was positively uncanny!

"I think," said he, when he had framed a suitable reply, "I think you are taking too much upon yourself! You are under-estimating most strangely the disadvantages of your present position. Forgive me for saying so!—but your ideas are crude to the pitch of absurdity. I ask you! Is there not something ridiculous in your undertaking to instruct me, who am Mr. Mayne's life-long friend and associate, in the manner I should use in approaching him? Gracious heavens! do you really imagine he would tolerate that tone for an instant? And do you really believe that your presence in any interview touching his private affairs would be—to put it mildly—appropriate?"

Allen smiled, unabashed. "There is no doubt something in what you say!—And yet," he added with a kind of chuckle, "I cannot help thinking that my presence would bring advantages outweighing its disadvantages."

"What advantages, pray?" cried Walter, red with indignation.

"Well!" replied Allen, still smiling. "I should bring to the task a spirit rather different from yours. Yours might be described as the official spirit. You would be apt, I think, to attach more importance to the procedure than to the results. You would be loath to take up any position from which you could not easily withdraw. Honestly, I doubt whether you would effect very much."

Walter emitted a sound of scornful impatience.

"Your method—the official method," continued Allen, "has a great deal to commend it, I know. I use it myself—when I am not particularly interested in *results!*"

"You and I are not likely to agree on points of general principle," retorted Walter with a chill disdain. "So the more closely we can confine ourselves to the actual question the better. That, fortunately, presents such very definite features that disagreement becomes, for rational human beings, almost impossible. The salient fact at the moment is the great difference in the positions which you and I hold in John Mayne's regard. John Mayne knows very little about you; and—to speak bluntly—if he interprets the story of Cosmo in the same fashion as Mrs. Pomeroy, he will hardly be disposed to give you a favourable hearing—to say nothing of permitting you to read him a lecture!"

Allen smiled. "It is strange when one comes to think of it!" he said. "You know very little more about me than John Mayne—or Mrs. Pomeroy; and yet, here you are, eager to conduct my defence!"

Walter opened his mouth, then checked himself, and became of a sudden preternaturally calm. "At any rate I do you the honour of brushing aside as absolutely preposterous. . . ."

"What?" asked Allen, leaning forward and fixing him with intensity.

The movement was so sudden that Walter actually flinched. A repetition of the gesture with which he had ended his last sentence was all that he could manage.

"I say: What?" insisted Allen.

Walter drew in a long breath. "I was alluding to the inferences which ... in your peculiar position ...."

"What inferences?"

"My dear sir!" exclaimed the other, flushing with sudden heat. "I refuse to be hectored! Understand this: if we are to discuss the matter at all, you must abandon your present attitude. Either you take this affair altogether too lightly, or else—from sheer loss of nerve—you are running to the other extreme."

Allen looked him straight in the eyes. "If anyone is taking this affair too lightly, it is not I, but you!"

The manner in which these words were spoken allowed of no misconceptions, wilful or otherwise. Out of the midst of Walter's anger and perplexity there arose an alarming conviction that a climax was being reached.

But what kind of a climax? And why must there be a climax at all? Was the man off his head?

"Explain yourself!" he articulated.

"I will!" returned Allen, speaking with vicious deliberation. "What you have failed, so far, to appreciate is this: If Mrs. Mayne doesn't get Eamor——"

"Eamor!" shouted Walter desperately. "I talking to you about Cosmo!"

Allen laughed, and said something which the roar and rattle of the flying train rendered unintelligible. But his laugh seemed terribly out of place. "Good God!" ejaculated Walter within himself. "I do believe the fellow is off his head!"

When the noise had somewhat abated, Allen leaned forward again. The incandescent gas-lamp in the ceiling put a greenish light upon his face, and a glitter in his eyes.

"Do you want the truth?" said he.

The menace in this was so unmistakeable that Walter felt no inclination to answer in the affirmative. Nevertheless, courageously, he nodded.

"Good!" cried Allen. "Good!"

For the moment there was no opportunity to say more. The train, which was racing with rising speed and clamour, along a downward grade, had plunged into a tunnel, the reverberations of which made intercourse an impossibility.

In a little while, however, the noise grew less over powering; a movement of Allen's showed that he was ready to resume; anxiously, but unwillingly, Walter bent forward to listen.

"Standish!" shouted Allen into his car. "The first thing to get quite clear between us is this:—I stand under suspicion of murder."

Walter started away.

"Nonsense!" he shouted back. "Nonsense!"

Again the din became insurmountable. He saw Allen fling himself back against the cushions. He saw Allen's mouth open in a monstrous, but inaudible laugh. Allen's eyes, too, were focussed upon him with glittering malignancy; Allen's face was lighted up by a diabolical amusement.

Walter shuddered. In an instant a heavy perspiration broke out over his entire body. A mist came down over his sight. He could not make out what was happening to him. He gasped for breath.

Fortunately, however, this weakness was only temporary. In a few moments he began to recover his senses; and, as his self-possession returned, he noticed that the heat and stuffiness of the compartment might well account for a high degree of physical discomfort. The ventilators had been left open; the air was filled with hot, sulphurous fumes.

Chapter 19

As soon as the train emerged from the tunnel, he became almost himself again. Letting the window down, he stretched towards it, and took a number of deep inhalations. The fresh, night air was delicious. But he was miserably aware that Allen was waiting; so, presently, he drew his head back, and with a gesture signified that he was ready.

Allen wasted no time. "I am not quite sure," he began, "whether you heard what I said just now. I said that in the first place——"

"I heard perfectly," interjected Walter with curtness.

"Very well!" And Allen paused to bestow upon him a long, strange smile. "Secondly, then," said he, "I would have you know this: Lilian Mayne is my mistress."

This time Walter was really not sure that he had heard aright. "What? What's that?" he stammered. The abominable grin appeared again. "Mrs. Mayne is my mistress!" Allen repeated, raising his voice. Walter drew back as if he had been bitten.

"And in the third place——" Allen went on. "But no! On consideration I will hold something in reserve. I have said enough to show that I am in earnest about Eamor. I consider that Lilian has a right to it. She and I need it. We mean to have it."

Walter remained dumb. Every one of his feelings as a gentleman was inexpressibly offended. He was outraged beyond speech.

His perception that Allen was, in some sort, acting a part—and intentionally over-acting it—did nothing to mitigate the shock to his sensibilities. The man was not less of a scoundrel for that, but simply a scoundrel of a more sinister kind. That he should be following a plan of intimidation was bad; that he should be doing so with brazen openness was worse. His behaviour enforced the conviction that his villainy was not pure mummery, but an illustration—caricatural, if you would, but still a fair enough illustration—of a real villainy underneath.

He found it impossible to doubt the truth of what Allen asked him to believe. A guilty relation between these two went far towards explaining what in Allen's past conduct, did, after all, require explanation. It showed why Allen had the future of Eamor so deeply at heart. It knit the whole situation together. It brought all the colours out, too; it made the picture complete.

Staring blankly through the carriage window, he projected against the darkness of the passing landscape a vision which might well have sprung from the imagination of the most sombre of the painters under the Inquisition. And whilst he gazed at his vision with consternation, the swaying and jolting of the express reminded him that he was being bodily transported into that phantasmagoric sphere of life. What, in God's name, awaited him at Eamor? There was no one in that house from whom he could expect support, sympathy, or even understanding. Not even from Madeline! The personages awaiting him at his journey's end were one and all subdued to the dreadful spirit of the place. He, Walter Standish, soon to be amongst them, but not of them, would move with helpless disconnexion amid a concourse of beings whose passions he could neither sympathize with nor even scarcely understand.

At last, feeling that his silence must not be extended any longer, he turned and said dully:

"Perhaps you will now explain what you hope to gain by this disclosure?"

"My hope," replied Allen coldly, "is that you will find it illuminating."

Walter marshalled his resources. "So far," he returned with a fine stubbornness, "so far you have done no more than display an amazing lack of wisdom and good taste. I choose to ignore completely what you have said about Mrs. Mayne. And, for the rest,—let me warn you!—you will be doing yourself a disservice if you persist in your present course."

Allen smiled. "A little while ago you were far from realizing that Mrs. Mayne and I are in earnest. I am sure that you now have a much better grasp of the situation. You certainly apprehend more clearly the temper of the persons with whom you have to deal."

Walter gave a short laugh. "My impression is that you have temporarily lost your balance.—You have conveyed nothing more!"

For a moment Allen considered. He had the air of a man who sees himself driven to taking further measures. "You think I have lost my balance," he pronounced slowly. "Well! that *might* follow as a result of prolonged companionship with Cosmo. Is that what you are thinking?"

Walter let this pass.

"Tell me!" Allen went on in a significant tone. "Should you have said that Cosmo was mad?"

"I have had small means of judging."

"Then you have *not* formed the opinion that he was mad?"

"I have formed no opinion," said Walter.

Allen smiled again. "Tell me this then!—What theories do you hold about his death?"

Walter sighed wearily. "Your questions are so obviously put with a childish—and perverse—intention that I must decline to answer them. I expressed my views at the beginning of this discussion, and I have not moved from them by one inch."

Allen threw back his head and laughed.

"Let me give you one last, solemn warning!" continued Walter with a sudden flare of indignation. "If your object is to intimidate me, you are heading straight for disaster!"

"A threat?" exclaimed Allen genially. "But what have I to fear? The gallows?"

Walter uttered an impatient ejaculation.

"What then?—A public accusation? An embarrassing notoriety? A scandal? The loss of position and prestige? The compromising of my future career?" He paused. "*I* have none of these things to fear. My humble position in the community has, you see, its advantages!"

Walter's face grew stern. "If not on your own account," he cried out with vigour, "then on Mrs. Mayne's account, it behoves you to take heed. In all this farce which you are choosing to play what pleases me least is your unchivalrous attitude towards her. Your attempt to coerce me is so foolish that I can afford to ignore it. You have a right to give a scandalous impression of yourself, if you will. But you have no right to drag Mrs. Mayne down with you. I am convinced that she would not willingly associate herself with you in your present tactics."

The light of temper flickered up in Allen's eyes. "You are talking nonsense!" he said quietly. "Lilian Mayne is a person of very different mettle from what you imagine. Be warned in time, my dear Standish! She won't shrink from any ordeal. And that is why I feel bound to give you some idea of what the consequences will be, if you shirk what we conceive to be your plain and simple duty. For heaven's sake, try to realize that we are not to be trifled with. What do we care about publicity, a ten day's sensation, and the rest! It is our intention—in the event of our losing Eamor—to leave this country for ever. We have no other ties here. We should set out blithely—without regrets! But not—no! not before making you pay the full penalty for——"

"Be careful!" interrupted Walter holding up his hand. "Be careful

Allen! This sounds almost like blackmail! In fact I should consider it blackmail, if you had the means of giving the least substance to your threats!"

Allen laughed. "You are asking me *how* we should visit you with retribution. But that I prefer to keep to myself. I can point out, however, that your position with John Mayne and his two nieces is not so secure but that we can throw you out of favour in an instant. We can show that you have plotted with us to keep Cosmo out of sight, that you were aware of his death, and that you—better than anyone else, excepting me, perhaps—have reason to believe he died a violent death."

"Preposterous!" ejaculated Walter, tossing about in his seat. "Preposterous rubbish! This really is going beyond all limits!"

"Am I lying then?"

"Since you ask me, I must say yes."

"Come! Come!" returned Allen good-humouredly. "Let us look at the facts?—Or rather, as it would be idle to review them all, let me merely ask: What about that letter?"

"What letter?"

Allen smiled. "My dear Standish, I am not unaware that Cosmo, whilst under my care at Tornel, was in the habit of writing very extraordinary letters. And he was always on the look-out for a chance to post these letters off to—well! to almost anyone! And these letters contained definite charges against me and Mrs. Mayne. They were letters, moreover, which, for all their oddness, were so circumstantial, so logical, so collected, as to exclude—or nearly—the hypothesis of madness. And finally, one of them, in the light of subsequent events, appears to have been—almost prophetic!"

During the course of this speech Walter had lost colour. His face was now working strangely. He seemed to be temporarily bereft of the command of his voice. After a moment Allen turned his eyes away and began looking through a despatch-case which lay beside him.

"I have here," he resumed with quietude, "the exact copy of just such a letter,—which was posted to *you!* And the counterfoil of its postal registration is here also!"

Walter's silence continued for quite another minute. Then he cleared his throat and said:

"It was unmistakably the letter of a lunatic!"

Allen looked up at the ceiling. "No! I don't think so!" he pronounced consideringly. "And I don't think others would think so! Really and truly, my dear sir, that letter, taken together with your previous knowledge of the case. . . ." His voice died away into stillness; his eyes dwelt upon Walter with a grave urgency.

"That letter," articulated Walter. "When did you find the copy of it?"

"I, myself, got Cosmo to make a copy of it. You see, I discovered and intercepted the original at the time. And then, after consideration, I let him post it."

"Why?"

"Simply because I wanted to share the weight of my responsibilities with a person of your judgment and worldly wisdom. I wanted your tacit approval. And, as you kept silence, I thought I had it. To be quite candid with you," he went on, "I have been greatly distressed—from the very beginning of our conversation—by your tendency to dis-associate yourself from Mrs. Mayne and me. That attitude of yours——"

A stifled exclamation interrupted him. "All this is monstrous!" cried Walter with a distracted gesture. "It's a perversion . . . a gross distortion. I have never had anything to do with Cosmo . . . I repudiate absolutely . . ." He broke off, choking.

The tone of Allen's reply was gentle, almost sympathetic. "Look here, Standish!—Try to put yourself in my place! Try to imagine how painful it has been for me to hear you disown your small, but legitimate, share of responsibility in proceedings which—all things considered—and due account being taken of Cosmo's physical and mental condition——"

With a movement of horror Walter again cut him short. "No, no!" he muttered, as though speaking to himself. "No, no, no!"

His need of an interval for recuperation was so obvious that, with a smile and a sigh, Allen desisted. For a while Walter gazed with staring eyes out of the window. Then he noticed that the train was slowing down; it was nearing a station at which it was due to make a halt. His heart leapt at the idea of continuing the journey in another compartment. He struggled to his feet.

"Standish!" said Allen with great earnestness. "I beg that you will not break off this discussion just at the moment when a better understanding is in sight. So far we have been largely at cross-purposes. I have put only one aspect of the matter before you. It has other aspects, which you ought to consider."

Walter looked down with a face of desperate indecision.

"In less than an hour," continued Allen in the same quiet tones, "we shall be at Eamor. And then—it will be too late."

These last words echoed forebodingly in Walter's heart. True it was, alas, that at Eamor in all probability it would be too late! Of what use to withdraw now? Nothing was to be gained; and something might be lost . . . The discovery of some mitigation, of some compromise, of some loop-hole, of some stratagem or device . . .

These inward counsels prevailed. Composing his countenance, he relinquished his grasp of the door-handle. Slowly he sank back into his seat.

"I will hear you," he said.

"Good!" replied Allen warmly.

In a moment the train moved on.

Allen leaned forward again. "Bear this in mind!" said he with a conciliatory smile. "Our object and our interests are identical. The only difference between us is on a question of method. Now, listen!" And for the remainder of the journey his persuasiveness was great.

Chapter 20

Together they drove up to the house; and, for his part, when he alighted, Allen was full of inward chuckles. He had been able to indulge a vein of humour that did not often find an outlet; and if he was a little apprehensive of the manner in which Lilian would receive the story of his long duologue, he could at any rate assure her that the conclusion had been satisfactory. For Walter had finished by coming to terms; assurances had been exchanged, which, if not exactly cordial on Walter's side, nevertheless put it beyond a doubt that he would do a great deal to avoid incurring the wrath of his undesired associates.

The chief factor, however, in Allen's pleasant excitement was the thought that his separation from Lilian was at an end. That raised him above all worries. And although not without the grace to perceive that his humour comported ill with the grim uncertainties of the general situation, he dared hope that Lilian would forgive him the high spirits which he felt unequal to concealing from her.

He was not disappointed. Ever since the receipt of his telegram she had been looking forward to his arrival with impatience. Her welcome was delightful. Nor was she unduly perturbed by his prompt, brief statement that Nina had discovered the identity of "Richardson" and Cosmo. She told him her reasons for suspecting as much already; and for believing that Nina had also informed John Mayne. He wondered a little at her equanimity. Indeed, she presently struck him as being almost too equably self-poised, almost too magnificently collected.

The fact was, that, not having seen her since the tragic period of Cosmo's death, he was as yet unaware that those days had marked a turning-point in her spiritual development. For forty-eight hours she had lived in a state of mental agony. Then, all at once the pain and the anxiety had left her; she had dropped into a preternatural calm. What was the significance of that serenity? She herself wondered. Life, Allen used to tell her, was all a game—a game of chance and skill, of luck and cunning—a game to be played with all possible zest, but a game, the issue of which you must be ready to accept with a shrug. That shrug, which you held in reserve, was everything. That shrug had enabled the French aristocrat to triumph over the rabble with their guillotine. And no advance of mind or heart would ever do much more than add an extra nuance to that shrug.

There was something in her temperament, no doubt, that rose responsive to this doctrine. Perhaps it had helped to fortify her through the weeks of lonely trial that were now drawing to a close. But she questioned whether she and Allen really started from the same temperamental basis. It seemed to her that in spirit he was younger than she—younger, too, than Nicholas.

In a little while they settled down to a more detailed exchange of news. On his side he had to give her an account of his conversation with Walter—and to convince her, if possible, that his procedure had not been unduly daring. She listened to the first part of his narrative with more amusement and a readier acquiescence than he had looked for. She agreed that no measures were too desperate for the emergency. But when he came to the point where her own name had been so startlingly introduced, her equanimity did, most certainly, desert her. Her eyes opened; her lips parted; she broke out into horrified exclamation.

But Allen hurried on. "My darling, wait a moment, until I have explained! What I said was unconventional, I admit. But let me show you how necessary it was! So far from being an indiscretion, it was a stroke of genius. It shook Walter's nerve more than anything else. The whole situation suddenly flashed out before him in a most lurid light. He saw us as a pair of Macbeths. He was aghast. Then and there he abandoned the notion that I might be persuaded to accept his good services for myself, without troubling overmuch about Eamor and you. After all, our actual relation does stand at the bottom of this affair. It was therefore necessary that he should be made aware of it."

But Lilian still gasped. "Your mistress! And to Walter! before whom I have always been so—so genteel!"

"All the better!" said Allen. "The shock was the greater. You stand before him now as a very Jezebel. And the more genteelly you behave in future, the more his flesh will creep. For all his man-of-the-worldishness, Walter remains very ingenuous at heart; and sexual misconduct inspires him with a particular horror which he is ashamed to confess to." He broke off with a low laugh. "As for his view of me, that leaves nothing to be desired. Nothing upsets Walter so much as a refusal to defer to the ordinary traditions of gentlemanliness. He is at last convinced that I am capable of anything."

"But then...."

"What then?"

"Mightn't he...."

"Denounce us? Make use of my admissions? Never! Such a decision is entirely foreign to his nature. Do you think his imagination fails to picture the dreadfulness of the scenes that would ensue? No, no! He isn't even tempted to denounce us. He is committed to quite another line. He still firmly refuses to take cognizance of anything that clashes with his benign view of the case. His parting observation to me was that he considered my words about you unspoken."

Lilian sighed, but with a kind of smile lurking underneath; and presently she allowed him to proceed.

Coming to Cosmo's letter—"I assure you," he said, "the effect of that was prodigious! And he is still wondering what other bomb-shells we may not explode under his feet. A little later I drew a bow at a venture and scored another point. I said something which implied that he knew perfectly well that John Mayne had a desire for information about Cosmo. And the unhappy man did not deny it. I am certain that he is mortally uneasy about his position with both John Mayne and Madeline. He apprehends that should any big storm take place, his ship would assuredly founder."

From this they passed on to a discussion of what they called "Cosmo's letter," although, as Lilian was already aware, that letter had been concocted and written by Allen himself. The idea had come into his mind upon discovering and intercepting a letter in very similar strain, which Cosmo had composed for the benefit of the police. At that time—about a fortnight before his death—Cosmo had become so unmanageable that Allen had almost decided to throw off his responsibilities by going to Walter and accepting whatever solution of the problem the latter might recommend. But that would have been the equivalent to giving up; and now he saw the means of sharing a good part of his responsibility with Walter without, the latter's becoming aware of it. Should the letter cause Walter to send for him, well and good; should it not, so much the better. It was an interesting experiment. Walter would have strong reason to believe that the letter was, and would remain, a profound secret to all but himself and Cosmo. For was it likely that the latter, who expatiated upon the stealth which he had to use in the composition and posting of his denunciation, and who professed himself to be in fear of his life—was it likely that he would be his own betrayer?

So the experiment had been made, and Walter had behaved as Allen had rather fancied he would. After much anxious cogitation, he had put the letter away in the most secret of his archives, and had then done his best to banish all thought of it from his mind. But, as Allen was able to point out to him in the train, the tragic sequel had brought his inaction out into an ugly light. And, contrary to his former belief, the whole degree of his complicity was known.

"Dear old Walter!" exclaimed Allen. "I am really getting quite fond of him! It is so pleasant to deal with a man whose mind represents the exact average. Walter is the average written large. Walter illustrates with absolute precision the norm of human intelligence, honesty, and good intention. Other persons stray from the mark in one direction or another; but Walter never. Such a man is a very bulwark in times of trouble."

Lilian smiled.

"My dear," Allen persisted; "Doesn't it give you confidence to feel him ranged on our side?"

"No," replied Lilian, still smiling. "Walter is, and always will be, a nonentity at Eamor."

"But——"

"For Nina—and even for Madeline—Walter, at this moment, hardly exists. We women," and she lifted her head ironically, "don't think very much of your Waller."

Allen explained that he was thinking of the pressure Walter could bring to bear upon John Mayne.

She knit her brows. "It is quite true that the John Mayne of old days would have been horrified by the prospect of his work going to pieces. But I don't think that remains true of the John Mayne of to-day."

"Oh, surely! You have often told me that muddle is his bugbear. Now, what Walter can threaten is—simply chaos!"

Lilian sighed. "He has changed!" she said in a low voice.

"As much as that?"

"I fancy so."

Allen was silent.

"I have a feeling," she added after a pause, "that all those things have lost their importance to him."

Allen pursed his lips. "What, then, is left?"

"I don't know. Perhaps—nothing!"

"My dear," said Allen after another silence, "if Walter can do nothing, who can do anything? Can I? Can you?"

She was looking straight out before her, and she continued in this posture for some moments before making her reply.

"It seems to me," she said slowly, "that everything depends upon what shape his . . . well! his despair, his repulsion, his . . ." and she raised her eyes to Allen—"You know what I mean!—It depends upon what he is coming to in the end. For some time already he has looked upon Walter as a fool; and I can't help thinking that Madeline is beginning to disgust him."

Allen gave a short laugh. "The question is whether you, Orissers, don't disgust him equally, in a different way."

"Quite true!" she sadly smiled. "That *is* the question."

There was an interval of meditation. Then Allen said: "I judge, from what you tell me of his condition, that whatever we do must be done to-morrow?"

"To-morrow!" she absently assented. "Yes, to-morrow."

After a moment she roused herself. "You must go to him—alone, first; then, if you think fit, call in Walter."

"Or you!"

She gave a shiver. "No! for pity's sake, not me!"

Allen looked at her thoughtfully. "If I do send for you, it will be precisely for pity's sake. Men are apt to turn to sentiment on their deathbeds. And then, Lilian . . ."

"He will not!" she replied with sudden passion. "No, no! That would be terrible. That must not be!—Allen!" she cried, her breast heaving, "if I thought you were going to play upon his feelings, I should forbid you to approach him! I swear to you, I will never accept Eamor from him unless he flings it at me with a snarl."

Allen looked at her for some moments without speaking. In his heart there was approval and admiration. But of this he gave no sign.

"Put your mind at rest!" he said at last; "I neither could, nor would——"

"Forgive me!" Her vehemence suddenly melted into contrition. "Forgive me!"

They smiled into each other's eyes.

"Lilian, you are what is called a hard woman, I fear."

"Hard?" And she gave a sad, little laugh. "Isn't it for his sake as much as for mine? Oughtn't he to die—game?"

Allen studied her in a kind of fascination. "I suppose he ought,—if he can't reach to . . . something else."

"There *is* nothing else," she returned simply. "Not for him and me."

Allen said nothing; and the colour slowly rose in her cheeks. "Are you thinking," she asked, "that there *ought* to be something else?"

He knit his brows in consideration.

"No," he returned; "I shouldn't say that."

Her looks remained fixed upon him as though she wanted something more.

At last he said: "If your differences were *only* personal or, so to speak, idiosyncratic, I should say you both ought to reach out after a sentiment which would transcend them . . . But your differences, if I mistake not, rest on fundamental antagonisms . . . implanted in the very heart of things . . . eternal antipathies, and condemnations . . ." He broke off; then added with a smile, "I believe in more Gods than one."

Chapter 21

After watching John Mayne and Nina disappear up the stairs, Nicholas remained in the hall for some minutes longer, struggling with a profound agitation. His previous suspicions that some calamitous revelation had been made were converted into a certainty; and he felt he ought to make a report to Lilian and Isabel, whom he pictured waiting in silent preoccupation for his return. But to go back to that dreadful, dusky little room was more than he could do. So he betook himself to Lilian's bedroom, intending to abide there until she came.

In the stillness and peace of that chamber his excitement gradually abated; and during the next half-hour he sank into an abstraction, listless, yet acutely receptive of the grace that surrounded him. The sweet, ordered living of which that room was an expression—the softness and freshness of its tints in the candle and firelight, the fragrance, the implicit suggestions of leisure and security which every detail conveyed,—all filled his heart with sadness, with a sadness made bitter by self-mockery.

The more deeply he became penetrated by the effluence of the scene, the more indistinct became his sense of its actuality. His spirit was projected into a sphere from which the present was apprehensible only in an essence as unsubstantial as the stuff of memory. His actual perceptions coalesced with the memory-images of his childhood and caught their poignant aroma. He played with the wisps of sentiment that blew across his mind. He pitied them—insignificant shreds of anguished feeling, alive only to the littleness of one small, perishing consciousness.

When at last Lilian appeared, he beheld her, too, from the remoteness of memory. She, with all this, to which she so exquisitely belonged, was an appearance in an epoch that had closed. She smiled and spoke, and her words barely reached him. She moved across the room, and he gazed upon her as he would have gazed upon her image in a crystal. The weary grace with which she bore herself seemed to incorporate the weariness of centuries; and that grace, again, seemed to him to be a thing of the past, transiently resurrected in a moment of enchanted retrospect.

Rousing himself from his preoccupation, he described, in a few words, what he had seen. She listened, glooming. The sound of her low voice, as she took counsel with herself, flowed like deep water about his ears. She speculated, she explored, she prepared. She brimmed with a profound and potent resolution.

But while one part of him was carried forward upon the current of her untiring, undespairing energy, another portion of his being, the innermost, remained aloof. It was poising high overhead in a timeless altitude of its own. He looked down upon her as a mountain-climber looks down into the village he has left. He heard and saw her from afar; and her ardour and her beauty were as chimes ringing distantly below— strong chimes, whose resonance, spreading thinly into space, tolled out the words: Vanity! Vanity!

The next day he secluded himself in the library. A night of wakefulness and violent dreaming had wrought a curious change in his mood. An obstruction had given way in some region of his brain; torrents of pent-up thought and emotion poured over the stormy surface of his consciousness. All the elements of his personality were in hurricane agitation; and over that submerged and desolated landscape ideas shot up like coloured rockets, filling his mind with successive showers of light. His old intellectual fervours burned fiercely. He tore open the parcels of books that he had brought from Tornel. Now reading and annotating, now pacing to and fro in ardent meditation, now writing at his desk, he journeyed hard through the domain of the mind. The afternoon slipped by as quickly as the morning. When dusk fell, he was still moving in a bright, remote world of his own.

Yet, for all this concentration, he could not entirely forget. Just as his bodily form crouched under the yellow lamplight, as if fearful of the darkness round about, so did his spiritual form crouch within the circle of its own defensive radiance, daring not to lift its eyes to the blackness of reality beyond. No! For among the images peopling that blackness there was one, he knew, of so appealing a presence, that, had he but looked up for an instant, his pupils would have become fixed.

In the night he had dreamed of Isabel, and in the morning he had covertly observed her. She had looked pale, and lovely in her pallor. Something, he fancied, must have passed between her and Lilian;— something, certainly, she had divined or learnt.

He was still sitting before the fire with a book, when he heard the door open softly behind him. Clenching his teeth, he refrained from any movement that would reveal that he had caught the sound. The door closed; and for a minute he dared hope the intruder had withdrawn. Presently, however, there was a rustle across the room, and Isabel appeared before the hearth.

Looking up, he intended to smile. But the duplicity required was too great. His eyes were as grave as hers. But hers were grave with candour, his were darkened by secrecy.

He could not smile; but in growing horror of the silence between them, he inquired whether Allen had yet arrived.

She answered with a movement of the head.

"And Walter too?"

"Yes." And she sighed.

Over her young bosom her dress fell softly like the soft plumage of a young bird. He looked upon her young, girlish body with a secret coldness. He was indifferent to it, just as he was indifferent to her young, girlish spirit. He saw that she was lovely; and his indifference filled him with anguish.

After a little she raised her head; her eyes wandered miserably round the room. "Lilian knows!" she murmured.

"Yes," he muttered back. "Lilian knows."

What more was there to be said? Why didn't she leave him? But— poor child!—whither had she to go? She was alone.

"Isabel," he blurted out, "where have you been all day?"

She made no answer. Leaning back against the mantelpiece, she seemed to have lost the sense of his presence.

A kind of desperation came over him. A laugh thrust itself forth from his lips; and, to his horror, he said:

"Are you unhappy, Isabel?"

The colour rushed into her face; resentment gleamed through her lashes. "Not particularly!" And in a low voice she added the words: "But you are!"

He winced. "No, no!" And his painful laugh sounded again, while with futile evasiveness he went on: "In some ways I'm glad that Lilian knows."

She turned her face away from him; her lips smiled faintly and sadly.

"As for Eamor," he continued with the same hopeless intention, "I think I have really given up caring."

After a minute she drew in her breath. "You've not been happy," she

328

said, "at any time."

For a moment he was speechless. Her eyes, directed full upon him, forbade misunderstanding. "What do you mean?" he stammered. "Not with you? Never? Not even *then?*"

"No!"

This was terrible, although he knew not why. She had plunged cold steel into his heart.

"But why?" he besought her. "Isabel, why do you say that?"

She continued to look at him in silence.

"But you are wrong, Isabel! You are wrong. And why do you say it *like that?*"

There was no answer.

"My God!" he exclaimed. "What is happiness? Happiness!" And he burst forth into savage merriment.

"It is everything!" she replied stilly.

It seemed to him again that she had struck him mortally. He made no movement. He no longer looked at her. For a minute more she stood there; then quietly she moved away. She passed down the room, he heard the door open and close.

Why did he not rise and pursue her? Could they not join their two lonelinesses into one? No! Each man lives and dies alone. Follow her? It was useless. What had he to say? All his life he had been journeying towards a spiritual death; and it seemed to have come at last.

Chapter 22

Late that evening he was still sitting before the fire, when the door opened and Allen looked in.

The room was lit only by a glow from the hearth, for his lamp had burnt itself out. For a moment Allen stood peering into the semi-darkness.

"I am here," said Nicholas.

Allen entered, closed the door, and took a few steps forward through the obscurity. Then, halting, he struck a light, and having advanced across the room, lit the two candles upon the mantelpiece.

Lilian had begged him to have a talk with Nicholas, about whom she was troubled. But he felt ill at ease; he did not know where to begin. During dinner the young man's taciturnity had bordered upon absolute rudeness.

"Do you know," he brought out abruptly, "you haven't spoken a word to me since I arrived?"

"I have nothing to say," replied Nicholas.

Allen seated himself on the other side of the hearth, he noticed that Nicholas's eyes were unusually bright, and that there was an unnatural tautness behind the apparent laxity of his pose.

"There is a verse in the Koran," said he, "which runs something after this fashion: 'When a man shall find nothing to say unto his brother, it shall be a sign that the end of the world is at hand.'"

The other laughed gently. "Very apt! Too apt, I'm afraid!"

"Oh, I'm not sure about that!"

Nicholas gave him a sarcastic smile. "You are satisfied, then, with things in general?"

"Satisfied? Not altogether!" returned Allen slowly. "And yet—to be frank—I am in a mood to be easily satisfied. You see—I am going to marry Lilian."

"That is excellent," exclaimed Nicholas, jerking himself up in his chair. "I hoped it was coming."

"You did?"

"Yes."

"Thank you," said Allen.

"I'll tell you one reason why," continued Nicholas after a pause. "I've been thinking about the future. I've had visions of Lilian living alone in a third-rate lodging-house in Tornel. I've seen her growing thin, tight-lipped, wrinkled, grey. I've seen the years pass, and Lilian dressed in shabby black, going about her business, always silent, always alone. And at last after a long time, for she is very strong—a hearse looms up out of the fog and halts before the house. It carries her away down the wet street. She gets a wreath from Walter, and that's the end."

"You haven't a cheerful imagination," the other commented after a short pause. "May I ask what you foresee for yourself?"

"Certainly!" And the young man sprang, unexpectedly, to his feet. "For myself I see something really good—nothing less than a complete regeneration! At present I am living within the narrow circle of my own petty, personal interests. I need to be shaken out of my egoism; I need to be thrown up against my fellow-men, and forced to compete with them in practical affairs. Thus only can one attain to a true conception of life. What I now shrink from as a dreadful calamity will prove to be a blessing in disguise. The time will come when I shall look back upon my past self, if not with shame, at least with an indulgent contemptuous-ness. A cheerful, manly, self-reliant young fellow, I shall be so much wiser then than I am now!"

Allen smiled uneasily.

"Yes," Nicholas continued, bursting into a loud laugh, "there's many a true word spoken in jest, isn't there? And that's because the truth is so often ridiculous. Don't I know as well as you that Time and the World work their will on us all? Life is a schoolmistress with certain lessons that she is determined to inculcate. It is absurd to protest that one considers those lessons better unlearnt. Life thinks she knows best—and she has a birch in the cupboard. Sooner or later one conforms to the maxims in the copy-book; and what one practises one comes to profess and believe. I have no choice but to convert my mind into a passable imitation of Walter's. I have no option but to live for the edification of Walter, and to the glory of Walter's philosophy. Moreover, as bitterness is always to be scorned, the quicker I can convert myself the better."

Allen said nothing. The young man's eyes were fixed upon him in a bright stare of hostility. The best he could do was to muster a friendly smile.

"I was thinking, this afternoon," Nicholas went on, "that Walter, you, and Cosmo, presented three interesting specimens of life's disciplinary results. Cosmo was the incorrigible bad boy, finally expelled from school. You began bad, if I understand your character aright, but scraped through to middle-age, when, learning to appreciate the value of mental inertia, you patched up a *modus vivendi* with your teacher. Walter, the good, smart boy, was ready from the very first to absorb all the lessons that life had to teach him. He accepted all the school standards without question; the school's conventions came to him as a second nature; the happy lad developed by quick, easy stages into the impeccable social automaton he now is."

Allen sat up in his chair. "When you have had your innings will you allow me to have mine?"

"Certainly. But one question before you begin: Has Lilian told you about me and Isabel?"

"Yes."

"Good!" Nicholas gave a short laugh. "That will help you to point your moral."

Allen frowned meditatively.

"It will be interesting," continued Nicholas, "to receive a lecture from a man without principles, without convictions, and without faith."

Allen smiled.

"From a man with nothing but a smile," Nicholas went on. "And that a smile which reflects nothing but the belief that he is a very good fellow at bottom."

Allen remained silent.

"In your mind," proceeded Nicholas with venom, "that irrational belief stands in lieu of faith, and conceals from you the fact that you have disentangled nothing, formulated nothing, found nothing. No! your mind is simply a welter of contradictory hopes and beliefs, from each of which in turn you manage to squeeze out just enough reassurance to tide over the discomforts of the moment. You take, indeed, a certain pride in your scepticism; but you lack the courage of scepticism just as you lack the courage of faith. So you shrug and say: 'One must live after all!' And you consider yourself a good fellow because you grant indulgence to others on the condition that they be as poor-spirited as yourself."

"It's not a case of indulgence," returned Allen with tranquillity. "It's just a case of instinctive fellow-feeling."

"And of what worth is that fellow-feeling?" cried Nicholas with scorn.

"*Quod ubique, quod ab omnibus . . .*"* said Allen. "Fellow-feeling, charity, love—name it by what word you will—it exists and it counts."

"Love!" exclaimed the other. "I thought we should come to that. Love! A word very dear to the godless. 'God is Love,' they say, when they wish to imply that He is nothing else. What is your Love but God shorn of all His finer attributes? Is there not a holiness of the mind, as of the heart? No, not for you and for your ilk! Love, under cover of which you discard one-half—and the nobler half—of human idealism— Love is enough for you! Moreover, when you say '*Quod ubique, quod ab omnibus,*' you lie. The cult of love as a be-all and end-all is narrow and new. It was invented by European civilization as a cloak for its soulless materialism. It is not even Christian. And in the great, ancient religions of the East love was assigned its proper place—honourable, but subordinate—honourable, *because* subordinate,—in a theogony that had a substance and a meaning,—in a doctrine less miserably derogatory to Humanity and Divinity alike than the pseudo-religion that goes by the name of Humanism to-day. What, I ask you, is the value, or the meaning, of the word Love irrespective of an enclosing faith? Is it what the Grand Inquisitor felt for his victims, while he tortured their bodies for the sake of their immortal souls? Or is it what Walter feels for *his* victims, whose bodies he feeds, while by his words, by his example, by his hopeless confusion of thought, and by the contagion of his despicable character, he stunts, starves, and misguides their souls? Love, in the mouths of the good folk of to-day, means Walter."

"My dear Nicholas," said Allen with a kind of groan, "I am getting tired of Walter. Let us talk about you for a change! And let me do the talking."

The young man twitched his shoulders impatiently. "Go ahead!" said he.

"Your position is this," said Allen.† "You live, like many moderns, on the higher cerebral levels of the mind; and those levels reflect not the deeper movements of the organic life, but the activities of the individual consciousness. We of to-day have lost that immediate unity with the life of the race which was so spontaneous in the minds of our ancestors. Each person has become an end in himself. A dualism has arisen between the animal life of the race and the volition of the individual.

---

* "Always everywhere and by everyone."

† (L. H. Myers' footnote): Acknowledgements are made to Professor John Dashiell Stoops of Grinnell College, Iowa. Cf. "The Will and the Instinct of Sex," *The International Journal of Ethics*, Vol. xxxii, No. 1.

The end of nature is no longer the object of man's will. But nature is not remade by the arbitrary personal philosophies of individual minds. Let man take warning!"

"Arbitrary," echoed Nicholas with anger. "Arbitrary!"

"Yes, arbitrary:" repeated Allen firmly. "And where the will of the individual conflicts with the will of the Great Mother there results a condition of chronic nervous and mental strain. Sex, disenfranchised, outlawed, excommunicated, builds itself a rebel citadel from which it raids the land."

"By me," said Nicholas, "sex is recognised, licensed, indulged. I claim only the right to despise it."

"Yes, in you it is Venus, not Isis—not Isis, the sacred mother of life, upon whose statue was engraved the words: '*I am that which is, has been, and shall be.*'"

"My dear Allen," said Nicholas, "you may admonish and adjure, but the will of the individual is as strong as the will of the Great Mother herself."

"I doubt it," returned Allen. "The energies of the will are in instinct, which belong to the organic life. The apostate will cuts itself off from the source of its energies. Mind you, I have no quarrel with the ego. The ego has come to stay. But if it is to develop fruitfully, it must desist from rebellion. After all, the apostasy of the individual dates from yesterday. It is no more than a backward eddy upon the great racial stream. The line of the modern introspective philosopher goes no further back than to the mediaeval saint and early Christian revolutionary."

"You say so?" cried Nicholas. "Then what of the myth of man's fall—the apple and the serpent?"

Allen shrugged. "That myth shows that the trouble was intuited a little earlier—say about 800 B.C. But I am dealing with Time on a biological scale. Moreover, up to a quite recent date the conflict between the instinctive objectives of race and the *a priori* schemes of the individual mind has remained latent and embryonic. To you and your like belong the responsibility of bringing it out into self-consciousness. It is essential that you should go one step further yet. You must come to realize where you stand. And then you will cease to be obdurate."

"You think so?" said Nicholas with a laugh of scorn.

"There can be but one end for those who resist. They will perish."

"Is that not what I myself have said? I have declared that Walter and Madeline shall inherit the earth."

"Madeline is not the true and only daughter of Isis, nor Walter the true and only son of Osiris. They are both miserably incomplete. At the present day we are in dire need of larger personalities, in which the individual elements of the mind, such as reason and will, shall be harmonized with the deeper instincts of race, to form one living whole."

"Look here, Allen," said Nicholas, with dull rage, "up to now I have been able to listen to you with respect. But if all this merely leads up to the assertion that those things which present themselves to us in our experience as incompatibles can be 'harmonized,' I shall beg leave to go to bed."

"No. Don't mistake me," replied Allen. "I am prepared to admit that man was born with the seeds of duality within him, and that, becoming self-conscious, he lives under a dyarchy. But I believe that the two parties in the dual control are not necessarily antagonistic. A little while ago," he added, "you denounced me for holding no faith. If I proclaim this belief—and cling to it as an act of faith—will you denounce me for that too?"

Nicholas gave an angry shrug. "The question is whether you, being as self-conscious as you are, can really possess any honest faith," he muttered.

"At any rate I am capable of holding some honest disbeliefs," returned Allen with a smile. "And I cannot believe that the race will ever degenerate into a society of Madelines and Walters. The suggestion is not an extravagant one,—that I admit. But——"

He was interrupted.

"The change," cried Nicholas, "would creep over mankind without mankind's becoming aware of it. Only a few individuals here and there would cry out; and their voices would fall upon deaf ears. Cosmo's was such a voice!"

"Humanism," continued Allen, disregarding this interruption, "humanism, in all its forms, I despise as much as you. But I do not fear it. As a creed it will only appeal to moral eunuchs—I mean to persons suffering from a deep, inward inhibition, which cuts them off from the true generative and social energies of the race. That class is driven to provide itself with an imitation of what it lacks. The intellectual who labours for mankind is a solitary and disappointed beast at heart. Children and animals shun him,—although he never loses an opportunity of patting them on the head. Such persons may lead civilization astray for a while, deluding it with what you have called the 'new materialism.' But that doctrine will never engross the whole of man's unconscious energies, nor satisfy the whole of man's semi-conscious idealism. You see," he added with a smile, "how far I am prepared to go with you!"

Nicholas passed his hand wearily over his forehead. "You began by stigmatizing the demands of the individual will as arbitrary," said he; "and you have alluded to the Great Mother as if she merited respect. But the individual has an intellectual conscience. His reason is obedient to precepts which are as authoritative to it as the instincts of the Great Mother are to her. Moreover, the laws which we obey with our self-conscious minds command our respect, and the instincts of the Great Mother do not. She may utter threats; but the mind will not respect her. She fails to command respect, because the individual has developed a sense of values, and of those values she is either ignorant or heedless.

"You are referring to our conscious values," replied Allen. "And those are shifting, artificial, and—not seldom—conceived for purposes of self-deception. But, *filii terrae*,* we live by our instinctive, and largely unconscious, values, which are the values of the Great Mother."

Nicholas sighed and yawned.

"You are tired," said Allen, rising.

"Indeed I am!"

"We will continue on another day—and on many other days."

"Perhaps," answered Nicholas.

"I wish," said Allen, looking him fixedly in the eyes, "I wish that you had shared certain experiences of mine in Babylonia and Egypt—and not only in Babylonia and Egypt, but also in Tornel." He paused reminiscently. "One occasion in particular comes back to me. Late one winter night I walked to the museum to fetch some papers which I had forgotten to bring home with me. I let myself in with my own key. The moon was nearly full and shining clear. I needed no other light to guide me down the gallery. I moved slowly forward, stopping every now and then. And, as I advanced, I was overwhelmed by a sense of awe. When I reached the bench on which you were sitting the other day, I let myself sink down upon it in a kind of trance. Opposite me was the lion-headed goddess, Sekhet. The moonlight slanted in upon her; and the awful austerity of that animal face struck terror into my bones. The human face can look austere; but no human face could ever express what was expressed in the animal face of that animal god. An aspect of Life's essential energies was revealed. And in the graven images of Thoth, and Ptah, of Seb and Set, other demiurges of the world stood present—stood around me in the solidity and stillness of black stone. And I felt that in my beating heart, and in my flowing blood, and in the people of

* "Children of the earth".

336

the city outside, and in all the life of the earth, those same energies were moving, august and resistless."

Chapter 23

During the last part of his journey to Eamor Walter found time to get over the first shock of Allen's disclosures, and even succeeded in repairing a good deal of the damage done to his self-esteem. He felt that his self-esteem ought to be proof against attacks such as this, for it was solidly established upon a fine fund of public regard. By making an insignificant draft upon this fund he could make good the loss which his private dignity had sustained. That loss had been inflicted by a person of no account, and, so to speak, burglariously. It was no more than an incident in his private life; his public life, his public honour were not affected.

If, deep in his heart, anger smouldered, he did not care to avow it; indignation was in place, but not anger. Anger was too nearly akin to hatred; and hatred was a sentiment which it was beneath his dignity to entertain.

Thus, partially assuaged, and keenly alive to the urgencies and exigencies of the situation, he forced himself to bury his resentment and to concentrate his mind upon the future. He condescended to listen to Allen. But while seeming to patch up an agreement, he privily marked out a provisional policy of his own. He foresaw many opportunities of evasion. Time was short. The complexities of character and circumstance were largely in his favour. It was unlikely that John Mayne would be capable, or wishful, of grappling with intricate affairs. There would be facilities for bringing about confusion and delay. The Orissers, however desperate, would find it hard to decide upon denouncing him, and harder still, whatever their cunning, to drive their charges home. Moreover, the Maynes, however imperious and impatient, would, even at the worst, find no handle for their wrath, no chink in the slippery surface of his elaborate and dignified explanations.

His meeting with Madeline was grave and tender. Her manner was softer than it had been for many weeks past. Grief seemed to have refined out of her the ungentle characteristic that he had latterly been given to deplore. Perhaps he had been unjust to her in his thoughts.

Whilst listening to her admiring description of her uncle's fortitude, he struggled hard to banish his preoccupations. He felt that her sentiments did her honour, and that he owed it to himself to respond with all the warmth of generous disposition. There were a number of pertinent inquiries burning upon his tongue; but he choked them down. He let her talk on. Thinking that there was a faint chance that Nina had not let her into the secret, he refrained from any allusion to Cosmo.

At last Madeline rose, declaring that she must return to the sick-chamber. Whereupon, in perfectly ordinary tones, he asked to see Nina.

"Now?" queried Madeline, halting on her way to the door.

"Yes, now!" returned Walter cheerfully. "She isn't busy, I suppose?"

Madeline hesitated a moment.

"Walter!" said she in a changed voice, "what a dreadful affair that, is—about Cosmo Orisser! I don't like to speak of it! I don't even like to think about it!"

Walter's heart sank, but he allowed himself no more than a sigh and a gesture of vague deprecation. "Your uncle?" he briefly inquired. "Has she told him?"

Madeline nodded with sadness. "Alas! she had to. It could not be avoided. The subject of Cosmo came up. And then of course Nina had to speak. Poor dear Nina! It was very hard for her. And poor uncle! He was terribly shocked. To think that Lilian had been deliberately deceiving him all these years by letting him imagine that Cosmo was dead! And then to keep the man hidden away! So near, and yet out of all sight and hearing! What a strange story, Walter! And the end—does it not seem to you—sinister?"

She was standing a few paces from him. Her pupils were dilated; her face had become tragic. "I don't know what to think," she went on, her voice sinking to a whisper. "But I know it makes me shudder!"

Walter strove to keep up a perfectly unmoved appearance.

"Dearest," said he, "you must not allow your imagination to run away with you. I have reason to believe that Nina's information is very misleading. There is, I am happy to say, a quite different reading of the whole affair;—I intend to explain this to Nina."

Madeline looked puzzled. "But surely——"

"I have just had a long talk with Allen," continued Walter, cutting her short with authority. "I travelled down in the train with him."

"Heavens!" the girl exclaimed, her face assuming a look of horror.

"Do you mean to say that man is actually in the house at this moment?"

Walter held up his hand in expostulation.

"My dear! Please! Please! There is absolutely no occasion for excitement. Keep your thoughts upon the sad duties that belong to you. This affair—which is largely one of misunderstandings—must be left in my hands. I say again, I have had a long talk with Allen. I speak therefore with some knowledge of the case. And although I am not at liberty to repeat all he said to me, I can assure you that—well! that the whole matter is susceptible of a much more satisfactory explanation than Nina is inclined to suppose."

So saying, he came forward and put his arm about her. "I want you, my darling, to spare yourself! You are already carrying a load almost heavier than you can bear. I want you to keep all your thoughts for ..."

"For *him!*" breathed Madeline softly. "Yes, Walter, I must!"

There was a feeling in Walter's tone, a purposefulness in his manner, which considerably impressed her. She relaxed in his embrace. But of a sudden, reverting to her previous line of thought, she drew herself away.

"Oh!" she cried, "I cannot bear to think of that man in the house! Surely he will not attempt to thrust himself in upon uncle—even now!"

"I shall set myself firmly against unnecessary and painful interviews," declared Walter with sternness.

She looked at him with an air of relief. "Yes, Yes!—Of course."

"I should even think twice before ..."

"Before going to him yourself!"

Walter nodded. "My presence could hardly fail to bring his mind back to worldly affairs. And it is proper, at this supreme hour, that his thoughts should go forward—not back."

Madeline lifted admiring eyes. "Walter," she murmured, "how very right you are!"

He smiled and kissed her lightly in a manner of dismissal. "Send Nina to me!" said he.

Left alone, he stood in the centre of the room and stared gloomily at the carpet. The strength of his anger against Nina revealed to him how desperately he had been clinging to the hope that she had not, after all, carried her tale to John Mayne. Wretched woman! all this mischief was of her brewing. Thank heaven, Madeline was of another mould!

Nina kept him waiting for some time. When at length she appeared, her measured movements and the self-righteous impassivity of her countenance carried his exasperation to the highest pitch. He determined to use a high hand. Most women would be intimidated; and this woman, for all her coldness and self-possession, was probably no exception.

It came about, therefore, that poor Nina, who thought she stood so well in Walter's books and had almost persuaded herself that her excuses would pass muster, received a decided shock. Walter's carriage of himself, which with Madeline had been sufficiently imposing, now became positively Rhadamanthine. He brushed aside all her explanations; he was little less than ferocious; and very soon the culprit, too abashed to give fight, was humbling herself before him. She was reduced, indeed, to bringing out her pocket-handkerchief and passing off her real mortification as distress at having incurred his displeasure.

When asked in what fashion John Mayne had received her information, she admitted that the old man had been greatly incensed.

"Against his wife?"

Nina hesitated guiltily.

"On what grounds?" demanded Walter with truculence.

"Well!" protested Nina, "he could not help feeling, I think, that Lilian had been wanting in openness." And then, recovering a little spirit—"The whole affair, you will allow, does wear a strange aspect!"

Walter made a gesture of exasperation. "Everything depends upon the angle from which you choose to look at it! You have, I repeat, been very rash in your inferences; very hasty in your judgments; very—" He broke off; it occurred to him that his excessive annoyance might ultimately engender suspicions in Nina's mind. After taking a turn down the room—

"I must tell you," he went on, "that as a consequence of not disassociating myself with sufficient distinctness from your views, I have had a narrow escape from putting myself seriously in the wrong. I sent for Allen in Tornel, and relying upon your statements, I made some rather severe criticisms of his—and of Lilian's—conduct; and I was obliged to accept correction."

He glared. And the look of intelligence in Nina's eyes showed him that he had been successful in misleading her.

"I am very sorry indeed!" said she apologetically. "Very sorry! And yet . . ." She paused, shades of perplexity and disappointment passing over her face. "And yet I cannot imagine how that man managed to explain away——"

"My dear Nina!" he interrupted impatiently, "to go into that affair again now is really more than I am prepared to do! This is not the moment. I refuse to talk of the case any further, unless"—and here he paused menacingly—"unless it be to free your uncle's mind of any mistaken ideas which you may have implanted into it. But," he continued after another telling pause, "I consider it highly improbable that he has accepted your version of the affair. And it is certain that his present condition absolves him from further mundane preoccupations. I shall therefore abstain from intruding myself upon him; unless forced to do so. I consider that his last hours should be spent in peace and self-communion."

He waited; and having received Nina's ready assent—

"I count on you and Madeline," he continued, "to keep his mind off all painful and disturbing subjects. Should Lilian—or this fellow, Allen—seek to break in upon him, the doctor would, I imagine, intervene with firmness?"

This suggestion made Nina look rather blank for a moment; but she presently agreed—and with warmth—that the doctor ought to be prepared to intervene . . . Only, she doubted his firmness.

Walter pulled his moustache reflectively. "I think you had better send him to me. I should like to have some closer information about your uncle's condition."

Nina nodded gravely. And then, feeling that the interview had come to an end, made as though to take her departure. But Walter detained her.

"My dear Nina," said he with a return to something like his customary benignity, "if I have spoken to you with some heat, you must forgive me on account of my concern for your uncle's peace of mind. I could not help feeling that you had been hasty in troubling him with particulars which a fuller knowledge and a broader vision of the case would have shewn to be unworthy of communication in this present juncture. It is difficult to see Life steadily and to see it whole . . ." He sighed. "But we must all strive after a true sense of proportion. What importance has this wretched affair that it should occupy our minds now, when the Angel of Death is amongst us? Later, certainly—when all is over—I shall be happy to go into the whole matter with you most carefully. In the meantime," he added, smiling, "you must take it from me that you have made a mountain out of a molehill."

Nina had not left many minutes before Madeline burst impetuously into the room.

"Oh, Walter!" she cried; "What have you been saying to Nina? The poor dear is in tears! You have hurt her feelings dreadfully!"

Walter felt a thrill of pride. He had been asking himself whether he had been wise in taking Nina so severely to task. Madeline's words gave him confidence; If Nina was in tears, his predominance over her was assuredly complete.

"My darling," he replied, "I hope I was not unkind. I was carried away by my sense of the untimeliness of her preoccupation with trivial matters—yes! matters wholly trivial in comparison with the solemn realities of the moment. I had to show her that she had jumped to hasty, ill-grounded conclusions; and was in danger of suffusing an atmosphere of hysterical unrest around a death-bed. It is difficult to see life steadily and to see it whole; but the presence of Death in our midst should enable us to do so."

Madeline looked up at her betrothed with admiration and not a little wonder. Nina, if not actually in tears, had emerged from Walter's room considerably upset. And this, combined with the gravity and authority of Walter's bearing, awoke in her heart a new feeling of respect for him. Of late she had been slightly piqued by her sister's attitude towards the man, who, after all, was shortly to become her husband. Nina's discomfiture was by no means disagreeable to her.

On his side Walter felt that he had made a very good start. He was imposing himself; he was raising the general tone of feeling. The springs of Madeline's sensibility were, he perceived, ready to overflow. Wherefore, to improve the occasion, he fell into a vein of reminiscence, recalling all the most glorious incidents in the long business campaign which his old chief and he had waged together. Insensibly he cast off his pomposities; and Madeline noticed that at moments he had to blink to keep down the moisture that gathered in his eyes. Her spirit rose on a wave of emotion responsive to his. The secret fund of resentment and mistrust which she had been accumulating against him during the past weeks, seemed to be dissipated for ever. She forgot the innumerable, dreary days, when her heart had cried out against him for enjoying a fugitive and comfortable virtue in Tornel, whilst she was struggling as best she could against corruption and intrigue at Eamor. She forebore to ask herself whether Walter was still liable to defer to the dictates of a cultivated priggery rather than to her desires. During the course of a long and feeling colloquy she yielded more and more to a delicious confidence in his masculinity; before they parted, she threw herself with a sob of emotion into his arms.

Chapter 24

Walter retired to rest that evening with his self-confidence considerably strengthened. But the next morning, after a poor night, his anxieties again got the upper hand. It was true that he had cowed Nina, infused a new spirit into his relations with Madeline, and given the doctor a better sense of the authority vested in his person. But these measures, as he now reflected, did not strike very deep. Though cowed, Nina would no doubt welcome an opportunity of retaliation; the doctor was not the man to be of any real support in an emergency; and it was by no means certain that Madeline's allegiance was strong enough, even now, to withstand any sudden and severe shock. Her quick temper was the chief peril. In a transport of rage and disappointment she might say terrible things—things that would create a chasm between them in an instant.

He apprehended that she was the last person in the world to listen patiently to argument. Subtleties of dialectic, that would be of saving value in a masculine court, would be utterly wasted upon her. She could easily be confused, but her confusion would not in the least abash her. It would not trammel her wrath; and her wrath would move with all the swiftness of her intuitions.

However, he had done as well as was to be expected. Looking back upon their colloquy, he could not but admire the fashion in which he had buttressed her faith in him without uttering a single sentence of dangerous self-commitment. On the contrary, he had succeeded in saying things of which *he* would be happy to remind *her*, should she ever accuse him of having failed in candour.

Everything, in fine, had passed so propitiously that he was resolved to leave well alone, and to see as little more of her—or of anyone else— as possible, until all was over. After taking breakfast in his room, he seated himself at a writing-table strewn with papers, and gave out that he was busy with urgent affairs. To his wonder and satisfaction he received no summons from the Orissers; and that, although the morning's bulletin was to the effect that the remainder of John Mayne's life had to be measured not in days, but in hours. Allen's margin of opportunity was, accordingly, very narrow; the chances of holding him off until it was too late were correspondingly good.

In the night he had awoken with an attack of nerves. The mystery surrounding Cosmo's death obsessed him. He had struck a light in order to study the old cutting he had made from a local paper. There it was briefly reported that the death of the man "Richardson" had been found due to natural causes. He read and re-read this statement as though it were an exorcism. He rejected Allen's veiled self-accusations in a frenzy of rage and disgust. Allen was an abominable scamp; but no more. And the gross aspersions on Lilian's honour, issuing from such a mouth, were worthy of nothing but scorn. "That's my attitude!" he defiantly declared; "and I am prepared to defend it before anyone!"

The long, slow hours of the forenoon were a sore trial. He could not blind himself to the fact that the situation, taken as a whole, was susceptible of a cynical appraisal. It was only by dint of persistent effort that he kept his better faith. Lilian and Allen might be greatly erring, but that was no reason for regarding them as villains in a melodrama; Madeline's passionate, undisciplined nature might yet create an obstacle to their union, but the affection they bore to one another was admirable and true. Nor was there any doubt that, given the opportunity, she would prove herself a good wife, a good mother, and a good citizen. As for John Mayne, one had to but turn over the pages of his life history to see what manner of man he was. A great character, with few faults that were not the almost inevitable accompaniment of greatness. Finally, with regard to himself, he had no intention of falling into the error of misvaluing his own excellencies; for that, he well knew, was the first step towards misvaluing those of others. Circumstances of an unusually trying character were imposing upon the several inmates of Eamor unusually exacting tests. It was only right to make the most liberal allowances possible. We cannot serve the ideal without conceding to the real; and this being so, expediency has its own idealistic value. It is for us to transfigure the world by our apprehension of it; and in order to do this we must have faith.

He would not quite confess to it, and yet he did believe in a personal God. If he did not pray, it was because he was sure that God was more touched by a pious determination to see what is as good than by any suggestion, however diffident, that the existent is susceptible of improvement. In any case, he was inclined to ascribe less efficacy to prayer than to the running commentary on life which is provided by a resolutely benign mode of vision. Thus, more tactfully, and with greater reverence, might one convey to the Almighty one's notion of what was befitting.

This method he was applying with particular insistence to the case presented by John Mayne. On arriving at Eamor, he had at once proceeded to build up in his heart the conviction that the old man had divorced himself from earthly cares and was preparing his soul for an audience with its Maker. Wherefore, instead of questioning Madeline, Nina, and the doctor about John Mayne, he had put a sanctified picture of the dying man before their eyes; and to his satisfaction they had said nothing, as yet, to contest its verisimilitude.

So far, then, so good. The actual appeared to be adhering to the line which he had drawn out for it; and every quiet hour that passed he could count to his gain. His programme was inactivity. But, as he soon found, inactivity, in its more masterly forms, puts a severe strain upon the nerves.

Luncheon he much dreaded, fully expecting to be invited into Lilian's sitting-room afterwards. However, to his immense satisfaction, he managed to slip up to his own chamber again, unchallenged.

Then began an interminable afternoon. No step approached his door. A deep stillness seemed to brood over the entire house. In the end, the isolation in which he was left became well-nigh insupportable. At about four o'clock he sent a message to the doctor to say that he would be glad to have another word with him. He did this against his better judgment; but his longing for news had grown irresistible; and he persuaded himself that he might be able still further to fortify the doctor's sense that John Mayne was *on no account* to be disturbed.

The moment his visitor appeared he regretted having sent for him. The little man wore a harassed look, which suggested that he had troubles, which he would not be sorry to share.

"Doctor," said Walter without losing an instant. "the patient's condition is, I take it, much t he same. It would be a blessed thing, indeed, if he were to slide peacefully and insensibly out of this world into the next—without pain or the bestowal of another thought upon earthly affairs."

The physician, a short insignificant-looking person of indeterminate age and aspect, looked up at him through his glasses, and fidgetted in gloomy indecision.

"I understand, Mr. Standish," said he at last, "that you are an old friend of Mr. Mayne's?"

Walter, with a quite novel unwillingness, admitted that he was.

"Well, sir," continued the doctor with eager, stuttering precipitancy, "I find myself in a difficult position. I hardly know what line to take; and I should be glad of your advice. The fact is that Mr. Mayne is not at all in the frame of mind that you suppose. No, sir! On the contrary! He is in an extremely excited state, Mr. Standish!"

Walter's expression became stern. "I am very sorry indeed to hear that, Doctor. May I enquire what is the cause?"

"For one thing—his use of stimulants."

"Stimulants!" ejaculated Walter with mingled surprise and relief. "What stimulants?"

"Well, chiefly brandy."

"Indeed! But—who has ordered him brandy?"

"Let me explain to you, Mr. Standish," said the doctor. And he proceeded to disclose that ever since the specialist's visit John Mayne, feeling that restrictions were profitless, had taken the law into his own hands. It was useless—nay, dangerous—to attempt to thwart him. Opposition excited his fury. The stimulants that he was taking fired him with an energy truly extraordinary in one so near to death. They appeared to enable him to gather into one short-lived flare the whole residue of his forces. But those forces, so extravagantly expended, must all the sooner come to an end.

Walter listened with dismay. He felt sure that this was the prelude to some appeal; but did not see how he could avoid hearing it.

"Is Mr. Mayne's brain at all affected?" he enquired after a few moments of reflection.

"No. He is greatly excited; but his brain is clear."

"Does he express a desire to see anyone—besides his two nieces?"

The doctor hesitated uncomfortably.

"Not so far as I am aware. But Mr. Allen has asked to see *him.*"

Walter was silent; then put the question: "Mr. Mayne has not expressed any wish to see me?"

"I don't think he has been told that you are here."

Walter looked up in surprise, but quickly turned his head away. "No . . . Exactly . . ." he murmured. "There is no reason why . . ." And he took a short turn down the room.

"Doctor," he continued presently, "it is certainly undesirable that Mr. Mayne, in his present excited condition, should have visitors."

He paused; but, when the other seemed about to speak, he hastily resumed.

"As you must already have become aware, there is a division in this household. Mrs. Mayne is not on the best terms with her husband. And I have no doubt that Mr. Allen has constituted himself her emissary. But I may tell you in strict confidence that it is certain no good could come of the interview which he is seeking. For this reason alone it is greatly to be deprecated. It could hardly fail to rouse Mr. Mayne to the highest pitch of agitation and—and distress; and this at a time when—" and here he fixed his auditor with an impressive stare—"when the consequences of such agitation might be fatal."

"As to that, anything—at any moment—may be fatal," returned the doctor querulously.

Walter continued to regard him with sternness. "What, then, is the subject upon which you wished to consult me, Doctor?"

"Upon this very subject."

"Well! I have given you my opinion—founded largely upon your own statements—but supplemented by my particular knowledge of the domestic factors in the case."

The other flushed and moved uneasily before him.

"Miss Mayne is placing me in a very difficult position, Mr. Standish. I have supported her with my authority up to this point. But if any further pressure is put upon me by the other side, I shall have to give way."

Walter felt his apprehension and annoyance rise. "Surely, my dear sir, you do not mean that Miss Mayne is placing you in a difficult position. Your position *is* intrinsically a difficult one. Miss Mayne and her sister are doing no more than offer you the advantage of their knowledge of the domestic situation. They are able to conceive just what this interview would entail. To what they have said I do not think I could possibly have anything to add."

The doctor passed his hand over his forehead.

"I have just been talking with Mr. Allen," he brought out at last; "and Mr. Allen insists on having an interview with Mr. Mayne within the next two hours. It also appears that Mrs. Mayne telegraphed early this morning to two eminent specialists in Tornel, one or both of whom may appear at any moment." He paused, eyeing Walter with an expression veritably tragic. "In these circumstances, as you will understand, I really cannot——"

With a gesture Walter cut him short.

"No one, Doctor," he said warmly, "could fail to recognise that you are striving, under very complex conditions, to perform your duty. But—" and he sighed deeply—"as you say, the position is difficult."

For a few moments he paced the room, a cloud of thought upon his brow.

"I understand that Mr. Mayne might collapse at any moment?"

"Yes."

"And is he aware that Mr. Allen wishes to see him?"

The other hesitated. "I am told that he is . . . But——"

"But it does not appear that he has any particular desire for the interview?" suggested Walter quickly.

"Well! I think it would be a good thing if you were to have a talk with Miss Mayne yourself," said the doctor after a pause.

Walter pursed his lips, and his face, after he had turned away, was expressive of the utmost vexation. It was clear to him that this man was of no character at all.

"Let me fetch Miss Madeline and Mr. Allen," continued the doctor persuasively, "and we will all four talk it out together."

"No!" said Walter to himself. "No!" But, instead of giving utterance to this energetic refusal, he gave himself the appearance of carefully weighing the suggestion.

"That, certainly, would be one method of meeting the difficulty," he returned; "but I doubt——"

As he was speaking, the door opened and Madeline showed herself on the threshold.

"Doctor," said she, "my uncle wants you."

For a few moments no one moved. The doctor's eyes had turned appealingly in Walter's direction; but the latter preserved an inflexible, expressionless silence.

"I am wanted?" murmured the little man at last. "Certainly! Certainly!" And he hurried out of the room.

So soon as he had gone, Madeline threw Walter a quick, mechanical smile, and vanished, closing the door firmly behind her.

Chapter 25

For a minute or more Walter stood motionless upon the selfsame spot. Then, with a deep intake of breath, he went over to the window and looked out into the gathering dusk. All at once he threw the window open with vehemence. A cool, damp air flowed into the room; and the smell of it filled him with a longing to escape. It struck him that he had not been out of doors all day. What he needed was a brisk walk, and, by Heaven! he meant to have it.

No sooner had he stepped out into the corridor, however, than he was assailed by a keen sense of wrongdoing. He felt sure that if he were met, he would be challenged, and his project frustrated. It cost him an effort not to slink along on tiptoe.

As luck would have it, upon turning a bend on the stairs, he came full upon Nina. She was hurrying in the opposite direction. She drew up at once, however, and eyed him with suspicion. Giving her a nod and a smile, he essayed to pass on.

"Walter!" she cried; and he had to halt. "Where are you going?"

It was to be seen that she had something on her mind. She had an unusual appearance of being flustered. For a few seconds, while he remained silent, she seemed undecided, then——

"Has Madeline told you?" she asked. "A most upsetting thing has just happened."

"What?" enquired Walter in his gloomiest tones.

"Well . . ." She hesitated again. "Uncle has taken it into his head again that he must go down to the Big Hall. He insists upon it. And . . . in his present condition . . . it's really dreadful!"

Walter continued to stare. Not a word escaped his lips; but inwardly he was full of lamentation. So this was the end of all their efforts to preserve the old man's seclusion. It was pitiful.

"Where were you going to?" asked Nina again.

"I was going for a walk," he returned sepulchrally.

"A walk!" ejaculated Nina, as if scandalized. "Oh, Walter, you can't do that! You may be wanted at any moment!"

There was no reply. For a few seconds longer Walter gave her the benefit of his disgusted stare; then slowly he turned himself round and marched back to his room.

The waiting began again, and it was worse than before, he could not help feeling that Nina, Madeline, and the doctor, were all, in some fashion, culpable. They had failed to hold up with sufficient authoritativeness before the eyes of Fate the pattern to which circumstances were beholden to conform. Why must John Mayne go down to the Big Hall? It was not reasonable. It was not proper.

No! things were not as they should be. And, first and foremost, it was outrageous that Walter Standish should be sitting helpless, inactive, unconsidered, and imprisoned, in his room, at an hour, when, for aught he knew, the whole of his future career was in the balance. The man of ability and character, the man of commanding presence, the man of influence and distinction, known to the world as Walter Standish,—this personage had sunk into the position of a nonentity. How had it come about? For the life of him he couldn't see. He was aware of neither weakness nor indiscretion; and his motives had been consistently good. Was it a weakness to be chary of thinking evil? Was it a fault to strive to upholster the harsh contours of life with a padding of good manners, good sense, and good will? And yet, here he was . . .

While he revolved these bitter reflections, the wintry daylight faded. His fire had died down; his lamp remained unlit. He lacked the energy to stir. A vacuous gloom descended upon his spirit. When, presently, there arose sounds of bustle and movement about the house, even that portent, grave as it was, failed to do more than ruffle the surface of his profound, melancholy abstraction.

Half an hour later a servant came to lay out his clothes. Automatically fulfilling the routine of life, he dressed and went down to the drawing-room. It was empty. There was nothing for it but to proceed to the Big Hall. As he advanced along the passage, a murmur of voices reached him. With a painful contraction of the heart, he strode forward.

The moment he pushed the curtain aside, his eyes fell upon John Mayne. The old man was reclining upon a raised couch in the middle of the room. A pedestalled lamp, standing above him, shone down upon his white, tousled head. His face glistened darkly against the pillows; its expression betokened excitement and strain. Behind him stood Madeline. Her colour was high; her eyes were bright.; he suspected her of being on the verge of an outbreak. Close by sat Nina, alert, watchful, self-controlled. Lilian was seated opposite, and Nicholas stood at the back of her chair. Shifting uneasily beside the couch were the doctor and the nurse. It was plain that they were remonstrating with their patient, whose manner with them seemed to be one of ironic jocularity. Evidently they did not dare push their protests very far for fear lest his arbitrary temper should flash out. Directly at the foot of the couch stood Allen; and it was to his figure that the old man's eyes constantly reverted.

The fevered atmosphere of the apartment caused Walter's spirit to sicken within him. To his quickened perceptions the scene revealed itself as being of dangerous augury. Whilst apprehending that nothing of vital import had yet taken place, he conceived that he might at any moment become the witness of a catastrophic explosion.

During the few moments of this distant survey, he passed completely unnoticed. The lamp standing at John Mayne's head being the sole source of illumination, the greater part of the hall was in semi-darkness. It cost him no small effort to come forward. When he had reached the foot of the couch, John Mayne's eyes rested upon him for several instants with vacant indifference. Then perfunctorily, he gave a smile and a nod,—no more. Walter returned the salute gravely and withdrew.

He withdrew in bitter sadness to the corner of the room where John Mayne's writing-table stood, and stared through the uncurtained window into the night. It impressed him as well in keeping with the general conditions that no one had taken thought to exclude the dim, depressing prospect without. Ragged clouds were hurrying across the face of the moon; the wind tossed the branches of the wet evergreens against the panes.

And the dying man's writing-table itself was in a disorderly litter. The central drawer was neglectfully left agape. In it he perceived his old chief's familiar appurtenances—the copper box containing clips, the seldom used paper-weight, the old-fashioned revolver, and the holder for a cigar. Those well-remembered objects had a strange power to move him. They were the only things in the house that spoke to him of the real John Mayne,—of the man who had once been his colleague and his friend.

He sighed, and at the same instant a faint stir, near by, brought his head round with a start. His eyes fell upon Isabel, who, lying back in a big arm-chair, had escaped his notice; the pale chintz of the chair blending with the light hue of her dress. He was seized with a moment-ary embarrassment. Certain things concerning her had been imparted to him by Madeline—things which had shocked him profoundly. He found himself eyeing her with constraint, reprobation, and curiosity intermixed.

After they had exchanged greetings, however, his stiffness wore off. He dropped into John Mayne's seat; and there they sat, united in a common aloofness from the rest of the gathering. Few words passed between them; but a melancholy was breathed out of her, which he felt, most unaccountably, to be attuned to his own. Whenever Madeline's voice rang out with agitated shrillness, or John Mayne sounded a loose, insulting laugh, it seemed to him that her spirit shrank with his in a sympathetic shudder of distaste. Indeed, during those few minutes that he spent in her neighbourhood, important movements took place in his heart. His disapproval of what he detected in Madeline,—the while she stood there with such a gleam in her eyes,—ceased to be moral in order to become deeper and more intimate. Something ugly and mean disen-gaged itself from her; and for the first time in his life he failed to persuade himself that this quality had a merely negative value. He could not see it as a symptom of her limitations; he saw it rather as something big and powerful, and as the source of her strength. He felt that she, and in a lower degree, John Mayne, were the active and aggressive forces in that group; and he shrank from naked contact with their spirits more apprehensively than from contact with the spirits of the others. Almost simultaneously, however, he perceived that these feelings were not to be encouraged. They were a disloyalty, not merely to Madeline, but to the life behind her. They involved a renegation of the whole, whereof she was an insignificant—but in his present view, a terribly illustrative—part. Taken in contrast to the Orissers, he and John Mayne and Madeline were allied—not, perhaps, in intention or even in conscious faith—but in the subconscious genius of their breed. They were united in one psychic organism, to whose purposes they were instinctively subservient. They were on the side of the angels—often disobedient maybe—but not, like the Orissers, dedicated by some inherent vice of nature to an everlasting contumacy.

Such was the disaccord within Walter's mind,—a disaccord of undefined sentiments rather than of thoughts. It caused him a discom-fort which he attributed to a flagging of his faith. This gave him an excuse for closing the inward debate. He set himself to regain the larger grasp, the nobler vision . . .

Perceiving that the group around John Mayne's couch was about to disperse, he got up, squared his shoulders, and advanced.

"Doctor!" he heard the old man say, "you can go and eat your dinner with an easy conscience. You have done your best. Now let me die in my own fashion."

There was a ring of finality in these words. But, although all had risen, no one seemed certain what to do next. With a commanding gesture John Mayne informed them. He signified that they were all dismissed—all save one. His heavy eyes fastened upon Allen. "With you," he said, "I wish to have a few words—alone!"

At this Madeline came forward from behind the couch. Her whole being was expressive of a riotous agitation. A torrent of indignant protest was about to gush forth from her lips. But Nina with a frowning look succeeded in checking her. She struggled with herself and held her tongue. Yet she was not resigned. Her eyes, half-challenging, half-supplicating, wandered round in search of assistance. For a moment they rested on Walter. Then, with a scornful twitch of her shoulder, she turned her back on him, and in silence followed the others out of the room.

Arguing hotly in undertones, she repaired with Nina to the drawing-room. There, presently, Walter joined them, and advised that they should pass up to their own quarters. But Madeline fiercely refused. What! leave that murderer alone with her uncle—beyond reach of all? Not for anything in the world. The suggestion was outrageous.

Her face worked so strangely as she spoke, that Walter abstained from all reply. He even let the word murderer pass without objection. Then and there he left her; and, in order to set everyone an example of composure, betook himself to the dining-room, where he made a short, solitary, and unhappy meal. Afterwards, returning to the drawing-room, he noticed that the sisters' fervid colloquy ceased abruptly as he came in. Some efforts were made on both sides to put up a conversation; but they failed; and the silence which settled down was painful in the extreme.

At last he got up and went out, closing the door carefully behind him. His patience was at an end. After a furtive glance round, he seized upon his coat and hat; with extraordinary swiftness and noiselessness he unfastened the front-door; and the next instant he disappeared into the sweet, damp freshness of the night.

Chapter 26

Lilian and Nicholas had withdrawn to the boudoir, where they sat for some while in silence.

At last Lilian said:—

"Nick, I think we ought to keep watch, so as to make sure that Allen is not interrupted."

After a moment the young man acknowledged this with an unwilling nod and rose wearily to his feet.

"Shall I go and sit in the long passage?"

"Yes—and if anything happens, come to me."

He left the room forthwith. On his way he encountered no one. Halfway down the passage to the Big Hall there was a shallow alcove, which contained a seat. He sat himself down and waited.

His mind was in a state of strained vacuity. When he asked himself what he was thinking about he could not say; and when he put his cold hands up to his forehead, he found it burning.

In this condition of semi-stupor he lost all sense of time. But every now and then a wave of anxiety swept over him, and then he would get up and pace to and fro in front of his seat.

Madeline and Nina had seen him pass. At intervals Madeline stole quietly to the entrance of the passage and watched him. But of this he was unaware. Idle dreams floated over the surface of his consciousness, whilst his mind, underneath, laboured with some momentous problem, which it was keeping jealously submerged.

Gradually, however, his suspense increased and invaded the whole of his being. For several minutes at a time he would stand staring at the dark, heavy folds of the curtain at the end of the passage. And, as he stared, he listened. After a while he drew nearer. But, every few moments, he stopped and listened again. In this manner he went forward until he was so close that he could distinguish every detail in the tapestry before him. But still no sound came to his ears.

Then he noticed that the curtain left a small gap on one side of the doorway; and, after some hesitation, he placed himself in a position to

355

peep through the chink. He found that John Mayne's couch came within the field of his vision. He could see Allen standing motionless beside it. Allen's back was turned to him. It was not clear what Allen was doing. He appeared to be looking down upon John Mayne in silence.

For a minute Nicholas's heart beat wildly. He fancied that John Mayne must be dead. But soon Allen stepped aside, giving him a view of the old man's head and shoulders, and showing him that his supposition was a mistaken one. John Mayne, it was true, had sunk lower upon his couch; his head had fallen forwards upon his breast; his eyes were vacant and unseeing; but, unquestionably, he was alive.

Allen had moved to a table near by and was engaged in measuring some brandy into a glass. His actions seemed to Nicholas to be singularly deliberate. Indeed, the whole scene appeared to him to be unfolding itself under conditions of time different from those ruling in the ordinary world. Time in the Big Hall seemed to be running down. The persons under his eyes were enwrapped in a silence and a lethargy which removed them into a dream-like sphere of being. He could not understand that, their seemingly unnatural tranquillity was but an effect of contrast produced by the rush and turmoil of his own subconscious mentation.

Presently Allen returned to the couch; and, to Nicholas's relief, John Mayne's hand slowly rose to take the glass presented to him. But. whilst he lifted his head to drink, his eyes remained fixed and staring. And, at last, when he broke silence, his utterance was so indistinct that Nicholas could not make out what he said.

The reply, however, was just audible.

"Yes," said Allen very slowly and gravely, "I think the end is not far off."

The old man groaned. "Yet still you plague me!"

"No," returned Allen gently; "I am not plagueing you. You have but to speak the word and I will go."

John Mayne closed his eyes and sipped at the liquor in the glass. The other stood silent, looking down upon him.

"Where is she?" articulated the dying man. "Why isn't she here? On her knees . . . on her knees——"

"Sir," returned Allen, "you know her better than that!"

John Mayne handed back the empty glass, and drew a breath of air deep down into his lungs. When he next spoke his voice had a new strength.

"Yes, I know her . . ." He paused. "And I know you. And you may talk and talk, but—with my last gasp I say it!—you are a scoundrel."

Alien's expression did not change. "At any rate I have told you the truth," said he.

"The truth!" And the old man actually brought out a choking laugh. "That's what they always say,—all the scoundrels!"

Again he seemed to lose the sense of his surroundings, but this time there was the light of active meditation in his eyes. After a while he drew another deep breath and said: "I feel better."

Allen was silent.

Slowly and fearfully John Mayne turned his head up towards him; there was a look of defiance and entreaty in his eyes. "These doctors," he pronounced harshly, "they know nothing! Fools! They know nothing! Perhaps, after all——"

"No," replied Allen sternly, "you are dying."

John Mayne's head rolled forward again on to his breast; and again he groaned.

Nicholas waited for no more. With throbbing temples he drew back and returned to his seat. There for another space he sat, motionless, staring into vacancy.

Once, for a moment, he became aware that Madeline was watching him. He saw her standing at the end of the passage. She scorned infinitely remote, he looked away and yawned.

At last he was aroused by the sound of a rapid tread. He saw Allen coming towards him. Allen looked grim; but, on reaching his side, he murmured. "All is well!" and, seizing him by the arm, hurried along down the passage. On the way they passed Madeline, who had at once started towards the Big Hall.

"All is well!" said Allen again, as soon as they were in the boudoir. "Lilian, you must go to him at once! And I must fetch Walter."

Lilian rose. She had the air of one obeying in a trance. Wide-eyed, she looked at Allen, and said nothing.

"I have shot my bolt," the latter continued. "I can do no more. I think you will find him ready to yield. But anything he may now do is liable to be contested by Madeline. However, Walter is executor. His presence will carry weight. He must be present."

"I will find him," said Nicholas, and left the room.

Allen put his hands on Lilian's shoulders. "My dear," said he, "go quickly! I am afraid you will find Madeline there. Get rid of her, if you can. But. if you can't, never mind. There is no time to lose."

After Lilian had gone, Allen joined Nicholas in a frantic search for Walter. At last servants were sent out to scour the grounds.

But before the missing man had been found,—and in what seemed an extraordinarily short space of time,—Lilian reappeared. As she emerged from the passage, Allen hastened up to her.

"Well?"

She was very pale. She smiled wanly, but with the light of happiness in her eyes.

"It is all over," she said. "Eamor is ours."

"What happened?"

"The mortgage is destroyed."

"Destroyed? When?"

"Just now. He made me destroy it before him—then and there. And my other debts, he says, are forgiven in his will." She raised large, weary eyes to his. "Doesn't that make me free?"

"Perhaps . . . probably . . ." Allen stopped and frowned. "Come to the boudoir. I must hear every detail."

Just as they were moving away, however, the front door opened, and Walter made a stately and deliberate entry. His deportment was instinct with that self-conscious dignity which a sense of guilt alone can confer. After bestowing upon Lilian an uneasy smile, he addressed himself conscientiously to the wiping of his feet upon the mat, and began carefully removing his out-door clothing.

At the moment of his appearance Allen's face had taken on a decidedly wrathful expression; but, after exchanging a glance with Lilian, amusement tempered the virulence of his regard.

"Standish," said he dryly, "I have been looking for you." And, without allowing Walter to continue the leisurely unwinding of his muffler, he haled him before Lilian, and bade him give an attentive hearing to what they had to say.

But Walter was still suffering too much from an embarrassed consciousness of truancy to make a very receptive listener. As he stood there, blinking solemnly in the lamplight, one could not but wonder how much he was taking in. It was not long before Allen broke off in a frenzy of exasperation.

"For God's sake, pay attention!" he cried. "Don't you see that every minute is precious? The moment you have grasped what the situation is, you, and Lilian and I, must go straight to the Big Hall and get John

Mayne to——"

He was in the middle of his sentence, when a startling interruption took place. Madeline, her face crimson with agitation, rushed into the hall. After looking wildly about her for an instant, she ran up to Walter and began dragging him away by the arm.

"My dear!" he protested. "Really, my dear child!"

"Come quick!" she gasped. "Quick! Uncle has had another attack! He's unconscious! He's dying!"

Fortunately, the doctor was at that moment coming down the stairs. He heard Madeline's last words, and hurried off in the direction of the Big Hall. Madeline followed, dragging Walter after her.

Chapter 27

"My dear," said Allen a few minutes later, "I want you to give me an account—as full and accurate as possible—of what passed between you and John Mayne."

Lilian looked up from the low chair into which she had dropped the moment they reached the room. She seemed to be overcome by a sudden languor. But Allen's tone brought a troubled light into her eyes.

"I will try," she murmured.

Nicholas, who was walking restlessly to and fro before the door, paused in his march. Allen, equally expectant, stood over her, waiting. But, while still continuing to look up at him, she remained silent.

"Well, to begin with," said Allen encouragingly, "Madeline was there all the time, I suppose?"

"Yes. She was there—all the time."

"But no one else?"

"No one else."

In the ensuing silence she caught her breath. "I am thinking," she murmured. "I am thinking."

They waited.

At last she sat up in her chair and, staring straight out before her, began speaking.

"It was like this," she said. "When I went in, I saw him propped up against the pillows, and Madeline hanging over him. With one arm he was feebly pushing her away. He raised his head and looked at me as I came up. He gave me one long, hostile look . . . Then he said to Madeline: 'Go to the cabinet and get out the title-deeds. The keys are there!' And he pointed to the table at his side. Madeline turned pale. At first, she pretended not to understand. Then she began to stammer out objections. But he checked her at once; and, seeing that resistance was useless, she mastered herself and obeyed. She unlocked the cabinet and fumbled in one of the drawers. I thought she was going to say that she could not find the deeds. But, after a minute, she brought back a packet tied up with a piece of tape. He took the packet; and, after glancing at the docket, said: 'Give them to her.' So Madeline came over to me and put the packet into my hand. I was standing by the fireplace. 'There are your title-deeds,' he said. 'And the mortgage is with them. You can take it out now and destroy it. That will settle the matter.' I could not answer; I said nothing. He glared at me angrily. 'There has been no registration of the mortgage,' he said; 'and I have made no mention of it in my will. Do you understand?' But I was still confused. I stood there, holding the packet in my hand, and looking at him. 'Burn it!' he called out at me so violently that he was taken with a fit of coughing. 'Burn it! Destroy it! Do you hear?' Then I undid the packet. I slipped the papers out from under the tape. The mortgage was among them. He was watching me. 'Is that it?' he asked; and then, as I hesitated;—'Read it out aloud!' he cried. He was trembling with exasperation. 'Go on! Read!'—I did as he told me; and after I had read a little way down the first sheet, 'There!' he said; 'that's enough, isn't it? Well, now put that paper into the fire.' Somehow I could hardly bring myself to do it. I was shaking. But at last I bent down and thrust the paper between the logs. I saw it catch fire. . . 'In my will,' he said again, 'I have excused you your other debts. Now we're quits—and you can go.'"

Having finished her recital, she drew a deep breath and closed her eyes once more. Allen remained standing before her.

"Well," he muttered at last, "I daresay that was the best he could do."

She raised her lids. Her eyes fastened upon him anxiously. "Aren't you satisfied?"

"Not entirely." He took a turn down the room, then halted before her again. "I wish Walter had been there. . ."

All at once Nicholas broke silence.

"What about Madeline?" he asked hoarsely.

She turned her head towards him. "Madeline?"

"Yes. What was Madeline doing while the mortgage was being burnt?"

She knit her brows; she seemed puzzled. Little by little a look of fear crept into her eyes.

Allen, who was watching her with intentness, stirred uneasily.

"I imagine that Madeline must have felt—and looked—somewhat annoyed," said he, with a questioning smile.

She put her hand up to her forehead. "At first . . . yes!" she pronounced brokenly. "At first. . . And then afterwards, I don't know . . . I hardly noticed her. . ."

Nicholas's face had gone white. His eyes glittered. "Did she seem to recover herself?" he persisted.

Lilian turned her head from side to side as if in pain. "I—I think she did."

The young man wheeled round upon Allen. "There you are!" said he in a voice of rasping bitterness.

Allen eyed him with anger.

"Nick, what do you suspect?" asked Lilian in an undertone.

"I don't know. Something!"

"Allen!" she cried entreatingly.

Allen frowned and bit his lip. "My suspicions?" said he. "I haven't got any suspicions. I merely think it not unlikely that Madeline and Nina will dispute the validity of John Mayne's action. John Mayne ought to have drawn up a deed formally renouncing his charge upon the estate. His verbal renunciation of his claims, accompanied by the destruction of the mortgage deed, is good enough perhaps; but—but where are the witnesses? Is Madeline's evidence likely to bear out yours? That's what I'm not quite happy about!"

Lilian, deathly pale, rose from her seat.

"I'll fight this, Allen!" said she.

"Yes," returned the other grimly, "we will!"

There was a silence. Then Allen addressed himself to Nicholas.

"Go to the Big Hall! See if John Mayne has revived—or if there is any chance of his reviving... Do you understand?"

"Yes, I understand." And the young man walked slowly towards the door. On the threshold he turned and faced them. "This was to have been the end! The end!" He sounded a dreadful laugh. "I tell you, this is only the beginning!"

Chapter 28

Nicholas walked down the corridor and crossed the front hall without encountering anyone. But, as he was about to enter the long passage, he drew up sharply. His ear had caught the noise of footsteps. It sounded as if a number of persons were advancing along the passage in company. John Mayne, he divined, was being carried back to his room.

Instinctively he recoiled. The empty drawing-room offered a refuge. He stepped in, leaving the door behind him only just ajar. A lamp was burning on the table by the fireplace. He went and extinguished it; then moved cautiously back through the semi darkness towards the thin ray of light streaming in from the hall.

There, by the door, he posted himself. The murmur of voices had become audible, and he could also hear the creaking of the invalid chair in which John Mayne was being wheeled along. In another minute the whole group emerged and moved across the hall to the foot of the stairs. Here there was a pause, while dispositions were made for the ascent.

His view of the scene was complete. Immediately before his eyes was John Mayne, whose nerveless body hung and lolled over its supports. From the old man's mouth there issued an occasional groan that was the voice, not of the mind, but of the blindly protesting flesh. His chin was resting upon his chest; his eyes appeared to be half-closed. Around him hovered the day- and night-nurses, whose starched dresses and white wristlets crackled and gleamed. A kind of inward elation, decorously subdued, found its outlet in a preternatural neatness and alertness. The doctor directed them. Master of the Ceremonies, Death's Majordomo, he ruled over the proceedings with a becoming austerity. Yet neither could he completely mask his elation. A complacent sense that everything was taking place just as Science had foretold beamed through his spectacled gaze.

In the background, with sombre, self-important faces, Walter and Nina were whispering together. Each was flattering the other by a marked deference of address. Madeline, who had been hanging on Walter's arm on her way down the passage, had hastened up to her uncle's side as soon as the chair came to a standstill. She was now leaning over him as though to extract a meaning from the inarticulate noises that broke from his gaping mouth. That posture of tender solicitude was not new to her. But in earlier days, when John Mayne had possessed the strength, he had revolted against it, and pushed her angrily away. Now he could do nothing. Under the compassionating looks of the nurses, she hung over him, her young cheeks rosily flushed, her lips pathetically quivering. When she drew back, it was to cover her face with her hands.

After the procession had moved on up the stairs and passed out of sight, Nicholas retreated into the darkness of the room behind, and let himself drop into a seat. "Those creatures that I have been watching," said he to himself, "are they monstrosities?—Are they beings outside the ordinary run of humanity? That scene, was it ingeniously staged as a derisive travesty of life?"

For a while he stared out before him, then rose to return to the morning-room.

To his surprise Allen was alone.

"Where is Lilian?" he asked.

"Upstairs.—She'll be down again presently.—Well?"

Nicholas described what he had seen. "But," he added, "I didn't hear Lilian pass by." And then—"How long have I been away?"

"Nearly three-quarters of an hour," replied Allen, whose eyes were resting upon him curiously.

Nicholas passed his hand over his forehead with an air of bewilderment.

"Lilian went up to see Isabel," said Allen.

Nicholas blenched. "What is the matter with Isabel?"

"Nothing—so far as I know. Lilian just went to say good-night."

As he spoke, he turned away, and began to walk slowly up and down between the fireplace and the window. He seemed to be musing; but every time he wheeled round he took a sharp look at his companion.

"So John Mayne is practically unconscious," he muttered. "Well, that means that nothing more is to be done to-night. But as early as possible to-morrow morning I shall get hold of Walter . . . Yes! Walter and I must have a talk together. It's for him to keep Madeline on the straight path. . . From now on, that becomes his particular job."

Nicholas smiled and said nothing.

A moment later Allen abruptly halted. "Damn it!" he exclaimed with a grin, "all this, you know, is quite amusing!"

Nicholas gave a shrug.

"It is," laughed Allen, chipping him on the back. "My dear Nick, it is!"

"All right. I'll take your word for it," returned the other dryly.

Allen laughed again.

"I'm afraid," said Nicholas, "that you'll get to the end of your laughter before you get to the end of your litigation with Madeline."

"No. We'll get the last laugh," returned Allen. "You just wait and see."

He kept a cheerful face; but, as a matter of fact, the prospect of going to law filled him with a sick disgust. He saw well enough that the case would be of a nature favourable to chicanery of every kind. It might be protracted over years. From court to court it would go. To what shifts would Lilian and he not be driven in order to meet the expenses? And while they frequented lugubrious ante-rooms and sat closeted with legal sharks, life would go by. Could any vista be more heart-breaking?

"I should like to ask you something before Lilian comes back," said Nicholas suddenly.

"Yes?" said Allen with an imperceptible stiffening of his whole frame. "Yes?"

"Do you advise me to marry Isabel?"

Allen uttered a short and slightly embarrassed laugh. "No!" he replied.

"Why not?"

Allen pursed his lips and turned away. "I can see you quite happy with a few books and some writing materials in a garret," he answered indirectly.

"And as for her?"

"As for her," began Allen, then broke off, for at that moment the door was opened by Lilian.

"Good-night, Allen," said Nicholas quietly and held out his hand. "Lilian," he went on; "I am going to bed." And having kissed his step-mother, he quickly left the room.

Lilian followed his movements with troubled eyes, and continued to gaze at the door after it had closed behind him.

"How is he?" she asked, turning abruptly to Allen.

"He's all right," replied Allen with curtness.

There was a silence.

"Do you know what he asked me just now?" said Allen presently. "He asked whether he should marry Isabel."

"And what did you answer?"

"I said: No."

Lilian moved to the fire-place and, picking up one of the ornaments upon the mantle-shelf, examined it intently. "Why did you say that?" she enquired.

"My answer was according to my conscience," replied Allen; and there was a touch of bitterness in his tone.

"Are you really satisfied with the result of your talk with him last night?" asked Lilian, after another silence.

"There was no result," returned Allen with a brief laugh. "There never is. But the talk was as satisfactory as could be expected. Each gave expression to his temperament. One never does anything more."

He ended in an absent manner, quite different from that in which he had begun; and then stood gazing meditatively into the fire.

"What is in your mind now?" asked Lilian softly.

"Nothing that would interest you."

"Tell me!"

"Well! it's merely this:—" And he had a slow smile.—"That talk left me wondering whether I am not a charlatan."

Lilian smiled, too,—but indifferently; and Allen quickly went on:— "Nicholas is suffering from fear of life. That's all. And one gets over it. I told him just now that he would be quite happy with a few books in a garret. That ought to comfort him."

"But is it true?"

Allen gave a brief laugh. "Maybe it is. In any case let him think it is."

With a sigh Lilian turned away; but, after taking a few vague steps about the room, she faced round resolutely.

"Isabel can never be to him what I am," she said.

He looked at her penetratingly, and yet as from a distance. "Can't she?"

"No," replied Lilian with a kind of sombre pride. "Never!"

Nicholas had gone up to his room; and there he sat before the fire which had died down to a red glow. He abstained from lighting his lamp; partly, because he preferred the darkness; and, partly, from a fear that Lilian, seeing the light under his door, might look in upon him on her way up to her room.

His misery had concentrated itself into a sense of its complete commonplaceness and futility. The Dark Night of the Soul . . . Spiritual Rebirth . . . how fatuous it all was! And the issue, no matter what, how devoid of true significance! Man's everlasting struggle to cast off the burden of Selfhood, and all the devious reasonings by which he sought to find glory in so doing; how vain! Allen strove in the name of the Great Mother; others in the name of Humanity, or Christ, or Buddha. All were homesick in Selfhood; all were whimpering for reintegration in the Universal. They were children that had wandered forth and become tired; they longed for the comfort of the Great Lap. And so did Nicholas Orisser. But how was he to deceive himself into thinking that this longing was a sign of grace? How could he make himself believe that the renunciation of Self was a victory and a glory, instead of a surrender and a dishonour?

It seemed to him that his spirit was broken, that he was ready for any treachery to the little Ego that was the cause of his pain. But he also had a conviction that that little Ego was too cunning ever to be captured. He could see it eluding, escaping, retreating, like an ignoble dwarf, deeper and deeper into the fastnesses of his being. Its citadel might be progressively battered down by the forces assailing it; but, with a grin of derision upon its face, the dwarf would slip away.

After sitting for a long while before his fire, he rose. It was now two o'clock in the morning, but he had lost all sense of time. He meant to go to Isabel and propose marriage. He had chosen his part. "I intend," he said to himself, "I intend to fulfil all the functions and forms of life in the most exemplary manner. I intend to detach myself from Lilian. I intend to earn money, to have children, to cast my vote, to drink beer—in a word, to play the man,—for as long as I have the courage—and the patience."

As he stood there a smile hovered over his features. "But my mate should have been Madeline," he murmured, "instead of Isabel. Madeline is such a fine figure of a woman! Largely planned, rich in vitality, abounding in the milk of human nature, opulent in femininity, the eternal child, the eternal mother, the guardian of the race.—Yes!" he went on, grinding his teeth, "it should have been Madeline! For gross she is, and crass she is, and mean and small and vile she is; and, by the grace of God, I should soon have killed her, or she me."

He opened his door, and groped his way down the dark passage. He expected to find a lamp still burning in the main corridor. But there, too, it was dark. And then, suddenly, the meaning of this universal darkness declared itself to him. John Mayne was dead. The sick man had become a dead man, who needed no watchers.

He began to consider what he should say to Isabel. Up to this moment he had vaguely supposed that the right manner would come to him by inspiration. But now, when he recalled their last words together, his heart sank. It was not his desire to influence her; but, he felt that he must, in fairness, let her understand that he meant to do his best "to make her happy." He must remind her, too, by indirect methods, that should Lilian, after all, secure Eamor, he would be quite well off. He must be very gentle, very composed, and quite matter-of-fact.

In spite of these resolutions, however, his heart was beating hard, when he reached the door of her room. Several seconds elapsed before he found courage to turn the handle. He entered with the least possible noise and closed the door behind him.

A bright wood-fire, which had evidently been made up not many minutes ago, illuminated the room. Isabel was in bed, as he had expected. She was lying still, as if asleep. Her face was turned to the fire light; and as he advanced, he saw that her eyes were closed.

For a minute or more he stood, at a distance of some three paces, looking down at her fixedly. Her face was visible in every detail, even to the lashes resting on the cheek. He could not detect any movement of respiration. He might have fancied her dead, had it not been for the pink of her cheek and the red of her slightly parted lips.

He moved quietly to the fire-place and sat down in a chair, from which position her face was still in view. But he turned his eyes away and stared into the fire. He was waiting.

He knew that her sleep was a pretence. He was certain that she had been wide awake, when he entered. From beneath her eyelids she was now, probably, observing him. He continued to stare into the fire.

The beating of his heart was audible to him. Now and again the logs crackled and fell together in the grate. But the stillness of the room was intense. He sat, wrapped in misery.

He was sure that she divined why he had come. Nor could he doubt that she now guessed what was passing in his mind. She knew that her pretended sleep did not deceive him. She knew that he was waiting for a sign.

Should no sign come, he must get up and go. He must give her time; but not too long. The ordeal must not be unnecessarily drawn out.

At last he rose and, standing still, fastened his eyes upon her once more. She did not stir. Very well: he was answered.

He left the room as noiselessly as he had entered. For a minute he stood motionless in the passage outside, listening. There was no sound within.

Very slowly and stealthily he moved away through the dark. He imagined her silently weeping. "But no matter!" he said to himself. "For I think she has chosen wisely. And her grief will pass."

Halting before one of the windows in the passage, he drew aside the curtain. He looked across a dusky sweep of lawn to a vague, dark boundary of trees beyond. The sky was suffused with a dull, blue luminosity. Vapours were drifting past, high above the earth, in a continuous, silent movement, suggestive of obscure adjustments preparatory to another day.

He had often looked out from this window as a child; but what came to him now was not the composite memory of those occasions, but the sharp, isolated recollection of one. Indeed, it was not properly a recollection, but a repetition, of that occasion. A Self, who stood outside all time, was saying to him: "Years ago I chose this moment as one of our meeting places. I built on it a cairn to mark my changeless identity. This is the moment in which, through all your disguises, you may recognise yourself in me, and me in you; and know that all experience is but a stripping off of veils."

And he seemed to hear himself answering: "Yes: that is the Truth: I see it." But even as he spoke, his unalterable Substrate sank beneath the waves. It sank into the depths where it abode, and hardly a ripple remained upon his brain to mark the place of its descent.

Chapter 29

Walter and the night-nurse were waiting in the room adjoining John Mayne's. They were waiting for Madeline, who, with the doctor, was watching at the dying man's bedside. The room, littered with bottles and medical appliances, smelt like a laboratory. Walter stood by the fire; he felt cold, nervous, and miserable. The nurse was occupied in heating some milk over a spirit-lamp.

It was long past midnight. Walter turned, now and then, to look at the minute-hand of the clock upon the mantelpiece. He was longing for the end of his ordeal, but he also dreaded the moment of Madeline's appearance. The presence of the nurse would make him feel awkward; and he was not sure that Madeline would give his attentions even a modicum of recognition.

The minutes dragged painfully by, until at last a dreadful sound issued from the next room,—a long, gasping exhalation of breath. The nurse, who had been bending over her lamp, straightened herself and looked at him significantly. He frowned and turned to the fire again.

Presently the door opened; and Madeline, advancing with small, uncertain steps, came forward into the room. She was followed by the doctor, who, after closing the door carefully behind him, gave a nod to the nurse and passed out into the passage. Walter put an arm about the girl's shoulders and led her gently up to a chair by the fire. The nurse pressed a cup of hot milk upon her. She refused it at first, then gave way, raising her eyes with a dumb, pathetic look of intelligence and thanks. Walter again laid a protective hand upon her shoulder; but the gesture was unconvincing, and it seemed to him that the smile with which she acknowledged it, was such as one might give to a well-meaning child.

She sat there, sipping her milk and staring into the embers. The nurse, who was busy about the room, presently remarked that she had made up a nice fire in Miss Madeline's bedroom and put a sleeping-draught beside the bed in case of need.

"Thank you, nurse," said Madeline in a faint voice. "But I shan't need anything. I am very tired."

Walter felt the nurse's presence increasingly irksome. But he could not help being aware that Madeline did not share this sentiment. He was conscious of a kind of understanding between the two women. They seemed to feel that death, like birth, was a matter within their especial competence; and he was vaguely irritated by the enormity of this pretension.

In a little while Madeline got up to go to her room. He accompanied her to her door and kissed her on the forehead. She smiled upon him kindly, almost tenderly. On his way to his own room he positively stumbled with fatigue.

Madeline made no haste to get into bed. Sitting before the fire, she brushed her hair with leisurely thoroughness, and, while she did so, the scene in the death-chamber re-enacted itself before her eyes. She had never seen a human being depart this life before. And John Mayne had not departed easily. Yet she was able to recall his agony without aversion or fear. No, rather she felt invigorated; she felt as might feel a priestess after the celebration of sacred and awful rites.

Before very long there came a knock at the door, and Nina entered. The glances of the two sisters wavered for a moment, as if neither was quite certain what manner to affect. Then Madeline smiled gently and put out her hand; she signified by this that she was calm, that her emotions were too profound for outward exhibition. Nina, looking relieved, took a chair on the other side of the hearth; and presently they fell to talking about the date of the funeral and about what they should wear for the occasion. The ceremony was to take place at Tornel; Walter had told Nina that it was his intention to leave Eamor early next morning to make all the necessary preparations. The funeral would of course be an important affair.

Madeline gazed deep into the fire while Nina was speaking.

"I suppose," she observed meditatively, "I suppose that means that *we* shall leave Eamor the day after to-morrow."

Nina murmured assent.

There was a pause, during which the girl passed her hand over her forehead, leaned back against the chair, and let her lids sink down over her eyes.

"And will it be—for ever?" she let fall beneath her breath.

Nina stole a glance at her and said nothing.

"Oh, my God!" said Madeline presently, "how thankful I am that *he* has escaped from it all!"

To this there was no response. Nina seemed to be inwardly bracing herself up; she had the air of waiting. Madeline, however, remained sunk in an apparent languor. So, after a while she, herself, stirred; with an effort she said:

"Well, my dear, something has to be settled—to-night."

Madeline opened her eyes. "To-night!"

"Yes, to-night. Walter has already been asking for uncle's keys. Before going to Tornel he will lock up the cabinet and put a seal on every one of the drawers. He told me this himself. He means to be very particular."

Madeline's face changed.

"Of course he's quite right," said she after a pause. "He must protect himself. He must not give Lilian any opportunity to find fault."

"Exactly," assented Nina.

After a minute Madeline rose and stood before the fire. Her brow had become lowering. It was very evident that some fierce emotion was rising within her.

She looked down with a face of tragedy. "My God!" she broke out. "When will this end? When shall we have peace?"

Nina remained silent.

"Not one minute's respite!" continued Madeline with a long, sobbing breath. "There lies his body hardly yet cold! But not one minute for sorrow—for prayer!"

Nina sighed and moved uncomfortably.

"Oh, the cruelty of it!" cried Madeline in a choking voice. She threw her head backward on her shoulders and again closed her eyes.

Nina looked harassed; but, pressing her lips together, maintained a resolute silence.

After a moment Madeline raised her lids.

"I am ready, Nina," said she in a tone of resignation. "But God knows I am tired, tired, tired!"

Nina drew in a long breath. "Well, my dear," she brought out at last. "I have been thinking things over; and I am not at all sure that—that we had not better. . ." She stopped short; she could not, after all, finish her sentence. She knit her brows and turned her face.

Madeline had thrown herself into her chair again. As she sat there, gazing into vacancy, tears gathered in her eyes and rolled slowly down her checks.

In silence they both meditated. The problem before them was, unquestionably, a hard one. The document which Lilian had destroyed in the Big Hall was only a draft. Madeline had found time, while standing at the cabinet, to draw the actual document out from under the tape, and to slip the draft, which closely resembled it, into its place. The real document, as Nina knew, was now locked up in the drawer of the desk that stood beside Madeline's bed.

After a prolonged interval the girl dried her face and got up. She walked over to the door; swiftly and noiselessly opened it; and looked right and left down the corridor. All was quiet and dark. Then, after turning the key in the lock, she went over to her desk, took out a long, parchment envelope, and tossed it onto Nina's lap.

"So this is what it comes to!" she said in a low, hard voice. "Because that murderer succeeded in bullying and browbeating a dying man, I am to allow Lilian to enjoy her infamous triumph!" She paused, then raised her arms aloft. "God in heaven!" she cried. "What a mockery of truth, and justice, and right! I, who hold her in the hollow of my hand, am to allow her finally to humiliate me!"

Her voice, still subdued for fear of eavesdroppers was vibrant with indignation and scorn. She stood over her sister like an angel of wrath. Nina stiffened, sturdily and sullenly defiant.

"You can do as you choose," she muttered.

"Ah! you say that!" cried Madeline. "But what you are aiming at is that I should throw that paper into the fire!"

Nina bit her lip. "Yes!" said she stubbornly.

Madeline turned aside with a bitter laugh.

"After all," continued Nina, "you can plead 'undue influence' without making use of that deed."

Madeline swung round, uttering a suppressed cry of rage. "That's nonsense! And you know it. It would merely lead to a quarrel with Walter. He would be against me. Everyone would be against me. You yourself would very soon advise me to desist. I should be made to appear mean, vindictive, mercenary!—Mercenary—I! I, who even now am willing to treat that vile woman with charity! For it is not as if I wanted to drive her out penniless! No! I am ready to be generous to her even now—in spite of all her past insolences—insolences which Christ Himself could hardly forgive!"

Nina picked up the deed and began coldly examining it. "I advise you to stop ranting, and to do a little thinking instead. To deny the whole story of the burning would be—well, too much! Frankly I doubt if you are equal to it."

Madeline's mouth hardened. "It would be my word against hers. Is my word not as good as hers? And then"—she pointed to the document—"there would be the deed itself to give Lilian the lie."

Nina compressed her lips and slowly shook her head.

"My story," continued Madeline, "my version of the affair would be that he gave her back her private letters, and made her burn *them*. You know, he, himself, burnt them the other day. I would admit that the deed had been produced and discussed, but I would deny that he intended it to be burnt."

Nina smiled bleakly. "Lilian is a clever woman. And you give her credit for some character, I suppose? Do you imagine she would sit down under that! No, my dear! If you want peace, that's not the way to get it."

"Madeline," she continued after a pause, "be reasonable! You are inheriting a fortune. What more do you want?—And then, consider Walter! Why risk a quarrel?" Her eyes rested upon her sister with a curious expression of cold, disdainful envy. "Marry him, my dear girl! Settle down and have children! Again I say, what more do you want?"

The moment she had finished, she looked away. She realised that her tone had not been judicious.

"Ah!" rejoined Madeline with all the bitterness of wounded pride. "How little you understand me!"

Nina was silent, searching for some way to repair her mistake. But she was not in time. All at once Madeline, now ominously flushed, turned full upon her and said:

"Look here, Nina! I am ready to give Lilian Eamor. But she must take it from me—as my free gift. On that I insist."

A gloom spread over Nina's countenance. She returned Madeline's regard with fixity. But it was with a kind of hopelessness that she replied: "My dear, you are over-excited . . . You are going too far . . . After all, the decision was Uncle John's . . . And he has made it. You must think of that!"

At these words the veins in Madeline's forehead began to swell. Her eyes became fixed and staring. For an instant she stood still, her whole body gathered together as if for some physical effort. She was searching for means to express the intensity of the passion within her. Then, suddenly, she rushed to her bedside, and, grasping her Bible, advanced into the centre of the room.

"I swear on the Holy Book," she cried, after pressing the Bible to her lips, "I swear that I truly believe I am carrying out Uncle John's real desires. I believe that his spirit is in this room and that he hears me! I believe—I *know*—that he does not wish, and never has wished, Lilian to triumph over me. He surrendered Eamor to her with a tortured heart! He did it because he is a man of honour—and a true follower of Christ! He repaid evil with good. His conscience is clean; his honour is saved. And now—now at last it is in my power to give him his reward." She paused, choking. "Nina, he is with us in this room! I can see him sitting in that chair. He looks at me and says nothing. He is too proud to speak, but his eyes speak for him. They rest upon me immovably, and they say: 'Madeline! I have played my part. I have satisfied my conscience; and Lilian now knows what I am. The rest lies in your hands.'"

During this speech Nina had sat bolt-upright, gazing at Madeline with a kind of disgusted wonder. After a dramatic pause, the girl came forward and grasped her sister by the shoulder; her strong, quivering lingers dug into Nina's flesh.

"Nina!" said she, "look me in the face and answer me this:—Do you believe that it was—or that it is—Uncle's true wish that Lilian should gain her ends?"

With a scowl Nina turned her head away.

Madeline straightened herself and dropped her hand. "Good!" said she. "You have answered me!"

Brushing the hair back from her forehead, she began to walk backwards and forwards across the room. Her bosom was heaving; she had to fight for her breath.

Nina still stared sullenly in the opposite direction. The silence continued, until at last, facing round with a gesture of contemptuous resignation—

"Very well!" she sneered. "What next?"

Madeline halted. Her passion seemed to have left her. She wore a look of exhaustion.

"My fear," pursued Nina bitterly, "is that you will fail. You are over-wrought. I can't trust you not to make some fatal slip."

Madeline drew in a long, sighing breath. "Heaven knows!" said she, "I am tired—wearied out! But I shall do my best, Nina! I shall do my best!" She paused. "Oh, Nina, you will help me, won't you? Don't misunderstand me, Nina! Don't hold aloof, thinking me a hypocrite! You know in your heart of hearts that I am not that! I am not made to stand by formulas and codes. They mean nothing to me! And I should only be insincere, if I pretended they did. But I have faith in my own heart, Nina! I believe in my love for Uncle John, and for you, and for all the dear ones at home. I believe in what is fair and right. And I *know* that it is not fair nor right that Lilian should triumph over us. And I *know* that Uncle John thought as I do.—Nina, I love and admire him for having done what he did. But—remember this!—I am not in his position. *I* never made any promises to Lilian. Besides, I am not intending to deprive her of Eamor, but only of an ungodly triumph over us. I swear to you, Nina, I could not give up now without despising myself for ever!"

Nina gave a short, graceless laugh. "I'll stand by you, my dear—of course. And after all, we shall not be committing ourselves irrevocably. I mean, if——"

Madeline was not listening. "Nina!" she interrupted with a terrible earnestness, "I cannot give in to Lilian, because I feel her to be bad. All that is good in me cries out against her. There is no generosity in her— no faith—no love! In her presence my heart shrivels up. If the world really is as she sees it, I would rather die than live!"

Nina sighed wearily. "What I was saying was this: if things go against us, we can always end the dispute. We can say to Walter: 'Lilian is lying; and her falsehoods naturally make us indignant. However— what passed in the Big Hall was very confusing (we must insist on that—the muddle, the ambiguity, the fact that Uncle John was hardly aware of what he was doing), and as it is just conceivable that she is really labouring under a delusion, we will give her the benefit of the doubt.' Do you follow me?"

"Then," Nina pursued, after a pause, "then we will go on to point out that, as we have never had any intention of using the deed for the purpose of depriving Lilian of Eamor, the question at issue is really just a question of honour . . . And, as Walter will be only too ready to give us his *private* assurance that he takes our word against Lilian's——"

"Yes," replied Madeline sullenly. "But then—what hold should I retain over her?"

Nina rose from her seat; she was visibly at the end of her patience. "For heaven's sake, don't be a fool, Madeline!"

Suddenly, unexpectedly, the girl burst into tears. "Oh, my God!" she cried, "have I the strength to persevere? How far can I depend on you, Nina? And how far can I depend on Walter? Poor Walter is so useless! It isn't his fault. He doesn't understand. He never will understand. He thinks he is so experienced, but he is really no more than a child! Oh, what would I not give to be like him,—a mere child!" She smiled through her tears. "He believes in laws and rules; and thinks everything is so simple. Nina! When I read about nuns in their convents, my heart aches to be with them. But the world is not a nunnery. . . No. . . And when you are in the world——"

Her voice died into a sigh; her eyes looked out sadly, unseeingly. She walked slowly up to Nina and clasped her in her arms.

The envelope containing the deed was still in her sister's hand. As soon as the embrace was over, Nina held it up and regarded it meditatively. "And now—as to this," said she.

"It must be put back into its place to-night," she went on, after a silence. "We can't keep it here. We can't produce it, casually, from your bedroom." And she sounded her short, dry laugh.

Madeline pondered distressfully; but in a minute her face brightened.

"Everything in the Big Hall was left in disorder.—The cabinet is unlocked;—and Lilian left the title-deeds on the table by the fireplace . . . There is an excellent excuse for going down!" Her eyes were full of eagerness. "Pray heaven, the title-deeds are still there!" she cried. "We will put them and the mortgage together in the cabinet—exactly as they were before!"

Nina nodded.

"Shall I go down—or will you?"

"Not you!" answered Nina grimly. "You are overwrought . . . And there is just a chance of meeting someone on the way."

Madeline kissed her again. "My darling! I knew you would not desert me!"

Quivering with restrained excitement, she stood by, whilst Nina made her preparations. The woman raised her skirt, and, after thrusting the envelope into her stocking, took several turns about the room to make sure the paper would not crackle with her movements. Next, she lit her bedroom candle, and waited till the flame was burning brightly; then she turned towards the door.

"Come straight back to me here!" whispered Madeline.

She nodded curtly.

Chapter 30

Candle in hand, Nina walked slowly down the dark corridor. Madeline's clock had told her that it was between three and four in the morning. She thought it very unlikely that anyone would be about. Nevertheless she did not relish her mission.

It was a long way to go:—two stretches of corridor, then the stairs, and, finally, the long passage. She forced herself to move with deliberation, and to assume an expression of tranquillity. The candle-flame, sheltered by her hand, threw all its light up into her face; she felt herself to be a target for unseen eyes. She felt that anyone, at any moment, might step out of the obscurity and challenge her. But she was ready. Her senses were on the alert. And she knew what to say.

Perfect silence, perfect darkness, preceded and followed her. She was glad that she did not have to pass by Uncle John's room ... He had been dead now for two hours. Yes; everyone, certainly, would be asleep. But—Heavens! how the stair-boards creaked! There was no preventing it. However—she was almost out of the danger-zone now. Once in the long passage she would feel tolerably safe. Then, the return journey over, how thankfully she would put herself to bed! And, next morning, she and Madeline would make themselves inaccessible to Walter. They would have headaches. Lilian would probably seize upon him, before he left the house, and get in her story. But no matter. The funeral would come next; and for the time being Walter would think mainly about that ... Yes; the funeral and that obituary notice of his would engross him ... Then he and the lawyer would return to Eamor, and read the will,—and find the deed! Tableau!—Or should Madeline prepare him?

Well! That must be carefully considered ... But in no case would she or Madeline need to return to Eamor after the funeral. No reason why Lilian and Madeline should ever meet again ... Much better not ...

By this time she had reached the threshold of the Big Hall. Pushing aside the curtain, she paused before the cavernous darkness in front of her. She held the candle aloft and peered about. First, she would go to the table by the hearth, where, according to Madeline, Lilian had put down the title-deeds. Overcoming her reluctance, she marched resolutely forward. But a shock of disappointment awaited her. The deeds had gone. A glance made that plain. Yet she remained hovering round the spot for some moments,—even searching on the neighbouring pieces of furniture and on the floor. Alas! there was no mistake! Either Madeline's memory had played her false or someone had been there already. The effect Madeline had it in mind to produce, was frustrated. The absence of the title-deeds would detract from the discovery of the mortgage; and Lilian's actual possession of them would lend credibility to her version of the affair. Wretched Madeline! She ought to have thought of those title-deeds before!

Nina sighed softly, and stood hesitating. Should she return and once more beg Madeline to renounce her scheme? She gritted her teeth together in an agony of irresolution. Fully competent to execute a pre-arranged plan with adroitness and precision, she was not quick to choose her part in an emergency; and her actual situation was by no means conducive to calmness of thought.

It did occur to her, however, that someone—one of the nurses, perhaps—might have tidied the room and placed the deeds on her uncle's writing-table. It was even possible that Madeline, in her agitation, might have put the deeds back into the cabinet, without retaining any memory of the act.

Slowly she directed her steps across the room. And, as she did so, she made her mind up. For good or for ill, she would put the mortgage back into the cabinet. She would accomplish, as nearly as possible, what she had set out to do.

When she had come to within a few paces of the writing-table, she perceived that its broad, leathered expanse was bare. A fresh gust of annoyance swept over her. But her resolve held good. Setting the candle down, she bent forward, extracted the deed from its place of concealment, and placed it beside her candle. Then she turned towards the cabinet.

At this instant, however, her senses received an impression which caused her to stiffen into immobility. From her appearance it might have been supposed that her ears had caught some sound. Yet, apart from the gentle rustle of her own movements, no noise of any kind had broken the cold, nocturnal stillness of the Big Hall. What, in point of fact, had arrested her was not a sound but a smell. His nostrils had detected the reck of a smouldering candle-wick. She stood quite still, her head thrown back, like an animal that scents danger. Did her own candle need snuffing? She glanced at it. No; the flame burnt clearly.

For about half a minute she abstained from all movement, excepting a slow turning of the head from side to side, while at the same time she avidly inhaled the air. So complete was the silence of the place that her misgivings almost left her. Almost, but not quite. Her reason still made question. That smell could hardly have been a delusion of her senses. And unless the whiff had emanated from her own candle, it must have been produced by somebody else's; and that other person could not have left the Big Hall before she entered it. No! the smell would have been dissipated before now.

It followed from this that someone, already in the Big Hall, must have heard her coming; and must have blown out his, or her, light; and must actually be in hiding near by.

With a quick gesture she picked the deed up from the writing-table. Lips parted and eyes narrowed, she stared warily about her. She was ashamed to take flight; she shrank with nervous dread from making a systematic search of the apartment; and she could not carry out her mission under an unseen enemy's eyes.

Another minute went by, and during this interval there gathered in her mind the absolute certainty that a human creature was in hiding only a few feet from where she stood. Someone was close—quite close—possibly behind those curtains . . .

She stared. And it came as a positive relief, when one of the curtains moved. She gathered herself together to call upon the hider to come forth. But before she could find utterance, the curtain was thrust aside and Lilian stepped out before her eyes.

After a silence—"What are you doing here?" she demanded with a gasp.

"And you?" returned Lilian.

"You hid!" brought out Nina, clasping one arm across her pounding heart.

"Yes. I hid."

In the ensuing silence Nina realized what was before her. The battle-alarm had sounded; the adversary intended to fight to a finish; that gleam in her eyes meant nothing less.

"Why did you hide?" she whispered. A whisper was all that she could manage. She was suffocating. At any moment she might faint. Her heart, the one weak point in an otherwise robust constitution, had failed her. She marked with dismay that, physically, she was unfit for her ordeal.

A faint smile appeared about Lilian's mouth. "I hid in order to watch," said she.

"My heart!" ejaculated Nina, and looked round for a chair.

"Sit there!" said Lilian, pointing. And Nina obeyed.

"You asked me what I was doing here," Lilian went on. "I came down to fetch my title-deeds." And she held out the papers in evidence. "Now tell me your business here!"

"You startled me," panted Nina. "You have made my heart . . ."

"I am sorry," returned Lilian coldly. "Please take your time. But— make sure of this: you shall not go back to your room, until you have answered my questions."

As she spoke, she darted a look in the direction of the hearth, on one side of which was the bell-cord. And almost at once the other guessed what was in her mind. "My God!" said Nina to herself, "her idea is to summon Walter and exhibit me to him with this deed still in my hand. She realizes that what she could do here and now, she will never get a chance of doing at any later time. To-morrow I should have a story ready. I should be in a position to quibble, and contradict, and deny. But now! Good God! What can I say or do? Besides, at any moment Madeline may come down to see what has become of me. And whatever I now say she will be liable, unknowingly, to contradict. Moreover, at the sight of Lilian here, she will certainly lose her head."

While these thoughts were racing through her brain, Nina gave herself the appearance of being in a half-fainting condition. There was no compassion discernible, however, in Lilian's face, as she watched her. And it was in the most peremptory of tones that, presently, she asked—

"What is in that envelope in your hand?"

Nina made no reply. She meant to enjoy in full the privileges of her disability. Covering her eyes with her hand, she continued to take rapid counsel. "It is plain," said she to herself, "that Lilian will now stick at nothing. Never has she used that tone to me before.—But, after all, what can she do? She is unable to summon Walter; the bell here is no use. It rings in the pantry on the ground floor. It might ring and ring for hours without arousing anyone. She is alone,—without witnesses,— helpless. In a minute, I will make my escape. No matter how! Appearances, as between her and me, have no importance. I shall get back to Madeline's room, and lock the door. Once there, I shall be safe. This heart-attack shall be my protection."

Slowly she rose to her feet.

"I came here to put away the papers, which . . . which had been left in disorder . . . and to lock up . . . the cabinet."

"I am asking you about that paper which you brought down with you, and which you are still holding."

Nina seemed not to hear. Her problem was to get away; but how could she take a single step to escape, without exciting active opposition?—opposition which might well lead to the rousing of the whole house.

With the same exhausted utterance she continued:—"Walter is going away early to-morrow. Everything has to be locked up . . . Madeline asked me . . . earlier in the evening . . . to see to it.—But I forgot."

She paused. Her situation would be improved, if she could manage to rid herself of the paper in her hand. And it occurred to her that she might yet—with audacity—dispose of it in accordance with her original purpose.

"If you have no objection," she went on, in a note of weary irony, "I will now proceed to do—under your supervision—what I came here to do. I will put this paper, and the title-deeds,—and anything else that may be lying about,—in the cabinet; and lock it up. The keys you can then deliver over to Walter, *yourself,* if you choose."

Lilian laughed. "The title-deeds are mine; and I am going to keep them."

Nina raised her eyebrows and gave a shrug. "Very well. I shall tell Walter to-morrow morning about—about this meeting. Keep those title-deeds by all means, if it pleases you."

She advanced towards the cabinet.

"Stop!" said Lilian. "I forbid you to touch that cabinet. Do you understand?"

Nina opened her eyes. "What does this mean?" said she in firmer tones. "You must be mad."

"What does it mean? You shall see!—Once again I ask you: What is that document in your hand?"

"This?" And Nina looked down at the mortgage with a little laugh. "This is—But no!—I deny your right to question me. I shall be prepared to answer any questions which Walter may care to put to me to-morrow. But for you to presume to catechize—to interfere with me—it is an impertinence."

Lilian's eyes blazed. For a few seconds she stood motionless. And Nina was seized with a new and undefined dread.

"Watch me!" said Lilian.

Leaning across the desk, she snatched up John Mayne's revolver from the half-open drawer. A small cardboard box of cartridges was lying beside it. These she took as well, placing them upon the desk beside her. Then she opened the breech of the weapon, examined it, and smilingly closed it again. "Loaded already!" said she.

At her first movement, Nina had quailed; but now, although her heart was in truth almost choking her, she succeeded in meeting Lilian's eyes with a look of contemptuous composure.

"I really begin to think you are out of your mind," she murmured.

For all answer Lilian wheeled swiftly round and flung open the window at her back. Seating herself upon the sill, she leaned out and faced towards the wing of the house, which, at a distance of some thirty yards, projected at right angles to the Big Hall. The movement revealed to Nina, in a flash, what her purpose was. The window of Walter's bedroom on the first floor presented an easy mark! The next instant a shot rang out and was followed by the tinkle of broken glass. Nina gazed in stupefaction and dismay. Having fired her shot, Lilian drew herself back into the room, snatched up the candle from the desk, and, holding it outside the window, called at the top of her voice: "Walter! Walter!"

A few seconds passed, at the end of which she turned round with a look of triumph. "He is coming," she said.

Nina's eyes measured the distance to the passage-way. Now, if ever, was the moment to fly. But wasn't it already too late? She reckoned that it was. Lilian had taken possession of her candle. The house was pitch dark. Her knees were trembling; her heart had begun its disordered racing once more. Walter, too, no doubt, was already on his way. And, finally, Lilian's eyes were upon her.

Chapter 31

Walter had gone to bed that night with a mind relieved of its heaviest cares. If what Lilian had told him was accurate, the question of Eamor was practically settled. With John Mayne's death, too, the situation entered on a new, and a less dangerous, phase. Madeline and Nina would be more amenable. A good part of the deference yielded to the dead man would be transferred to the dead man's executor. It was true, Madeline had not yet declared herself on the destruction of the mortgage-deed; and it was possible that she would be tempted to question the validity of her uncle's action. But he made no doubt that she would give way to his arguments against carrying this plea into court. He could show her that such a proceeding would be certainly discreditable and probably abortive.

The same considerations held good, when he turned to the affair of Cosmo. He need not apprehend any serious trouble from Nina. He was in the position to observe, with a fine trenchancy, that John Mayne had given evidence of taking exactly the same view of the case as he did: the old man's decision in regard to Eamor was presumptive proof that he absolved both Lilian and Allen from blame. Let Nina, then, take warning! It was dangerous to spread grave charges which one was quite incapable of substantiating.

In fine, neither the Maynes nor the Orissers were likely to set their minds upon making further trouble. Squabbles over minor points would no doubt arise; but both parties would be predisposed to accept his arbitrament. Henceforward his wisdom, experience, and authority, would receive due recognition.

Soothed by these comfortable reflections, it was not long before he fell into a deep sleep. When the crack of Lilian's revolver and the rattle of falling glass startled him back into consciousness, he had the impression that he had only just closed his eyes. He awoke perplexed, horrified, but lucid. He realized that someone outside had fired at his window. Something, too, had fallen onto the foot of his bed, and he rightly surmised that it was a piece of plaster from the ceiling. Then, to his amazement, he heard Lilian's voice calling him. She seemed to be in the garden. He jumped up, went to the window, and peeped cautiously out between the curtains. He saw Lilian with her candle standing in the window of the Big Hall; and he gave—very unwillingly—an answering shout.

All this passed so rapidly that he had no time to consider the meaning of the occurrence. But now, as he stood shivering by the window, his thoughts began to spin round in riotous speculation. What, in God's name, had come to pass? He couldn't form even the remotest conjecture. The only thing that stood out clearly was the unpleasant necessity of going down to the Big Hall at once. There was absolutely no way out of it that he could see. He must go—and quickly.

Having lit a candle, he wrapped himself in his dressing-gown, thrust his feet into slippers, and opened the door. The silence and darkness of the house were decidedly uninviting. Could he, without looking a fool, arm himself with the poker?—he feared not . . . Besides, whatever dangers might be awaiting him, he didn't intend to measure his strength, physically, against the enemy. No! he would rely upon the moral effect of his interposition. His dignified presence was all that could reasonably be expected of him.

Candle in hand, he walked firmly and swiftly down the corridor. It was desirable to get this extremely unpleasant experience over as quickly as possible. But he wished he had taken the time to brush his hair. He began smoothing it with his hand as he went along.

Turning into the landing at the head of the stairs, he came full upon Madeline. She had apparently been leaning over the banisters. She seemed to be listening for some sound from below. It was evident that she had heard him coming, for she gave no start on his appearance.

"Walter! Where are you going to?"

She spoke with a certain sharpness, and instinctively he answered in the same tones.

"To the Big Hall."

"Oh!" She stared straight into his eyes. "Why?"

He took a moment to reply. Her question made it plain that she had not heard the pistol-shot. But, then, what was the meaning of her presence there? Her face was flushed; her demeanour displeased him; he could see that her collectedness was the effect of a deep secret excitement.

Instinct bade him be canny. "From my window I caught sight of a light in the Big Hall. I am going down to see what it is."

A look of annoyance flashed, betrayingly, across her face and she gave a short laugh. "It's only Nina," said she.

"Nina!"

"Yes. Nina has gone down to tidy up." And she proceeded to give an account of Nina's mission.

Walter studied her coldly. Her manner had become pleasanter; but he was not taken in. She could not efface his first impressions. She had been decidedly put out by his coming. And she still resented his presence. At the back of her eyes there lurked mistrust and hostility.

He heard her out in silence; then said:—

"In any case, I'm going down." And he suited his action to the words.

"My dear!" cried Madeline. "Why? You will only startle her. Why not wait here with me?—She'll be back in a moment."

Walter gave her a look over his shoulder and let his eyes speak. Silent, he went on.

"Oh! very well then!" Madeline called after him. "But I'm coming with you." There was temper in her voice,—temper and perhaps something more.

He faced round sharply. "Madeline, stay where you are! I don't wish you to come. I have my reasons."

His visage, illuminated by the candle in his hand, was so expressive that she stopped short. She was warned. She was almost intimidated.

The change in her countenance was not lost upon Walter. He allowed his words time to sink in, then continued his descent. No footsteps followed. He had triumphed. She had submitted her will to his.

This incident did not detain his thoughts long, however. As he proceeded down the long passage, his mind was entirely engrossed by what lay before him. Nina! Nina and Lilian together! In such a place, at such an hour, it was indeed an ominous conjunction! And then, the revolver!—A chill ran down his spine. He thrust his terrors from him with a fierce, but ineffectual, indignation. What! In the twentieth century! In the heart of civilization! Pistol shots! It was monstrous!

He encouraged his anger, for it detracted from his fear. Those two women,—were they no better than savages? Letting off revolvers at night! What did they mean by it? By Jove! Unless something very serious had occurred, he would let his wrath fly! What if he should find that they had put him through this exquisite discomfort for a mere bagatelle? By Jove! They must not push him too far. A little more, and he would wash his hands of them all, even of Madeline! He had always known that this was not his milieu . . . No, no! This intriguing, this brawling—it was crude, indecent, vulgar. . . It was not the kind of thing that a fastidious, cultivated man of the world would put up with. Imagine Henry Portman *dans cette galère!* Damn it! One just couldn't! But how would Henry have acted differently? Would he have retired from the whole hideous imbroglio long before this? But wouldn't that have spelt weakness rather than strength? Consider what was involved!—an old, time-honoured partnership, important business undertakings, huge philanthropic enterprises,—the achievement of the past as well as the promise of the future,—public as well as private interests! Would Henry have sacrificed all that?—as well as a fortune, a career,—and his betrothed?

It was hardly to be believed. And yet, on the other hand, look at this! Slights! indignities! ignoble scenes! Revolver shots in the middle of the night. And possibly . . . What?—Ah! in another two seconds he would know. Courage! In all probability this alarum had been caused by some trifle,—a women's squabble, which he could cut short with peremptoriness. Yes! he would strike shame into both of them.

Chapter 32

Having crossed the threshold of the Hall, he stood still for a moment to take a survey of the scene.

A candle, placed on the corner of John Mayne's writing-table, was the only point of illumination in the whole apartment. Conspicuous beside this candle was the figure of Lilian. She stood erect, facing the interior of the Hall, which was lost in absolute darkness. Upon the fringe of this darkness, and immediately opposite her, sat Nina, whose chair was at some four yards' distance. Nina sat upright and motionless.

The candle-flame was wavering in a light draught, which came in through the open window behind the writing-table. The faces of the two women were indistinct; but, as far as he could see, they were both outwardly calm; and both appeared to have been awaiting his arrival in silence. He noticed that the revolver lay upon the writing-table within reach of Lilian's hand.

After a moment of stern scrutiny, he advanced.

"What is this?" he enquired in a hollow voice.

Their eyes rested upon him with fixity. They made no movement.

"What is this?" he repeated.

Lilian took a step forward. "I will tell you!" and she drew in a long, unsteady breath.

He waited. His eyes travelled from the one to the other. Their self-possession was becoming an offence to him. They were misdemeanants; he was their judge; and yet, in this silence, they seemed to be taking his measure.

"Walter," said Lilian in a low, controlled voice, "you have already heard about the burning of the mortgage. You know what passed in this Hall, a few hours ago, between John Mayne and me ..."

He frowned; he hurried her forward with an impatient nod.

"Well, a little while ago, remembering that I had left my title-deeds down here, I became uneasy. I thought they would be safer in my hands; so I came down to fetch them.—I found them;—here they are!" And she showed the packet in her hand. "Then, as I was about to go back to my room, I heard someone moving down the passage. I blew out my candle and hid behind that curtain——"

Nina rose. "If your object in coming here was as innocent as you make out——"

"Yes, why did you hide?" asked Walter sharply.

Lilian set her teeth. "Let me—please—tell my story! You can put your questions afterwards."

Nina rose with decision, at the same time uttering a brief laugh. "Walter, if you don't mind, I will go. My object in coming down here was simply to tidy up. In the confusion of the scene which took place just before my uncle's collapse, papers were scattered about the room,— and that cabinet was left open. Whilst he was alive, my uncle entrusted the handling of his papers to Madeline and me. I considered it nothing less than my duty to put things in order, before handing the keys over to you in the morning." She came forward holding out a bunch of keys. "Here they are!—And as for this envelope, which, so far as I can make out, is the whole cause of Lilian's excitement, I found it——"

"No, you brought it down with you!" interrupted Lilian with an intense, but restrained, vehemence. "I saw you take that envelope——"

"Stop!" cried Walter holding up his hand. "This is just what I am not prepared to put up with! Unworthy wrangling!" He paused impressively; then, concentrating the severity of his regard upon Lilian: "Am I to understand that you deliberately fired at my window with the sole object of bringing me down here to listen to this trivial dispute? Have you forgotten that it is barely a couple of hours since . . ." He broke off with an exclamation of disgust and faced round upon Nina. "Give me that paper, Nina! I will see to the locking up of the cabinet. And if this miserable discussion is to be renewed, let it be renewed later, under less unseemly conditions."

Heavy was the silence which followed these words. Walter dared hope that his immediate and pressing aim would be accomplished. His desire to bring the scene to a speedy close was considerably strengthened by the fear lest Madeline, unable to restrain herself any longer, should put in an appearance.

For some moments the three stood looking at one another. Then Lilian again found her voice.

"Walter! there will be no wrangling, if you will let me speak. In two minutes I shall have said what I have to say. And I demand that Nina, as well as you, hear me out."

She spoke so quietly that it was difficult to refuse. Besides, Nina had made no movement to give up the envelope. He scowled, irresolute.

A gleam came into Nina's eyes. "You may say what you choose," said she, addressing Lilian. "But I refuse to stay." And she began to move towards the passage.

Stepping swiftly forward, Lilian placed herself once more between Nina and the doorway.

"Walter!" she cried. "I call upon you to find out what that envelope contains, before she leaves this room. I demand it! I have reason to suspect trickery."

There was another silence. Walter's face had turned quite white. After a moment he said:

"Give me that paper, Nina! Then Lilian will have no further excuse for opposing your departure."

For an instant Nina hesitated; then she handed Walter the envelope.

"One moment more!" said Lilian, speaking with rapidity, and still barring Nina's exit. "I give you fair warning, Walter, that Madeline and Nina intend to make trouble about Eamor. And I believe that a great deal hangs upon that paper which you now have in your hand. Am I right, Nina?"

There was no answer.

Walter's expression now became truly extraordinary. Coming slowly forward, he placed himself in a position where he could see Nina's face.

Lilian fixed her burning eyes upon him. "You now have an opportunity, Walter, which you will never have again. For your sake as well as for mine, I implore you not to let it pass. Don't examine that paper yet. But insist upon Nina's telling you plainly what her intentions are."

A pregnant silence followed,—a silence longer than any there had yet been. Walter, as well as Lilian, now stood between Nina and the doorway. The latter's hand was clutching at her left breast; her respiration was short and fast; but her face was hard-set. Alternately she regarded Walter and Lilian. And sometimes, for an instant, her shifting glance darted over their shoulders towards the curtain behind.

"My intentions?" she articulated at last. "I am not sure that I understand ... I am not sure ..."

She was looking hard at Lilian as she said this. Her lips were twisted in a thin, uncertain smile. It seemed to Walter that her eyes, which, when they rested on *him,* were cold and unrevealing, had taken on another expression for Lilian. For the latter they now appeared to contain a message of intelligence and invitation.

After the lapse of another minute Lilian suddenly turned towards him.

"Walter!" said she, "I would rather you did not look inside that envelope yet. It might contain papers that are private. It may be that Nina and I have misunderstood one another."

Having spoken these words in a loud, firm voice, she once again directed her gaze straight at Nina; and to her she said:

"If you are wise, you will let me have a few words with you,—in private,—over there." And she indicated the further end of the Hall. "A few words between you and me might suffice to clear this matter up,—without Walter's intervention after all."

Walter's eyes had opened wide. His countenance showed him to be under the influence of a very singular blend of feelings. But he held his tongue.

Lilian stepped up to Nina. "Quick!" said she in a low voice, "before Madeline comes in!"

This speech Walter pretended not to hear. His fear lest Madeline should burst in upon them had become agonizing. He had an overpowering instinct that her advent would bring about a catastrophe. Ostentatiously he thrust the envelope into the pocket of his dressing-gown and turned his back upon his two companions. At the same time they drew a little apart; but, before Nina had taken many steps, she stopped and faced round.

"Walter!" said she, raising her voice," I want to tell you now,—before having my talk with Lilian,—that her suspicions are absolutely unwarranted. I, for my part, believe that Uncle John intended her to have Eamor. I cannot say exactly what Madeline's views are; but I am certain that she will ultimately come to my opinion."

Walter turned sharply about. "Lilian, do you hear that?"

"I do," was the reply, made in the same ringing tones. "I do. And it relieves my mind of a great anxiety. I understand," she continued after a brief pause, "that Nina means this:—" She paused again to pick her words with the extreme of caution. "Neither she nor Madeline will throw doubt upon the significance of what passed in this Hall a few hours ago, when John Mayne summoned me here. That is to say, neither his intentions, nor his mental lucidity, will be questioned?"

Nina cast a rapid glance of alarm at the curtain over the doorway. But the next instance her countenance became firm.

"No!" she replied. And then turning to Lilian:—"Your suspicions," she added with a sneer, "are quite beyond my comprehension."

Dissimulating the immensity of his relief, Walter gave Lilian a disdainful smile. "I think you owe Nina an apology," said he briefly; and once more he turned away.

As soon as they were outside the range of his hearing, Lilian came close to Nina, and said in a low voice:

"Madeline is on the other side of the curtain, isn't she?"

"I think so. I saw it move."

"And she will abide by this?"

Nina shrugged.

"That paper, now in Walter's pocket—it is the real mortgage-deed?"

"Yes."

"Then what I burnt was just a worthless copy?"

"How should I know what you burnt?" returned Nina with insolence.

Lilian smiled and bit her lip.

"That deed must be handed over to me before we leave this Hall!"

"Certainly," replied the other with calm; "but Walter must never know what the envelope contains. And you will, please, say nothing about my having brought it down from upstairs. Is that agreed?"

"Yes."

"We will tell him that the envelope contains private papers—nothing to do with business . . . My only fear is that he may insist . . ." And she looked anxiously over her shoulder.

Lilian considered. It was true that Walter, feeling that the danger was over, might, later on, be moved to make an assertion of his damaged authority.

After a minute she smiled. "No!" said she. "He will not insist. I can prevent that."

"How?"

"By hinting that the envelope contains papers about Cosmo Orisser."

Nina drew back sharply, with narrowed eyes.

"He has no wish to hear anything more about Cosmo," continued Lilian. "Nor have I."

Nina's air was frigid. "The subject is certainly not a pleasant one!" She paused malignly. "However," she added at last, "so far as I am concerned, it is closed."

While this conference was going forward, Walter moved over to the big stone hearth and stationed himself before the white embers. A grey light had begun to filter in through the windows of the Hall. His candle, which he had put down upon the table beside John Mayne's couch, showed him the brandy-bottle, the medicine glasses, the disordered coverlet, the crumpled pillows:—unlovely reminders of the dead man's recent presence. The gloom upon his brow deepened and he lowered his head. In that hour success as well as failure, dying as well as living, seemed to him to be vain and paltry affairs. Fruitlessly did he try to ease the sickness of his spirit with the reflection that the crisis, seemingly, was turned, and a new era dawning. Ah, but what a cheerless dawn it was! And what a poor heart he brought to the greeting of it! Madeline, whose image should have been standing at the gates of the future, radiant and reassuring, still offered him a figure of menacing uncertainty. Did he keep faith in her? And was his obstination to do so a sign of grace or of disgrace?

While the two women were murmuring together, it was not towards them, but towards the entrance-way, that his anxious glances were directed. How came it that the girl had not already appeared? And when she did appear—for he made sure that she would—what treatment could their poor, ill-used love expect to receive at her hands?

It was a bitter thought that Lilian, who so little deserved to gain her ends, had—with his ostensible favour—secured them. She was saved. But was he? Madeline would answer that. It remained for her not only to determine the future, but to put an irrecusable interpretation upon the past. Under the cynical eyes of Nina and Lilian, their love, their idealism, their pride and self-respect, would stand either justified or degraded.

Well! Let this be the decisive test! Should Madeline comport herself as he hoped—why then, all the ambiguities of her previous behaviour should be forgotten. Yes, absolutely! He had to insist on this, because he was aware of one problematic point, to which—unless he should now register a vow to the contrary—his thoughts, in the future, might have a troublesome tendency to revert. For the fact was that a thin, uneasy suspicion *had* once or twice flitted through his mind that Madeline might, conceivably, have followed him, after a discreet interval, down to the outer threshold of the Hall; and that she might have stood there, wavering; and that she might have overheard a part of the conversation within. But, if this hypothesis did lurk in the nethermost regions of his consciousness, it was not one that he felt called upon—or even entitled—to entertain. No! that suspicion must be banished. He had already endured enough, without loading himself with supererogatory qualms. Not a little was it costing him to stand aloof, while those two women bargained—darkly and unlawfully—over questions which, by rights, should have been resolved by him, upon accepted principles, under the light of day. For, if to stand aloof, was, perhaps, not in itself dishonouring, to stand in the dark, to accept during ignominious delays the position of blind man in a game of blind man's buff, to be suspected of taking peeps underneath the handkerchief, whilst waiting until the right, the satisfactory, denouement had been manoeuvred into his grasp:—wasn't this carrying forbearance almost too far? Indeed it was! And he didn't mean to cheat himself of his reward. If, in the end, his hands should close felicitously upon a Madeline offering justice and proclaiming peace,—why! then, he was not the man to let doubts that belonged to yesterday, overshadow a hard-won happiness.

Such were his reflections during this interval which was now drawing to a close. He saw Nina and Lilian begin to move back towards him. He braced himself for their reception. But, before they had taken many steps, his attention was violently deflected. Rapid footfalls sounded in the passage. His head went round with a jerk. He was just in time to see the curtain fly aside and Madeline sweep into the Hall.

The manner of her entry was not lost upon him. But what was he to make of it?

Chapter 33

A few paces from the threshold Madeline came to an abrupt halt. Her eyes had fastened upon Lilian; astonishment was displayed upon her face. After staring for a moment, she turned her gaze questioningly upon Walter, and hurried up to his side.

"Walter dear, what does this mean? Why is Lilian here?" Her voice was low and a little breathless. As she spoke, she laid an appealing hand upon his arm. Very different was this tone from that which she had used at their encounter on the stairs.

Overcome by the complexity of his emotions, Walter was dumb.

She seemed to take his silence for reproof. "I couldn't help coming down, Walter! I became too anxious at last! I thought something dreadful must have happened. Tell me quick! What *has* happened? Why is Lilian here?"

"My dear," said Walter, finding his voice with difficulty, "it was like this: Nina and Lilian met here—unexpectedly . . . And—from what I gather—a misunderstanding of some kind arose. But very soon . . . I am happy to say . . ."

He broke off. The two others were now standing by. He drew himself up. He fixed them with an air of severity, and cleared his throat.

"Well? What is the result of the conference?—Indeed, I think I need hardly ask. Unless I am much mistaken . . ."

A brief nod from Lilian supplied an assent. Nina, who remained a little in the rear, was lookingly meaningly at Madeline. He perceived that her eyes conveyed both a warning and an invitation. Didn't Madeline catch that look? And wouldn't she—oh, wouldn't she!—go over to Nina, and let *her* have the first word—in private?

He took a step towards Lilian, at the same time laying a hand upon Madeline's shoulder and giving her a gentle impulse in the desired direction.

But alas! the girl clung.

"I don't understand! Walter, what was the misunderstanding about?"

He screwed up his face with a perplexity, which, if humorous, was also wholly real. "What was it about?—Do you know, I really can't tell you!"

"Do you mean to say you don't know?"

"No, I don't!" And he gave a little laugh. "You had better ask Nina."

This was spoken lightly. But his nervousness was too acute not to show through. He looked hard at Nina; but her countenance had become absolutely wooden. And the acme of his discomfort was reached, when Madeline, suddenly detaching herself, stepped back, measured him up and down with big, reproachful eyes, and said:

"Oh, I am sure you know *something*!—Is it that you are afraid of telling me? Is it—can it be—that you lack confidence in me, Walter?"

A silence followed these words. They entirely confounded the unhappy man to whom they were addressed; and he was not sure that the two others were much less put out than he was. Madeline's demeanour was absolutely baffling. Why had she ignored the invitation of Nina's look, and the slight, but appreciable, shove of his own directing hand? Was it possible that she was heading, half wilfully, half blindly, for a catastrophe? And, if so, why were the others content to stand mutely by?

"My dear child!" he ejaculated. "Lack confidence in you!—What do you mean?"

The heat of an unfeigned emotion was gradually deepening the hue of Madeline's cheeks. She seemed to welcome his disclaimer, but to be still far from satisfied. Walter, however, could find nothing more. His wits had scattered. He was completely out of his reckoning. Nina's unhelpfulness exasperated him to the pitch of frenzy. He glared at her, and received no response.

The fact was that Nina had fallen into a mood of sullen, helpless disgust. Neither she nor Lilian had been deceived for more than an instant by the appearance which Madeline had given to her entry; nor were the springs of the girl's present behaviour too deep for a sisterly insight. If Lilian's grasp of the situation was not yet quite assured, Nina's was. She understood that Madeline had accepted defeat, but required to make a virtue of what she at last felt to be a necessity. It was an imperative demand of her inner nature that she should offer herself, at this supreme juncture, some striking scene in homage to the fineness of her feelings. Furthermore, the scene must be so contrived as to eradicate from Walter's mind any misgivings or suspicions that might be lurking there. She couldn't be content to accept the benefit of any doubts. Her smarting pride demanded that Walter should have faith in her, and should, moreover, give shining evidence of his faith. She couldn't let the great drama close with the appearance of his sharing, even partially,—and no matter how tacitly—the conception of her held by the other two. No! Walter must speak, and in no uncertain voice! So far his utterance had been pitifully weak.

In the present pause, which further exhibited his embarrassment, she felt her anger rise. Her betrothed was failing her. She couldn't prompt him. That would spoil everything. But while she waited, helpless, in her heart she uttered threats. Let him take heed! He was on his trial. There, before him, were two cynical and soulless women, who defamed her in their thoughts! Did he associate himself with *them?* Was he ashamed of testifying for *her?* Fool! And coward! A little more, and she would show both him and them that she could stand alone. She would cast him off, publicly and finally.

Lilian's voice broke in upon her fierce, silent comminations.

"If you had been here a little earlier, Madeline, you wouldn't, I'm sure, tax Walter with a lack of confidence in any of us. He has given ample proof of confidence simply by leaving Nina and me to settle our misunderstanding by ourselves. At our request he has not even looked at the paper over which the trouble arose. The fact is——"

A murmur of impatience stopped her. The intervention had been timely; but that voice grated on Madeline's nerves none the less.

"Walter!" she cried; and then stopped, choking.

"This is how it was," resumed Lilian hastily; "I misinterpreted Nina's manner, when I questioned her about that envelope. And now we want to ask Walter to give it back to us—-to me rather—without looking inside it.—Walter," she went on, with a turn of her head, "if we give you the assurance that the papers in your pocket are private—if we declare that they are wholly and solely concerned with someone—who—"

Again she was interrupted.

"Show me the papers," cried Madeline in a tone of command; and her eyes fastened upon the envelope that Walter was now fingering dubiously.

If the latter felt any hesitation, the nod which Lilian gave him—a nod which Madeline fortunately did not see—enabled him to overcome it. He handed over the envelope with a gesture that left nothing to be desired.

Lilian drew a deep breath. "Madeline," said she, "I jumped to the conclusion that the papers in that envelope had something to do with Eamor. And so we went on at cross-purposes—Nina and I,—until at last I asked her point-blank whether she had any intention of disputing your uncle's last actions; and then——"

"Stop!" cried Madeline, now flushing to a deep crimson. "From you I refuse to hear a word more!" And she wheeled round upon her unfortunate fiancé. "Waller, I have to put you a question!"

She paused. Her whole being was shaken by an almost delirious excitement. "Walter!" she cried in thrilling accents. "Have you at any time this evening suspected *me* of—of——"

She was unable to finish. Not only was she well-nigh incapable of speech, but there was no idea in her mind distinct enough for articulate expression. Her eyes, however,—charged with a dreadful intensity of menace and supplication—conveyed a sufficient meaning.

In the ensuing moments Walter's mind performed prodigies. He realized that, unless he could speak the word, he was lost. She asked: Had he suspected her of——? Merciful heavens! Of what? That blank provided a God-sent loophole. Besides, in any case, "suspect" was surely much too strong a term? Aye, he was saved. Saved! For he could—and he would—and forthwith, most magnificently he did—step for ward and in a solemn voice reply: "Never, Madeline! Never!"

Indescribable instant! At those magic words Madeline's entire frame relaxed; happy tears gathered in her eyes; a smile of tremulous thankfulness spread over her upward-turned face.

And what pride, what tenderness, in Walter's answering smile!

Slowly she moved towards him. He took her hands in his. Rapturous silence!

But all was not over yet. And what had to come was unexpected, even by Nina.

Lifting her head with a movement in which humility and pride were marvellously blended, Madeline addressed herself to the other two.— "You have heard what Walter says.—Well! now I have a confession to make to him; and I wish you also to hear it.—Walter!" And she clasped her hands together upon her breast. "Walter! For a few unhappy minutes this evening I was foolish and wrong-headed enough to think of questioning uncle's decision. I argued that his mind was weak,—that he had been unable to resist the pressure put upon him. I told myself that his noble resolution had not been freely made. Oh, I was foolish, foolish! In my heart of hearts I knew all the time that he was never more strong and generous than at that very moment! Yes! His last act was one of perfect self-fulfilment. He had learnt to forgive—and in the end he proved it!"

Burying her face in her hands, she broke out into hysterical weeping.

The envelope containing the mortgage-deed had dropped onto the floor. Walter, his arm round her shoulders, guided her gently away. In silence they passed out of the Big Hall. Nina, whose face during the last few minutes had worn a positively sick expression, followed at a discreet interval. Lilian was left alone.

Chapter 34

The grey of dawn, filtering through the December mists, slowly gathered in the empty hall. Mild and damp was the air; mild and indifferent the light. Another day was commencing. And that day was to witness the departure of Walter, Madeline, and Nina, from Eamor.

There were no good-byes. In silence and unattended, the three stepped into a closed car and were driven off. Passing down the familiar drive to the lodge gates, they abstained even from looking out of the window. Few words were exchanged; and those few bore no reference to their departure. They would not honour the occasion with so much as an allusion to it.

John Mayne's coffin followed them to Tornel the next day; and two days later the funeral took place. Allen and Nicholas attended it, but not Lilian. And on his return to Eamor, Nicholas found that Isabel had gone away. Lilian assured him that the parting had been as easy and amicable as could be desired. Nor did he disbelieve her. Isabel had all the natural dignity of her stock. Moreover, he felt sure that if her experiences at Eamor had hurt her, she had quickly and instinctively decided not to grieve over her hurt. When she had rejected him, she had rejected all her possible misery as well. In his aching heart he made her great reparation. His thoughts of her were admiring. The stings of life could not poison her; its stains could not penetrate her. She was almost unalterable. To change involved a concession to experience which it was not in her nature to allow.

When John Mayne's will came to be read, it was found to contain no unwelcome surprises. It satisfied Walter in every respect, save one. It left two or three openings to Madeline to put forward claims, which, if admitted, would still have afforded her some "hold" over Lilian. This, later on, led to several painful tussles. But Walter supplemented his natural tact with more than his usual courage; and he got his way. Madeline's resistance had force of habit rather than force of will behind it. It contented her that her every concession should illustrate her magnanimity and give evidence of Walter's masterfulness. Their differences, accordingly, had the happy effect of fortifying the conviction of both that he was her predestined governor and moderator through life.

Six weeks after John Mayne's death, when it had become clear that no serious trouble was to be expected from Madeline, Lilian and Nicholas set off for a tour on the continent. And not long after their return, Lilian and Allen went through the ceremony of marriage.

As the winding-up of John Mayne's estate proceeded, the last links between the Maynes and the Orissers withered away. Very soon the names of her old enemies were no longer to be heard upon Madeline's lips. And Walter respected this silence most scrupulously. He was not so foolish as to imagine that it was the silence of forgetfulness.

His own marriage turned out very happily. His courageous belief that Madeline would make a good wife, a good mother, and a good citizen, received a well-merited and conspicuous justification. She bore him two children; she directed his household with ability; she gathered a little salon, in which persons of note—be it social, artistic, literary or scientific—were all equally honoured, and all, apparently, at their ease. But, above all, she was indefatigable in the humanitarian cause. She vied with him in public spirit. When, four years after their marriage, he received a peerage, it was generally conceded that they both richly deserved it.

For his part, it was very rarely that Walter allowed his thoughts to stray backwards. Of undesired memories only those that clustered round the name of Cosmo kept the power to cause him an occasional twinge of disquiet. In the most secret of his archives was a large envelope with the superscription: "To be destroyed, unopened, at my death"; and this contained a cutting from a county newspaper, two or three letters from Lilian, and the strange communication which he believed to have been penned by Cosmo himself. These papers he longed to destroy; he could conceive no circumstances in which he would regret having done so. Late one night, after Madeline had retired, he look them out with the intention of thrusting them into his study fire. But his hand would not perform the act. The instinct of caution, which made him preserve every relic of his past life, as evidence to which, in an emergency, he might wish to resort for purposes of self-exoneration,—this instinct was too strong for him. So the hated envelope went back into its hiding-place, a counterpart to the hated memory locked away in the deepest dungeon of his mind.

In the meantime life at Eamor flowed on smoothly enough. Allen abstracted sufficient time from his archaeological studies to attend closely to the management of the estate. To his surprise he discovered in himself good administrative capacities as well as a shrewd practical imagination. It was not long before he demonstrated that the estate's long-standing unprofitableness was due chiefly to neglect; and presently he succeeded so well with his drastic reforms and innovations that a substantial revenue began to flow in. There was no longer any doubt but that Lilian would be able to maintain her establishment on the same liberal footing, as in the old days.

With Nicholas Allen stood on terms of deep understanding. But their intimacy, although it went far in some directions, halted abruptly in others. For one thing, he censured the young man's obstinate refusal to enter the world. And Lilian's efforts to change her step-son's mind were, in his view, strangely half-hearted. He disapproved of her acquiescence, seeing in it another indication of sympathy with an attitude towards life which he condemned.

It was, indeed, gradually borne in upon him that she had drawn from her life-experience lessons which he would rather she had not drawn. She had reached serenity; but it appeared that in so doing she had parted with something which he valued even more. The conceits and vanities which are proper to the human animal, and which keep the airy spirit thrall to earth, she seemed to have lost them. And this led him to the reflection that whereas a man is prone to attach himself to mundane things by vanities of the intellect, a woman must be bound by some fond vanity of the heart. But didn't she, then, love him? Poor Allen! It was but slowly and reluctantly that he accepted the comprehension that he could not exact from her the kind of love which anchors the spirit to material things. The trouble was that he had no fundamental need of her. All that he needed, fundamentally, was his work. He never had been—he never would be—dependent on human relationships. So he left her too free. She was attaining to a self-sufficiency which went further than his. He needed the world of time and matter as stuff from which to distil the abstraction of his thought. She, like an Indian Yogi, was learning to need nothing. And this detachment of her innermost self from the seduction of persons and things, was the more baffling in that it proceeded concurrently with a ready obedience to the demands of every-day life. That she was moving through the world under an artificial impulse from the *conscious* will, and that her serenity was the serenity of a mock life, were truths that gradually became almost certain to his intuition, although no substantial evidence was forthcoming. In his mind he compared her with the typically "good" woman, the selfless soul, who lives "for others." Had she conformed more closely to this pattern, he could have reproached her with it. He could have told her that she had reached her admired goal by a secret road of disenchantment and defeat; he could have assailed her serenity by telling her that it was hiddenly tainted by the knowledge that it was only a consolation prize. But she was at once too honest and too sophisticated to be the dupe of her own apparent virtue. She was even careful not to carry exemplariness too far. She exhibited just the saving egotisms and frailties; and she exhibited them so naturally, that his belief that they were deliberately permitted, was never given outward plausibility. Yet, at moments, a tranquil irony showed from her eyes so plainly that he could imagine her saying: "What have you to complain of? Don't I give you everything just as you would find it in the innocence of unselfconscious nature? Why should I restart the creaking mechanism of my humanity, when I can produce the required appearances without it? Do I make any exhibition of superiority? Or is the personality I reveal so unconvincing that you needs must probe through the mask into the emptiness underneath? No! Then, if I am empty, that emptiness is my legitimate secret. What is reality but a set of appearances to which one lends one's faith? Be at peace, my good Allen! Allow yourself to believe in the personality which I exhibit. What am I—apart from what I seem—that you should seek after the hypothetical ghost?"

Two years after their marriage he took her away with him on an archaeological expedition into the wilds of Peru. He wanted to see how she would bear separation from Nicholas, who was left by himself at Eamor. He hoped, too, that she would respond to the rougher contacts of the world in such a manner as to quiet his haunting sense of her aloofness. Nor was he entirely disappointed. She surrendered with such fullness to the distractions of an active life, that it seemed a little unreasonable to cling to the idea that the more important part of her was the surrendering—not the surrendered—part.

On their return, however, his earlier persuasions regained all their former strength. If she had been happy sharing his labours and hardships, she was equally serene in the dreadful peace of Eamor. Perhaps he had been counting on some change. At any rate, when he perceived that there was none, a subtle conversion, equivalent to resignation, took place in his own heart. He concentrated himself more than ever upon his work. His old rooms at Tornel had not been given up; and he gradually fell into the way of spending most of his time there. In fact, his life began to run once more along the grooves which it had followed prior to the arrival of Cosmo.

In the early days of his marriage, he had looked doubtfully upon the close association of Lilian and Nicholas, not—he honestly believed—because he was jealous, but because each fortified the other in a course which it would have been hard to pursue quite alone. Perfect solitude is very different from *une solitude à deux.* Not for one instant did he suspect disloyalty on the part of either. They would have no secrets; they would exchange no criticisms; they would formulate no private understandings. But it was equally certain that their spirits communed; that their ideas met; that their silences had the same significance; and that the same charity which bade Lilian mask herself from *him*, invited Nicholas to view her disenchantment and compare it with his own.

So this was the end. When he resigned her to her destiny, he also resigned Nicholas to his. The last vestiges of reproach and condemnation faded away from him upon a certain day in late autumn, soon after his return from Peru. He had arisen from a long spell of study, and wandered forth onto the terrace; where he leaned in meditation over the stone balustrade. The declining sun was sending a faint, golden glitter through the barrier of the trees. The air was without a stir. Heavy was the silence.

After gazing absently before him for a while, he made a determined effort to detach his mind from his work. And presently he succeeded. He became gradually aware—and very intensely aware—of the forms and colours of the world about him. He became conscious of the small sounds, far and near, that gave depth and extension to the pervading stillness. He felt the presence of the house behind him, and the presences of the huge, ancient trees.

Then, after an interval, he became aware of something more. He noticed that over the lawn, under the shadow of the trees, Lilian and Nicholas were sitting. It surprised him that he had not noticed them there before. But they were sitting very still.

For a long while he gazed at them with intentness. And at last, when he turned to go back to his work, there was heavy sorrow in his heart. But it was a sorrow so deep-seated and so mute, that he could almost call it peace.

About L. H. Myers

Born in 1881, Leopold Hamilton Myers was the son of FWH Myers, one of the founding members of the Society for Psychical Research and author of *Human Personality and Its Survival of Bodily Death* (which LH Myers compiled, and later abridged for a single-volume edition). His mother was the photographer Evelyn Tennant Myers.

Born wealthy, and marrying into yet more wealth (he married the daughter of railway tycoon General William Palmer), Myers nevertheless had a lifelong dislike of the privilege and elitism he found in Eton and Cambridge, both of which he attended, and, later, in the Bloomsbury group, with which he was, for a while, associated.

A constant contradiction, Myers espoused socialism while being part-owner of one of the most expensive restaurants in London; he loved his wife yet had a number of lengthy affairs, for at least one of which he set himself and his mistress up in a second home. He used his wealth to support those he believed in (for instance, anonymously funding George Orwell's move to the South of France for his health), and had a number of close literary friendships with, among others, LP Hartley, Olaf Stapledon, and David Lindsay.

During the interwar years, Myers enjoyed a popular and critical success as a writer, with his novels *The Orissers* (1922), *The "Clio"* (1925), *Strange Glory* (1936), and the quartet later collected as *The Root and the Flower*: *The Near and Far* (1929), *Prince Jali* (1931), *Rajah Amar* (1935), and *The Pool of Vishnu* (1940).

A combination of disillusionment with the War, the failure of his socialistic hopes for Russia, a self-imposed isolation from his wealthy friends, and fear of an upcoming operation led Myers to take his own life in 1944.